Shelbourne

CRAIG PHOENIX

Kirsten Vaughan – This book is dedicated to you, for your help with 'Ushered'. A bit late, I know!

Acknowledgements

Tina Rolph – Thank you for your invaluable feedback and support with this book.

Dad – Thank you for your comments and feedback.

Trudi Couldridge - Thank you for the hours we spent with the cover, we got there in the end.

Helen Deione – Thank you for your help.

Lynne Simmonds – Thank you for your comments and 'smiley' faces.

Lauren Hainsby – Thank you, your feedback was invaluable.

Hannah Campagna – Thank you for your love and support. Love you xx

Chris Izod, James Moore, Kim Tobin – Thank you for taking time to pose for my photos, much appreciated.

*Magick – The spelling of Magick comes from the early modern English. It has been utilised by various practising 'philosophies of magick' over the centuries to differentiate themselves from other belief's. Some have used it to distinguish between theatrical magic of magicians and the ancient art of dark magick.

1

Peter surveyed the meandering crowd gathering in the hall. The sound of scraping chairs on the parquet flooring was like a jubilant fanfare. Voices reverberated around the vast hall as the audience talked excitedly whilst taking their seats. Curiosity to see Beryl Wallace in the flesh was high, and Peter had certainly judged the book-buying public accurately. Intrigue surrounded the process involved. How did Beryl talk to spirits? People wanted to know. He was confident this PR exercise for her third book was going to be successful as the hall bustled with people. Cyril's first book in his own right was coming together nicely, yet a title seemed elusive, the working title was 'Samuel Preston' but it didn't quite have the right 'hook' to it yet.

Beryl's second book 'Justice for John Johnson' had re-opened John Johnson's case and was now being talked about in the press with much being made of Beryl, both good and bad, with some saying she was a hoax. Peter knew these events were a chance for her to demonstrate that the process was legitimate, especially, as it was going to be her last book. He needed to make sure it generated enough interest to keep this and the first two books selling for as long as possible. He held doubts as to whether Cyril would attain the same highs as Beryl but it was worth a shot, after all he was a talented writer. Deep down Peter didn't really care what people thought, he just wanted to sell more books and he would do almost anything to reach this end.

This was the first night of the tour and he was a little anxious as he watched from the side of the small staged area at one end of the hall. A long table and three chairs were set in readiness with a jug of water and three glasses neatly placed in the middle next to a note pad and pencils.

The audience occasionally glanced at the small stage for the

1

long anticipated sight of Beryl Wallace. Peter had decided it would be better to have the book-signings afterwards, thinking that people would be keen to buy the books, especially if they could get them autographed. Reluctantly Beryl had courted the press as she was obliged to do, but she couldn't wait for her writing career to end and Cyril to take up the mantle.

Peter reflected back to his first sight of Beryl in her parlour two years previously when he had been talked into visiting her by his dear friend Edward Grace, an effeminate thin-looking man who walked with a cane and had a Panama perched precariously to one side of his head.

She had almost wafted into the room, her bare feet just brushing the thin pile of the jaded brown carpet. Her delicate five foot four inch frame had silenced the intimate gathering. Pulling the shawl, draped around her narrow shoulders tighter, she pinned her long bleached-blond hair to her back. She had cut quite a weak character, nothing like the picture his imagination had painted, her bright brown eyes only just managing to give her pale complexion a brightness it otherwise lacked.

Her nephew, Cyril, a meek looking character with lack-lustre eyes, kept notes of each meeting and would do so for the duration of the tour.

Gathering his thoughts Peter strolled purposefully onto the stage raising his left hand high in the air to quieten the audience. One or two heads turned immediately before, slowly, the remainder caught on and the hall gradually began to tingle with silent anticipation.

Clearing his throat, Peter began quietly "Thank you... mm...thank you...err...ladies and gentlemen, thank you." His authoritative voice had lost its usual confidence and wavered at his discomfort with public speaking. He had run over and over in his mind the opening remarks but suddenly nerves were getting the better of him. Clearing his throat again only made his voice rise sharply, causing the audience to laugh, making him blush. A tremor rattled his first few words. "Thank you, ladies and gentlemen for your time here tonight. I just wanted to say...to say..." a bead of sweat trickled down his forehead as his mind went blank, everything he'd prepared had vanished temporarily from his thoughts. He counted silently to two allowing the words to find their way back "...that when I first heard about Beryl Wallace I was intrigued, I had heard through a friend of mine about her particular..." he paused for a nanosecond to emphasize his words "...'gift' and was more than pleased when I finally got to witness the incredible scene at first hand." Peter relaxed as the audience became engaged by what he was saying.

Unbuttoning his royal blue pin-striped suit jacket and displaying his matching waistcoat, he took two steps forward, edging closer to the front of the stage.

"There we were...seven of us...all gathered in this tiny room, nothing spectacular about it, just an ordinary room, sparsely decorated, with chairs and a writing desk. Then this woman walked in. At first, I was amazed to see someone so mundane and normal looking." A murmur from the audience signified that he was winning them, he had found his rhythm. "We watched and waited with bated breath. I don't know what I expected that night, maybe fireworks or spirits to suddenly start flying around the room." Peter smiled at his own mockery then let it ebb away. "But when she started, the hairs on the back of my neck stood on end."

Peter let the audience picture that for a moment before continuing. "The air in the room was palpable, as a cold sensation engulfed us. Her voice was delicate and shy. Not at all, as I had expected."

He paused again, taking time to look around the audience, as if studying them.

"There have been many stories in the press calling her a phoney, a hoax, a liar. But, I swear to you...that what you hear tonight will be the truth and nothing but the truth, as God is my witness."

"Bullshit!" came a cry from the back of the audience. A young man in his twenties stood up as the audience turned to see who had spoken.

Peter was prepared for this, "you do not believe, sir?" he called.

"You are full of shit," the man growled, kicking his chair across the back of the hall, before heading towards the door.

"Then why did you come tonight, sir?"

"Nothing on TV." The audience tittered.

"Are you a beer drinker?"

The young man turned to look at Peter, "what if I am?"

"Did you like it the first time you tried it?"

Astounded the man spoke, "what on earth has that got to do with it?"

"Did you like beer the first time you tried it? Or did you feel that it was an…acquired taste?"

"You're full of shit!" The man had gone red, he knew he had not liked beer the first time he had tried it, in fact not even the second or third time, but it was what his friends were drinking. The audience were staring at him and he felt their pressure.

"All I am asking is for you to open your mind, sir. You have turned up here tonight, haven't you?"

"Well as I said, I had nothing better to do," the man mocked, smiling, the audience didn't share his joviality.

"Very good sir…but, if at the end of the evening you are still a non-believer I will…," Peter paused.

"Will what?" the young man interjected, trying hard not to let his bravado fade in front of everyone.

"I'll buy you a party seven." The audience laughed.

The young man stood contemplating his next move. He didn't want to look foolish or ignorant but a party seven sounded good.

"Alright. You're on. What have I got to lose?"

"Thank you, sir."

After allowing the man to collect his seat, Peter addressed the rest of the audience. "I believe that she will amaze you all tonight. Enthral you. You will get a chance at the end to speak with Miss Wallace and ask her to sign any books you may wish to purchase from the stall at the back of the hall." A couple of heads turned to locate the trestle table piled high with its wares. "So I will say little more about her." He paused to take in every pair of eyes in the hall, making sure he had them where he wanted them.

"I think we are ready for Miss Beryl Wallace."

2

Beryl and Cyril sat in the small room that had been set aside for them to use as a dressing room, she was going through her regular routine whilst Cyril watched his aunt anxiously. She had never held an evening with so many people in attendance and he wondered if any spirits would come. When the tour had first been mooted they had said to Peter that spirits were unpredictable but he had brushed the comment aside with indifference, seeing only pound signs. Unrelenting Peter had pushed on with the idea. Finally, Beryl had agreed on the understanding that Cyril would have his chance at a solo writing career. What had punctuated matters making them worse was that the tour had been mentioned to both Cyril and Beryl at lunch by Edward Grace, and not by Peter.

***

"Hello Edward. How are you?" Edward was already sitting at a table of a bistro café called 'Food for Thought' with a glass of Chardonnay reflecting the dazzling sunlight that shone beyond the plate glass window. He stood up to greet Beryl taking her hand gently in both of his well manicured hands.

"Very well, very well indeed. It's good to see you again. A shame it is under such circumstances."

"And you. I am very sorry about my telephone call earlier."

"Don't mention it, Cyril," Edward acknowledged, indicating for him to sit. "I understand. I only wish I had spoken with you before you had signed with Peter for the first book and maybe explained what it could be like. I do so hate mixing business and pleasure. I had only intended for him to come along and relax. He is a dear friend and I know he struggles with trying to live up to his father's image. I thought it might be something different. Open his mind to the world outside of work."

"I must admit to seeing a different side to him today," Cyril imparted.

Edward looked at the young man sitting opposite him, how

he had grown up in the last two years. One thing that hadn't changed was his loyalty to his aunt, he could see that in his eyes.

"Yes, he can be a bit insensitive, but unfortunately that is business and he is trying to make money, like us all, I must say."

"I'm sorry. I shouldn't have spoken with you about him, he is a friend." Beryl apologised.

Edward stopped her before she could say anymore. "Nonsense, nonsense. I know he has faults and I am sorry that I couldn't advise any different, a contract is a contract."

"I know Edward, I know. I feel so stupid getting myself mixed up in it."

Cyril interjected. "It's my fault really. I talked you into it. I wanted it. I wanted my stories to be more than just empty words on a page, I wanted them to breathe and..."

Beryl placed her hand on Cyril's.

"I could always have said no."

"Beryl is stronger than you think." Edward smiled. "But look at it this way, and as much as it pains me to say it, you only have the third book to do and then you can walk away from it all. Fade back into anonymity. You will still have the royalty cheques coming in for the rest of your lives so you can still do good with the money. This publicity circus will be over soon enough. I have seen it time and time again."

"Thank you," Beryl said. "Shall we order? This is my treat."

"Nonsense," Edward exclaimed heartily.

"Now, Edward, please let me do this, you have been a godsend and I would like to offer you my thanks."

"One objection is considered good manners, two would be rude. Thank you," Edward replied.

"Now, where is the waitress?" Beryl said aloud.

As if on cue a short plump lady waddled over, "what can I get you?" her quiet polite voice enquired.

"Another Chardonnay for my friend here," Edward tipped his glass in thanks. "Cyril?"

"Beer, please."

"Campari and soda for me. What are the specials today?"

The waitress ran through the specials and then remembered that she hadn't actually brought over the menus and rushed away to fetch them.

"So, Beryl, when can I expect your usual Wednesday evenings to start up again? I do miss them."

"Yes, I have been neglecting my regulars."

"It's quite alright under the circumstances, I'm sure."

"Yes, but I do miss the intimacy and hate having to try and cram twenty people into my little parlour. I always think everyone is so uncomfortable. A part of me is wondering who is there because of the books and who is there for what the evenings are about."

"I liked it when there were fewer people." Cyril added.

From nowhere a man and woman approached the table. There was a brief awkward silence as neither would be the first to speak, taking it in turn to nudge each other.

"May we help you?" Edward offered politely.

"Are you Beryl Wallace?" The young woman asked her voice trembling with nerves, her face turning crimson.

"Yes, this is my Aunt, Why?" Cyril's words came out rather harshly.

"Could we get your autograph?" Beryl stared at them incredulously and slightly embarrassed as other diners started to take notice.

"It is considered rude to interrupt someone's private lun..."

"Thank you, Edward." Beryl placed a placating hand on his forearm. "Of course I would, just this once though. Would you like my nephew's as he writes the books?

"Really?" The woman turned her attention to Cyril and started to go all doey eyed.

"Of course," Cyril said uneasily as the woman continued to stare at him. "Have you got something for us to sign?

The man fumbled around in a cotton bag he had been carrying, pulling out a copy of 'Justice for John Johnson', handing it to Cyril who then passed it to Beryl.

Almost gushing, they left excited at their reward for being brave.

"I'm sorry about that Edward. See that's what I have grown to dislike. I am just an ordinary person. I don't understand this fascination people have with celebrity. Surely it's the books they want. The stories?"

"Unfortunately, they want a little bit of you as well."

The waitress reappeared with the drinks.

"Are you ready to order?"

"Sorry, no. Can we have a few more minutes?" Cyril answered. They all sat in silence perusing the menu.

"What did you think of Peter's idea for the third book?" Edward asked guardedly.

"What idea?" Cyril said hurt. Edward instantly realised that Peter hadn't spoken to them about the third book.

"I should not have said anything."

"I thought we would be doing the one I am working on at the moment, about the mobster," Cyril added firmly.

Edward, feeling torn, wanted say more but did not want to betray Peter.

"Maybe you are." Beryl and Cyril stared at Edward who uncomfortably sipped his wine. "He wants to do a tour, a writing tour," he finally gave in.

"How would that work?" Beryl asked curiously, amazed at such an idea.

"I don't know to be quite honest." Edward decided that he ought to play dumb. "Maybe it would be best if you ask him yourself."

Beryl sensed Edward's unease and, not wanting to upset him, changed the subject. "So what are you having Edward?" Her mind was curious as to Peter's plans and no longer on the meal.

"Well the soup of the day for starter sounds nice."

"Yes it does. I'll have the same," Beryl agreed distracted. "Cyril?"

"Prawn cocktail, I think, followed by a fillet steak."

"I think the chicken cordon bleu for me please, Beryl."

"Yes, that does sound good, but lamb for me. Now where's that waitress?"

***

Cyril had been sure they would be publishing Samuel Preston's story, but Peter has pushed through with this writing tour, although he had conceded that Cyril could use 'Samuel Preston's' story for his first book, which had placated him. Cyril continued to watch his aunt as she proceeded with her prayer for guidance and protection from evil spirits, followed by a short meditation to enhance communication with her three spirit guides, her Great Grandmother Irene, Matthew - a farmer from the 17th Century, and Graeme, a vagrant who had died on the streets of Victorian London. It was a routine she had followed ever since he could remember, it opened a connection, formalized events.

"Are you ready Auntie?" Cyril asked as they listened to Peter's voice growing in stature, his confidence growing, his opening comments capturing the audience.

"Yes, I think so. Although a little nervous. I don't know why, it is not something that is new to me."

"I suppose it's just different from the parlour."

"Yes, you are probably right. But as long as my guides are here, then everything will be fine."

"Come on, that was Peter introducing you."

Reluctantly Beryl rose, remembering her first meeting with Peter in her parlour; he had been a non-believer and had been caught off guard when the first spirit was for him.

***

"I am getting the name Maria...and a dog, does that mean anything to anyone?"

Fred, another regular of Beryl's, dipped his head wearily, he so wanted to have contact with his wife, who had died from cancer. Everyone else glanced questioningly at each other waiting for someone to acknowledge.

"Ah... might be Mariana and a ca...no definitely a little dog, he is standing here now." Beryl turned to face the door she had entered through and bent down. "Lovely patchwork brown and white King Charles Spaniel."

"Judy". All eyes turned to Peter who had put his hand to his mouth too late to stop the words escaping. "Oh my god," Edward stared curiously at his friend, surprised and pleased by the sudden outburst.

3

Beryl looked at Peter. "This spirit belongs to you?" she paused. "There is a man with the dog. A short stocky man with thin grey hair."

"That's Uncle George," Peter stammered, hating to be in the spotlight, especially when it wasn't expected.

"He is nodding. It is your Uncle George. He says..." Beryl listened carefully. "He says you need to tread carefully. There are many things you don't understand and you must leave well alone. Oh!" Beryl stopped, shocked. "He warns you not to be like your father. The dog is barking. He is going. He sends his love."

"But I don't understand. Ask him what he means?" Peter's voice rose impatiently.

Beryl paused, "I'm sorry, he has gone."

"Gone. What do you mean gone?"

"I'm sorry but spirits will only come as they see fit, I cannot control them, I am merely a channel."

Peter sank back into his chair, his mind racing back to a childhood he had long since left behind.

"You're honoured Peter, I have been coming for nearly two years and no one has spoken to me," Edward whispered.

"I don't...I can't believe it. Not Uncle George, I thought he hated me." The words faded as more thoughts cascaded through Peter's head. "Judy chewed up my uncle's copy of the book, 'Mariana', which was a gift to my aunt just before she di...passed away."

Edward smiled half-heartedly at his friend.

***

"Are you alright auntie?"

"Yes I was just thinking of that first evening when we met Peter."

"It's seems a long way away now."

"Yes," Beryl replied, missing the intimate gatherings.

10

The odd uneasy clap resonated around the hall as Beryl walked out from the wings, accompanied by Cyril, whose shoes clicked on the wooden stage, making him self-conscious, whilst Beryl's bare feet made no sound. Beryl took centre stage and Cyril sat on the chair nearest to where they'd entered, leaving Peter to take the one furthest away.

Beryl stood for all to see, her hands at her side, trembling slightly with nerves. She took a long slow breath, searching her mind, trying to focus it, finding it hard to hear her guides as the pressure of expectant eyes watched her, hampering her normally fluid connection.

Murmurs could be heard from the audience.

"What's going on?" an old gentleman asked of his friend.

"Don't know Bert. But isn't she meant to be doing something?"

"Well I think it's a load of rubbish," one woman stated, a little louder than she expected.

"Then why did you come, and why did you drag me down too, Sarah?"

"Shush," a stern looking woman commanded the husband and wife.

Two minutes turned into five. Beryl became uncomfortable as people started to fidget. She fought to stay calm but nerves were getting the better of her. She was only doing what she did normally, but tonight it felt so different, so much more difficult.

Peter looked at Cyril, who watched his aunt anxiously, pencil poised.

Beryl finally felt her spirit guides close to her again and relaxed. Her soft voice broke through the quiet chatter of the audience, now pleased that something was happening, although they strained to hear her.

"The spirits are with us now. Just..." Beryl leaned to one side as if listening to someone who was shorter than her. "...I am getting a woman by the name of Nancy, does this mean anything to anyone?" Silence engulfed the hall. "She does not belong to..." Beryl stopped abruptly her face turning pale. Cyril tensed as the audience gasped in unison. Beryl visibly relaxed. "You are welcome here. I have another spirit who wants to tell his story. Please, use me as your instrument," she sensed the spirits aura, "to guide me through your life. Help me to assist your passing over... I can feel you, your presence. Do not be afraid, these people want to know your story, please tell us."

"This is such bullshit," came a call from a lone voice in the audience.

Beryl ignored it and carried on. "Please tell us how and why. We will not judge you. Please tell us your name..." Beryl hesitated. "You seem distressed, anguished. You are amongst friends here...please. I want to help you. We want to know."

The audience sat forward intrigued.

Beryl's face and voice slowly changed, her soft pleasant features took on a hard edge, her eyes darkening, her voice growing deeper much to the amazement of the audience.

What's to tell?

Beryl questioned, although the voice was not hers.

"Booo," yelled the same audience member, yet he didn't move to go.

"Shush," called another couple of people.

Beryl was back, her voice normal, her tone sympathetic. "Please tell us, it will help you move on. Sometimes it unlocks the shackles that bind you to this mortal place, allowing you to..."

Maybe I don't want to move on. Maybe I don't deserve to.

Instantaneously her demeanour changed, the audience rocked back in their seats, incredulous. The air around them chilled, making a couple of women pull there coats tighter.

Peter smiled as he saw the audience react, it meant they were being drawn in. Pound signs flickered up in his mind.

"What is your name?" Beryl's tone was soft and tender again making Peter remember the night he had first seen her, how inexplicably he had been caught under her spell, despite the fact that he didn't want to believe.

Beryl's voice changed immediately as the spirit communicated through her.

It's not important anymore.

"What do we call you?" Beryl's voice was rough and angry.

It doesn't matter.

"Don't go…" Beryl pleaded, "…stay…tell us about yourself." There was a long pause as she walked to the edge of the stage. For a moment Beryl seemed to have lost whatever connection she'd had, but slowly the spirit started to talk freely through her.

The voice lost its sharpness as the words tumbled out.

I used to work days.

The spirit paused.

I used to have a wife. I used to have kids.

A minute passed as Beryl stared off to the back of the hall.

"Is that…?" Someone started to say.

That was a long time ago. They are gone now… along with any sense of pride I had. And I was proud.

Adding more softly.

A proud father. A proud husband. A proud home-owner until I had the sap sucked clean out of me and I sank to depths I never thought possible.

I live…lived on the Shelbourne Estate, not a very nice place to raise a family or attempt to live in peace. I knew of people on this estate who had died from starvation because they were too scared to go out.

Too scared!

Beryl's voice reverberated around the hall. Tears started to run from her eyes as the anguish the spirit felt cloaked her.

How can a thirty-five year old man be too scared, of a seven year old, but that's how it became?

I saw grandmothers out walking with their grandchildren, grandmothers before they're thirty.

Beryl's voice became tormented.

It's a joke; they smoked, they drank, they couldn't speak the Queen's English. Half of them were too stoned to know what day of the week it was unless it was benefit day.

I watched the estate decline for four years. Four years!

Beryl sat, legs dangling over the edge of the stage.

It was a nice place once, when I moved there, it was full of promise and community spirit. The old and the young living contentedly side by side. It's astonishing how quickly things can change, how quickly depravity takes a hold, how sick people could really be.

I was happy. Then I joined the other side, pushed too far. That's when I took action. I wanted to see the estate back as it was, a nice place to be, a nice place to live.

I'd lost so much that was dear to me, my wife, my kids, my job, my dignity.

The spirit paused.

My self worth. I wanted them back and I was going to take them.

I couldn't remember most of the time, who or what I used to be.

It would have been my son's eighth birthday. That was the day that changed my future, my destiny and set it on the course that led to my demise. I stopped being afraid, I stopped caring anymore. Another car was in flames, barely thirty feet from my front garden.

Slowly the venom in Beryl's voice grew.

A stolen car! Someone's hard earned money, taken by mindless arrogant yobs with nothing better to do. I wanted to turn the tables. I wanted them to be afraid. I wanted to show them what it felt like.

The hall went quiet and Beryl's head lolled to one side before her body started to roll backwards allowing her head to bang on the stage floor, breaking Cyril from his note-taking. For a split second Peter and Cyril looked at each other in astonishment.

4

Peter ran to Beryl, reaching her only a second before Cyril, who barged Peter out of the way. Lifting her head off the floor Cyril tentatively nudged her shoulder as Peter checked her pulse.

"Auntie Beryl?"

The audience viewed the scene in silent curiosity.

Beryl's eyes blinked wearily open as she focussed on Peter leaning over her. She looked drained, sapped of all strength. A new twist, Peter thought, smiling with pleasure that she appeared to be getting into performance mode for the audience. Peter glanced at his watch, it had lasted barely fifteen minutes. Was she done for the night? Trying to conceal a sneaked look at the crowd he wondered how they would react, and panic started to sweep over him.

Cyril helped Beryl up, her legs like jelly. The audience watched unsure what was going on.

"I don't understand, Cyril," she muttered. "I have never been so sapped of energy."

"Maybe it's nerves." Cyril said leading her from the stage.

"There is something very familiar about the spirit, Cyril," her words were starting to get lost amongst the murmuring crowd who were wondering what was going on. Peter noted the glances at watches and he felt the pressure mounting.

"Sorry Auntie. What was that?"

"It's probably nothing." Had she imagined the familiarity? What was it about this spirit that made it feel so different to others she had communicated with?

Peter took centre stage uncomfortably, clearing his throat to quieten the growing mumble of voices.

"I'm sorry ladies and gentlemen…mmmm…but it looks as though Miss Wallace is…" Peter contemplated the words he needed to use, although the audience had not paid he could feel their unrest "…exhausted." The audience uttered their disappointment and Peter racked his mind for words to appease the restless crowd as the noise of disgruntled people grew. "Look, sometimes the spirits can take a lot out of her. Yes, she might be able to continue if..."

"If what?" a gruff voice, hidden amidst the throng of people, called.

Peter clasped and unclasped his hands. Maybe this hadn't been such a good idea. He knew he would have to do something, then inspiration struck "Look, ladies, gentlemen. Maybe if we just take a short break..." but already the scraping of chairs was reaching a crescendo. "...please, ladies and gentlemen... if we..." His voice was getting lost in the noise of marching feet, although after a few short minutes the exodus subsided leaving nearly half the audience still awaiting his suggestion. Pleased, he sighed heavily. "Thank you. Thank you for your patience. Please, just...I will..." Peter dashed off stage.

"Cyril, is she alright?" Peter expressed his concern as he burst through the door to the dressing room.

"My aunt is tired, physically drained. She says that the spirit that has connected with her is strong. Well you saw that. He is full of rage and anger and it took a lot out of her, Peter. Something I have never witnessed before." Cyril wiped his brow with his handkerchief.

"But she has never had a problem before. I've seen her talk for hours. I don't understand."

"I know that. And she knows that but she can only do what she can do." Cyril spoke sternly, his brow furrowed.

Flustered, Peter spoke again. "Well, what shall I tell the audience?"

"I don't..." changing tack. "...Peter we did say that this only works if the spirits are willing and no guarantees can be made. Auntie Beryl is my first concern. She has never had a spirit take control like that and it concerns me. I don't know if this is such a good idea anymore."

Peter looked anxious as he observed the room. "Where is Beryl anyway?"

"She went to the toilet, she'll be back in a minute." Almost on cue Beryl walked in behind Peter.

"I am ready again now."

"Are you sure Auntie?" Cyril passed Beryl a glass of water.

"It's fine. Maybe just nerves. I'm sure it will be alright."

Peter relaxed as he left the room to face the waiting crowd. Beryl drank heartily.

"Are you sure you want to continue? You look quite pale."

"It is fine Cyril, please don't worry yourself." Her words didn't quite have the impact she had intended but Cyril didn't question her further and they joined Peter on stage, much to the appreciation of the remaining audience.

Inside Beryl was trying to fathom why the spirit had a familiarity about it? It was as if she knew the spirit, as if it was as familiar to her as one of her guides, yet, however much she racked her brain, nothing came forth.

5

"Ladies and gentlemen, Miss Wallace is ready to continue."
There was the sound of a lonely clap. "Thank you," Peter added
half-heartedly.

The audience watched in silence as Beryl took to the stage,
her mind clearly uneasy. Something about this spirit made her
wary, there was an anger, a regret, and a deep sense of loss, very
powerful emotions on their own, but when combined, wielded
an extraordinary power. Beryl had never been so completely
taken by a spirit, spirits emotions were in their words and not
in manifestation. She had been disturbed to find herself sitting
on the front of the stage, unaware that she had even sat down,
her memory blank for those few minutes except for the nagging
feeling of a connection.

She thought back to her parlour when Peter had first turned
up, it had all been so innocent, no pressure, the evenings could
take their own course.

***

"I see a new face amongst us," her soft voice had drifted like a lazy
summer breeze dancing amongst the trees. Beryl smiled warmly
at Peter. "I only hope that you have come with an open mind. I do
not promise to be able to answer your questions or even provide
the guidance you may want but, if the spirits are willing, my
guides and I will do our best." Beryl hesitated, tilting her head to
one side, as if listening to someone.

Peter folded his arms curiously, watching Beryl perform,
wondering what he had allowed Edward to talk him into.

"We are fortunate tonight as my guide tells me we have a
visitor already who is anxious to speak with someone."

Peter scoffed quietly in disbelief. What an act he thought. Fred's
face lit up in hope whilst Beryl tried to conceal her sympathy for
him.

"I am getting the name Harold. Does that mean anything to
anyone?" Blank faces met Beryl's gaze. "He is in an army uniform

and walks with crutches."

Still silence blanketed the parlour. "I am not getting anymore. If this spirit doesn't belong to anyone then I will ask him to go." A few seconds passed and no one acknowledged. "Then I ask you to go…with our love."

★★★

It was so easy then; people didn't expect results everytime. Maybe this spirit was connected to this hall in some way and that was why he was coming through so strong.

Although still drained, she had felt obligated to continue. Her spirit guides were faint, as if being blocked by an invisible wall and that made Beryl edgy. The sea of faces stared expectantly at Beryl as she became aware of the spirit again. Inside she fought to control it but the immense strength overpowered her as she absorbed its' energy. Breathing with difficulty her demeanour physically changed.

Cyril stared on, concerned. He remembered the first time he had seen her bind with a spirit, Beryl's fingers had contorted, she had rocked slightly back on her heels as she sank deeper into her trance, her toes curling up, whilst her body trembled slightly as the temporary joining had taken place. Yet she always had control. What was different?

Cyril pondered whether he should try and stop this. He looked at Peter but as he went to say something Beryl spoke…

I watched from my son's box room window, the lights were off. I didn't want anyone to see me, my face hidden by the thick, dirty net curtain.

Beryl became physically choked by the anguish she felt. The spirit continued unabated.

Mentally, I made notes of what they looked like, every ugly detail of their horrible annoying faces, whilst they stood smug in the knowledge that nothing would ever happen to them. There would be no repercussions. This would just be another night of entertainment, like watching TV was for most people, most normal people.

I reflected on what normal used to mean to me. A memory of a time so tranquil, and pleasant, and yet so far away. A tear brushed down my cheek. I found it hard to believe I still had the capacity to shed a tear. I thought I'd cried them all out, shed the last one a long time ago

6

The group of youths. No, I can't call them that. That would imply that they were human. Wolves! Yes, wolves! That's far more apt. Nothing more than wolves sucking the marrow out of existence, tearing at the very threads of life, my life, and all life surrounding them.

I counted seventeen wolves rallying round the burning mass, jeering and laughing. In the distance I could see people's curtains twitching as they watched in horror as another nail was banged firmly in the proverbial coffin of this estate. This was just another tortured night watching and waiting to see who would remain unharmed and unaffected. Like me, most dreamt of leaving the estate and living in a quite cul-de-sac somewhere else. The innocents betrayed by a society that no longer seemed to be able to control the anger and abuse. Human rights only managed to protect those that broke the law, leaving law abiding citizens destined to be drowned in the excrement that was left.

It hurt me inside to watch. I'd suffered so much pain, but there was little I could do.

Twenty minutes passed before an explosion rocked the house catching me unaware, waking me from my hypnotic stare into oblivion, making me almost pull my protective net curtain down. One of the wolves, a shaved headed one, saw me. My pulse raced. I had their attention now, I was their next target.

Shaved-head pointed up at the window and to me, hiding behind it, then gave me the finger. He had the upper hand. I was scared. I had seen what they could do.

Attracting the attention of the rest of the wolves I knew it would be a long night on a knife edge, although part of me didn't care anymore, the dead part of me – the lonely defeated part.

Predictably the focus changed to me and the house that used to be my home, the burning car, a forgotten distraction. I can hear them still, baying at me, their war cries like thunder in my head.

The first stone hit the window and ricocheted off inoffensively. I cowered back into the room falling backwards onto my son's broken, rotting, empty bed, the pungent smell of urine and faeces, a token of what the wolves thought of other people's possessions. They had been in here before. I was shaking, terrified, knowing what the wolves were capable off. A thud shook me and it was quickly followed by the sound of breaking glass, a half brick just missed me, landing on the floor.

I was sweating, my hands shaking. The noise from the wolves was worse now, they were so close. I sat up, putting my hands to my ears, gently rocking backwards and forwards with my knees tight to my chest, desperately trying to shut out the howls of the wolves. This torment was fun to them. I heard more missiles hit other windows of my house that was like my prison cell - soon to be a coffin.

In the distance there was a faint wailing of sirens. Finally, the police were turning up. The police, what a laugh, like sending children to do a man's job. The Marines or the SAS would have been more appropriate. The police couldn't handle the wolves. The police tried, but they were out-numbered and out-weaponed. They tried to avoid coming onto this estate, every day it got closer to becoming a no-go zone, a war zone - we would become the forgotten ones in time. When they did turn up it only had the affect of scattering the wolves back to their bolt-holes temporarily whilst they sussed out the situation and planned their next strike.

I had witnessed stand offs between the police and the wolves. The wolves stood invincibly whilst the police visibly shook, knowing what they were letting themselves in for - they had repercussions if they didn't follow protocol. Eventually the police would retreat off the estate for their own safety – they wanted to stay and fight, return some law and order – but it was a monumental task and only managed to entertain the wolves. The wolves returned to their lairs on the estate to the welcoming embrace of motherly or fatherly adoration, the congratulations of a job well done.

What could the police or fire brigade do? They knew that there were innocents involved, but they had to consider their own lives as well and as much as they may have wanted, they couldn't legally touch the wolves, bureaucratic nonsense and red tape had gone too far. Do-gooders tried to protect the innocent and instead all they did was make it harder to control the minority, the wolves. Democracy ruled by minorities!

I heard a knock at the door. The outside noise had quietened, the wolves dispelled for a short respite. The police were doing the rounds looking for witnesses. People who were brave enough to stand up and be counted.

The fire brigade had got the burning car under control. We were all too scared to say we saw anything. Irony – we wanted this sort of thing stopped but no one would put their necks on the line. A few had, and died shortly afterwards, now the rest of us had learnt not to.

The second knock on the front door was harder. I walked to the top of the stairs and looked down to see the shapes of police officers outside. They called my name, they knew me, they knew my history. My name didn't mean anything to me anymore. An identity lost in the realms of time, I believed I'd become a statistic. I watched as the officers realised, as much as they wanted to help, it was a lost cause. Still they tried a few more times to rouse me. But I wouldn't speak to them. That time had gone. Dejected they left.

I went to what used to be my bedroom at the front of the house and watched as they knocked on other doors. They were met with the same response. There is a mutual understanding that just holds the estate in the gridlock and depravity that exists on this night and every other night like this. 365 days a year, Christmas does not give relief, drink and drugs fuelling the wolves, loose fireworks that wreak havoc. Police talk about community spirit and togetherness, but when people are too terrified they have got an impossible task on their hands and I sympathise with them. It won't change how I am towards them though. I have paid the bitter price.

It is late and while there is the lawful presence outside, the estate is in relative tranquillity, briefly – the wolves can't be bothered to attack the police, blessed relief.

Tired and thirsty I headed off to my bed.

My bedroom was now in the cold draughty loft. The only place I felt relatively safe from the wolves. Every night I hauled the ladder up behind me replacing the hatch, pretending I'm not in, wishing I wasn't. If the wolves entered, as they so often did, then I might escape unscathed. A part of me wanted them to end my miserable existence but I fought that thought as something still kept me going. I didn't want to give them the satisfaction of beating me. In the sanctity of daylight I will patch up the broken windows. Daylight doesn't change the estate, it just seems less frightening.

I felt safe in my loft space even though there was not a large amount of room, it was boarded roughly. Everything of value to me was up here, photos, laptop, kettle, crockery, cutlery and clothes. Not much to show for fifteen years in this house, but then I didn't have much of anything *left, the few clothes I owned were piled neatly in one corner and once a fortnight I'd go to the laundry and get them cleaned.*

This particular night as I lay down in the dark contemplating the future, I resolved to change things. For seven months I had lived like this. Haunted by the memory of my life before. Haunted by the sounds of a happy home, haunted by my own inadequacy to protect my family.

Beryl laid down on her back at the front of the stage, fluffing up imaginary pillows, much to the entertainment of the audience who sniggered quietly.

I lay in my uncomfortable makeshift bed. It was September and reasonably mild, I was not looking forward to the winter, although I had a heater, when it got really cold it would provide little in the way of real warmth. I had done my best to insulate myself from nature's elements but there was only so much one could do without money. I hadn't worked for three years. The factory closed. The main source of work for the area, 10,000 people lost their jobs in one fell swoop. I tried anything to avoid claiming benefits but I couldn't even get a job cleaning toilets; over subscribed with applicants I was always the last in line and eventually as depression took its hold I had stopped trying.

The factory closing was the first nail in the coffin for this area as houses became worthless, mortgages higher than the true value, negative equity became a byword. A good majority of the 14,000 people crammed onto this estate had lost the last mainstay of their income.

The ideal of Shelbourne was to be a community of its own, united. Well, they got that right - united in terror. Run by the wolves. It didn't take long to get that way. A single incident would lead to recriminations and as the police investigated each one so a backlog would build up, the police couldn't cope, ordinary law abiding citizens started taking the law into their own hands, exacerbating the situation. That was when the wolves really took a hold.

Beryl lay quietly and the audience looked on, wondering if she was finished, whispers broke the silence. She spoke again.

This particular night, something filled me with a new determination. Deep in the recesses of my mind came the rumblings of an idea. I would surf the net to look for the answers, for help. I didn't know what I would be looking for but hoped the search engines would throw up something.

A noise downstairs interrupted my reverie.

Beryl sat up.

7

The wolves had got in again. Making their presence felt, using terror to silence me, keeping their identities hidden from the police. They would smash anything that I hadn't taken up into the loft, tables, chairs, even light bulbs were targets.

In the sanctuary of my make shift bedroom I was relatively safe. I extinguished the light. I dared not move for fear they would find me. Listening, as they did their worst, hearing them call me, not by name but by every profanity their unimaginative minds could think up.

Beryl hugged her knees close to her chest as if creating a zone of safety.

The anger welled up inside, I wanted to fight. My fists were clenched tightly as I heard the splintering of wood.

Crash! Another bit of my life decimated. It was three in the morning and it would be another half an hour until they got bored and left.

As I listened to the destruction a powerful urge gripped me tighter, the resolve to try and do something. A determination to change things. An idea festered away in my mind as yet unclear but there all the same. Tiredness abated, I surfed the net which was my only lifeline to the outside world, from my safe haven. A new calmness engulfed me.

Staring at the blank dialogue box I pondered what to type, letting every bad thought of what I'd like to do to the wolves course through my veins. I typed in 'Deathwish' just because I knew of the films – loads of junk information about Charles Bronson came up, some with very tenuous links. I tried 'revenge', useless sites about the definition or games, or shops. I opened one about curses and that started to conjure up thoughts about the magick they depicted. I typed in Voodoo, because I saw it on a page, endless lists appeared, from books to people offering their services, even experiences. I ordered a couple of second-hand books hoping I had enough money left from my benefit cheque to pay for them. I typed in 'rituals' and got everything from Pagan to Satanic. I became engrossed as life started to course through me. I felt alive again. It was not until I heard the dawn chorus outside that I guessed what the time was. In total I had ordered eight books including the Satanic Bible. One thing that seemed to be prevalent was that it was more about belief, an understanding of ones self and harbouring all that energy to focus it on the work that was needed.

Leaving my safe-haven in the roof I surveyed the damage downstairs. There was excrement on the kitchen worktops. Someone has urinated on the battered sofa in the lounge, and the back door kicked in. But, rather than the usual heavy sighs followed by the long deep depression. I smiled. The course was set. Their comeuppance assured in my mind. If only they knew.

Beryl flopped exhausted onto the floor.

Cyril rushed to her aid immediately, placing his arm gently round her back and pulling her into him. She rested her head gently on his shoulder and lazily opened her eyes.

"Are you okay Auntie?" Cyril couldn't hide the concern in is voice.

Awestruck the audience started to applaud, showing their appreciation, which momentarily lifted Beryl's energy, but in her head the room started to spin.

"Cyril can you…" She blacked out.

Peter stepped from behind the table gathering his thoughts to address the pleased crowd, allowing himself a moment's congratulatory pat on the back at the success of the evening, but there was the promised book-signing still to do.

"Ladies and gentlemen, thank you for your appreciation. I can assure you that Miss Wallace is perfectly alright." He didn't know whether she was. "Now, if you would like to read more from Miss Beryl Wallace then there is a small stall at the back of the hall where you can purchase copies of her first two books, 'Anne Farmer' and 'Justice for John Johnson'."

"I still say it's all a load of rubbish," the young man from earlier shouted with less conviction, not wanting it to appear that Peter had actually got the better of him, although Peter was surprised that he had remained whilst the others had left.

"Very well, sir, you are entitled to your opinion. But have you not been entertained? Have you not listened, gripped by the tale Miss Wallace has portrayed for us?"

The young man shifted uncomfortably in his chair aware that there were many sets of eyes looking at him.

"Well, it was alright, s'ppose," he mocked begrudgingly.

"I do have one question, Mr Phillips," spoke a gentleman sitting in the fifth row, the remaining strands of his hair plastered to his scalp. "What is a laptop and the...what was it she said...mmmm...ah, that's it," he said clicking his fingers, "surf the net?" There was a general murmur from the rest of the audience eager to hear the answers.

"Yes, well." Peter searched for an answer or something he could say glancing to the door where Cyril and Beryl had disappeared. "Well," he cleared his throat. "To be honest, I don't know." Regaining his composure he continued more confidently spinning a yarn. "You cannot always know where a spirit originated, so there can be colloquialisms that are unfamiliar. It is probably something mundane like a book or a game. As the spirit has not given us where he resides, I mean resided, or rather where Shelbourne was located, it keeps us in the dark. I'm sure it will all become clear in due course of the story." The answer was not what the man wanted to hear but it seemed to pacify him. "And sir, if it does not, then I will make sure these terms are explained in a reference section at the back of the book." The audience looked a little let down by this but didn't know what else they could do except to take it at face value.

Peter left the stage hoping that someone would not remind him about the book-signing session that had been promised.

***

Beryl and Cyril sat in the dressing room. Beryl had finished two glasses of water by the time Peter entered smiling.

"Well, I think we can say that was a resounding success."

"Peter…" Cyril started.

"Cyril!" Beryl pleaded, feeling that her nephew might say something untoward, knowing that this situation had soured somewhat since the initial discussions about publishing the stories of spirits had been muted.

***

"Excuse me, Mrs Wallace."

"Miss Wallace," Cyril corrected, closing his pad and gathering up his pencils, noting that he didn't like the conspiratorial look

Mr Phillips had, a smugness that he tried to hide.

"Sorry, Miss Wallace. Forgive me." He spoke with a suave sophistication, the epitome of charm. "I was very fascinated by the story of Anne Farmer that you told this evening. As well as intrigued by the reminder of Judy, my faithful friend." He brushed a mock tear away. "It really caught my imagination. The emotions of such a young girl going through so much trauma. Devastating. Her story had a poignancy about it."

"The truth often has, Mr Phillips."

"Peter. Please, call me Peter." Pausing he watched Beryl for tell-tale signs that he was winning her over, moderating his tone accordingly. "I saw the way it affected everyone in the room, including myself." Edward, who was standing nearby, now knew where this was going.

"The point I am trying to make is that I would very much like to hear more of Anne's story, if I may." Cyril held his notepad tighter to his chest. "I think...if I may be so bold as to say that it could be worthy of being turned into a book." He saw the astonishment and horror on Beryl's face as she glanced at Cyril.

"Please, don't get me wrong, Miss Wallace." He was losing her. "You see I think it would be a great tale for the young people of today who are having a hard time at home. Help promote family values. Let others learn from her."

"I know it may seem strange, Mr Phillips." Beryl emphasized his name, she didn't like to call strangers by their first name so soon after meeting them, and something about Peter made her want to keep her distance. "But I do not do this for profit, it is a calling. The small donation you gave at the beginning I give to the church. I was fortunate enough to be left this house when my parents died. I have a very meagre existence, I do not care for possessions."

Peter was losing control of the situation. "I understand that, and I appreciate your view, but I feel there is a multitude of young girls who might benefit from Anne's sad and unfortunate tale. Yes, I'll admit the money means something to me, after all, I am a businessman at heart." He smiled warmly showing a set of yellowing teeth. "But if I can do something to help the young at the same time then I feel we could both benefit."

Peter had a winning patter when he turned on the charm and he could see Beryl contemplating his idea. Her brow furrowed as she looked towards Cyril who was now standing at her side. Now for the winning statement he thought.

"Think of the young girls…" He remembered what she had said about the donation from this evening and quickly added "…or the church, that you could help with the money you could make. I will even put you in contact with organisations that could do with the sort of money we could be talking about.

All I am asking, at this stage, is that you give it some consideration, Miss Wallace."

"What do you think, Cyril?" Beryl asked. Peter's words hadn't managed to convince Cyril of his sincerity.

Peter knew how to play this. She was on the edge and with a beaming smile and eye contact he said. "No need to make a decision tonight. Please, take my card and we can talk more another day…or evening. I would very much like to return, if I may? I do think Anne's story, especially if the rest is as poignant as tonight's episode, could touch the hearts of many and reach so many unhappy girls."

Cyril showed Mr Phillips and Edward Grace to the door. Peter shook Cyril's hand firmly as if sealing a deal.

"Goodnight Edward. It was nice to see you again."

"Goodnight Cyril. Beryl was magnificent tonight, and I look forward to next week."

Cyril closed the door and looked at his hand in mock disgust, trying to dismiss the man and his offer. But as much as he had taken an instant dislike to Mr Phillips he knew the rewards would allow them to carry on with the charitable work helping those less fortunate than themselves, and ultimately that was what his aunt wanted. He looked at his pad and flicked affectionately through the handwritten pages of scribbled notes with a new pride, pride that his notes could be turned into a book.

***

"Now do you think you can go out and do some book-signing?" Peter added without thinking.

"My aunt is exhausted." Peter's smile evaporated. "I have never seen her quite so tired after a session, and she has never been so animated." Cyril became more confident. "No. I don't think she can."

Beryl looked pensively at Cyril and stroked his arm, she was physically exhausted. Peter stood shell-shocked.

"But the audience is expecting her out there to sign books."

"I realise that, but I don't think it is a good idea. Not tonight."

"Peter, please pass on my apologies," as Beryl spoke she seemed to struggle to get her breath. "Maybe we should have done the book-signing beforehand?"

Peter looked deflated but conceded reluctantly.

"Very well, if you go back to the B&B, I will talk with the crowd."

"Thank you," Cyril added curtly.

Peter smiled and bid both a goodnight before returning to the stall.

"Where can we get the books signed?" A lone voice beckoned, grabbing everyone's attention. A tall burly man stood in front of Peter.

"I can see how disappointed you all are and it was planned that Beryl sign all her books sold at these events. But unfortunately I couldn't predict how ill she would be."

"Ill?" a woman questioned.

"Yes, I'm afraid Miss Wallace is feeling a little under the weather, she was before we started this evening, and so I have sent her to her room to rest."

"Bloody typical," the man said, disgruntled walking off, startling Peter.

He watched as more disappointed customers left the hall.

8

When Peter finally made it back to the B&B he couldn't help but feel flushed at the success of the evening, the books sold like hot cakes. Although he was very tired he found it hard to sleep as the excitement at the prospect of more money coursed through him. He was so glad that Beryl had taken up his book offer as it was giving him the success that his father had attained yet had been so elusive to him. When Beryl had arranged a meeting to discuss publishing the books it had been like a joyous cry. In the dark Peter replayed the meeting back in his head.

***

Sitting behind his father's old leather-top desk he perused the contract he had ready for Beryl. It was a standard contract, a three-book deal, with plenty of tie-ins to make sure he could get his money's worth. Suddenly the intercom screeched to life.

"Mr Phillips. Miss Wallace & Mr Hewington are here," Peter's secretary said professionally.

"Thank you Valerie. Send them in." Peter said excitedly, placing the contract back in his desk drawer, before adding, "And bring some tea in." 'Manners' would impress Beryl and create a good impression. "Please."

Peter had been in a good mood since Beryl's phone call the day before, delighted that she had even entertained his idea. He knew now that he had her exactly where he wanted, unless he said something completely offensive to her moral standing, then he knew she would not sign a contract with him. Although he had a good feeling about this meeting, he didn't want to push the contract just yet, in case she baulks at the formality so soon, unless it felt right to do so. There was definitely something about her stories that would capture the public's imagination, more so than any other authors he had signed to Phillips Publishing and Literary Agency (a business that had been set up by his father in 1936, for all manner of technical manuals needed at the time. Only in later years had it moved into works of fiction).

As the door opened Peter cursed himself for not opening it, creating the impression of a gentleman. Jumping up from his green leather swivel chair he hurried to greet his guests.

"Miss Wallace, welcome. Come in," he added more formally. "Cyril, pleased to meet you again." Peter shook Cyril's hand firmly. "I see you have brought the notes with you. Excellent, excellent. I was amazed at the notebook my driver brought over yesterday." Cyril smiled meekly, still unsure what to make of this businessman, his initial distrust of him waning.

Cyril looked around the opulent office with its shelves upon shelves of books all neatly arranged. The desk was perfectly organised with everything in its place. He had expected piles of paperwork strewn across it.

"Please, take a seat. I must admit I was a little surprised, but pleased, when I got your call yesterday, I think this project is very exciting." Peter was finding it hard to stifle his excitement. This felt like the time he signed his very first author, a proud moment for him that had been met with a modicum of excitement from his father. His father had shaken his hand as if a stranger. It had taken the wind out of his sails at the time, his father never got excited not even when that particular author, Jack Hamilton, had made them a small fortune before going on to sign with a bigger publisher.

Now though he had complete control and sometimes he found it hard to hide his delight, he knew a good story when he heard it.

"You have my nephew to thank for that, Mr Phillips." Cyril still clutched three notebooks tightly to his chest and looked awkwardly at Peter. "He convinced me of the good work that we could do if we made any money."

"Miss Wallace, I don't believe it is a question of 'if' but more 'how much'. Just from the short extract of Cyril's work I have read so far I can tell that Anne's story is more than worthy of a…"

"And, as I was going to add. The people we might be able to help. I am not familiar with the ways of business, Mr Phillips, but believe in honesty from the outset. Therefore, I would like to make one point perfectly clear at this point and that is I want Cyril to write the book. He is a very good story-teller, he has a natural way with words and, as he has been part of the initial process I think he understands the spirits. He has been present at all the evenings." Cyril turned crimson.

Peter looked at both his visitors. "I don't believe that will be a problem. From what we discussed yesterday on the phone and the initial notebook I would be inclined to agree. It takes talent to take notes and turn them into a well-crafted book and Cyril certainly has that."

A knock at the door stopped Peter in his tracks.

"Enter."

Valerie walked in pushing a trolley on which were three bone china cups and saucers accompanied by a large teapot and a small plate of digestive biscuits. Valerie caught Cyril's eye and smiled, he timidly reciprocated.

"Thank you, Valerie." Valerie passed out the cups lingering momentarily longer when it came to Cyril and, with a little smile, resumed her duties. It was a moment that didn't go unnoticed to all in the office.

"I like to look after my authors, Miss Wallace, as they are essential to the success of this business. We have nearly forty years experience and in that time have created a respected reputation in publishing. I believe in looking after my investments."

"Thank you. It is difficult for me to believe that enough people would be interested in reading these stories, Mr Phillips, so forgive me if I seem a little hesitant."

"I completely understand, Miss Wallace." Peter rocked back in his chair knowing that she was, in theory, looking for guidance. "I also understand that you don't know me as we have only met once. So I have invited a good friend and acquaintance of mine to join us - Edward Grace." Beryl's eyes lit up as she knew him to be a lovely gentleman. "I thought it might be nice if we met for lunch and that way you could discuss with him any doubts you might have, therefore enabling you to make an informed decision."

Beryl looked to Cyril who seemed more relaxed at the

mention of Edward Grace who had been coming to Beryl's evenings for about a year, on and off.

"Can I ask a question?" Cyril asked, his voice languishing above a whisper.

"Of course you can, Cyril," Peter answered brightly.

"Will I have to work here?"

"Well..." Peter folded his arms and rested his elbows on the desk. "First, I will read through what you have got, as I prefer to take this project on personally. Just to see where there might be room for slight adjustments."

"But you said you liked the way I write."

Beryl eyed Peter cautiously.

"You are quite correct Cyril, however, even the best authors need someone to oversee their work." Peter continued before Cyril could interrupt him. "I have no intention of changing the story or your style just moderating it here and there to suit the audience."

Cyril looked hurt and rested his right hand protectively on the notebooks that he had placed on the desk, the move was noted by Peter.

"Look, I think the best thing might be," Peter paused, in part for effect, and in part to work out how he was going to play this. "Yes, just hold on a moment." Peter pressed the intercom bottom, it crackled into life. "Valerie, would you mind coming in please?"

Valerie entered a few seconds later and Peter saw Cyril's face brighten, he knew then he was onto a winner.

"Valerie, would you be so kind as to show this young man round the offices and introduce him to Arthur." Then, standing up to encourage Cyril to go with Valerie added. "Arthur is one of our best, I like to call them advisors, he helps my authors with the little finishing touches, he will help explain what I mean by changes."

"Come with me Mr Hewington, I'll show you around," Valerie said flirtatiously, trying remain professional.

"Please, Cyril," Valerie smiled, and Cyril reciprocated.

As they left Peter offered Beryl another cup of tea.

"Thank you," Beryl said taking the offered refill. "Mr Phillips, thank you for allowing my nephew to take a look around, I feel it is important that he feels comfortable that his work is being looked after." She paused, "There is one thing."

"Yes, Miss Wallace?"

"You have made no mention of a contract." The statement caught Peter off-guard yet he managed to look unfazed.

"You are quite right. I would normally be talking about a contract, about now, with my clients, but..." Peter was a little unsure about this woman in front of him, he was usually very good at reading people. At first she had seemed quiet and demure but it belied her acumen of how things worked. "I want to be sure you are happy, like all my authors, at how or rather at what pace everything is going. I shan't lie to you, Miss Wallace, once the process starts it can be pretty daunting. I need you to believe that I will be there every step of the way to help make the road as smooth as possible."

"I see. And the contract?"

"It is a formality that can be addressed at a later date, when you are sure. When you are happy."

"That's very considerate, Mr Phillips." Peter smiled, now he wasn't sure if he was winning or not, she was very difficult to read.

"Miss Wallace, please help yourself to biscuits."

9

The Community Village Hall, Rattlesden

The atmosphere was electric in the hall as Peter watched the ambling crowd hovering around the bookstall at the back for the second night of the tour. Inviting the press to the first night had ensured that the tabloids exploded with reviews. Many quoting the reactions from their own astrologers, who knew nothing of spiritualism but were the closest to hand to offer any opinion at short notice, despite not being present. Peter was ecstatic, whether the opinions were good or bad didn't matter, he knew they would grab people's attention and arouse natural curiosity. Beryl had already garnered press attention from the first two books, and with 'Justice for John Johnson' kicking up a press frenzy opening up an old police case, things couldn't be better.

The ambient noise rose above normal conversation level. Peter had drafted in help to organise teas and coffees; another money spinner. The bookstall, run by Adele and Tracy, had already seen excellent sales of Beryl's books on the first night, and Peter was wondering whether it would be a prudent move to bring in books from the rest of his stable of writers.

In the dressing room Cyril looked at his aunt, her eyes were dull, her complexion sallow.

"Are you alright?"

"Tired, very tired. I didn't sleep well in a strange bed." She didn't want to let Cyril know that the connection she had felt with the spirit was what had kept her mind racing half the night, frantic because she couldn't fathom why she felt the familiarity.

"I know what you mean. I ended up working on 'Samuel Preston' for the best part of the night."

"And how is it coming along?" Beryl asked wearily.

"Good. I'm pleased with it. I've done a few of the re-writes that Arthur suggested, still got a few to do, oh, and I finished the notes that Peter wanted, to recap the story so far. Do you think you'll get the same spirit again?"

Beryl looked forlornly at the wall behind Cyril's shoulder. One night and already she was shattered from the tour. She did feel the spirit was close by, a strange ominous presence that she couldn't shake.

"I think I will. I don't know why, but I think I feel him close by."

"That's good isn't it?" There was a hint of caution in Cyril's voice.

"Yes, I guess it is," but her answer didn't have the impact it was meant to and Cyril saw the pressure she was under.

Peter had pushed the book-signing to the beginning of the evening. Questions had come quick and fast from the crowd, as well as demands for autographs. Peter had even mocked up a cover of what would be Cyril's first book and this was gaining interest, which managed to put Peter's mind at rest as to whether it was a good idea to take on Cyril's book project.

Now the crowd sat holding their signed copies in anticipation of seeing her work first-hand. The mêlée quickly hushed as Peter took the stage to make his opening remarks which included a summary of the first night, compiled by Cyril, that way everyone had an idea of what had happened. Peter hadn't questioned whether the same spirit would return for the second night, however, when he stood centre stage he too felt some of the pressure Beryl must have felt, a little part of him even wondered whether he had been foolish to ignore Beryl's warning that she may not always get the same spirit.

Peter's mind was a hive of activity as questions raced round inside. How would it look if they got a different spirit? What would people say? How would the evening pan out? This summation would be useless?

He gulped, knowing he could do little now other than to proceed as planned, reading out Cyril's summation. The audience showed their appreciation with a generous round of applause making him feel a little easier.

As Beryl took to the stage she gasped, Cyril instinctively put his arm around her.

"What's wrong?"

"He's closer now, I can feel him."

"Do you want to go on? Can't your guides hold him back?"

"He is too strong for them. I'll be fine, I'm sure." Beryl gently pushed Cyril away from her and shuffled forward to take centre of the stage area which was only a foot above floor level, leaving Cyril momentarily at a loss. As Peter sat down he prayed that the same spirit was here. The audience took a sharp intake of breath, holding it briefly before letting it out again.

Beryl stood with all eyes upon her; she could feel Cyril's eyes piercing into her back. She knew he was there for her. The latent spirit's presence was all around her like a dark menacing cloud. Filled with trepidation she started to take a deep breath, but before she could finish the spirit had taken control, eager to tell his story. The voice that projected was a mix of Beryl's and the spirit's. The dark tones resonated around the hall. All Cyril could do was make notes and hope that his aunt would be okay.

Beryl edged closer to the front of the staged area, it seemed the spirit wanted to perform, knew he had an audience.

The next few days were quiet for the estate. I'd boarded up the window and back door which made the house feel even more like a dark dingy prison. It was pointless replacing the glass panels, for as well as the expense, it would only give the wolves more power to intimidate me. In my mind I thought if I left the boarded up windows on show they would think I was beaten and hopefully leave me alone to fade away.

The books I bought were delivered a couple at a time and made a pleasant change from the bills and demands that seemed to arrive in their multitudes. It was pleasant to have a purpose, an interest to occupy the hours of the day. I studied the books diligently, like a keen scholar, a few of them were self-published and not very well proof read, spelling mistakes littered the pages.

Some had lots of useful information, others just seemed to be full of dialogue that went nowhere and said very little. I pulled out the information I thought might be important and discarded the books I thought were rubbish.

In my safe haven I went about making an altar, as described in 'The Grimoire of Anthony Jenkins, mentor of Dark Powers', using the black candles that had been included. I had also ordered one of the gypsy curse kits that I had found on the internet, it contained white candles and a protection spell, just in case the law of nine should truly exist. It stated, that if a curse was invoked for revenge and was not honestly warranted then the curse would return nine-fold to the instigator.

My altar looked simple and rather silly. I'd drawn a pathetic looking pentagram on the floor in felt tip pen and labelled Gods' names at certain cross-sections as described in the books. A part of me wondered what the hell I was doing. Had I truly lost my mind?

With nothing left to lose though, experimentation didn't seem like such a bad idea. What else had I to do? I racked my brain for something simple, a test, a gauge, nothing was forthcoming, so reluctantly I left my safe haven to wander around the rest of my prison, looking for inspiration.

Beryl paced the stage, head down, her body language sullen.

I sat on the lounge floor.

Beryl sat down.

Watching day fade to night. The familiar outside noises of battle cries and baying wolves penetrated my cell as I wallowed in self-pity.

A quick movement caught my eye and I saw a mouse scurry across the floor. I watched as the mouse stopped and stood up on its hind legs to study me in the dim light, its nose twitching.

Taking pity on it, I picked up a stale crumb of bread or biscuit from the floor and offered it to the mouse. A Mexican stand off ensued as the mouse eyed the proffered morsel of food, nose twitching as it picked up the scent, but wary of the giver. I kept as still as I could and then very hesitantly the mouse scampered forward, stopping every few steps to check it was still safe.

After a long time, and when the mouse was just a few inches from my hand, it launched itself at the food, but instead of just biting at the crumb, it bit my finger. I swore, instantly retracting my hand. A globule of blood emerged from my finger which I sucked on impulse, the bite burned. The mouse scampered to the far corner of the room to nibble on the crumb held firmly in its mouth. I lunged at it in anger, shouting my disgust at the creature.

An idea struck me and I went to the kitchen to get something else. It had never occurred to me how desolate my food cupboards and battered fridge, which despite the wolves' best efforts to destroy it still effervesced life. Searching around I found a cube of chocolate that had fallen down the side of the fridge.

Sitting back down in the lounge I waited for the mouse to return. Only a few minutes passed before the mouse picked up the scent of more food. His nose twitched as he emerged from underneath the threadbare carpet. Once again we had a stand off. Time passed until, finally, the mouse found the courage to come closer to take the food from my hand. As it took the proffered chunk I managed to trap it inside a clear plastic tub I held hidden behind my back. I smirked at how easy it had been. Carefully sliding the lid underneath I listened to the brute scampering around looking for a way out - I almost felt sympathy for it, trapped like a prisoner. Trapped, like I felt I was. After punching a couple of air holes in the lid I went upstairs to the loft to contemplate what to do next.

Thinking long and hard about what I could try on the mouse, I watched it as it systematically checked the container for a way out.

"It's not nice is it?" I mocked, as it sat still in one corner, was it curious about its fate? I noticed its rapid breathing so punched some more air-holes in the lid. "Don't want you to die on me, do we?"

A wry smile crossed my face as I decided what I wanted to try. The more the idea rattled around inside my head, the angrier I became and the less sympathetic I was for the mouse.

I was almost ready, ready to plunge myself into the dark world. Take action against my protagonists. I sat back and let the pleasure flow through me, it was the happiest I had felt in a long, long time, ever since I had lost my wife and kids. Practice was essential to see if the magick really worked or if it was all blarney.

I picked up a T-shirt from my small pile of clothes next to my bed and wrapped my hand in it, then, opening the lid of the plastic box I grabbed the mouse tightly and with a pair of tweezers yanked out some hair, I didn't care that the mouse was clearly distressed at the process. Replacing the lid I placed the strands of hair on my altar.

I took my place in the pentagram. Lighting the candles I switched out the light and commanded forth the powers of darkness, starting from the north and working my way round counter-clockwise to the east, emptying my mind I focussed my thoughts clearly on the mouse, concentrating. A surge of energy made me feel euphoric, sending shudders pulsing through me. I didn't really know if I was doing things or whether my imagination or part insanity was playing tricks on me. But it felt real.

I watched the mouse and thought of the suffering I'd like to see. The mouse started to run round in circles in its plastic prison, obviously flustered. Abruptly it stopped. It looked at each corner, sniffed and ran faster and faster.

It was working, it was working, I thought, as jubilation flooded through me. It started to convulse. Carried along with the moment, I imagined myself crushing its tiny heart, joy oozing through me. The mouse keeled over, it chest hardly moving, its tail jerking and flapping around. Then all went still.

I stared in disbelief, pleased at what I had done. I tapped the box – nothing! The mouse lay motionless. I can't remember how long I spent going over and over what I had done. I felt guilt start to ebb its way into me but then I justified that the mouse deserved it, it had bitten me.

A wail of sirens and the jeering of the wolves woke me from my reverie and getting up I banged my head on a rafter, something I hadn't done for a long time. Feeling the bump on my head I felt the first trickle of blood. I cursed the mouse. Everything was the mouse's fault and in my fury I kicked the plastic box across the floor where it hit the bare brick wall with the mouse's body bouncing around inside. I snorted my satisfaction and left my safe haven.

From the bedroom window I could see a column of flames behind the houses that stood on the far side of the green. In a distant street, I guessed, another car was on fire.

A group of wolves stood on the green drinking cans of lager and laughing.A solidly built man, walking his dog on the pavement, tried to pretend they weren't there but the wolves saw him. I saw the desperation on the man's face as he tried to ignore their jeering taunts. One of the wolves, with a studded collar round his neck, threw a crushed beer can at him. The dog yanked at the lead as if to play catch with the can which landed a few feet away. Pulling the dog to heel the man marched on, head down, pace quicker. He knew better than to have a confrontation with the wolves even though they only looked like teenagers.

Standing in the bedroom I watched on for another hour.

One of the wolves, with jet-black-hair, lay down on the grass, as if to go to sleep, leaving the others to slowly drift off, laughing and joking.

They had this estate eating out of their hands and they knew it. My distaste was like salt in my mouth and I muttered my condemnation.

Jet-black-hair remained on the ground even as the first spots of rain fell. A part of me hoped he was dead, wished he was dead, it was what he deserved. But twenty minutes after the rain had started to fall like stair rods he got up a little dazed, and walked off.

I went back up into the loft and to my disgust found the mouse scampering around his box. Deflated, I sunk down on my bed and listened as the rain hit the tiles. Had it all been in my mind?

10

After a time, I picked up the tub and studied the mouse as he sniffed at the air holes looking for a way out.

"So much for dark magick, eh! Or, are you a cat from a previous life. Still got your nine lives left?" I muttered cynically.

Placing the box on the altar I went downstairs to fetch an egg cup of water to place in the mouse's new home. I'd seen enough pointless suffering and didn't see the need to force anymore upon this animal. It drank immediately.

Beryl eased herself down onto the floor, oblivious to her actions.

Laying down on my bed I watched the flames of the candles flicker against the eves of the roof, my mind full with thoughts of anything but where I was and who I was, and slowly I must have drifted into sleep.

I was in the kitchen. The sun was streaming through the window Samantha was boiling an egg for my breakfast.

"Mark," she said, her soft voice like a dream.

"What?" I replied, scoffing down the last remains of my cereal.

"You know we talked about having a family." She scooped the egg from the water and placed it into an egg cup with my name on it.

"Yes. We said we'd wait a couple more years."

"Mmmm, well in that case we should have stopped practising."

"What?" But the reality hit me of what she was implying. "You're pregnant?" I said, astonished.

"Uh-huh. Three months gone. I didn't want to tell you sooner because I wanted to be sure." Samantha was carrying my egg to the table when I jumped up and hugged her tightly sending the egg crashing to the floor where it remained intact by pure fluke. "Careful," she reprimanded me playfully.

"I don't care, that's great news. Anyway it's hard boiled." I picked it up. "See just the shell brok....ah...ah..." I juggled the egg as it burnt my fingers, before throwing it on the table, as it landed the yoke oozed out of a crack and I woke up with a start with the realisation that I

hadn't closed off the gate to the other world.

With second thoughts I decided I couldn't have opened it in the first place, I had no power.

Hours drifted by with the mouse in the background scrabbling at the sides of the box, looking for escape, eager to go back to its family just as I wanted to get back to mine.

When I finally found the motivation to get up I reluctantly re-read the books for want of something better to do. What had I done wrong? There was no real ritual except what you made up, certain elements had to be present and I needed the Gods on my side. 'Belief' seemed to be the key. I questioned whether I had really allowed myself to be totally submerged in belief because of the lethargy I was wrapped up in.

Picking out a couple of flakes from a cornflake box I opened the lid to feed the mouse.

Beryl entertained the audience as she went through the motions.

As soon as I lifted the lid of the plastic box slightly the mouse struck out and went for my finger, sinking its teeth deep into my skin. I withdrew my hand instantly but the mouse gripped tightly and I cursed it as I dragged its body through the tiny opening. Raising it to head height I watched as it hung on refusing to let go, I cringed as the pain intensified.

I shouted a profanity shaking my hand vigorously to try and loosen the creatures grip; still it clung on. Finally, I let out a cry like thunder and squeezed his tiny body with my free hand, its eyes bulged and finally it let go, its body wrestling to get free from my grip.

I threw it with all my might, across the loft space, but rather than lay lifeless where it landed it seemed to mock me by standing up on its hind legs, twitching its nose. I lunged towards it and banged my head on the rafters, again, which only managed to infuriate me further.

Peter watched on as Beryl lunged across the stage, concerned at first that she might hurt herself, Cyril stopped making notes curious at her sudden motion.

"Auntie Beryl?" he called. She didn't respond, but continued with her dialogue, her face showing real anger, focussed at a point somewhere across the stage area.

A stream of abuse, similar to what the wolves use, escaped my lips. The mouse scurried around looking for escape from the bellowing noise.

My mind started to conjure up all sorts of images about the mouse as I continued to mutter my annoyance, sucking my bitten finger, trying to stem the blood flow. I imagined that I was sucking the life force out of the little creature, and quite suddenly, the mouse stopped as if struck by indecision. Remaining still, it visibly contorted in an unnatural way. I sucked harder, staring at the blasted creature, tasting the blood in the back of my throat, imagining it was the mouse's last breath.

In my crazed mind I pictured the mouse being flung against the brick wall and pinning it to it like a poster. I thrust my hand towards the mouse to get a reaction from it, wanting it to scamper away for its life. Instead, the mouse vaulted across the loft space and hit the end wall. I didn't even flinch, as if it had been expected. I watched as its head twitched, I squeezed my left hand tightly and watched the blood form a tiny red ball on my skin; I imagined crushing the mouse's heart. The mouse's eyes popped out of its tiny head, hanging like tentacles on the optic nerves and shock registered within me, breaking my anger, the mouse's body fell dead onto the boarding - this time he really was dead.

Stunned, I had a million thoughts rushing through my head, shock and excitement at what I had, seemingly, done. Questioning whether I was losing my sanity, imagining it. After a few minutes staring at the lifeless body I crawled over to it and checked the physical evidence, tentatively prodding it to make sure it was really dead. It was incredulous that I could do such a thing. Was I pleased or frightened?

After a while I went through the motions of closing off the gateway, believing I had really manifested some sort of power, almost content with the knowledge that I had achieved something, even though I wasn't sure how or why.

'It worked,' I said disbelievingly. If this was all true then all I needed was a definite plan of action.

Beryl fell exhausted to the floor, a cold sweat on her brow, her face ashen. The audience paused in silence. Whatever had happened in the hall held everyone spellbound. Cyril and Peter rushed forward to help her.

"I say Beryl, that acting is just perfect. It is really drawing the audience in."

Beryl's reddened eyes fixed onto Peter.

"I'm sorry Peter, but this isn't right, it has to stop." Cyril spoke unaware that the front rows of the audience could hear him, and they stared up, astonished by the comments.

"We can't just stop now," Peter added. But before Cyril could reply the audience broke into applause.

"It's alright Cyril. I'm fine." Beryl's whispered, her voice dry and hoarse. She placed a hand on his shoulder for support.

"But..." Beryl put her hand up to quieten her nephew before he had time to finish his sentence.

"Well, I think another successful night," spoke Peter brightly, but his cheerfulness was quickly cut down by a sullen glance from Cyril who helped Beryl back to the dressing room.

Ashcroft Guest House.

"How is Beryl?" Peter asked, drinking a glass of brandy. "You sure you don't want one?"

"No thank you, it doesn't agree with me. She is tired. I put her straight to bed. Peter I know this is a liberty but would it be possible to have a couple of days rest? She has never been like this after an evening. You've seen her yourself, with Anne Farmer. She was never animated and only a little tired."

"I know Cyril and it is terrific, the audience absolutely love it." Peter stopped, realising it was not what Cyril wanted to hear. "Look the halls are booked and whilst I agree she does look extremely tired, I have paid out money, the adverts have been placed. How do you think the public will react if she doesn't appear?"

"Well maybe she could just do the book signings."

"I don't think the audience will be happy with that, they have come to see her perform."

"She is not a puppet you know." The words came out angrily. "Sorry."

Peter looked at Cyril, whom he knew not to be an angry person.

"How about if I cover the cost of the hall?" Cyril added.

"That's very noble of you." Peter rolled his brandy round the glass and took a large draft. "I'll see what I can do, but I can't promise anything."

"Thank you," Cyril said, relieved.

"Now, how are those changes to 'Samuel Preston' coming and any ideas for a title or at least a sub-title? I think if you are to break out from under your aunt's name we can't really run with just 'the name', people won't believe the books to be any different."

"I'll be honest, I am struggling with that."

"Well, there's still time yet." With that Peter drank down the rest of his brandy and got up. "Goodnight."

"Night." Cyril sat in the empty bar area of the guest house contemplating the name for his first solo book and wondering what price his aunt was paying for allowing him the chance of a solo writing career. He knew it was the only reason she had agreed to do the tour. He wished he had been stronger at the meeting.

***

"Beryl. Cyril. Good morning. Thank you for coming in. I realise this has not been easy but I hope you see I have come to a compromise that may suit both of us. I have spoken with Edward." Peter saw Beryl acknowledge the comment and in some way it lightened her frosty persona, "and he has helped me understand something."

"He is a lovely man," Beryl added.

"Yes." Peter sat back down behind his desk. "Let's get straight to the point shall we?"

"Please."

Peter felt himself growing weary of Beryl. "As I have said before, and you have agreed, a contract is a contract. I can't back out of it, it wouldn't be right. Now I know Cyril would like to run with the mobster book which he has researched."

"I have almost finished the initial draft. I would have brought it in..." Cyril said excitedly before Peter raised a hand to stop him.

"As I have said before I do not think it is the right kind of story for Beryl's readers." Immediately Peter could see Cyril stiffen. "But, I have a suggestion that I hope will suit all parties."

"We are listening, Peter."

"I would like you to write the third book on a tour." Beryl and Cyril looked at each other, as it confirmed what Edward had said, disappointing both of them. "Beryl, you said to me that you missed the evenings you held in your parlour and the fact that so many people wanted to come along, and that your little room is no longer big enough, following the success of 'Anne Farmer' and 'Justice for John Johnson."

"Yes, but I don't s..."

"I will hire halls…"

"A hall. It's a bit impersonal. Ed..." Beryl tried to interrupt.

"It is the best way I can think of to allow your public to see you in action but also keep a modicum of structure to the evenings."

"But how it would work?"

Beryl had hated the idea when Edward had accidentally mentioned it, yet she knew her contractual obligations. Peter decided the fact that she had not dismissed the idea totally, gave him hope of an amicable conclusion and he started to lighten as he explained his idea. "It would work exactly as your evenings would, except on a larger scale. Then we write the story of whatever spirit contacts you. The advantage being, that some of the book-buying public will feel involved in the process."

"So we travel from hall to hall and I write the story."

"Yes, Cyril."

"So, what about the mobster story?"

"This is where I, compromise, we do a fourth book..."

"So this is where this is going." Beryl went to get up. "Come on Cyril I think enough has been said."

"No wait. The fourth book will be under Cyril's name and will be his chance to establish himself independently, and yes, it gives me something in return. Cyril has an excellent way with words and I don't want to lose that talent, maybe this is one way that we can all work this situation to our own ends."

Peter could see Beryl fighting the idea, but he could also see her warming to the fact that it gave Cyril the chance he deserved.

"I see. But what if we don't get a spirit with a story to tell? It is not an exact science Peter, there are no guarantees. Each place may invoke a different spirit. What then?"

The idea of a different spirit in each hall had not occurred to him and he thought about how to rationalise it.

"Your guides, they are always with you wherever you go aren't they?"

"Yes."

"Then the spirits aren't necessarily tied to the one spot are they? I mean Anne Farmer wasn't tied to your house and neither was John Johnson."

"No. True."

"So if we do this, then I can write my own stories and you'll publish them?" Cyril was caught up in with the idea of being a name in his own right.

"Yes, Cyril. Providing they are good enough. And then you can use any spirits' stories you might have to base them on. It would keep a certain theme that has already been established with your aunt's stories but with a twist of your imagination too. And research."

"Peter, I do not wish to trample over your idea, but I don't think it will work. I do not always get spirits who have a story to tell. You have published two out of about five over the last fifteen years. I think you will have a very disappointed audience if they do not get a story, or even one that starts but we never hear from the spirit again."

"I understand," Peter said but he wasn't really listening, "Beryl, but we can have a book-signing session and maybe you could do readings as well. It is also a chance to quell the rumours that people think you are a fraud."

"Frankly, I do not mind if people think I am a fraud. That is their prerogative."

"But it will help establish Cyril, as he will be on stage taking notes as always. It would open that opportunity for him."

"I see," Beryl said.

Breaking from his own thoughts Cyril added. "I think my aunt is right, I do not think it will work, spirits are unpredictable. We have had evenings when almost nothing has happened. People have been disappointed then. How will a hall full of people react? Just the book signing at Grindley's the other day was daunting." Cyril could see his chance slipping away.

Peter had an idea that maybe she could just make something up, but as quickly as it came he put it to one side as he knew her principles. He slouched back in his chair.

"Okay, I admit I do not have all the details worked out but I think it is the best way forward from here."

Beryl could see that Cyril was excited by the idea of establishing himself independently, and he deserved that. It all sounded quite plausible but scepticism of its success was still strong inside her. One thing it did show her was that Peter was thoughtful, to a degree, after all. He had already pressed the point of the contract and a third book but this was his way of trying to compromise without pursuing a legal argument and she admired that, it showed integrity.

"I think a few more details need to be ironed out first, but, I'll go along with it if you will seriously take Cyril on."

"Definitely." Peter beamed relieved. "Thank you for listening. Now, Cyril, you bring in what you already have on the mobster story and hopefully we can coincide publishing it with Beryl's third book."

"Will do. Thank you so much." Cyril jumped up and shook Peter's hand vigorously, momentarily forgetting the trade-off his aunt was making.

"You're welcome."

As Peter showed them out he asked Valerie to get Edward on the phone.

11

Higham School Hall, Market Harborough

Peter managed to delay the move from Ashcroft guest house for another night, allowing Beryl the rest she needed. Stating in a press release that she had fallen mysteriously ill, knowing it would kick up even further interest, whilst Peter had openly voiced his discontent about postponing one night. Beryl's impending retirement was making headlines, which was more free publicity as far as Peter was concerned, along with stories of whether she was genuine or not.

Experts were being dragged out of the woodwork to cast their own aspersions on Beryl Wallace and her so called 'gift'. Peter decided he needed to arrange for more books to be delivered to the next event as Adele and Tracy found themselves on the receiving end of a frenzied assault of book-buying by an ever-eager audience captivated by Beryl. It was beyond Peter's expectations. Other books from Peter's stable of writers would also be delivered, although these were just bunce and not his major concern for this tour, but at least people would see the names and titles.

Peter paraded the hall like a proud father, informally greeting people, sniffing out members of the press who he thought had, turned up surreptitiously with their so-called experts at their sides. He welcomed them, any publicity was good. Peter gave a little knowing smile to someone he recognised.

"Evening Terence. Come to check it out?" Peter beamed.

"Well, we can't have Phillips Publishing House and Literary Agency having all the kudos, can we? Anyway Peter you know us press we like a good story as do our readers." He raised an eyebrow. "So is there anything you'd like to tell us about this..." Terence searched his note book. "...Beryl?" The comment was loaded with cynicism.

"Beryl Wallace is the real deal." An air of confidence exuded from Peter.

"Well, with two top-selling books you would say that." Pulling Peter to one side, out of earshot of anyone else. "Come on, what is she? Where did you find her?"

Peter smiled broadly. "Terence, ever doubtful as usual. Just sit back and enjoy. You'll be amazed."

"We'll see. We'll see. Can I get an interview with her afterwards?" Terence looked on hopefully.

Peter merely looked at his watch and left the question unanswered. "Nearly time dear boy, please, take a seat." He guided Terence to a nearby chair and then left him.

***

In the dressing room Cyril looked at his aunt with concern.

"Auntie, are you sure you want to continue? I don't feel good about this."

"Stop fussing," she placated. "I, we made an agreement with Peter and I shall stick to it." She smiled and stroked his hand. "It's fine. Everything will be okay. We'll just..." The door flew opened and in walked Peter with a beaming smile.

"Have you seen the newspapers this morning? They can't stop talking about you. Not quite front page news but close enough. How about that? And the press are out there tonight as well, good, good, good." His jubilant voice was met with a wall of silence that he didn't seem to notice. "I've had to order another 400 copies of each book to be delivered to Shrewsbury. I can't wait to get this one out. You'll be rolling in luxury..." He stopped realising what he was saying and the fact that money meant nothing to them. "Well, are you both ready?"

Beryl stood up confidently. "Yes. We are both ready. Aren't we Cyril?" It was a rhetorical question and Cyril barely muttered his acquiescence.

"Good." Peter left the room to take to the stage for his introduction.

***

"Good evening ladies and gentlemen...and members of the press." He caught Terence's eye. "It is so nice of so many of you to come out on a miserable night like tonight but I can promise you, you won't be disappointed."

"We better not be, I'm missing me darts night for this," came an off-hand remark, followed by a slapping noise.

"Stan, you're so embarrassing. One night, I'll…" The woman hushed as all eyes looked upon her and her husband.

"Yes, well, as I was saying, you won't regret it. Now I'll just bring you up-to-date on the story so far…" Peter proceeded to read out the notes that Cyril had prepared whilst the audience sat, intrigued.

"Just one thing before I bring Beryl Wallace on stage, this book will be available early next year along with Cyril Hewington's first book under his own name." There was a tender gasp from the audience. "Now, without further ado. Miss Beryl Wallace." He looked over at the side of the stage.

Beryl walked with a heavy heart, Cyril staunchly at her side, her face slightly sullen as she felt the spirit close by, its sombre dread like a heavy cloud in the hall. Cyril took his place at the smaller than usual table, shuffling his pads and pencils, preparing, whilst Beryl took centre stage in readiness.

The ominous presence started to seep into Beryl. She winced as she fought for control. She hoped the spirit would fail to appear tonight, what a blessed relief that would have been but he was there and, with a pang, his familiarity slipped over her like a cloak. She had prepared a little ceremony, a protection spell for tonight, something that would hopefully stop the spirit taking her so completely, but before she could instigate it the spirit was upon her.

The hours slipped by. I was immersed in my triumphant euphoria. If all was to be believed then the magick really did work. Was I a natural? Where did this latent power come from? Had I got it from my mother? What was she?

I had no definite plan of action yet a frenzied sense of power gripped me, an all encompassing power lifting me up to higher realms. Life seemed good again. It held value for me at last. My appetite was back with a vengeance. I didn't have much food in the house so I had to suffice with a bowl of stale cereal.

The excitement of my achievement left me with an inept ability to concentrate fully on a plan. If I could wield that sort of power then anything was possible, I really could make a difference, I could beat the wolves.

Could I harness this power when I needed it? If not I might end up in all sorts of trouble.

A slip of an idea entered my fevered brain as I visualised the face of the wolf from the other night, a clear picture in my mind. I had nothing physical of Shaved-head only his image indelibly etched in my mind. Would a drawing work? I didn't know but it was the best I could do. Not being a great artist I sketched a likeness as best I could on the back of an envelope.

Beryl mimed drawing in mid air.

I felt alive with excitement that I was doing something positive, putting things right, fighting for my freedom and my peace of mind.

Then doubt entered my head and I tried to usher it away - the mouse, it hadn't worked with the hair that I'd taken, yet it had worked when it had bitten me. Did I need physical contact? Or, was it the anger that had given me the belief, the power, the rage. Yes, the rage! Had I mistaken that for passion, or commitment, allaying any doubt that I could do this?

I looked at the pathetic sketch in my hand then thought about my family.

We stepped through the door. It was the first day we could bring Joshua home from hospital. He had been born two weeks early and they had kept him in to make sure he was strong enough.

I was so nervous that I held him like a delicate china doll, too scared that the slightest movement would break him. Samantha smiled at me, she had a glow about her, this was her chance, our chance to make our son's life so different from how our own lives had been. We had spent the months leading up to his birth decorating the box room, swamping it with cuddly toys and everything we could think of to spend our money on. We wanted him to have everything that we never had.

The first time I placed him in his cot, I stayed and watched him sleep, I must have been there a long time because eventually Samantha came in and placed her arms around me.

I turned and told her, "I love you."

She smiled. "I'd like a daughter."

"What now?!" I said sarcastically.

"No silly. You know what I mean."

"If she turns out anything like her mother, that would be great."

I held Samantha so tight I thought she might burst, I wanted the moment to last forever.

Abruptly the memory faded and I felt the emptiness, the solitude of my life surrounding me; their faces and voices just bitter memories. A sting of a tear reminded me of the desolation of the estate and my home, and how the wolves had wrecked everything that was precious to me racking me inside. Raw emotion was congealing, focussing my thoughts. I could see every piece of blatant vandalism I had ever witnessed. I let the energy fill me up inside like a well of raw power, erupting, projecting the hatred that consumed me at the rough image of Shaved-head. I opened the gateway, following the ritual I had set for myself, my crazed mind seemingly under control, rage boiling just under the surface.

Taking a pen knife from my pocket I slowly and playfully made cuts within the sketch. At first tentatively, thinking about them, planning them, placing them, then slowly the anger manifested itself and every cut became more frenzied. Despite only having a sketch in my hand I could see Shaved-head in person, his physical body. Every ugly feature engraved in my memory from that night, the sneering evil eyes that mocked me, that preyed on weakness, the baying call as his shouted profanities landed at my feet. I could see him being torn to pieces, blood everywhere, a concrete floor, a sea of crimson. I saw the pieces of him scattered over the floor like rubbish.

The sketch lay in shreds on the floor of my safe haven, spots of blood littered some of the shreds, and when I studied my fingers I saw tiny nicks I had made on my own hands. So engrossed by my rage I hadn't felt their pain, detached from it for a minute or so, before it started to register. I examined the cuts as if they were insects, then I couldn't help but smile, this turned to laughter, a maniacal laughter. Was I crossing over into madness? As the laughter died away a warm sense of justice eased through me.

Beryl stood centre stage revelling in the euphoria that the spirit felt. The audience was not sure if she had finished and just as one person started to clap, she spoke again, the fervour gone from her voice.

I closed down systematically thanking the gods from each point on the compass, letting my energy dissipate, the euphoria faded as I took in my surroundings and I realised that nothing had actually changed. Had I expected to find my family around me, all ensconced in the lounge playing happily? They weren't! There was just the desperation of my own surroundings. My delight had completely evaporated.

I scoffed at whether I had actually achieved anything. What was I doing this for? What did I hope to achieve? I wasn't too sure of the consequences and although part of me didn't care, my curiosity was pricked. How would I know?

I went downstairs and started to tidy up my prison cell, return it to some semblance of a life I once knew and would love to experience again. As I tidied, a sense of loneliness encompassed me, how I missed the company of others. How I missed my family. I was sad again and the impetus I had gained, vanished.

The night was quiet, unusually quiet for the area –feeling slightly uneasy. It was nice though, as it should be. I almost believed I could sleep on a normal bed tonight if I had one that had not been decimated by the wolves.

The uneasy serenity was shattered by the sounds of sirens as two police cars hurtled passed the end of my cul-de-sac. Jumping up I ran to the window and could just about see their lights flickering against the night sky. I heard two more police cars, shortly followed by an ambulance.

Something nagged at me to venture from my prison cell. A brave move during the day, let alone at night, yet a strange bravado hugged me and I let myself indulge it. At the end of the road I turned right following the flashing lights littering the sky. The road then turned sharply left and after a quarter of mile there was a fifteen storey block of flats called Shelbourne Heights, a small attempt to make them sound like plush penthouses, they probably were nice – once! They housed some of the worst wolves. A real den of iniquity, some flats still remained burnt out, where the wolves had taken revenge on those who stood in their way.

From a distance I saw the emergency services hesitate, their uniforms made them easy targets, only having strength in numbers, they entered.

A crowd had gathered outside, an unusual sight unless it was a crowd of wolves. These families wouldn't normally dare venture where emergencies services were, too afraid of getting caught up in a backlash.

I surreptitiously joined the crowd and waited with baited breath to find out what was going on. What could unite such a big crowd making them feel comfortable with being out like this at night?

12

Two police officers and a paramedic came out and retched into the flowerbeds that had once been well tended. My first thought was that it was probably from the putrid smell of the degradation and squalor that existed in these blocks, the excrement and urine filled stairwells and corridors, remnants from the drug users.

The three uniforms drank some water provided by another paramedic. I could see the disgust in their eyes as they perused the gathered crowd. I couldn't blame them but I wanted to shout out 'we're not all like that' knowing it would make little difference. They stood talking with each other, wary of the gathering crowd.

Ten minutes later a stretcher was wheeled out with a female strapped to it, she looked young, her two-tone hair matted and untidy, her face contorted in what could only be described as fright, she was placed into a waiting ambulance which promptly left.

I was tempted to ask if anyone knew what was going on but I fought it, uneasy about engaging in conversation with strangers. I wanted to remain anonymous.

A coroner's van turned up about an hour later. More people had gathered. Typical, a death has to occur to unite people. How sick is everyone? Finally I got bored of watching and went home and had one of the most peaceful night's sleep I'd had in a long time.

I dreamt about my son, my daughter and my lovely wife. We'd gone camping in the New Forest, one summer, the four of us with our Jack Russell, Smudge, so named because of the smudge of white he had on his back. That was the last year we had him as he unfortunately got run over just before Christmas.

Samantha was in the middle of cooking breakfast one morning when the tent inexplicably collapsed sending up a gust of wind which blew the stove out and sent our breakfast all over the ground. Josh, Clare, and I were on our way back from the shower block when it happened, we couldn't stop laughing as Samantha was engulfed by the giant canvas. We had to help her fight her way out but as we were in stitches it was quite a battle. Every time we thought we were close, Samantha found herself caught up in another fold of canvas. Samantha didn't see the funny side at first, more concerned about setting fire to the tent. Though when she saw that we couldn't stop laughing she started to laugh too. Eventually we all lay on the ground crying, tears of laughter running down our cheeks, much to the bemusement of the campers around. Those were good times.

We did wonder why it had collapsed and that mystery was solved the following night. I'd been woken up in the early hours of the morning.

"Samantha. Can you hear that?"

Groggily she replied, "What is it Mark?"

"Can you hear that?"

"Where's it coming from? Where are you going?"

"Outside to see."

"Take this." Samantha handed me a torch. I crept out of the tent only to find Smudge awake and pulling at the tent pegs. It all became clear that he thought it was a game. After that I let him sleep with the Josh and Clare, they loved it and it meant the tent stayed up.

Two weeks of bliss is how I remember it now, but I have no one to share it with. Even when it rained for two days we were still happy, we played games, Samantha was very inventive and had endless energy and enthusiasm for us all. If it wasn't for my precious Samantha, the children and I would have been bored and probably have got on each others nerves. She bought out the best in me, in everyone. That's why it is so hard now they're gone.

My life stopped when she went, ceased to exist, a grey barren land filled by the eternity of days and nights all mashed into one, an endless stream of nothing.

Beryl was kneeling on the stage crying, heart felt sobs, causing one or two of the more sentimental audience members to reach for their tissues.

Waking up, the memories dissipated quickly and reality set in. I wondered if the police were still on the estate. As I looked out of the bedroom window I saw there were more people out and about, scenes like I hadn't witnessed in months, possibly years. Had there been a new world order? It tricked me into believing that maybe I was safe and so I ventured out, again walking to the block of flats. The police were still present – which in itself was unusual – they would normally have been run off by now. I watched as curtains twitched. Front doors *slowly opened; neighbours came out and talked to each other, openly, all the years of mistrust wiped away, temporarily an amnesty. The gossip hotline fuelled once again as news circulated Shelbourne like a hurricane. Although I didn't like to talk to anyone on the estate anymore I felt that I could today.*

I watched for hours, forgetting where I was, caught by the eerie tranquillity that eclipsed the estate. Amazed by how I didn't feel threatened. I overheard one of the thirty-something grandmothers talking to someone on her mobile. The gossip was that one of the wolves was dead, mutilated. 'Mutilated', she repeated, shock present in her voice, not just dead, but mutilated, I thought it was a strange word to use. There was no firm information, the police had not said anything, they were following procedures and asking questions, which lacked the sincerity that a discovery like this would have provoked anywhere else in the world. The girlfriend who was with the wolf had been taken to hospital in a state of shock, too traumatized to talk or go home, her hair had reportedly turned white overnight.

An even rarer sight was that of reporters hovering on the estate, vultures looking for a story. I watched as they knocked door to door, some people answered but, after introducing themselves, found the doors slammed in their faces. That tended to be the innocent ones – the ones who wanted life to be normal and away from all the violence that manifested itself here. The ones that did talk tended to be the wolves' families speaking with pride, enjoying their two minutes of fame – pleading innocence as if they had never caused any pain or suffering and didn't know anyone who would ever do such a thing. Their sons and daughters were guilty and they knew it. Others looked through their windows and ignored the press. The police still had Shelbourne Heights cordoned off. A heavy police presence remained throughout the day and well into the night.

Back at home I tuned the radio onto 'News 24', hoping to get some more details. Mystery surrounded the incident which the police were treating as 'suspicious', that's all that was said at this stage.

It must be hard for the police to pretend to be interested in solving a case when they were probably just as pleased as some of the thousands of residents on Shelbourne that there was one less wolf. I was pleased that finally a wolf had got his comeuppance and shamed that it hadn't happened earlier. I wondered if it had happened earlier then maybe, *just maybe Shelbourne would not be where it was today.*

Nearly two days later the police left the estate and in those two days hardly a peep came from the wolves, their usual bravado gone. Maybe they were scared? A crack had almost appeared in the heavy black cloud that hung like the grim reaper over Shelbourne.

The press had finally been released some details. It appears that fourteen year old Jack Jones – JJ to his friends - had quite literally been ripped to pieces in a dark recess of a stairwell. His girlfriend, Joanne Marshall – also fourteen, had witnessed the whole event unfold. However, she was now in intensive care after suffering a mild stroke thought to be brought on by shock, still unable to state what she saw. Police believe she saw the attacker or attackers but was too petrified to go for help or even scream. It wasn't until a neighbour heard someone crying that the alarm was raised.

The police were baffled by the events as no murder weapon has been found and no DNA other than Joanne Marshall's had been found at the scene. Police appealed for witnesses and that was met with a wall of silence. Shelbourne was that sort of place. Justice would be meted out by the family and friends.

After the police left, the estate could so easily have gone into meltdown, exploded in a ball of fury, but an uneasy calm enveloped it.

Me. I was pleased with myself because when I saw the photo of the wolf concerned - it was Shaved-head. Did I feel guilty? No. Did I actually cause it? I couldn't be sure, I certainly wanted it. I certainly felt that much animosity towards him. I wanted to believe it was me, believe that I could harness that sort of power. The girlfriend was an innocent pawn- maybe? More likely she was just like the rest of them. Justice was mine in the end, that's what I believed and, that would allow me another peaceful night's sleep.

Beryl collapsed on the floor physically exhausted. Cyril ran to her aid offering a glass of water, which she drained quickly. Helping her up, they walked back to the dressing room. Silence filled the hall as Peter scanned the hungry eyes in front him, even Terence appeared lost for words for a change - that pleased him.

A scraping of a chair broke the silence, unlocking the voices that were quick to discuss this mysterious Beryl Wallace and after a short applause, Tracy and Adele were besieged with eager punters who hadn't bought books before, wanting to buy everything they could by Beryl.

Terence hovered near the stage as Peter made his closing comments, before following Beryl and Cyril into the dressing room.

"Brilliant. Absolutely brilliant, the audience loved it. Even the press seemed captured by it. The acting you do is just…just…"

"I am not acting Peter." Beryl's voice was just a whisper, which Peter didn't hear over his own excitement.

"Sorry, Beryl?"

"My aunt says she is not acting."

"Whatever, the audience are loving it. Now, there are quite a lot of press out there and I think it would be a good idea for you to talk with them."

"I am…"

Cyril interjected. "My aunt is far too exhausted, I will take her back to the B&B if you don't mind?" It was more a statement than a request for permission.

"But the press, this is important Cyril, I have already cancelled one event."

Cyril tried to control his annoyance, he knew he needed Peter on his side if he was to persist with a solo writing career, but also he had his aunt to think of. "Yes, and I, we appreciate that, but my aunt is very tired. That is not acting out there, the spirit is…"

Beryl placed a hand on Cyril's arm, stopping him mid flow.

"Please, Peter, I need to rest." Beryl spoke slowly and quietly, making Peter momentarily feel guilty about pushing the matter.

"Oh, very well. Cyril, please take your aunt back the B&B." Peter handed Cyril some pound notes for a taxi. "I will see you at breakfast."

"Thank you, Peter," Beryl muttered appreciatively.

Peter left the room disappointed.

13

Peter entered the main hall from a side door and was immediately snared by Terence, who unsuccessfully tried to drag him away from his fellow reporters.

"Mr Phillips," came the cattle call from members of the press.

"How long can you keep this pretence up?" Archie Dukes of the Mirror added

"Yes, when are you going to come clean, Peter, this is all a publicity stunt isn't it?" Terence cajoled.

Peter found himself backed against a wall. Grabbing his breath he eyed them all one at a time until they all hushed waiting for his reply. "This is no…"

"Come on Peter, don't give us that rubbish…"

"Please, please." Peter raised his voice, attracting the attention from the milling audience. "What you have witnessed here tonight is no publicity stunt. What you see is real. We at Phillips publishing do not employ such marketing tricks, we produce quality material for the reading masses."

"When can we speak to Miss Wallace?" bellowed James Hartridge of the Evening Press, interrupting Peter.

"Miss Beryl Wallace is very exhausted. These evenings take a lot out of her. She has retired to her room for the night."

"Hogwash, he just doesn't want us to find out the truth," Archie piped up, followed by a general consensus of agreement, but as they turned Peter spoke again.

"Gentlemen of the press, you will make whatever you want of this event, but the honest truth is that most are sceptical of what they do not know. I was…at first. But, also…I watched each and everyone of you here tonight, I saw your reactions." He waited. "And you believed." Peter let the words hang in the air before stepping through them to head to the book stall at the back of the hall, pleased with himself.

"How is it going Tracy?"

"I've never known it so busy, we are going to need more

books at this rate."

"I would never have believed it if I hadn't seen it with my own eyes," Adele chipped in.

"Good, good, keep up the good work, there'll be a bonus for you both at this rate." Both girls shared a pleased look, it wasn't very often that bonuses had been talked about and they were happy at the prospect.

"Where's Cyril gone?" Tracy asked nonchalantly, remembering the first time they had met, when Valerie was showing him round the premises.

***

"So, have you worked here long?" Cyril asked, feeling himself get hot under the collar as they left Beryl and Peter talking in his office. They were heading along a narrow corridor with framed book-covers on the walls.

"About two years," Valerie said flirtingly. Cyril couldn't help but notice how her brightly coloured thigh-length dress clung to her well proportioned petit frame, especially as he was a clear foot taller than her.

"I hope you don't mind me asking?"

"You can ask me anything, Mr Hewington."

Cyril felt himself going red.

"Cyril, please."

"Ask away Cyril. Anything." She turned and smiled at him before opening a door which led into another office with two desks. Unlike Peter's office this one had paper strewn about the place. "This is where Arthur Dalton works." There were rows and rows of filing cabinets with 'in' and 'out' trays on top, overflowing with thick wads of paper bound together with elastic bands. "Arthur?" Valerie called looking around the empty office. "Oh well, he is normally here, maybe he is making a coffee." She sat on the edge of a desk facing Cyril, crossing her legs allowing her dress to ride up even higher. "So what did you want to ask me?" she said expectantly.

Cyril gulped, as his insides churned up.

"You have got gentle looking eyes. Do you know that?" Valerie asked as Cyril became more uncomfortable. "So, what did you want to ask?"

"What's Mr Phillips like?" The words got caught in his throat and his voice broke mid-sentence.

"Is that all you want to ask?" Valerie asked Cyril suggestively.

"Well I was wonde…"

Suddenly the door flew open and in walked Arthur slurping his coffee from a mug that looked as though it hadn't been washed in weeks. His long lank hair, unkempt beard, thick heavy sweater and corduroy trousers, gave him the look of a yeti- type creature.

"Hi, Valerie. Showing off those lovely pins of yours, eh?" his broad Yorkshire accent filled the room.

"Well if you've got it flaunt it, that's what I say." She aimed the comment at Cyril who didn't know where to look.

"Aye and ain't she got it?" The question was also directed at Cyril who was still looking dumfounded at Arthur who was making his way to the desk that Valerie wasn't sitting on. "I understand that you be the young fella who needs my help writing words."

Cyril baulked. "No, Mr Phillips said he liked my writing but it might need a little polishing here and there."

"Aye, that's what I meant."

Cyril looked horrified.

"Don't worry about him Cyril, he's quite loveable once you get to know him and he doesn't take advantage of you." The statement was loaded.

"She'll get yer into trouble given 'alf the chance. Won't yer love?"

"A girl's gotta have fun."

"Aye. Anyways Cyril, let me put yer mind at rest. Come here and I show yer 'xactly what I mean about words."

Cyril looked at Valerie, who raised her eyebrows and bit her lower lip seductively.

Arthur grabbed a manuscript from a large pile and plonked it heavily onto his desk, then sifted through a pile of books on the floor.

"Now, this is what we're presented with and this is the finished product and what I do is…" Arthur started to demonstrate his craft whilst Valerie sat studying her bright orange nail polish.

Twenty minutes later they left Arthur and made their way to the warehouse. "See, Arthur knows what he's talking about. Lots of authors are concerned at first in case Arthur changes their writing style, but he doesn't, he just helps to maintain the power and pace of the story, it's quite a gift he's got really," Valerie said, leading Cyril down a staircase.

"Has he written any books himself?" Cyril asked, excited now at the prospect of working with Arthur who had shown how he can turn a simple story into a compelling read.

"No. It's quite funny really, I asked him that very question myself and do you know what he said?" she added in playful tones.

"No. What?"

"Take me out Friday and I'll tell you," she said, turning on him so he couldn't ignore her flirting.

"Why would he say... oh. Okay, you're on." Cyril couldn't believe his luck, he had never had much success with women and certainly never been asked out by any. Valerie smiled flirtatiously and turned to open the door to the warehouse. "So what did he say?" Cyril asked, following her.

"He said he didn't have an original idea in his head, but loved the fact that he can help to turn other people's ideas into something outstanding. Mr Phillips' father employed him about twenty years ago straight from school. Anyway, this is the warehouse. Tracy and Adele run it mainly with the delivery driver, Stan.

Cyril was amazed to see so many boxes of books neatly stacked on racking, just waiting to go out. On each rack, above the pallet, was neatly written the author's name in large print with the book titles listed after.

"Wow!"

"Hello? Oh, hi Val how are..." said Tracy, poking her head round a pile of boxes. "...and who is this handsome stranger." Tracy was tall and slender wearing jeans and trainers and no garish make-up which seemed to be all the rage.

"This is Cyril" Valerie said, grabbing his arm and smiling. "Mr Phillips wanted me to give him the tour. Where's Ad?"

"Around somewhere you know what she's like."

"So do you send all the books out?" Cyril was finding it hard to hide his attraction for Tracy. He had thought Valerie was nice but Tracy was gorgeous, with deep blue eyes, smooth delicate skin and full luscious lips.

When she spoke he found it hard to listen to what she was actually saying. "Adele and myself, yes. We telephone the book stores and then prepare any orders for Stan to take out, it's not rocket science but it does mean we get to read a lot when it's quiet. Do you want me to take you through the process? Come on I'll show you." Tracy went to grab his arm, clearly reciprocating Cyril's attraction.

"Thanks." Valerie held Cyril's arm tighter, looking disgruntled at Cyril's obvious attraction to Tracy.

"Is that the time? Gosh! Mr Phillips will be expecting Cyril for lunch, sorry Tracy," Valerie said curtly only too aware that Tracy fancied Cyril as well.

"Better go then." Cyril said lamely still looking at Tracy who didn't turn away. "Nice to have met you Tracy." Cyril held out his hand but Valerie spun him round firmly.

"Come on, can't keep Mr Phillips waiting, you'll get me in trouble." She dragged Cyril back into the stairwell then insisted on walking ahead of him so he could see her walk up the stairs, to take his mind off of Tracy, which it did. "Quite a ladies man aren't you?" It was a pointed statement.

"No. Sorry, I didn't mean to upset you."

"Who's upset? Not me," Valerie quipped nonchalantly.

Cyril shook his head, bewildered, eyeing Valerie's behind as it swayed seductively in front of him. At the top of the stairs she suddenly stopped, making him crash into her.

"Sorry," Cyril said whimsically.

Valerie pursed her lips. "Like what you see?" Cyril felt himself going crimson. "You'll have to wait 'til Friday. Come on."

***

"He has taken his aunt back to the B&B," Peter replied.

"I told you Trace. Look, he has hardly spoken to you in the last two years. He is not interested."

"He is. He just doesn't know it yet," Tracy replied to Adele.

"You might as well start packing up and I'll see you at the

next venue. You know where it is?"

"Yes," they replied in unison.

"Good." Peter walked off.

"Why is it we have to stay elsewhere? Cyril will never get the chance to ask me out at this rate."

"Dream on girl, dream on."

14

Cyril sat staring at Peter's back as he gave an excited fever-pitched synopsis of the previous parts of Mark's story whilst the audience drank in the details, quite taken by the tale. Cyril was disconcerted with how the events were progressing, and how they were affecting his aunt, who seemed a little withdrawn. When she had spoken, her mind appeared to be consumed by the spirit.

She had touched on the familiarity that she had sensed, even some kind of attachment, but with no location other than Shelbourne they had little to go on. Cyril was perturbed by how Mark absorbed Beryl so totally in his world, acting out the role so intensely; this had never happened before, Anne Farmer and John Johnson had merely used her as a channel.

Beryl sorely missed the evenings in her parlour which had become a distant memory. She would welcome the quiet evenings, even with Fred Dunton, who kept coming hoping for a last chance to speak with his wife, despite her saying her goodbyes before the cancer took her, but she still felt that she was doing him good in some way. Here she was just a freak show undermining everything she stood for. She knew it would be over soon and Cyril could take on the mantle he so deserved, but that time couldn't come quickly enough.

Peter had made a point that he wanted Cyril already seated on the stage before he gave the summaries, thereby giving Beryl full star appeal. It was something she wasn't happy about, but Peter was in charge and, reluctantly, both had agreed.

As Beryl took to the stage she nodded to Cyril but her eyes lacked their normal sparkle, an apprehension rested there. One thing Cyril was relieved about was that Mark, whilst taking her over, didn't seem to be doing any harm - a minor blessing.

Beryl took her position with her bare feet causing the odd murmur from onlookers, who thought it strange. She breathed out in readiness, sensing Mark's eagerness to continue his story.

It was circulating that the wolves were baying for blood. It even reached my isolated ears. It was the first occasion in nearly a year that I had spent any time in my garden, or jungle – which is what it resembled. I had overheard a couple of people talking behind my rear fence, about how revenge was going to be meted out.

A new sense of hope took hold, drowning me in its warmth; it was good and I indulged it by trying to clear the jungle, turn it back into a place where I wanted to bask in the sun.

The small victory had gone a long way to satisfying me but, in a way it was such a big step. A wolf had at last felt the wrath, which was what I believed his own curse of nine. This gave me a new resolve, a resolve to make a difference, to change my life, my circumstances, take back my life. The garden was a good place to start, so much could be achieved for free, yet it could make such a difference, embracing nature. It was part of the outside world, something I had not belonged to for so long, yet it was there for the asking, for the taking.

With only the few broken tools I possessed I worked a full day in the open air, drinking in its' refreshing nectar. Progress was slow but I didn't care, it was still progress and in the glorious sun until it slowly descended from the sky, disappearing behind the houses. Even then I didn't want to stop. It was hard yet rewarding work. Surveying my efforts it didn't look like much, but inside it was a breakthrough.

That night I even dared to sit downstairs for the evening, soaking up the splendour of how physically tired I was from doing a good days work. A smile sat caked on my face. If I'd had a beer or a bottle of wine in the fridge I would have opened it, but they were luxuries I could no longer lavish on myself. It was madness to let my mind wander to the thought of gainful employment, yet, in the shadow of my one day's work, anything seemed possible 'that really would be a milestone' I thought. Dare I think, then, about relocation? Dreams, just dreams, but such special dreams. My mind filled with the laughter of my children playing, I could almost feel Samantha next to me. Contentment spread through my whole being.

"You've done well. It is nice to see you taking pleasure in the garden again, you were so good with plants. You always had the gift." I felt

Samantha's hands massage my aching shoulders, soothing them.

"Thank you. We should have a barbecue to celebrate, the kids love to hear the burgers and sausages spitting in the flames."

"And jacket potatoes wrapped in silver-foil with their crunchy skins."

"The kids love to eat with their fingers."

"We should do it again. I love you, Mark." Her memory faded.

Strange, that a small victory could produce such a grand future. I embraced every thought and listened to the relative tranquillity that cloaked the estate, it was truly amazing, Utopia!

It was another two nights before the silence was broken. The wolves were back with a vengeance. Watching from my lounge window I saw someone's rubbish bin set alight before a lighted milk bottle was thrown at a house across the green, by a wolf wearing a hoodie. My heart jumped into my mouth as the bottle smashed through the window sending shards everywhere, shredding the net curtains behind. A bright flash erupted as flames engulfed the window frame and curtains, within seconds the flames were ten feet high licking the front of the house, scorching the upstairs. 'Hoodie' laughed as screams erupted from the house. Children's screams. They echoed through the night, haunting it like a ghost. My heart sank with sadness, I wanted to help but, in truth, I was too scared and so stared forlornly from my window, racked with anger. Hoodie rejoined his pack as they all sat smugly on the green, toasting their success with cans of beer.

Anger from my own uselessness boiled away inside and for a split second I forgot the possible danger and dashed to the front door. This was the reaction from the old me, the me that would have run and helped the victims, the one that would have saved a life, not to be a hero, just to help someone. The screams had fallen silent. Inside, I choked, wondering whether the occupants had perished. I hoped they had got out despite the fear of possible further attack from Hoodie and his pack. With one hand still on the catch of the door, I hesitated, I knew the consequences of helping and knew better. But to stand and watch from the sidelines, I was sickened not only by the wolves, but by myself, my cowardice. Something inside struck a chord banishing all hope that I had built up over the last two days.

A wave of melancholy washed over me and despair depleted the positive energy. I wanted to fight it but my heart was over-ruled by *my head. The dark cloud loomed over me, darker and more ominous than before. If I could have cried I would have. I struggled to open the front door, fighting with myself, scared of being seen. As I did, I saw some neighbours venture towards the burning house. The wolves rose instantly daring them to continue.*

15

I slammed the door in disgust and ran to the bedroom window upstairs to watch the scene outside. Someone from the burning house finally ran out onto the green with their clothes on fire. The screams will haunt me forever. The figure fell to the ground and rolled around to try and extinguish the flames. The stand-off with the wolves and my brave neighbours came to a head when one of my neighbours attempted to break through the wolves defence, he was tripped and set upon by the pack, the others then steeled forth to save him from the beating. The wolves were vicious and blows rained down on my neighbours as they finally broke through, visibly injured from the pummelling. But it was all in vein as the burning victim now lay motionless on the ground.

To add insult to injury the wolves then started to hit the burning body with whatever they could find nearby, half bricks, bits of fence, anything. It was gruesome to watch the delight with which they continued. My neighbours backed off not wanting to take any more punishment. To the wolves it was a game as they kicked the burning mass, trying to avoid setting light to themselves.

How could I have just stood and watched?

An uncontrolled rage welled up inside me and before I knew what was happening I had left all logical thinking behind and was running towards the burning mass on the ground, a curtain I'd torn down in haste, in my hand. But before I could get close enough, a fist struck me full in the face, sending me reeling to the ground.

Blearily, I heard sirens in the distance causing the wolves to walk away nonchalantly. Still dazed and angry, I instinctively grabbed for the wolf that had struck me but only managed to catch the bottom of his jeans with the tips of my fingers. He stumbled but still managed to kick out at me which enabled me to grab for his ankle more firmly, dragging him down. The other wolves were too far away to notice their fallen comrade. As he hit the ground he swung his body round to try and kick me again with his free leg, fighting to get free from my grip. Lashing out violently his kick made contact with my hands, the heel of his shoe tearing at my skin. I held on for as long as I could, battling the

71

ferociousness of the kicks, but after much struggling he broke my hold and ran into the night, minus one shoe.

As I lay there surprised by my own bravery, my own stupidity, I saw the fire brigade arrive. I didn't want to be questioned so retreated quickly to the safety of my cell, not realising I still held the wolf's shoe.

The taste of blood filled my mouth and on closer inspection, in what was left of the bathroom mirror, I saw I had a cut lip and a loose tooth. I rinsed the blood out of my mouth before watching the fire crew go to work on the house fire. The police had also arrived to give their support.

It took the fire brigade two hours to control the flames and then they stayed till morning to make sure all was safe. Four more bodies were brought out of the smouldering shell of the house and added to the one on the ground. Once again the police did the rounds, only to be met with the wall of silence.

The hold the wolves had was incredible.

Despondency enveloped me. I stared at my reflection, a good long hard look. My lip had swollen rapidly and a bruise was starting to show on my cheek. My back had started to ache where I had fallen so hard. I heard Joshua's voice break my thoughts and I dropped the shoe.

"Daddy can we go out and play football, please, oh please, Dad. Can I? Can we?"

"Of course we can Josh, just check with your mum when dinner will be ready."

"Hooray, I'm playing football." Josh ran out of the bathroom and disappeared.

Choked, I let out big sobs and fell to my knees, my head narrowly missing the sink. On the floor I curled up in a ball. I remembered it so clearly, the flashback fresh in my mind. One day in our lives. One happy day.

I must have fallen asleep because, before I knew it, it was night again. Getting up I scraped a meal together and ate because I knew I needed to, even though my resolve, my new strength, my new focus, had vanished. I'd allowed myself to be beaten again. Walking aimlessly about the house I let the loneliness creep in, seep deep into my soul like an old friend.

In the doorway of each bedroom I stared at the empty space that greeted me, picturing the scenes that would have played before my eyes two years ago, that should have greeted me today, the raised voices, the laughter, the innuendo, the simple smiles, the simple pleasures.

In that instant a cruel violent thought shook me. What was I thinking? I had the means to sort this out!

It was time again. Time to dish out the medicine.

I had no clear idea of what I was hoping to achieve this time, just like last time. The only problem I could see was that I didn't recall a face, it had all happened so quickly. Was the shoe enough? There was only one way to find out. I hoped the magick would work like a blood-hound tracking its quarry. I thumbed through the books for inspiration. I needed something, something to focus upon.

In my mind I conjured up an idea and prepared the altar as my thoughts became clearer, I knew what I wanted to accomplish. This was all still so new to me that I didn't know how much control I had. I looked up a Voodoo enchantment and changed it to suit my needs. Holding the shoe, I focussed all my energy on it. Opening the four gates I was sure I felt a charge around me as a faint citrus scent wafted in the air, I tasted blood again in my mouth. I visualized the scene – the wolf kicking me and then running away. I commanded forth the power of the gods from the four points of the compass and asked them to do my bidding. As the power rose, the shoe began to grow warm in my hands. I spoke aloud my commands, my spell, my thoughts, my deep, dark thoughts. A white searing heat transferred to my hands yet didn't seem to burn them, then in a blinding flash was gone.

I closed off the session thanking the four Gods then lay back on my makeshift bed looking at the shoe, wondering whether it would work as I hoped it would.

One of the teachings of the books was the belief that you should not feel guilt afterwards. Dealing with magick was more a facility to unlock our darker, hidden, side, hidden in every one of us. To unlock a power that over the centuries had been pushed aside and forgotten, except for the few enlightened ones among us.

These pieces of magick managed to instil a positive energy in me afterwards, a feeling of accomplishment, of satisfaction, a heightened sense of being, fusing every nerve in my body. With this new positivity I could work at getting my prison cell back to a home and the next day, I continued my work in the garden.

As the sun shone down on my naked back, it felt so good, life was *good again. A voice behind broke my reverie, it was my neighbour.*

"Hello," shock evident in the greeting. "It's been a while since we saw you out here." Jim was a retired postman who had lived in his house since Shelbourne was built. He could remember a time when Shelbourne was the ideal. Now his house had security cameras and alarms. He rented a garage off the estate to store his car overnight, not daring to leave it parked out the front of the house, and he never went out after dark.

I stared at him for a short while. It had been so long since I had spoken to someone, without anger or frustration. Jim's welcoming smile started to fade. "Sorry, yes." was my brief reply.

"It's a lovely day." Jim beamed. Two years ago conversation would have been easy, now I seem to have lost all my socials skills.

"Yes," was my awkward response, followed by silence.

"Anyway...it's good to see you again." Jim hesitated then pulled away from the fence.

"Thanks," I muttered. Jim was a lovely man, always had been.

Then he returned to the fence, there was something he wanted to say, he stood behind one of the half broken fence panels that separated our gardens. He still wore an old shirt and cardigan as always when in the garden, and the same ones for as long as I could remember. "Did you hear about that...that..." he searched for a suitable descriptive word. "Yob? For want of a better word."

"Jack Jones. Yes. Shame." The sarcasm in my voice was not lost on Jim.

"No!" Jim's eyes widened. "Not him. Although, I do share your sentiment. I'm not a malicious man but he did deserve it. Maybe not quite that extreme but hey-ho, what can you do, life is so vicious these days. They all deserve it." His eyes looked lost for a second.

My curiosity was pricked and I went over to the fence. "What were you going to say about them? I call them wolves, it seems apt somehow, but maybe that's unfair to wolves."

"Wolves! Yes," he toyed with that image, "anyway, it seems that this yob got into a fight with someone with a machete or sword, or something like that anyway, seems he lost his left foot, lopped clean off. Was lucky he didn't bleed to death. S'ppose that's what they call poetic justice." Jim stood silently letting it sink in. "You alright?"

"Couldn't be better, Jim. Couldn't be better." My face contorted into

a curt smile as I tried to think whether the shoe I had was indeed the left shoe.

"Glad to see that's cheered you up anyway. Can't say too many people are upset by it. It's a shame to be like that though really. Shouldn't need to be."

"Hopefully things will start to improve round here. That's three now isn't?" I was finding it difficult to control my excitement, I needed to confirm what I hoped was true.

"Three?"

"Yes, Jack Jones, his girlfriend, she sounds as though she's in a bad way, and now this one."

"Yes I s'ppose so. As long as it doesn't lead to all out war." With that he wandered off back into the house. "Nice to see you outside again, anyway." That last comment was delivered with heart-felt pleasure.

"You too."

Rushing inside I bubbled with nervous energy. Making my way up into my safe haven I scoured the floor for the shoe, almost in awe I saw that it was the left shoe. Breathless I smiled. I'd done it. Again! I decided to study the books a little harder and see what other delightful remedies I could conjure up to cure this estate.

16

"Hello, Auntie Hilda?" Beryl pushed two coins into the slot of the payphone.

"Hello. Who's this?" a frail voice asked.

"Beryl. Beryl Wallace." Hilda was eighty-six years old and lived in London in a high rise block. It had been nearly seven years since Beryl and Cyril had visited and, Beryl could feel the guilt searing her. There was a pause and Beryl wondered whether Hilda's memory was going.

"Oh, hello dear," she brightened. "How are you? I was just saying to Bert only last week that we hadn't heard from you in quite some time."

"How is he?"

"He is not so good. He finds it hard to walk these days, so hardly leaves the flat. Peggy just curls up by his feet and keeps him company when I go out."

"Can I ask you something Auntie Hilda?"

"Of course you can dear."

"I have been talking to a spirit, by the name of Mark, and he feels familiar to me, but I can't place him and he doesn't tell me anything useful about times or dates. Do you know anyone from our family's past called Mark who lived on an estate called 'Shelbourne'?"

"No dear, I can't say that I do. It is certainly not ringing any bells, hold on, I'll ask Bert." Beryl could hear the phone being placed on the telephone desk.

The pips started to go so Beryl pushed three more coins into the slot. A minute passed.

"Beryl?"

"Yes."

"No, we can't think of anyone that we know of and we have never heard of an estate in London called that."

"Okay, thank you. I'll make sure I come and visit you shortly. I have to go as I am running out of coins. Sorry to make it so short. I'll call again. I promise."

"Alright dear, you take care and give our love to Cyril."

Beryl pressed the button for the next call and dialled. The phone rang and rang.

"Five-five-nine-three-two."

"Henry?" Beryl said, melting as she heard his voice.

"Hello. How are you and how is my grandson these days?"

"We are very well. The marrows and tomatoes you gave us last time we visited were delicious. We have still got some left."

"Good, I have got some nice winter potatoes coming through, I'll put some aside for you." Beryl wanted to chat but was aware that she didn't have much change and the warmth of Henry's voice made her wish she was back at home.

"Look, I'm sorry I am going to have to be quick as my money is running out. Do you know if any of our family have ever lived on a Shelbourne estate, especially a Mark?"

The line went quiet. "I don't recall that name, Cyril's grandmother would have known, god rest her soul. Sorry I can't help."

"That's alright, just thought I'd ask."

"So how are things going with the book tour, I have been following it in the papers..." The pips started to go. Beryl frantically searched her purse knowing she didn't have more change but wanted to talk, the line went dead.

The Working Men's Club Hall, Shrewsberry

THE EVENING HERALD,

Fact or Fiction?

Tuesday I witnessed the 'supposed' sensation that is Beryl Wallace who is taking the literary world by storm. Phillips Publishing and Literary Agency started a tour a week ago, promoting last year's best selling author.

What did I witness? Well, in my opinion it was pure

sensationalism. This woman, Beryl Wallace, took to the stage like a great actress playing out a well structured story, dreamt up before this tour and invented to fool the audience, 'suckering' them in to sell more books. She creates quite a spectacle on stage strutting about 'supposedly' possessed by a spirit. What a lot of hogwash. Nothing more than a 'publicity' stunt. If you want to waste your evening then go and see this woman.

Margaret Williams

Cyril gave the newspaper to Peter who was sitting drinking a cup of tea "Did you read this? My aunt looks like a fool. It was not meant to be like this."

"Cyril, Cyril, this is good for us…" Peter spoke calmly.

"Good! What's the matter with you? My aunt is not some freak show for everyone to laugh at like a circus performer. People obviously don't believe her. This is not what she does. This is not what I thought it would be like." Cyril tried to be adamant but his voice trembled as he tried to hide his nerves.

The door to the largest dressing room they had had so far (and the most sparsely furnished) opened. "Cyril, what's wrong?" Beryl enquired.

"I was just telling Peter about the papers." Cyril tried to keep his voice level but his emotions were ready to burst out, angry that his aunt was being portrayed as a fraud. Angry in part with himself as she was doing this for him, he hated seeing her so consumed by Mark.

"Why, Cyril?" Beryl noticed the paper that Peter clung to. "Oh, you are not worried about that are you?" Her voice was placating. "Cyril, you take it too personally. I've been called worse. They don't understand, that's all, it is just envy." Her tone became more pointed. "Isn't it Peter?"

"Yes. Any publicity is good and the hall tonight is full. If used correctly you can use it to draw attention to the causes your aunt supports." Peter smiled meekly at Beryl.

"Yes. Anyway Peter, do you mind if we prepare ourselves?" Beryl shot a 'just get out of my sight' glance at Peter which belied her demure, gentle façade, making him feel awkward, prompting him to get up and leave.

"Now Cyril…"

"Auntie, this is ridiculous, we shouldn't be doing this."

"Cyril. Yes, we should. I want to see you make a success of your writing and if this is the small sacrifice I have to make then so be it." She placed her hands gently on his shoulders, attempting to look him squarely in the eye despite craning her neck as Cyril towered above her.

"But I've never seen you so exhausted." Cyril's voice had lost all its fight.

"Don't worry about me, I'm fine. But think about your future, when talking with Peter. He can guide you and you need him on your side."

"I know, I know. But…" Beryl's eyes spoke volumes, and Cyril knew to leave well alone. "I'll go and get ready." He left the room, leaving Beryl contemplating what was going to happen tonight. The two phone calls she had made earlier had yielded no answers and had only upset her, she missed her family.

Still bewildered by the spirit Beryl took to the stage after Peter's introduction which, once again, had taken on a form all its own. The newspaper articles had only managed to add fuel to the fire, giving Peter the incentive to embellish Cyril's notes, almost to the point of mimicking some of Beryl's actions, as she had portrayed Mark's story, making the audience laugh at his antics.

'How he had grown from a shy public speaker to enjoying the attention?' Beryl thought as she walked on stage, again wary of Mark. He was there, she didn't need her spirit guides confirming it, and they couldn't give her any more information than she already knew. She needed to reel it – him – in a little, for her own sanity. As she approached centre stage gone were her perfunctory preparations, Mark didn't care for formalities, he wanted to tell his story and Beryl was his channel.

She stood ready. "Mark, I know you are there, can you please tell me..?" It was too late for the questions. Beryl desperately wanted to know, When? Where? But she had gone, again.

The more I thought about it the better I felt. Although I could hardly believe the magick was working, a euphoric feeling engulfed me. I would never have believed anyone if they had said I could do it. But here I was. It was working. It must be, how else could I explain it? I was on the edge of madness, except that the picture was clear, clearer than it had ever been before. If I was really doing this, then anything was possible, I could really make a difference. Here! Now!

But where did the power come from? I had never known my parents as I was given up for adoption at birth. Maybe they had had a latent gift. I had once tried to find out about them, in one of those moments when I thought I wanted to know. I asked questions but was met with blanks, either the authorities didn't know or they didn't want to tell me for some reason. It hurt. I pushed for answers but was met with dead ends. It made me angry, but in the end I had to abandon my search.

Regardless of where it came from, I seemed to have a definite power, self-belief which my early experiments had lacked. I needed to feel the hatred welling inside me, gather it up like a ball and then focus the raw energy and turn it against the wolves rather than destroy myself with it.

If I could get closer to the wolves, discover their identities, find the ring leader or leaders then I could pull the rug out from under their feet. Normally, if a leader fell then the group would flounder, and that would mean easier pickings as the pack started to splinter, scattering like leaves in the wind.

It's strange - I thought I had lost the will to live when my family had gone, but somehow it had always remained...and now... now there was hope, I was sure of it.

I searched through my books for a protection spell, something that might help if I left the sanctuary of my prison cell. Excited by the power I believed I had mastered and the prospects of what I could achieve with it. Adrenalin pulsed through my brain making it hard to focus, nervous energy trickling through my trembling fingers. None of the books offered any specific spells.

With resolution, I knew I had to take my chances.

Early evening was the best time to roam the estate to look for the wolves, as during the day they tended to be sleeping in their dens. There were one or two places I knew of, which had become 'no go' areas pretty much as soon as the wolves had started to grow in size and reputation. These were dark, concealed areas. Out of the way places. The estate was meant to be the icon of modern design but had just provided the means for elicit trading and other activities to go *unnoticed. For years it had never really affected the rest of the estate, there was a hidden black market which everyone knew existed. I think it even made the estate a better place to live. There was a hierarchy, a code, stick to it and nothing bad ever happened to you.*

That was a time when criminals seemed to have a different mentality. It was never mindless, more calculated and carefully executed, with the minimum of fuss, away from an audience. The wolves today didn't care for discretion. They didn't worry about flaunting their crimes.

In an ironic way, crime needed to exist for utopia to be attained - it worked, people felt safe, community was strong, you left your front door unlocked, let your children play outside, you knew what was what.

How irrevocably things change.

Standing on the threshold of what I hoped would become my home again, I was scared and thoughtful. I knew what I was doing. I had never been a brave person, although I stood up for myself when the time was right and the situation necessitated it. I believed it was better to walk away from a physical fight. Tonight I could be walking into one.

17

Standing at my window, I watched the daylight fade as night smothered the estate. It had been ages since I had gone out in the dark. It terrified me, concealing people in shadows. Most of the street lamps had been broken and never repaired, it was a pointless task.

Preparing to start my journey, I knew a weapon, or some means of defence was essential, something, just in case. Was my confidence fading? I didn't know, but a weapon seemed logical. A claw hammer! It was easy to carry and to use and I still had one.

I was heading to the far side of the estate, at least a thirty minute walk away, involving some alleyways or 'walkways' as they were referred to when the estate was originally built. The first of these was diagonally opposite my home and my heart pounded a tattoo inside my chest as I approached it.

Stepping into the alleyway every noise that echoed off the hard surfaces was magnified by my imagination. Voices behind me made me freeze. What was I doing? I searched for somewhere to hide. There was nowhere. As I turned to head back home I saw three nine or ten year old kids, they petrified me.

How had I got here? I could feel fear rising inside. I remembered the hammer, the claw of which was held securely in the palm of my right hand with the handle stowed safely up the sleeve of my jacket, little comfort if I was too terrified to use it.

I stood my ground out of terror rather than confidence, gulping down air. My pulse raced.

They walked by me, ignoring me completely, I didn't exist to them.

For a few minutes I thought how foolish my mission was. How could I do what I wanted to do when I was scared to death of three nine or ten year olds? I knew that if I returned home, all was lost. I wiped the sweat from my brow with the back of my hand, nearly gouging my face with the claw of the hammer.

Continuing through the alley, every muscle was tense, every step deliberate. The sound of breaking glass caught me off guard. I let the hammer slide down, it fell quicker than I expected and I couldn't stop it *from crashing to the ground with a metallic chime. Fear prevented me picking it up as I backed against the wall to my right where I remained frozen rigid against the cold brick. Rational thought escaped me and a warm sensation ran down my leg and I knew I had wet myself.*

Looking at the hammer on the ground, I felt my courage ebb away.

Minutes passed and still no one appeared in the alley.

I breathed slowly fighting my own panic, telling myself there was nothing to worry about. I bent down to pick up the hammer, questioning my sanity in choosing to pursue this plan, to come out here at night, on my own. I wanted, needed, to make a run for it.

I started to run, my footfalls were heavy on the ground, echoing around me and making it sound like I was being chased. Without thinking I had become disorientated and had run to the wrong end of the alley, further away from my sanctuary, my prison cell.

Loud raucous voices abruptly cut through the night air, amazingly my irrational act had actually been the right one as I took a sly glance over my shoulder and saw the wolves enter the alley from the same end that I had entered. My heart jumped into my throat, my limbs screamed for me to move faster. I started to stumble as I picked up the pace, finally breaking into a sprint. I willed my footfalls to be silent. I heard a shout behind, 'After him!'.

Every fibre in my body screamed at me to move knowing this could be the end. I ran. I ran as fast as my legs would allow, out of the alley and into the street beyond, shrubs and trees passing like fleeting snapshots. Thoughts of refuge gnawed away at me, I needed to hide. I was already out of breath and knew I couldn't run much further. A metallic chime signified to me again that I had dropped the hammer, my only protection. Too frightened to stop and pick it up I carried on running my breathing coming hard and fast. My lungs fit to burst. The wolves were still behind me, their voices like war cries in the air.

Out of the corner of my eye I spotted some bushes to my left, behind a small front garden wall that stood barely three feet tall, I dived headlong into the thick bushes, not caring whether I was injured as long as I kept out of sight. Desperately I tried to quell my breathing, laboured from the effort of running and panic. The branches dug in, snagging my clothes, my weight breaking some of the smaller ones. Finally, I lay on the ground, hidden in the dark shadows. For an instant I thought that this might be my final resting place as the heavy footsteps of the wolves grew closer. The more I tried to control my breathing, the heavier it seemed get and I feared the wolves would find me. As they drew closer I heard one of them pick up the hammer. They started to bate me.

"Look what we have here, eh? Coming prepared now. That's not very nice now is it?"

Even though fear gripped me I became aware of the damp ground beneath me and how uncomfortable it was, as old drinks cans dug into me, their crumpled edges like dull knives. I tried to turn over to relieve the pressure of a stump digging into my ribs, the rustle of a crisp packet sounded like a firecracker in my hiding place, and any second I expected to see the wolves peering down at me over the wall.

Their laughing and joking had ceased and their footfalls seemed to go quiet, were they gone? I let the first wave of relief wash over me. It faded just as quickly when I heard a front door open.

"Get out of my garden," the booming irate voice of the garden's owner commanded. Through the stems of the bushes I could see the outline of a large well-built man with tattoos covering both forearms, he was holding a baseball bat.

"Just get inside granddad, before we're the last people you ever see." The wolves laughed hideously. I prayed the man would do as they said but his bravado had got the better of him and he stepped across the threshold of his front door into the onslaught of the wolves.

"Get the bastard," was the jollied war cry.

Cowardly, I watched the full horror of the attack from the relative safety of the bushes as the man vainly tried to swing the bat at the lead wolf, who wore gold rings and a black leather jacket, but another wolf, with a missing tooth and a large pointed crooked nose, grabbed it from behind preventing the swing. I saw the glint of metal as Goldrings raised the hammer, my hammer, and brought it down sharply on the man's shoulder. I remember hearing the squelch as the hammer made contact. As he fell to the ground a second blow rained down on his head.

Silently I retched, my insides twisting in agony, the smell hit my nostrils and I was forced to retch again. My conscience gnawed at me, I had brought the weapon of destruction, if it hadn't been for me, the man might have stood a chance.

He tried to fight bravely but within seconds of the blow to the head, the battle was lost. Gradually Gold-rings and Crooked-nose were joined by the others kicking and stamping on the man who now put up no resistance.

As they walked away from the bloody mess, Gold-rings spat at him.

"Serves you right," the others laughed as they all moved off.

The man had been my saving grace, in their show of violence they had forgotten about me.

Screwing my eyes tightly shut, I kept the sobs of regret to myself, listening for the retreat of the wolves.

When I left my hiding place I noticed the hammer discarded on the pavement next to the victim, they didn't care. I looked at it and then at the bloody mess that was the man, full of disgust, full of regret. Instinct made me pick up the hammer.

A shout from behind shook me from my self pity, I turned and then ran in the direction the wolves had gone, I knew what it looked like, but would anyone believe the truth? I didn't know. I had to get out of there.

The voice behind continued to shout for me to stop but I kept on running. I was innocent, even though I looked guilty.

I didn't know where I was going, I just ran as fast as my legs would carry me. I wanted to go home but the most direct route was the way I had come. Circumventing the estate was my only option now.

At the end of the street I saw Gold-rings and the rest of his pack and I ducked out of sight behind a low wall. They were kicking a fence panel and passing round cans of beer. I was stuck in the middle, between a rock and a hard place. Trying to keep out of sight, hidden by the shadows of darkness, knowing that my foolishness had led me here and that this could finally be my end, all the good I had wanted to achieve backfiring and costing one man his life.

I waited in the shadows on tenterhooks. It was the longest ten minutes ever and I was relieved when, finally, the wolves started to move on, leaving the fence panel in tatters. Mindless violence, simply mindless.

As Gold-rings walked away, he briefly glanced back, I studied him more closely, his cropped hair had an ugly scar cut in, about four inches long, just above his right ear, which had six piercings in it, his small nose looked as though it had been squashed flat giving his face the appearance of a cartoon character that had had an anvil smashed into it. Gold-rings threw the empty beer can into a front garden before opening another, which he pulled from his pocket. When they were out of sight, I collected the can.

Forty-five nervous minutes later I was back in my prison cell, smelling awful, my clothes dirty. The ache that I hadn't achieved anything, except to get someone else killed, racked me.

'How did I get here?' was the question rattling around my mind.

I should have helped. At that moment my insides churned up as the emotions gripped me and I vomited, leaving a vile taste in my mouth and tears running down my face. Maybe if I'd helped he would have stood a chance? Maybe it would only have resulted in me being killed as well. Maybe that would have been better for everyone? I paced the house in a hopeless fervour too disturbed to sit still, too irate to settle.

I was trying to be a saviour. Why? You need to be brave to be a saviour.

I'd forgotten about the beer can until I decided that maybe the only way I could find peace of mind was to avenge the man's murder.

In my safe haven, I placed the beer can on the altar and opened the gateway to the gods using the ritual I had established, beckoning forth the power and commanding them to do my bidding. Picturing the wolf's face as clear as day, I focussed all my inner strength and pent up frustration on what I wanted to achieve. I looked at the beer can and concentrated hard. First I imagined the beer can as Gold-rings heart, crushing it flat then ripping out his soul with my bare hands. I went through the motions in the air totally engrossed by my controlled rage. As a finally decisive end, I twisted his head sharply left until I heard the crack and his neck snapped like a twig.

18

Closing down the portal, I relaxed once again, satisfied that I'd done what needed to be done. A part of me thought that maybe the two instances before had been just coincidence. After all, I was a novice. How could I have such power? Yet how could things have appeared as they did, two wolves suffering in a manner that I had pictured, believed? How could I be so strong and powerful, yet not walk down an alley without soiling myself?

An hour later I heard sirens in the distance, my curiosity urged me to investigate but my cowardice kept me indoors.

A day later I found out the man they had beaten had indeed died from his injuries. It would have been a miracle if he had survived. He left behind three kids and a girlfriend. Although I felt guilty a sense of survival told me it had been necessary, otherwise I would have been lying there too. I could not save this estate from beyond the grave.

Save this estate. Me! It's saviour?

Mark relinquished his hold of Beryl and she reeled onto the floor, her limbs too weary to control. Slamming down his pencil Cyril rushed to her aid, her voice was so faint.

"Cyril, is that you?"

"Yes Auntie." Cyril snapped a disgusted look at Peter, who was in awe of her performance and the money he was making.

The audience hesitated, not realising it was all over. Slowly, a ripple of applause ran through them and grew as some of the audience took to their feet, showing their full appreciation.

A cry of 'phoney!' was drowned by the noise of clapping and the perpetrator left, shaking her head.

Peter took centre stage, holding his hands out at about waist height to quieten them "Ladies, gentlemen. Thank you."

Cyril helped Beryl up and led her from the stage. He was finding the situation more and more uncomfortable, his aunt had always been strong and in control. This time the spirit was leading her, taking her so completely.

Cyril had grown up with Beryl from the age of eight, after

his mother had been murdered. She was a stickler for honouring agreements but, despite possibly curtailing his own future, he wanted her to stop this, she was worth more than any money.

At home, when people came to witness the phenomenon, sometimes the evenings would be fruitless. The spirits didn't always want to speak. People left disappointed but they would return another night. Now this was more of a business, the pressure was on to perform. And Mark always managed to find her, every time, no matter where they were.

The evenings were certainly capturing everyone's imagination as books flew off the stand at the back of the hall. Peter couldn't have been more delighted.

***

Back at the B & B, Cyril made his aunt a cup of herbal tea and set her down to rest. He had so many thoughts he wanted to express but instead sat silent and forlorn as she too seemed lost in her own thoughts. Finally Cyril left his aunt so she could sleep. She hadn't said a word just laid down on the bed and closed her eyes. It was so unlike her, and it worried him.

Cyril paced his room, his mind racing as to what to do.

Friday 20th October 1978

Peter yawned as the rap at the door disturbed his sleep. Cyril had fretted all night, winding himself up so tight that he could no longer contain his concerns about how the tour was affecting his aunt. He had got dressed and made his way down to Peter's room.

"Hold on a minute," Peter called wearily from beneath the warm covers, "It's too cold," he shivered, poking a foot out. Unlocking the door he saw Cyril standing there frowning. "Cyril! It's a bit early isn't?"

Cyril's stern demeanour lessened as a bout of guilt for waking Peter hit him. "Oh! Sorry…but Peter, I need to talk to you about my aunt."

Peter said wearily, "If you must, come in, but couldn't it have waited?" Peter sighed, closing the door behind Cyril, who didn't answer. "What exactly can I do for you? We have a long journey ahead of us and I need to make some telephone calls."

Cyril struggled to find his voice, the fight evaporating under Peter's authoritative manner. "I don't want my aunt to go on with this anymore, Peter..." The words were fraught with nerves and anxiety.

Peter stood looking at Cyril rubbing the sleep from his eyes, feeling around the bedside table for his glasses. "Go on."

"Well...with this book-writing tour, it's...it's not right... something's not right. I have never seen my aunt so shattered after a session. This spirit, this Mark is sapping the life from her. It's doing her no good. I know we made a deal but..." Cyril's emotions began to take over. "I'm concerned for her health, Peter." Cyril's voice belied the sentiment his words warranted and he knew he was not stating the case as confidently as he had planned over the last two hours.

Peter sat down on the edge of the bed, lighting a cigarette, not paying very much attention, but listening nonetheless. He exuded an air of authority and Cyril's protests began to lose force without him actually saying a word.

"Cyril." Peter blew the smoke out. "Look, I understand where you are coming from and I see your point. I don't want to say this, but, we have a contract, we made a deal..." He took another draw of his cigarette. "Beryl, your aunt, agreed to this and you have your book to consider."

"I know, but."

"Cyril I have already cancelled one event so she could rest. I am not unreasonable, am I?"

"No."

"Look. I have done and will do my best to make allowances for her tiredness but we have an audience to satisfy, therefore, I need you both to stick to your end of our deal. I have invested a lot of money in this and in you. Please don't throw it back in my face." He let the words sink in, watching Cyril cogitate them. "Now, if there is no more...we will meet down stairs at..." glancing at his wrist he realised his watch was on the dresser, then picking it up stated, "nine-thirty?"

Cyril was about to answer but hesitated too long.

"Good. Now if you'll excuse me, I need to get dressed and make those telephone calls I mentioned."

Cyril left the room, utterly deflated. "Damn," he muttered outside Peter's door.

"Cyril?"

"Oh! Morning Auntie."

"What are you doing?"

Cyril looked back at the door. "Oh, nothing. Just showing... giving some notes to Peter."

"Come on, let's have some breakfast."

Cyril glanced at his watch. "But it's only eight-forty, Peter said we'd meet about nine-thirty."

Beryl looked at her nephew discerningly. "Well, I am hungry. Now, if Peter wants to wait until then, so be it. Personally I'd rather have mine now with my nephew." She looked at him as if to say 'well?'.

The door opened and out walked Peter in his dressing gown with a towel draped over his arm and a toilet bag grasped in one hand. Beryl and Cyril stared at him.

"What?" asked Peter self consciously.

"Nothing, come on Cyril." They walked down to breakfast leaving Peter pondering the strange look they had given him. He shook his head and made his way to the bathroom at the end of the landing.

Peter ate breakfast on his own before seating himself down in an area of the lobby set aside for the payphone. Taking out his address book he dialled his friend Edward Grace's office. After three rings the phone was answered by a woman.

"Good morning, Grace and Family Printers."

"Good morning. Is Edward there, it's Peter?"

"Just a second I will check."

Peter pushed five more ten pence pieces into the payphone and waited.

After a few more seconds the woman was back. "Just putting you through."

"Peter," came the pleasant cheerful greeting, "how are you my dear friend? Certainly making a splash in the papers, have been keeping quite an eye on your little tour."

"Thank you. I'm good. Book sales are excellent. Has my office placed the next orders?"

"Yes, I had an order cancelled from another customer so I have managed to slot you in its place for next week, as we already have the tapes we need. They should be with you the following week. Is that suitable?"

"That's fine Edward, thank you, just send the invoice to the office as usual. One other thing, does your cousin still work for the government?"

"I believe so, yes. Why?"

"I was hoping that maybe he could do me a favour and try to locate a…" Peter flicked to the front of his address book. "… Shelbourne Estate."

"Whereabouts?"

"That is just it, I don't know, the spirit refers to it and I am trying to establish that it either exists today, or may be a defunct estate somewhere. I know it's a bit vague but I have not got any more information than that."

"Alright, I'll see what Chris can find out. Have you got a number I can contact you on?" The pips sounded and Peter pushed five pence into the slot.

"I'll give you a ring in a couple of days or give my office a ring, I am checking in with them every day."

"Very well. Take care Peter and I will speak with you soon. I look forward to reading more about your tour in the papers."

"Thank you Edward, cheerio."

"Bye."

The connection was cut and Peter sat for a couple of minutes wondering where Shelbourne would be. The tour meant they were missing their usual games of snooker and he thought he owed Edward a great deal as without him, Beryl probably would not have signed a book deal.

***

The Lancaster Rooms was a restaurant in Alexandra Street, Southend-on-Sea a short taxi ride from Peter's offices. It was set above a snooker hall and was decorated very much in the style of a gentlemen's club, the tables lavishly set with crisp white linen tablecloths and silver cutlery. Peter didn't usually take prospective authors there but he felt if he could establish a more intimate gathering it would conclude the deal, and with Edward there Beryl would feel at ease.

Beryl and Cyril felt out of place as most diners were businessmen in suits and ties and they had only dressed casually, but smartly, for their meeting with Peter.

As they waited to be seated Beryl spied a familiar face, Edward Grace, sitting at a table, seemingly waiting.

"Look Cyril, there's Edward."

"Ah, already here, good. Shall we?" Peter said guiding his guests towards Edward, who rose as they drew close.

"Good afternoon Beryl, what a pleasure." He took her hand and placed his cheek to hers. "Cyril, how nice to see you again." They shook hands firmly.

"Thank you Edward, how are you?" Cyril replied, as Edward pulled out a chair for Beryl.

"Very well thank you. Peter, you didn't say we were having guests for lunch. How very remiss of you."

"Didn't I?"

"No." Then, speaking directly to Beryl. "Now, if you've had a meeting with Peter you must be parched, so let's get some drinks." Edward raised his hand to grab the attention of a nearby waiter.

"I'm sorry Edward, I could have sworn I mentioned it."

"No, you said they were coming to see you but…forgive me Beryl, how rude to talk about you as though you are not here."

"No, not at all. Always the gentleman, which, is so nice to see these days."

Peter felt a little under pressure, trying to create a good impression yet Edward was so natural at it.

"Good afternoon gentlemen and lady," said a waiter dressed in black waistcoat and bow tie handing out four menu's, starting with Beryl. "The soup of the day is Cream of Tomato with Basil. The chef's special is Beef Wellington. Would you like to see the wine list sir?" The question was directed at Edward but Peter answered.

"Actually, I think champagne might be more the order of the day."

"Very good, sir."

"Please, Mr Phillips I have…"

"Peter, please call me Peter." Beryl furrowed her brow as if considering the matter.

"Beryl, please forgive my friend here, he is trying too hard. He means well enough, just like his father." Peter looked abashed. "I am guessing he is delighted at the prospect of a business relationship? But he forgets that sometimes formalities need to be a part of that, to keep everything professional."

"Thank you Edward. But I think it should be me apologising. I am not used to such elaborate surroundings or business, or rather social business, I guess we can drop the formal titles as we might be working together a lot and it can get a bit tedious."

Peter visibly relaxed. "Champagne, please waiter."

"Peter, if I may say, I am not one for drinking at lunchtime, usually, but, if I am to have a drink could I request a Campari and soda please?"

"Certainly Miss…Beryl, order whatever you like. Edward, a glass of champagne?"

"No, I think I'll just have a glass of Chardonnay, Peter."

"Cyril?" Peter offered.

"Could I have a glass of wine please?"

"Certainly. Red or white?" Edward added jovially.

"Oh, mmm, I don't know." Edward could see Cyril's slight embarrassment.

"Might I suggest a glass of house Chardonnay, it is a light fruity wine that I think you might like."

"Thank you. Yes, I'll have that please." Cyril eyed the cutlery settings, confused by the multiple sets.

"Very good, sir." The waiter left, manoeuvering efficiently around the tables which were filling up fast with the lunch crowd.

"Edward, I am sorry I didn't get a chance to talk with you Wednesday evening, I found it a particularly draining evening and I do so enjoy chatting with you afterwards."

"I understand completely Beryl. Nothing like a chance to put the world to rights. I must say I can't wait to see Anne's story in print. I am correct in guessing that was what you were discussing earlier and what this lunch is about?" Edward asked. Nothing had been concluded in Peter's office but now, seeing Edward with Peter, filled Beryl with a sense of trust and she nodded her agreement."I think it will go down a storm. Let's hope Anne is willing to finish telling her story." That thought hadn't occurred to Beryl or Cyril and their expressions showed their concerns.

"I'm sure she will," Peter chipped in, sensing a slight tension.

"Yes, I'm sure she will. It will help her attain peace, the poor girl," Beryl continued.

"You must be very excited to think that your work will be in black and white for everyone to read, Cyril," Edward asked.

"Valerie introduced me to Arthur, who works for Mr Ph…" He stopped himself then looked at Peter. "I mean Peter. I couldn't believe how good he is with words. It's incredible. He showed me 'Visible' by John Kilkenny, I mean I didn't get to read that much of it but it was amazing to see how he transformed it into what it was, is."

"He is a very clever man," Peter started. "My father took him on as a weekend boy a long time ago now." The memory came flooding back to him of how his father had gushed about him at home and how he had wanted his father to talk that way about him. "He caught him reading one of the many discarded manuscripts one day. It was rubbish as far as my father was concerned, so he said to Arthur that he could keep it if he liked. Arthur was delighted, and went home and read it in one week. When he came back in the following weekend he wouldn't stop going on about it to my father, saying what a great story it was. My father told him that it had no pace, the characters were weak and the plot had no substance. Arthur tried to convince my father that it did but it just needed a little sorting out. He wouldn't leave it be, so eventually to shut him up my father told him that if he could do better he should re-write it, expecting this to be the last of it. He only went home and did it. In two weeks as well! My father placed it to one side saying he would take a look, but every weekend when Arthur came in he would ask whether my father had read the manuscript. He always had an excuse."

"Sounds a bit unfair," Cyril interjected.

"He was Cyril, or at least he could be. Once he made up his mind that was it with my father. Anyway, after about three months of Arthur pestering him, he did finally sit down and read it, he could not believe the transformation and then he understood what Arthur had been going on about. Unfortunately it was too late to sign John Kilkenny as he had already been signed to another agent, but my father offered Arthur a full time job straight away, he knew talent when he saw it. So Arthur reads any new manuscripts and those that have potential, but where the writer lacks the skill, Arthur steps in, he gets a small credit inside the cover and the author gets his or her name across the cover."

"But doesn't he mind that he never gets the recognition."

"He says he likes the anonymity Cyril."

Beryl was pensive for a moment, wondering how publishing Anne's story might affect their lives.

"Being famous is not all it is cracked up to be, just look at the papers. Sounds like he has the right idea," Beryl said.

"You could be right there Beryl, but some people crave that sort of attention," added Edward.

"Do any of the authors mind, Peter?" Saying Peter rather than Mr Phillips felt strange to Cyril as if he had crossed an invisible line.

The waiter appeared carrying a silver tray and started handing out the four drinks. "Are you ready to order yet sir?" he asked Peter.

"Not just yet, can we have a few more minutes?" Peter replied.

19

Nantwich Village Hall

Beryl stepped out of the back door of what was being used as a dressing room (but was nothing more than a kitchenette) to take in the cool refreshing air. The journey to Nantwich had been made with the minimum of conversation, each consumed by their own thoughts. After checking into the Abbotts Guest House and immediately transferring to the hall, Beryl had needed some fresh air after the book-signing and before taking to the stage. Her thoughts were full of her own reluctance to carry on with the tour although she was intrigued by Mark, who was proving to be a very strong force. She still couldn't fathom the connection, the familiarity, like a memory hovering just out of reach. It was something she had not encountered before. She understood Cyril's concerns and was pleased he was watching over her – she was proud of her nephew. Silently she condemned her own foolishness for honouring her contracts – she just wanted her quiet life back again, she missed it with a vengeance.

Cyril had spent quite some time staring out the window of Peter's Jaguar, his mind whirring, turning over all that this latest book seemed to be entailing, and the fact that it allowed him to follow a solo career as a writer. He couldn't escape the undue stress being caused to his aunt by the curious spirit, Mark. Things were so much better when it was just Beryl and him, in the parlour with a few guests - nothing untoward ever happened. Beryl would communicate the stories whilst Cyril made notes, it had been cosy, personal. Beryl would let her delicate tones invoke a sense that this was a special occasion, a private situation. She had never shown any signs of strain. This Mark certainly gave Cyril the heebie-jeebies, something wasn't right. His aunt's voice took on a dark sinister note with an almost rasping feel to it. Her body was used as a tool to convey the sentiments of Mark. She was totally absorbed, every movement, every step, her face showing every emotion. Mark sapped her energy, consumed her, he had witnessed the difference, each night a little more of her going as she went under. To the audience this was entertainment, to Beryl, it was all very real. Cyril dared entertain the thought that Mark was trying to become real again, through his aunt. Was it possible?

Peter drove with a half smile on his face for the whole journey to Nantwich, this was business, that's all, profits were going to be good, he had even received pre-orders for the new book. His conversation with Edward had filled him with hope that soon he would know where Shelbourne was, and maybe, once that was known he could arrange a short stop for this tour there, that really would be a boon.

Peter entered the dressing room as Cyril meticulously organised the summary notes of the story so far. Taking one look at Cyril he remarked quietly, "What's the matter?"

Cyril silently responded with a shrug of his shoulders, somehow he knew Peter was not interested in what he had to say, after all, he had tried already – albeit rather sheepishly. Beryl entered the dressing room and immediately picked up on the fraught silence.

"Everything okay?" she enquired.

"Fine," they both replied in unison, looking at each other in defiance.

"Good, then I am ready."

Cyril declared to himself that he needed to speak with someone, and soon, before it was too late.

Peter's introduction was received warmly by the attentive audience and soon Beryl was deep under the dominance of Mark, centre stage.

I was awoken from my slumber by a loud crash that seemed to be just outside my house. I didn't know what the time was but daylight was showing through the gaps in the eves. Climbing down from my safe haven I stared out of the main bedroom window, concealing myself as best I could behind the curtains that hung lank, lifeless and dirty. A feeling of tenderness came over me as I remembered how much love and attention Samantha had put into them when she had made them.

Looking across the square, nothing seemed out of place, it looked normal, groups of wolves huddled in the middle of the green, smoking, drinking, swearing. One couple were fornicating against a tree oblivious to anyone around them, she looked disinterested whilst he concentrated on the task at hand, his own satisfaction.

I couldn't see where the crash had come from. There was no movement, it was as if I was the only one to have heard it.

It came again, this time the whole house shook. I was puzzled, there was no smoke, no running, the wolves usually ran to wherever the action was. What was different?

Out of the corner of my eye I saw Jim and Eileen leave their house. Jim slammed the door closed behind him, making my prison cell shudder, attracting the attention of the wolves on the green, even the two fornicating gave a sideways glance, but didn't let it interrupt their rhythm. Jim was carrying a piece of wood. I became very scared for him, I had never seen him angry or upset in all the time he had been my neighbour. He was the prime example of cool, calm and collected - no room for irrational thought. I watched as he stomped off down the alley that I had braved two night's ago condemning one man to his death. Disappearing out of sight, Elaine followed, trying to placate her irate husband.

A strange stillness settled in the air. I could feel it even from the confines of my room. The wolves stayed where they were, other residents skirted the massive green in the middle of our square, anything to avoid confrontation. They tried to act as though they weren't scared but they were terrified, like everyone else on this estate, yet it was natural to portray confidence in the hope that it may just prevent experiencing the wrath of the wolves.

Over the tops of the trees, when the clouds let it, the sun occasionally hovered lazily into view. Anyone passing would have thought this was just another 'Pleasant Valley Sunday' as The Monkees once sang. If only it were. That must have been the picture they had in mind when the estate was first planned. A home, a place to be sought after, people on waiting lists just get the chance to live here. Instead people that didn't own their houses were on waiting lists to escape, those that did hoped someone was brave enough (or hadn't heard the awful truth about Shelbourne), to buy their house so they could escape this hell hole.

I stood watching for what seemed an eternity, time ticking slowly by, images blurring in front of my eyes as I stared off into the distance. This was how I used to spend my days, trapped in a dark place, my eyes vacant, as if in a trance hoping that death would consume me.

Jim & Eileen came thundering back through the alley. Jim's cheeks flushed, his face contorted in anger and Elaine in floods of tears. Jim still held the piece of wood in his hand. Just before entering their home, Jim did something that I would never have expected, he turned to the wolves shaking his head and shouting his disgust.

I willed him to stop for fear of reprisals but he appeared to have lost all reason. A couple of the wolves stared back then laughed mockingly. Jim, about faced and walked indoors. The house shuddered again as he slammed the door shut.

My curiosity was pricked, but still I just stood and looked. My experience from two nights ago still fresh in my mind and, although I didn't think it possible, I was more scared now than ever before.

How could I be petrified of leaving my own house?

Dismayed, I wandered through it, trying to find a better time, a time when life was so different, when I was so different.

I stood in my daughter's bedroom. She had been just five years old when she had been taken from me, my blonde-haired princess with blue eyes that shone like diamonds, a bright smile that could light the darkest of rooms. The pink wallpaper peeling, odd pieces ripped off – the wolves had done that along with scrawling their marks all over it. In my mind I could still picture her playing innocently on the carpet with her Barbie doll that we had bought her for her fourth Christmas. Her 'My Little Pony' bedspread which was adorned with hundreds of cuddly toys. I used to come in to say goodnight to her and sometimes I'd have to search long and hard to find her hidden amongst them. As I kissed her she would murmur sleepily 'night' and roll over, hanging tightly onto her favourite, a cuddly white rabbit with big fluffy ears and massive feet, called 'Mincemeat' – so called because when Samantha and I had bought him for Clare, it was her favourite food at the time. I smile at the randomness. Sometimes I stood listening to her breathing and Samantha would wander up behind me and wrap her arms around my waist.

"You don't have to watch her sleeping you know. She is quite safe."

"I know...but,"

"But what? You afraid she might disappear in the night?"

"No. She just looks so peaceful."

"It's a shame she sometimes isn't like that when she's awake, it's alright for you going to work. You don't see what the kids are like during the day, after school."

"But I would love to swap places with you."

"Would you now?" I turned to face Samantha. "I bet you wouldn't be saying that after a week, it's not all fun and games when the kids are arguing about what to watch on TV. "

"Yeah, you wouldn't change it though would you?"

Samantha thought for the briefest second, "I wouldn't change anything about our lives, even the bad starts we both had. It's what makes us complete."

"You're right."

"Don't make it sound as though that never happens!"

"Yes, boss!"

"Oi, you." She dug me in the ribs.

"What?" I replied sarcastically.

"Don't take that tone with me mister, otherwise you might lose these." She put her hand to my crotch.

"Okay, okay you win."

"Good. Now, take me to bed whilst I still fancy you." She kissed me on the mouth and I pulled Clare's door to.

At least no harm could ever come to them now. If only I had gone too. Spared this life, but it was always my choice, my choice to stay despite how desperate things got or how deep in depression I sank, my choice to stay and face the music.

Downstairs, I looked out over my garden, the garden I had started to clear, a small glimmer of hope in the desolation. A clear indication that every once in a while the fogginess of depression would clear and hope would be rekindled. Trouble was, the depression was never far away. Was it depression or just a kind of numbness?

Opening the back door I stepped out into the freshness, blowing away the stagnant air that lay dormant in my prison cell.

"Why, eh? Why? Bloody why?" I froze temporarily, a nervous reaction whenever a loud voice was close to me.

Looking over the fence I saw Jim's red flushed face. "Sorry?" I enquired.

He didn't look at me, just carried on ranting, digging up his flowerbeds destroying the hard work which I knew he had put into them, mindlessly turning over the soil, burying the plants, destroying them. "I'll never understand. Never! I'll never bloody understand. They won't be happy until they've destroyed every bloody thing, living or dead. Brain dead morons, the lot of them, and I had the chance to leave, but did I take it? Did I ever! Stupid, I was so stupid, I must have been bloody crazy to stay. A fool! What have we got? A home worth absolutely nothing! The police won't or can't help. Can't afford to go anywhere else! What a way to stick out retirement. We were going to do so much."

In all the time I'd known Jim I had never seen him as fired up as he was today, he was a placid, helpful man, he hated swearing and 'bloody' to him was damn right offensive.

"What's happened?" I offered.

He turned, his eyes showing his fury.

"Didn't you hear it? Are you really that shut off that you don't pay any attention to what's going on? Maybe you have got a lot to be sorry for, but how can you just…" the tirade stopped mid sentence and Jim stared at me, his eyes immediately losing the rage "I'm sorry, it's just…I don't know."

Head bowed I spoke softly. "I know. What's happened?"

A minute's silence passed between us then almost reluctantly. "You know our friends Maud and Arnold?" I nodded, I think somewhere in my mind I did know them, once. "Well it was their moving day today." Jim was physically choked and it took a couple of minutes to compose himself. "They were all packed up, van almost ready to go. I mean you know how hard it is to get anyone to come onto this estate let alone a removal van" the words got stuck in his throat. "Well…they were just about to load the last bit of furniture when one of those… those…BASTARDS…Yes! Bastards!" he spat the word out. "Drove a car right into the back of the van. Right into the back of the van! Can you believe it? And as if that wasn't enough, he even reversed it out again, drove round the block and straight back in again. Took out the whole side of the van out on the second assault. Almost killed the driver and his mate. Unfortunately, the bastards survived. The rest of 'em just watched and laughed…and applauded like it was some kind of event. Maud and Arnold are devastated, everything they had, smashed. Just like that. What could make someone do that to another human being?"

Jim forced the fork he was holding into the soil and stepped closer to the fence, the relief of talking to someone showing on his face as his brow softened.

"They didn't even have a buyer for their home. They were just going to leave it and rent it out to the council if they could. And do you know what else?" This was a rhetorical question so Jim could find the strength to carry on. "The bastards got out and laughed. Laughed, it's just a bloody game to them. It's like being in a prison you're not even allowed to leave. What the hell have we all done to deserve this eh?" Jim struggled to keep the tears from falling.

"Where are Maud and Arnold? Did someone call the police?" I knew these were stupid questions as soon as I said them.

"What use would the police do? They're too scared to come onto this estate unless they come in groups or in full riot gear and then they don't do anything." Jim wiped his eyes with the back of his right hand. "When the removal men were picked up they took Maud and Arnold with them. Arnold was a broken man. Why?" The question floated in the air for a little while as we stood not saying anything.

What could I say?

Finally Jim spoke again. "I thought I'd seen him at his lowest, but no. Only a handful of unbroken things remained. The rest will be in flames tonight, well what they don't nick first."

Jim's voice became quieter still. "Eileen wants us to leave. Tonight! I don't have the heart to tell her we can't. We've got nowhere to go. I contacted the council a couple of months ago. Do you know what they said?" I shook my head. "'You've got your own house so we can't possibly house you.' It's a joke, a bloody joke and we're the butt of it. We've got no money anymore, no living family. This is what it has come down to. What do we do?" Jim looked defeated, his shoulders drooped as he walked back into the house without another word.

I watched through their kitchen window as Jim took Eileen into his arms and she cried her heart out on his shoulder. I felt his grief well up inside me.

Jim's brother had once offered him the chance to move in with him and his wife when they bought a retirement bungalow in Bournemouth, which had a small annexe. At the time Jim thought *things would improve and didn't want to lose money on the house. His brother bought a retirement flat instead and used the extra money to go on cruises, enjoying their retirement until they died in a car accident six months later. Jim was a proud man and didn't like to ask for help despite the fact that he would always offer it himself. I don't really know what happened to the inheritance, I didn't think his brother had any children. I couldn't see why Jim & Eileen couldn't cut their losses.*

That's what I should have done.

I hoped for their sakes, he took that option. There was nothing here for them except more misery and heartache, but where would they go?

The sun was going down and a cold wind was kicking up so I went back indoors to stare at the stack of letters piled on the kitchen table, red bills, credit card applications, readers digest letters.

I used to be so organised and orderly, Samantha used to joke that I was the housekeeper, she was the homemaker. I made sure we never went without. I always said that it was the best way, she didn't deny it, she was a brilliant mother and wife, money was secondary to family. We had the right balance.

20

Cyril helped a weary Beryl to the dressing room as the audience showed their appreciation, leaving Peter to close the evening with a few remarks.

"Thank you ladies and gentlemen, thank you." Slowly the applause died down "For those that haven't yet bought books there is still a chance from the stall at the back of the hall." He smiled at his own poetic words. "There are books from the many authors I represent," The scraping of chairs proved to him that they had only come to see Beryl, but he was happy with that.

Leaving the stage, he went to join Cyril and Beryl in the dressing room.

"Well, that was another successful evening." He beamed as he entered. "Oh." The room was empty. He noted that their coats were gone and he presumed they had returned to the B&B. "Oh well." He decided to find out how Adele and Tracy had done.

Saturday 21st October 1978
Dronfield Junior School Hall, Dronfield

Inside my house I let the night slowly consume me as I sat on the lounge floor nibbling at the small tea I had prepared. Staring into oblivion, listening, whilst life outside continued. My mind drifted to Jim & Eileen, Maud & Arnold, the sadness, the loss, the emptiness that they must have felt. I thought of my own plight, my own journey and how, if at all, it could have been different.

If Samantha and the kids were still here, would I have the guts to leave everything, to get away, sod the financial obligations? If only I could take back time. Through the walls I could hear Jim & Eileen arguing, a very unusual occurrence, in fact, I couldn't remember them ever sharing a cross word. The angry words were just an audible whisper through the brickwork, but I felt saddened by how times can change people.

The previous night I had been overwhelmed by strength and power, only to fall prey to cowardice, two opposites of the spectrum in a short space of time. Deep inside, I wanted to be the saviour for this estate, bring my family back and live out the dream that Shelbourne promised so many years ago. Could one person do it, on their own? In the madness on which I bordered, the answer was yes. In reality, was it possible or was it too much. Magick, rituals, incantations, they worked, didn't they? They seemed to. Was I imagining it? If they did, I didn't really know how. Was I any better than the wolves? Revenge - was it sweet justice or was I just condemning myself further along destiny's path?

Things might have been so different if I'd known my parents. When I was younger I hated them, whoever they were, for abandoning me, leaving me in a world with no one to guide me. How could they do that? When Joshua was first born I saw this tiny bundle and my heart felt so much love that I started to rethink the old question of how my parents could have abandoned me as they did. No names even listed on my birth certificate, it was as though I was an immaculate conception. What makes people want to do that?

At dark times like these I still felt betrayed and bitter, even the wolves had someone.

What was I fighting for? Why was I fighting? Why wouldn't death come and take me? Life had nothing left to offer.

Beryl sat at the edge of the stage, deep in thought, her sad eyes searching the space over the audience's heads, whilst they sat in an uneasy silence, curious to know whether that was it for the evening; a couple of them noted the time on their watches, not even five minutes had passed. Peter looked at Cyril, who acknowledged him but proffered no answer to the silent question. A slow mumble started to grow within the gathered crowd, a discontented muttering, growing in volume as two minutes turned to three minutes, then to four.

Someone had to act.

Why me? The wolves were so strong.

The audience were caught unaware as Beryl broke into her stride again with Mark speaking through her.

The leaders, they held real power, they didn't hide behind a wall, fearing for their lives, worried that their identity might be discovered. Instead they thrived on the notoriety their lifestyles provided. I began to wonder how many followed just because it was safer to do so, easier to follow than to fight. How many would run and hide if the leaders were defeated?

A raw energy gripped me as I concluded that I needed to get closer. I pushed aside any guilt about the fallen wolves, they deserved it. Every last venomous bit of hatred returned tenfold.

My melancholy gone, I let the euphoria of hate envelop me for a short while. Then, curiously, I wondered how many of the wolves wanted out but didn't have the guts. Forced to endure the life that had grabbed them, taken them by the scruff of the neck and dictated what they must do. How many of them were weak and easily led?

NO!

The audience visibly baulked as the exclamation filled the hall. Mark's voice fused with rage.

They had choices likes us all. If they didn't want to go along with the other wolves they only had to fight, if more had, we wouldn't be in this mess. Yes! Yes!' with each 'yes' the energy returned to my body, the confidence, the bravado. 'This could be done, but I needed help'

I needed more people on my side, but how could I go about recruiting people? What if they thought I was insane? Was I insane? Probably! It could get even worse. Or could it? I didn't have any friends, Jim and Eileen were the closest I had, if any, but I barely spoke to them. Any friends we had were more Samantha's and when she had gone, they soon went, or I drove them away – it was difficult to tell in the haze that surrounded those times. Twisted memories, memories of what I think happened intertwined with the actual events. Sometimes, in those early days I believed I had deserved it, it gave me a strange sense of reason.

Leaving my half-eaten tea, I went up to my safe haven to scour the net.

From somewhere in the middle of the audience a lone man shouted, "excuse me, what is 'the net?'". Peter offered no answer, only scanned the people until he locked eyes with a rotund gentleman wearing large round gold rimmed glasses, he nodded his acceptance to answer the question later.

I didn't know exactly what I was looking for so, for a while I sat looking at the screen, the cursor blinking at me. For reasons unknown, I finally typed in 'cults', there were over 400,000 references. Did I think that was what the wolves were? Trying to narrow it down with specifics I only managed to increase the number of entries by 300,000. It was hard, as I didn't know what I was looking for. Opening a couple of entries I noted key words that kept appearing, shining like beacons in the bulk of text.

The hours drifted by and I didn't seem to be any closer. Only more baffled by the endless entries of people who seemed to have lost touch with reality and living in a sort of twisted nightmare. Maybe that was what I was doing, but still couldn't admit it to myself?

Nearly two days of fruitless searching passed before I even came close to finding what I was looking for, and then it was only because I had mis-typed the word 'Devil' adding an extra 'v'. 'Devvilian Demonic & Satanic Archangels'. The graphics made my tired eyes ache even more as the lurid red on black shimmered in a kind of haze, and the site drew me in.

It detailed rituals that had been performed and the results they said they had gained. A certain ethos about them caught my attention. Maybe it was because I felt an empathy with them. They detailed a cause that mirrored my own - proclaiming that they only use 'The Source' as they put it for saving society and were willing to help others with a like-minded spirit. There was a message board which I thought long and hard about adding to.

Reading some of the others messages I started to form the beginnings of my own twisted entry.

'The ethos of man, woman and child has been sapped dry, the marrow is desiccated, the evil in man needs to rise to combat the evil that is inherent in the world. The time to dance with the devil is now. Long live the dark lord, rejoice his time, join in the cleansing of the world. I have a job to do but a sole footman needs his brethren'

I re-read my entry and wondered what I was doing and what I expected. Had I lost touch with reality? I left my email address and pressed send.

There was a murmur from a couple of members of the audience, 'A what address?'

I sat back and wished I could change decisions I'd made, bring my family back to me. Take them to a different place where everything would be okay. I wanted to say how sorry I was, sorry for everything, that thought beckoned a forgotten memory.

"How could you forget Mark? Our anniversary." *Samantha's voice was hoarse from crying.*

"A couple of the guys just invited me for a quick pint to celebrate our bonuses."

"Do I mean that little to you? What about our daughter? When she is born are you going to forget about her as well?"

Samantha was six months pregnant and feeling the strain of her second pregnancy. I had vowed to be more attentive.

"It's not like I go out a lot." *As soon as I said it I knew it was like red rag to a bull. But as she went to vent her tirade a sharp pain gripped her and she held her precious bundle.*

"Mark! Oh, my god Mark." *Panic raced through me.* "Call an ambulance."

I stood looking on in disbelief.

"Call a bloody ambulance.!" *Samantha's cried.*

I ran to the phone and dialled 999 and within half an hour we were in the hospital. I held her hand so tightly.

"I'm sorry, I'm so sorry. I won't let it happen again." *She didn't answer me, too concerned about our unborn daughter. Finally, after a restless, anxious night the doctors gave us the all clear.*

I woke up crying, and for an instant not sure where I was, the darkness was a cloak smothering me. I wished it would. Samantha's hand had felt so real. I screwed my hand into a ball and willed myself back to the dream, but to no avail.

21

When reality hit, I knew it was shopping day, a day I dreaded as it meant leaving the house. My benefit was paid direct to my bank account and I could afford the few supplies I needed.

Readying myself for shopping was like getting ready to run the gauntlet. I knew I'd encounter the wolves on the way to the shops, and that alone, even in daylight, scared me. Stepping outside, a wave of nausea washed over me, I remembered the alleyway a few nights ago. I made sure the door was secured behind me even though I didn't really have anything to protect and a locked door would not prevent the wolves from entering if they really wanted to. Across the green were two female wolves sitting on a garden wall, one with long greasy black hair and a pale complexion, the other had a braid in her auburn hair and a nose ring. They gave me a cursory stare then carried on kissing, it was only for show, a game they played, it attracted the attention they wanted and gave them a reason to fight. I recognised one of them as one half of the couple fornicating a few nights ago. They stopped kissing and laughed.

A man walking his dog tried to skirt round them. "Wanna watch mister? Cost fifty?" said Pale-complexion. With that she shoved her tongue in Nose-ring's mouth "Well?!" The question was an angry one. The man baulked. I thought I knew what was coming next as Pale-complexion left the embrace of Nose-ring and stepped towards the man. The Alsatian growled a low menacing growl, baring his ferocious teeth, spittle hanging liked ripped leather from its jaw, the lead taut as the man struggled to keep hold of the dog.

The stand-off had started. I could feel the indecision of the man, 'to let the dog go or not?' From nowhere Nose-ring pulled out a seven inch hunting knife and knelt down to face the dog, eye to eye.

"Wanna try it pooch?" The man pulled the dog back as it fought to break free, snapping and biting the air. Nose-ring stood up "Come on slut, can't be bovvered to waste the energy."

"Oi! Bitch, who you calling a slut? You tart!" replied Pale-complexion, pretending to be hurt.

"You! Now come on take me back to yours and shag me." The two female wolves strutted off, laughing, arm in arm. The man relaxed, glancing over to me, our eyes met, we both knew what the outcome would have been if he had let the dog go, yet we both also knew that we had wanted it to happen. Society would have been against him and his dog, they would have been the ultimate victims.

The main supermarket was a mile away. Friday night used to be our shopping night. Samantha and I would take the kids with us and make the shopping trip last the whole evening. We'd stop off at the park that was just a little further on from the supermarket, let them run around and wear themselves out, then have fish and chips in paper from our regular shop that was now just a blackened burnt out shell, set alight one night by a disgruntled wolf.

Clare and Josh used to throw half of their chips to the pigeons.

By the time we'd get to the supermarket the kids were quiet and did as they were told, sometimes they fell asleep in the trolley seats which allowed us to finish our shopping in the shortest possible time and with the minimum of fuss. The kids actually seemed to look forward to Friday nights because they were fun; they were allowed to use their fingers to eat with and we didn't care if they played with their food. It was Samantha's idea, she just knew the best way to do things.

As well as the estate, the wolves now controlled the park, many of the gardeners had been attacked or bullied, so now no one looked after it. The council had allowed it to become a wasteland. The playground was now full of broken bottles and covered in graffiti, the swing seats had been broken and hung lifelessly. The grass was a foot high, the paths cracking as the ground reclaimed them for its own.

"Oi, arse-face nice rucksack. Did mummy buy it for you?"

I tried to shut out the verbal abuse that showered me as I walked the streets, they didn't even know me, but that didn't stop them. The abusers laughed as I walked on. I would never contemplate making this journey in the evenings now. The evenings belonged to the wolves, the daytime bearable only because the majority of the wolves slept.

The rucksack was to carry my shopping, it was safer. About a year ago I was chased by the wolves, fearing for my life, I dropped my shopping bags as they became awkward to carry whilst running. The wolves weren't interested in what I had bought just kicked it to smithereens, jumping on whatever couldn't be kicked apart. I went hungry that week. The rucksack was cumbersome and heavy at first but it meant I could run if I had to, albeit a little slower, but I knew fear would drive me on. And would I care if I died?

I returned home without incident, but as I walked to my front door I glanced at Jim & Eileen's house. A strange sense of foreboding kept me staring at it for a long minute. I put my groceries away, mostly up in my loft for safety, and then went out into the garden, still puzzled by Jim and Eileen's house. Their house looked quiet and peaceful, too peaceful and quiet.

The curtains! That was it. They were still shut. It was not like them at all, especially at 1pm.

Curiosity made me climb over the fence to peer through the glass, looking for a crack in the curtains, but there was none. I tried the back door, it was locked. Rapping on the glass I waited – no response. I tried again, still no response.

An uncomfortable feeling rose within me, but as I climbed back over into my own garden I wondered if maybe they had left in the early hours of the morning. I hoped they had. 'Good luck to them'. Anything has got to be better than here, this place, this hell hole. I knew it would not be long before the wolves would notice the deserted house. That thought horrified me. Jim & Eileen kept it so nice, the garden was always well tended, the rooms cleaned thoroughly every week without fail. I could only guess that they must have travelled light, probably a heart-wrenching decision after the arguments.

At least they'd got away, maybe they would arrange to come back and collect everything else. The important thing was they were safe.

Up in my safe haven I checked my computer, a dialogue box confirming that I had mail. I clicked on 'yes' to view.

Another murmur rose from the audience but Beryl carried on.

'The Dark Lord rises and takes us under his guise to do his bidding. Brethren of the Magick possess the tools to do his work. We must unite when a fellow brother calls. Invite us to your altar so we may rejoice. "Spirit of Four".'

I stared at the email for ages, nervous energy flowing through me, amazed that I had a reply. I looked at it for ages questioning whether I *should respond. What did I expect?*

After careful consideration, I typed my reply and looked at it for an eternity, it contained my telephone number so they could call me. I knew I had to talk with them first. 'This was it'. My thoughts ran to Jim & Eileen, Maud & Arnold, then to my wife, Samantha, my kids, Joshua and Clare, and as a tear slid down my cheek, I hit the send key.

Beryl lay exhausted on the floor as the audience broke into rapturous applause at her performance, with some standing, enthralled by the tale they had been told and how well it had been acted out in front of them, the passion and conviction. As Cyril escorted Beryl back to the dressing room, Peter addressed the gathering.

"Thank you. Thank you. I know some of you have questions. Especially over some of the terms used tonight, I can assure you we are looking for those answers and at the moment all we can surmise is that they are colloquialisms. I'm sure by the time this book is fully written we will print the answers to your many questions."

This satisfied some people, others just shook their heads disapprovingly "Just a way to sell books. Stan."

"Yep. I think you're right Derek, fancy a pint at 'The Hound'?" "Good idea."

After Cyril had made sure Beryl was comfortable in the dressing room he went to listen to the mingling crowd from behind the door.

"Don't believe a word of it Agnes. But wasn't she good?"

"She was amazing. I really believed it for a moment. I don't care if it was all made up, best night's entertainment I've had for ages."

"Come on let's buy the books, one each, then we can share them,"

"If it is as good as that then it'll be well worth the money."

Cyril felt hurt for his aunt, and guilt that she had done this for him. He glanced at Beryl who was laying stretched out on a settee. She wearily smiled at him. "Don't worry, as long as they are happy." She beckoned him over to her and placed a hand firmly on his shoulder as he knelt down beside her, he knew that meant she didn't want any silly talk from him.

"Look, I've got to go out. Are you alright going back to the B&B with Peter."

"Met a girl, have you, Cyril? Mind you I have seen the way that Tracy looks at you."

Cyril blushed and smiled awkwardly before leaving, not wanting to elaborate.

22

"Thank you for seeing me so late at night."

"That's quite alright. Father Andrew had said you were quite concerned and needed a friendly ear." Father James passed a cup of tea to Cyril as they sat in a plush lounge with ornate furniture.

"As you know my Aunt is Beryl Wallace."

"Yes, cooking up quite a storm from what I hear."

Cyril half-smiled. "It's just..." Suddenly he was lost for words. "My aunt has always been able to talk with spirits. It has never been a problem, they never want to harm her or anything." He took a sip of tea. "But this latest spirit, Mark," he stopped "It's not like the others, it...he seems stronger, he actually seems to possess her."

Father James physically withdrew at the mention of possession it was not something he had ever encountered. "Possession, you say?"

"Yes, but only for a short period of time. But I am concerned that one day it will not be just for a few minutes. At first I wondered if he was trying to be real again. If that makes sense?"

"I have never heard of a spirit coming back in to the real world. I have heard stories of possession, history is littered with them. I know the church has people who deal with that sort of thing. It is not something that I have ever encountered."

"But the spirit tires her, wears her out, she can barely stand afterwards. I don't know what to do."

"I am quite sure that no harm will come to her. Despite the stories and glorifications that films like to make of such instances, they are ...well I have only ever heard of one or two situations that have turned extremely nasty." He paused, watching Cyril nervously bite his lower lip. "I can see you are very concerned and whilst there is very little, I, myself, can do, I will inform the Bishop of your concerns, and maybe he will ask for an investigation. In the meantime I will pray for her and for guidance." Father James, could see anxiety riding Cyril like an angry dog. "Look, I will make sure that the Bishop sends someone, he owes me a favour. Now have you got details of where the next events will be?"

"Thank you. Yes, I wrote out a list, here, just in case." Cyril handed a folded piece of paper to Father James who scanned it meticulously. "I didn't know who else to turn to."

"Our doors are always open for those in need. And unfortunately, open or not, it doesn't stop some from coming in anyway." Cyril had noted the splintered wood on his way through the chapel door.

"I'm sorry to hear about that. Did they take much?"

"Nothing of real value. Anyway that is not why you are here so I will not burden you with our troubles. Now let's go into the chapel and pray for your aunt."

Sunday 22nd October 1978
The Congregational Hall, Cheadle

Cyril smiled sheepishly at his aunt as they sat quietly waiting for Peter to announce that it was time.

"Are you alright Cyril? You've hardly said a word all day. It's not like you to be so quiet."

"I'm fine," he replied curtly, making Beryl squint at him curiously. "Sorry. I'm just..." he left the sentence unfinished.

"It wasn't that girl was it?" Beryl said, remembering the last time he had been this quiet was after the date with Valerie.

***

Cyril spent hours getting ready for his date with Valerie, checking his watch almost every minute so he didn't turn up early or late. She had said she'd be ready at seven-thirty. Beryl had given him some extra money from his trust fund, left to him by his parents, on top of what she usually gave him.

She was so pleased to see him go on a date, it finally meant he was breaking free. She adored her nephew but knew he had to be his own person, and the book 'Anne Farmer' may be the catalyst to trigger that break. She had even been shopping with him, upon his request, so he could get some new, trendy, clothes, not that Beryl knew much about being trendy.

As he stood in front of the mirror he eyed his neatly cut short hair and wished that it was longer, in line with fashion. Since the date had been arranged he had noticed a lot more about the world outside of his life with Beryl, jading his confidence, how very different he was to people his own age.

"You look very handsome," Beryl glowed.

"I don't know. Is it me though?"

"Believe me, when Valerie sees you she'll gush at how handsome you look."

Cyril looked once more at his reflection, the loud orange paisley patterned shirt was a stark contrast to his usual pastel coloured shirts and tank top, with brand new flared 'Huggie' jeans. He had even stretched his budget and bought a black three-quarter length leather jacket and 'Old Spice' aftershave.

He glanced at his watch quickly.

"Oh god, I'm going to be late," he said, panicking.

"Have a nice time and I don't expect to see you before midnight. I won't wait up." She knew she would but wanted him to know that he should enjoy himself.

Cyril quickly checked his pockets for keys, money and her address then ran out the door leaving Beryl to close it behind him.

The walk helped to calm his nerves until he was within a few doors of Valerie's house.

"God, what am I doing. Flowers! I should have bought flowers. Damn!" he muttered. "It's too late now, just knock on the door, you'll be fine. But what do I say? Oh god, why I am doing this?" He checked the address once more and looked at the doors, stalling the inevitable.

He hesitated before ringing the bell, preparing in his mind what he was going to say.

The door opened and Valerie stood there in a white mini dress and knee high white boots. The dress fitted snugly and emphasized all the right curves and he found himself looking at her breasts which looked as though they had been squeezed in. He went red when she spoke.

"Punctual, I like that in my men."

'My men', Cyril thought, before replying. "I was always taught to keep good time." 'Oh my god how naff did that sound?'

"Good." She paused, looking at Cyril. "No flowers?"

Cyril blushed, he couldn't believe how bad this was starting. "No. I…"

"I don't like flowers anyway," Valerie said off handedly, implying the opposite and Cyril knew it. "So where are we going then?" Valerie slammed the door and grabbed his arm, turning him on the spot.

"I thought we'd go to that new place in Hamlet Court Road, you know, the Italian place."

"Ooh, a man with taste."

"That's a nice dress. You look nice." Cyril tried to sound confident but everything sounded lame.

"Just nice eh! I'll have to try harder next time," she said sarcastically, with a hint of playfulness.

'Next time, next time! Nice! Come on Cyril'

"I mean beautiful, really beautiful." It sounded contrived.

"It's a bit colder than I thought it would be."

"Yes. That's why I bought this jacket. Do you like it?"

Valerie gave him a sideways glance. "Yes. I should have brought mine." It was a loaded statement.

Cyril caught on and took off his jacket and placed it on her shoulders.

"You're not very good at this are you?!"

Cyril wondered whether she was asking or telling him.

"I'm sorry, no." He bowed his head.

"Relax, I'm not going to bite. Well not yet. But you never know your luck."

Cyril smiled awkwardly and physically relaxed.

"So how long have you worked for Peter?"

"Ooh, Peter is it. 'Us' minions have to call him Mr Phillips or sir." Cyril felt awkward again. "About two years. I did my Pittmans' shorthand and typing and his was the first job offer I got. It's alright. Keeps me in money and keeps my father off me back."

"Your father?"

117

"Right little tyrant sometimes. 'You must pay your way through life, you can't sponge off us', and all that bollocks."

"Oh." Cyril was taken back by the language and realised what a sheltered life he lived at Beryl's.

"Thought you could take me to 'Spirals' afterwards, it is a real cool bar, they play some really good music."

"Okay," Cyril agreed, wondering whether he had brought out enough money.

***

"Well, here we are." Cyril opened the door for Valerie, who walked through without a thank you.

Cyril followed and they were led to their table, which he had reserved earlier in the day. As they sat down Valerie handed Cyril's jacket back to him. He placed it on the back of his chair then held Valerie's chair out for her, again, he didn't get a thank you.

The waiter hovered with some menues.

"Would you like to see the wine list sir?"

In the hope of trying to appear sophisticated, Cyril replied, "Yes please."

"Ergh, no thanks. We don't want any of that gnat's piss. I'll have a snowball."

"Oh." Cyril felt embarrassed

"And for sir?"

"A beer thanks," Cyril answered shyly, deciding that he didn't actually like Valerie's personality, she was a little too brash for his liking and he still had the rest of the evening to go. She certainly looked attractive and had a good body but her manners left too much to be desired.

By eleven thirty Cyril made his excuses and left her to party the rest of the night away at Spirals with the other men whose attention she had garnered, she seemed to be having a good time and he didn't think it would matter if he was there or not.

***

"No." Cyril humoured her and then adding to change the topic, "Just, stuck on a part of Samuel Preston. Still can't think of a good sub-heading."

"It will come to you. Don't worry, just let it come to you. I have faith it will."

Peter walked into the kitchen that was being used as a dressing room, both Beryl and Cyril looked coldly at him and his smile slowly waned. "What's wrong?"

There was a pregnant pause and then Cyril briskly stood up. "Nothing, Peter, we were just getting ready, weren't we, Auntie?" Beryl acknowledged with a nod of her head.

"Good," Peter spoke, rubbing the palms of his hands together in a gesture of pleasure "Well the hall is full again so I'll go out and introduce you. Have you got the…"

"Here you go." Cyril thrust two bits of paper into Peter's hand before he promptly left, leaving the two staring meekly at each other.

"You're worried aren't you? Don't be, you worry too much. It will be alright. Although this spirit is powerful…more powerful than anything I have dealt with before, I don't get the feeling that he means any harm." Beryl walked over to Cyril and held his hand in both of hers, to comfort him.

"But…" She didn't let him finish the sentence, just placed a finger on his lips to quieten him. At that moment they heard the crowd in the hall fall silent as Peter's booming voice addressed them. He had grasped public speaking with a vengeance and seemed to enjoy being the centre of attention for the few minutes he had.

"Come on then, s'ppose we ought to go out and get ready."

"Yes, Cyril, you go. I'll be out in a minute." Beryl was tired but happy that things were not as bad as maybe they had first appeared, after all, the audience did seem to enjoy it, even if they didn't necessarily believe. That was their prerogative, she thought.

As Cyril left, she sat down again and spoke a little prayer aloud, gripping a silver cross she now wore around her neck. But she could still feel Mark's presence growing like a formidable dread.

23

My phone sounded its loud morning chorus, waking me from my fretful slumber. Through bleary eyes I saw that it was five in the morning. It had been so long since it had rung that it took nearly five rings for me to register the noise. It was almost pointless me having one really but it was pay as you go so it wasn't costing me anything..

There were baffled glances from some members of the audience at the phrase 'Pay as you go'.

"The Brethren are here to answer your calling." The deep gravel tones hung in my ears before the line went quiet. The abruptness with which I had been woken made it difficult for me to gather my thoughts, at first I didn't understand what the voice meant.

"Your Brethren, The Power of Four are here," the gravel tones stated more forcibly.

"Er yes, what? Yes, yes, where are you? When do you want to meet?"

"Brother, we are here. Now!" I was puzzled. "Let us in, so we may start."

The phone went dead. I sat still, mystified and dazed. How could they be here, I hadn't given them my address? Wearily, I climbed down from my safe haven to the front door expecting to find nothing, confirming that I had indeed been, or was, dreaming. But everything I touched, the wall, the ladder, all felt solid and far too real. I rubbed the sleep from my eyes.

As I neared the front door I could make out the shapes of three dark shadows beyond the obscure glass, backlit by the early morning haze. A thousand thoughts rushed through my head, my heart pumped at a rate of knots. Gulping, I cautiously opened the front door, expecting to wake up in bed again. The daylight dazzled my eyes and I blinked as the three figures remained still, like doom, waiting to make their move.

Swallowing hard, I was lost for words, frightened almost, with hardly any information they had located me. How? The three figures stood proud, looking at me, waiting, expecting. I hadn't envisaged it would happen like this, it had only been two days since the emails and part of me thought it was all just some sort of joke. But they were here, before me.

Their eyes penetrated my soul as we stood sizing each other up, anticipating the next move, shivers running down my spine.

I greeted them with a timid, 'Hello'. They said nothing just continued staring at me. Then the broad shouldered one, with cropped hair and dark eyes, wearing a full length black leather coat, motioned with his head for the others to follow him as they pushed past me, striding confidently into the lounge. Two of them carried holdalls, one had short cut, mousy hair and wore a trendy causal jacket and scarf over his crisp white T-shirt and black jeans. He also carried a small suitcase, and what looked like a laptop carry case; he reminded me of a mature student. The second one with a holdall was taller, nearly six feet two, and had a scar cutting an ugly line down his left cheek starting just below his eye, his hair was matted and unkempt, his blue jeans had various stains on them. He wore a dark sweatshirt and had unusually long fingernails.

Following them into the lounge I watched as they busied themselves. Dark-eyes spoke with a gravelly voice, portraying the character of someone who had survived many battles. "This is Scholar." He pointed to the one who looked like a mature student, who was already booting up his laptop. He loosened the tartan scarf that was wrapped around his neck as he worked.

"This is Scratch." He pointed to the one with long finger nails whose eyes were sunken, dark sockets full of mischief, his mouth was turned up in one corner which gave the impression that he was grimacing.

"And, I'm Whispa." I took in his broad shoulders and realised how formidable he looked, as though he could handle himself should the need arise. The stubble on his chin was at least two days old, even though his head was cleanly shaven. His voice demanded obedience. All in all, they looked intimidating and I began to wonder what I'd done. Whispa spoke again, his thunderous tones filling the room like a god.

"The fire shall reap them all." He came in close to me "The fire shall reap them all." Taking my right hand in both of his he stared long and hard into my eyes, his grip tightened and I tensed every muscle in my body as I tried to pull away. Fear rooted itself deep in my core. When finally he let go, he spoke again. "You are strong brother and it will be

a pleasure to serve with you." He laughed heartily. "Do you have any food, drink? Our journey has been long and we are famished."

"I...I only have tea...or coffee, sorry I don't have beer or spirits." It sounded flimsy, even as I said it. Suddenly, I felt compulsion to ask them to leave. I was scared. What would Samantha say if she saw this?

"Don't fret Brother." Whispa's piercing eyes ran through me.

"Tea will be fine. Whispa really shouldn't drink, he gets a little wired and you need a clear mind when dealing with the 'Dark Lord'." Scholar's words carried like a cold winter chill. His laptop was whirring away on the floor, also open was the suitcase, inside were some clothes and buried below them various books, large tomes, the like of which I had never seen before. He took each out carefully, placing them on a protective cloth he'd laid out in front of himself.

"So how 'bout this tea then eh?" Scratch slapped me on the back and marched me into the kitchen, his hand massaging my right shoulder, sizing me up.

"Sorry, the kettle's upstairs. I'll go and get it." I said trying to quell the nervous tones in my shaky voice. Scratch crooked an eye at me. "It's a long story."

Scratch eyed the kitchen. "I guess it mus' be. Ain't they all. We go' time." He smiled showing a line of crooked yellow stained teeth. He left me in the kitchen as he walked back into the lounge. I heard them all talking

"Scratch mark and cut out the star in the carpet. We'll place the altar against the wall," Whispa said.

"I can feel the degradation of this 'state, like a putrid pit of hell," Scratch said feverishly.

"Scholar..."

"Yes, I know Whispa. Check and see what I can find out."

"We'll align the Dark Lord tonight. I think he'll be pleased..." Whispa stopped

"I fink you right there. What is it Whispa?" Scratch imparted.

"I'll check on our friend, he doesn't seem pleased to see us."

I realised that I had been eavesdropping on my guests. Whispa appeared at the lounge door.

"I'm just...kettle, tea." I felt like I was the guest.

I trotted up the stairs to get the kettle believing I was in over my head. *They looked every inch the capable warriors I had wanted, but now they were here, my mind filled with odd questions 'Would I need to pay them? I didn't have any money. 'What would they do if I didn't?'*

Shaking, I started to ascend the ladder to the loft. The realisation that I must have lost my mind completely hit me. I stopped on the third rung from the bottom and hugged the ladder feeling my stomach turn over, a knot growing tighter and tighter.

"You have an altar?!" It was more a statement than question from Whispa and it caught me by surprise, making me almost lose my footing, Whispa grabbed my arm with a powerful hand, steadying me.

"Up there." I pointed into the loft. He looked at me.

"Do not fear us." His voice penetrated my soul.

He pulled me from the ladder and made his way up. Half way up he stopped and looked down at me "It will get better. We're your Brethren now, no need to fear us. Our guerdon is what we take."

I was too spooked to clarify what he meant. What did he mean 'Our guerdon is what we take'? Had he known what I had been thinking? He must have. Now I would not even be able to relax in my own prison.

"Our reward. It means our reward." Whispa spoke before disappearing from view and returning a few seconds later with the kettle and assorted accoutrements.

Downstairs I made tea and coffee, anxious and wary of what was going on around me. In the lounge a large section of carpet in the shape of a five pointed star had been cut out. Some of the books I had bought had been brought down from the loft. Scholar was scoffing as he read some of the titles, before throwing them like unwanted waste, into the corner of the room. Scratch was making an altar on the floor in front of the wall opposite the window, using a red velvet cloth. Thirty-seven black candles stood proudly on discs, some were on the altar and others placed in what looked like random places around the room.

On the bare floorboards within the star Scholar was marking out what he referred to as the 'Eye of Rabion'. I had read about that in one of the books Scholar had discarded. He looked up at me.

"We need to align the Dark Lord with our location and focus his power. Whispa said you set up your altar in the loft."

"Ain' that a long story," chipped in Scratch, smirking to himself. They were mocking me.

"You have a lot of power. Whispa can tell, he could feel it when you

contacted us. But an altar needs to be grounded, a basement is best, but as close as you get is fine. Most use our website as a source of fun."

"Mumbo Jumbo ain't it to most." I could tell Scholar hated being interrupted, by the scowl that he threw at Scratch.

"As I was saying, most expect a bunch of weirdos in…"

I half smiled but caught myself.

"You can laugh. It's good to laugh. But only with us…not at us." Whispa issued his retort firmly, but then his eyes lightened and he laughed. "It's a foolish man who can't see the lighter side to the darkness."

Concern consumed me. I had invited these people into my life, complete strangers, and here they were treating me as if I was one of them. Why?

It was all starting to feel a little too surreal, a vivid dream that I might wake up from. I pinched my arm.

"The Brethren is real, my friend. Do not fear us, we are here because you wanted us." I looked at Whispa and, although I heard his voice, his lips did not move. "Tell us your story." Whispa smiled, a line of perfect white teeth with bright eyes, making me feel at ease. They busied themselves and, as they did so, I told them of my plight, my story, the estate and what I wanted to accomplish. I explained about my life here in this house and how it had all changed, about my wife and kids. They let me release the emotion that was like a coiled spring inside. It felt good releasing all the pent up frustration, anger and depression.

Whispa appeared to absorb it as if his inner being needed it to survive. I talked for about an hour and a half by which time the sun was high in the sky. Looking through the window I noticed it was a beautiful day outside and, for the first time in ages, the weight on my shoulders had been lifted, the dark clouds driven from me.

"Please now take your place at the star of Filgoria whilst we focus the strength of the Dark Lord and tune in our minds." Whispa indicated where I was to kneel.

24

I knelt down, sitting back on my heels, as the others were doing.

Scholar stated matter-of-factly, "First we recite an Echobian Key," his sing song voice filled the room with masterful precision.

"Hold my hand and place your left on the altar so we can complete the circle of Jecia," Whispa instructed.

The atmosphere in the room became heavy, fortified with an unnerving energy. Something was happening and I didn't know what, these three people were in my house and I felt I couldn't change that, even if I wanted to.

In my head I heard Whispa. "The Faith, have faith. Control comes with faith." Whispa's grip on my hand tightened, he was almost crushing my fingers. In the distance I could hear a low persistent rumbling. The flames from the now lighted candles danced around, even though there was no breeze.

I sensed the rumbling getting closer, yet it didn't get louder, a presence enveloped me.

"Concentrate my friend." Whispa's voice was once again in my head. I did as instructed.

In unison Scratch, Whispa, and Scholar started to chant out loud in a strange language that I had never heard before, yet I found myself speaking it with them, calling out the words clearly and distinctly as though it was as familiar to me as speaking English.

"Kuwitiem piwarna wadibo ol druppkhan. Pitiyé graglodium" I felt an energy come to me in short bursts like a heat, but without the burning. The candles dimmed and then went out, leaving the room cloaked in a dim, dirty twilight.

All was quiet but I could definitely feel a presence in the room, something inexplicable and ominous, searching, feeling, crawling around. Whispa, Scholar, and Scratch were all looking at me. Whispa was still holding one hand, my other on the altar. My skin started to crawl and itch, my heart pounded, throbbing like it would explode. Struggling to get my breath, a suffocating force held me. Panic frenzied my mind and I stared in bewilderment at each of the strangers, in my lounge, believing them to be the last faces I would ever see.

Inexplicably a serene calm came over me and I passed out.

Beryl collapsed on the floor where she remained motionless. Peter teetered on the edge of his seat before moving to help her. As soon as Cyril noticed, he slammed down his pencil and ran to his aunt.

"Auntie, Auntie?"

Peter was a second behind Cyril.

"Beryl. You okay?" His polite tones lacked any sincerity.

The majority of the audience gasped whilst the rest sat quietly watching, believing it to be part of the act.

"I hope she's alright." A woman in her forties said to no one in particular.

"Did you feel that?" A stout looking gentleman stated.

"Yes, yes Bill, I certainly did. Definitely something there. I have never been to an evening where the spirit has been so strong." His rather large friend replied.

"She's the real deal alright. I don't doubt that for one second Ron."

"Auntie? Auntie?" Cyril called, ever wary of what Mark was doing to her. Beryl wouldn't come round. Cyril hugged her close to him. "Auntie, please wake up. Wake up. Please?"

The audience's faces registered that something was terribly wrong.

"Is there a doctor in the house?" A man in the fourth row called out

The question was met with no response.

Cyril grew apprehensive, although he could find her pulse.

Beryl's eyelids flickered.

"Auntie?" he called, relief flowing through him.

"Cyril," she coughed and spluttered.

A sigh ran through the audience.

"It's all part of the act," said a woman harshly, who sat in the second row gathering her handbag from the floor. "Good though, wasn't it Sarah?"

Beryl looked into Cyril's eyes. "I feel so weak." Her words were a whisper for him alone to hear and, with that, Cyril slipped his right arm under her knees and scooped her up off the floor in one swift motion, faltering only briefly as he stood up.

Beryl slipped her arm around Cyril's neck, drained. She had felt every emotion, the sadness, the insanity, the clarity of thought, and the anger. She hoped that by telling this story Mark would move on, yet he stayed and grew in strength. She didn't know how much more of this she could take.

A slow ripple of applause started.

"Thank you," Peter started.

"Excuse me. What's a laptop?"

Again Peter fobbed off questions from the enthused audience about 'laptops' and 'pay as you go' as mere colloquialisms, in truth he was just as curious and was hoping to have some answers himself – soon.

***

"Here, have a glass of water."

"Thank you. I feel so weak." Cyril poured a glass of water from a jug and handed it to Beryl. As he let go of the glass it slid through her hands hitting the floor and dispersing its contents. "I'm sorry," Beryl stated feebly.

"Don't worry, I'll get you another one." He picked the glass up from the floor. "Luckily the glass didn't break."

"Small mercies, eh!" Beryl stated dryly, bewildered that Mark could take so much from her.

"I think…" Cyril started, but Beryl, placing a hand on his arm, stopped him. She knew he was going to talk about cancelling the tour. She had made an agreement and would honour that. As she drank from the proffered glass, she remembered her conversation with Cyril after the first night Peter had come along to the parlour and touted the idea of writing a book.

***

Beryl had made tea whilst Cyril lit a fire in the small lounge at the front of the house. By the time Beryl walked in with a tray of tea and biscuits the fire was roaring away filling the room with its warm glow.

She placed the tray on a small coffee table in the centre of the room. "We'll just let it brew for a few more minutes." She said, handing the biscuit tin to Cyril. "I have got your favourites in there, Bourbons."

Cyril took the tin enthusiastically and pulled out two, proceeding to munch on them like an excited child before returning his gaze to the dancing flames.

"I do wish Fred would come to terms with the fact that Diane has gone, it does concern me so that he refuses to move on."

"I know Auntie. I suppose hope is keeping him from breaking down."

"It will do him no good in the end. I only wish there was something I could do to finally get him to admit that." Beryl poured the tea into two china cups, plopping two lumps of sugar in one, before handing it to Cyril, who stirred it vigorously.

"Thank you."

"You'll wear the pattern off them one day," Beryl said sternly, sitting down on the settee with her own tea.

"Sorry. What did you think of Mr Phillips?" Cyril said, slurping his tea. He was not good at hiding his thoughts or feelings from Beryl.

"You think I should go ahead with it?" Cyril shrugged and grabbed another biscuit from the tin he'd placed beside his chair. "I have to admit any money towards a good cause is truly worthy." She paused, "I just don't know about him, there seems to be something, just a feeling I have."

Cyril knew his aunt could be very perceptive about people and she was very rarely wrong.

"Businessmen always scare me. They always look so stiff, as if they are hiding something. I don't trust them normally but it just seems too good an opportunity to miss. You have always said that you wished you could have helped some of the people you talk with before they'd passed on, or at least similar people before it is too late. Maybe with this offer you could. I have all the notes. Maybe making them into a proper story could be my contribution," he said, delighted at the prospect.

Beryl looked at Cyril and sipped her tea, she knew what he meant by that comment. "You just being here is your contribution to this household." Cyril had mooted on various occasions that he felt he was not pulling his weight when it came to the household finances. "You look after me. We have money to get by on. Anyway, one day you'll meet someone and then I won't be so important to you, so I want to take advantage of you whilst I can, because then I will have to look after myself," she said playfully. She could see that he wanted to do it. He had a good way with words and she knew that he would make a great storyteller given the chance.

Cyril looked at his closed notepad sitting on the footstall on the other side of the fire. He had another twelve like it in his bedroom, he loved making notes, loved hearing stories of the lives of the spirits, in different times and places. He did feel that in some way his notes were pointless when they just sat there doing nothing, only to be read by him. Now he couldn't decide whether it was that thought making him want to take up Mr Phillips' offer or whether it was the fact that the money could help so many people on top of their usual charity work for the church.

They both sat in silence watching the fire dance over the coals. Cyril poked the fire and a spark flew out onto the hearth.

"Do you think Anne would like her story told to the world?" Cyril said suddenly.

"That's a very good question, Cyril. A very good question." Beryl sighed as she finished her tea. "I suppose I can't see any harm in doing it. You do have all the notes. I mean if people are interested. And, yes, the money could achieve so much."

Cyril couldn't help but smile, his words, in print.

"I will give Mr Phillips a call in the morning and maybe we can go and have a chat with him at his offices." Beryl could see that Cyril was delighted and that pleased her. "Do you want another cup of tea? I'm sure there's enough in the pot," Beryl said.

25

I woke with a start not knowing what had disturbed my sleep, but knowing something had. I found myself in my daughter's bedroom. I had got so used to my draughty safe haven that this felt strange and instantly I was plagued with strong memories, reminding me of why I also preferred my safe haven - giving me distance from the ghosts of my family.

Another memory snagged me, a recent one, Whispa's voice.

"You need to sleep with the memories in order to grow above them. Face the demons that torment you. All of them."

Through the torn shreds of the net curtains that remained I saw the night sky outside, the stars hidden by soft clouds that hung like marshmallows, the moon painting their edges in a silvery glow. It was a haunting picture and I watched, hypnotised by the tranquillity of it.

The house breathed and I took it in, it's life force was real inside me, we were at one and it felt strange, it wanted to be alive again, it needed a family.

Lying on the makeshift bed, I tried to remember what had happened the previous night. Had it all been a dream?

Sitting up, I convinced myself that, yes, it had been, just a wild vivid dream.

"Can you the feel your Brethren?"

"What? Who's that?" I blinked my eyes a couple of times to be sure I was awake. Looking around the darkened room, there was no one else.

"Feel the power."

My pulse started to jump like a hyperactive child, tiny pearls of sweat formed on my forehead, my hands became clammy as I rallied my thoughts. "Who's there?" My voice stronger than the question behind it.

Had I finally crossed into insanity?

Pulling my knees up to my chest, I hugged them tightly and shifted back towards the wall under the window, staring into the empty space that was once my daughter's bedroom. Minutes passed and when nothing presented itself, I relaxed.

Stirring my weary body I walked to the door, my actual movements seemed to be a split second behind the thought as my head throbbed, every movement painful. The room started to spin. I grabbed for the door handle, my hand missed, or, did it go through? I wasn't sure. The pit of my stomach started to churn, the room spun faster and I became unsteady on my feet. I tried again for the door handle and this time caught it in my clammy hand. I wrenched the door open almost banging my head on it and stumbled into the hallway, the woozy feeling dissipated and everything felt normal again.

Pulling the door closed I remembered the room, fall of the joys of my daughter, her giggling voice as I used to blow raspberries on her stomach. The sound of her voice, as she talked to her dolls and cuddly toys, then, as she would say 'Goodnight Daddy', a heartbreaking softness in her voice that was full of innocence.

"Daddy, Daddy play with me. I'm having a tea party. We have got 'gons'" I smiled as I remembered Clare having problems with saying scones, I couldn't remember why, and that thought twisted like a bitter knife.

"And who's coming to tea?"

"You are silly. Mincemeat, and Barbie, and My Little Pony, and Big Ted."

"Are they all eating scones as well?" I replied playfully.

"Gons, not what you said," she corrected me. And the memory was gone.

I made my way downstairs as quietly as possible, listening to the house which was bathed in darkness. In the lounge the altar was still set up. It was real. I started to remember. The ceremony. My three guests. It had happened. In the back room, my old dining room, there were signs of my three guests, their makeshift beds made up on the floor, yet they were nowhere to be seen. I believed I could tell whose bunk was whose by the way they had been left. Scholars - neatly made and with a pile of books stacked with the largest at the bottom, a small pile of clothes sat at the foot of the bed. Scratches - a scrunched up mess of blankets and clothes. Whispa's - a rolled up sleeping bag and nothing else.

Back in the lounge I switched on the light, it gave me a sense of security. Studying the five pointed star cut out of the carpet and the red painted eye in the middle, a peculiar feeling took hold. As I moved closer, an inexplicable euphoria, a heightened state of non sexual arousal enveloped me. Energy flowed, electrifying my senses, the hairs on my arms stood on end. I trembled as a cold shiver coursed down my spine.

The front door slammed shut and I turned sharply, my heart in my mouth.

"So, you do feel your Brethren?" spoke Whispa, beaming a hearty smile at me from the doorway before he entered the room.

Scratch followed him and I saw Scholar walk past to the back of the house.

"This 'state is rancid," Scratch imparted.

Finding my voice, "I know." The words faltered slightly. "I call them 'the wolves'. They always hunt in packs. There is a leader, I just don't know who, they won't be happy until they've sucked all the marrow out of life."

Scholar had come into the room. "We ready then?"

"Ready for what?" I said, looking at my three guests in turn.

"A lil' exploring." Scratch raised his eyebrows to emphasize the excitement in his voice.

"I don't know if I can go." I paused, taking in the puzzled stares I was getting. "Last time I…" I started to explain.

Whispa put his hand on my shoulder. "Feel the power running through you." I could. I really could. Whispa's voice rattled round my head, even though his lips didn't move. His voice, just like earlier when I had woken up, like an inner conscience. He smiled at me again and left the room.

Scholar approached me. "The invocation ritual we performed last night not only directed the Dark Lord's power to us here, but it will help unite us so we can protect each other."

"Should need arise," Scratch emphasized.

"Oh!" I didn't know what to say. I was now submerged into something I knew very little about. "Okay," I said, sounding more sure than I felt.

"Good," Scratch beamed.

"Of course, that's not from everything," Scholar added nonchalantly.

At those words I sank back down again.

"We are not immortal," Scholar added.

Whispa glanced at his watch. "It's time to leave."

I knew my comrades needed to witness the wolves behaviour first hand and as I was ushered through the open front door I found the prospect daunting.

The night air was cool and our breath rose in small clouds until it dissipated high above. As a group of men, I knew we would attract the unwanted attention of the wolves. They might see us as a threat, or a challenge that needed to be dealt with.

We were barely out of the front door when I was proved right. A group of three wolves spied us, one had multiple gold earrings hanging in both ears which glinted in the moonlight, another was carrying a four-pack of beer with one open in his hand, the third had a thick square jaw that looked like it was carved from stone. I caught the gaze of Four-pack before quickly diverting my eyes and lowering my head, hoping, praying that the inevitable wouldn't happen.

"Look what we have here." Square-jaw spoke, his voice caught between puberty and manhood and belying his looks. Thrusting my hands deep into my jacket pockets, I fell into line with my comrades, my Brethren, who all walked proud, they didn't care what attention they attracted.

They ignored Square-jaw, he was just an annoying little noise.

Square-jaw walked boldly towards us, standing in our way.

"I said, 'what do we have here then?'" He was tall for his early-teens age but it was comical the way his voice didn't match up to his stature and broad build. We stopped and he paced round the four of us whilst Gold-earrings and Four-pack watched on. My three Brethren did nothing. Inside my heart was pounding, a knot starting to tighten in my stomach. "What! Don't ya speak? Cat got ya tongue?" The goading was directed at Whispa. "'ere Flick whadya reckon?"

"Gut'em like pigs." Gold-earrings laughed, spurred on by Four-pack, who drank the last of the beer, before crushing the can and throwing it in our direction. It was a statement of bravado.

"You don't want to do that." Whispa finally spoke, the words thick like treacle.

"Oooh! It does speak," Four-pack announced, swigging from another can of beer he had just opened.

"Now, if you don't mind we'll be on our way." Whispa was calm, not even a sign of any tension.

"Maybe I do mind," Square-jaw challenged.

"No. You don't," Whispa commanded, inching towards him. Square-jaw appeared to shrink in stature.

Trying desperately to maintain his image. "Well, maybe just this once."

"Thank you," Whispa replied sardonically.

"Mack, what you doing?" Flick sounded incredulous.

"Just leave it," Square-jaw snapped.

"Leave it. What's wrong with you?"

"Come on, let's go," Whispa commanded.

I marvelled at what had just taken place and tried to stay alert in case of retaliation as we moved away.

We walked towards the alley where I had wet myself, still watched by Four-pack. Flick and Mack were arguing with each other and, slowly but surely it was getting heated. I caught a flash of light on metal as Flick produced a knife. The alley loomed like an ominous tunnel.

26

Scratch took the lead, with Scholar filing in behind, then myself, then Whispa. Scratch knew where we were heading and walked with confidence.

As we approached the far end of the alley we saw another group of wolves causing a nuisance not far from the crime scene where I had caused a man to be bludgeoned to death. The tape cordoning the area flapped in the slight breeze. One by one the wolves noticed us and stopped what they were doing.

"I smell fear," Whispa said under his breath. The wolves held back, standing their ground on the other side of the road to the entrance. Spreading out on the pavement we continued walking in pairs.

Without warning a half brick landed a few feet in front of us. Scratch and Scholar stopped immediately. I wanted to run, my life was in danger and a warm sensation ran down my leg, embarrassment coursed through me. I didn't want this sort of attention. Yet I had invited it when I first contacted my Brethren. Scratch walked towards the group of wolves, who stood stock still in silence.

"Wasn't me gov,'" a medium-built wolf announced. He had carefully crafted hair with a black streak of lightning dyed into it down one side. His nose looked as though it had been broken more than once, his arm muscles bulged beneath his dark T-shirt. Scratch stopped in front of him.

"What wasn't eh?" Scratch's voice brooked no insolence.

A stand off.

I had never seen anyone face the wolves like this. Scratch held no fear and the wolves themselves were not openly intimidated by Scratch. Each sized up the other. Scholar moved to the right of Scratch and a few paces behind, busying himself making notes in a book.

"What you writing mister, last bollocks and testicles?" Hysterically the wolves cackled at their own humour but, as the laughter died away, they seemed uneasy. I watched a couple of them moving their feet in a strange nervous shuffle. They were itching for something to happen but the head wolf, Bulging-muscles, was still playing his game. The wolves were not used to a show of strength and they were thinking hard about their plan of action. Without any audible command, the wolves formed a formidable line in front of Scratch, standing shoulder to shoulder, ready for action. For a few seconds the stand off continued in silence.

Scholar was still writing or sketching in his notebook, it was difficult to tell which. Scratch eyed the line of wolves, male and female, standing united.

'What are we doing?' I thought to myself, battling the urge to run.

"Scratch is 'seeing', an ancient form of viewing another's mind." Whispa answered my question using telepathy, his talent scared me.

Scratch pointed to one of the younger wolves, she looked about ten, dirty and scruffy. "Come here." The female wolf looked nervous, but no one moved. She waited for back-up, none was forthcoming. Tentatively she took a couple of steps towards Scratch before an arm shot out and barred her progress.

"If u wan' her you'll 'ave to come froo me." This came from Bulging-muscles. The girl physically relaxed. The rest of the wolves suddenly found their voices and started to jeer and cajole.

Scratch, unperturbed, stepped forward and made a grab for the girl. Bulging-muscles launched himself at Scratch. Scratch struck out with his left hand catching Bulging-Muscles at the top of his windpipe, with the webbing between thumb and forefinger, temporarily winding him and sending him crashing to the ground. Scratch pinned him down as he struggled to regain his breath. The rest of the pack stepped back, amazed at the power and speed with which Scratch had struck.

Scratch lifted Bulging-muscles' head off the ground, drawing it closer to his own. He was still fighting for breath and his gargled gasps were short. The pack didn't know what to do and just watched. Scratch drew his finger nail across the left cheek of Bulging-muscles, who howled in pain as thin wisps of smoke rose. Scratch released his grip without saying a word, got up and walked back to where we stood.

Scholar snapped his notebook shut and spoke loudly to the fallen wolf. "You are a marked man, I would leave if I were you." Then placed the notebook in his pocket.

The line of wolves had broken to create a circle around their fallen comrade who was trying to pick himself up and regain some composure. I caught his eye in between the bodies around him and for a *split second I saw vulnerability, but that was soon overcome by flashes of anger at being made to look a fool. The pack tried to help him to his feet but he fiercely rebuffed their offers of help.*

In an attempt to save face he shouted at us as we walked away, I was the only one to turn to look at him. My Brethren ignored the threat and, after the display I had seen, I was not surprised. It was a little unnerving that I didn't know the full ability of my Brethren but I was pleased to be with them, and a little in awe of how much they could achieve without great effort.

The estate was a labyrinth of streets and footpaths. We visited places where people had been killed or tortured, dark places that normal people stayed away from, garage blocks that lay desolated and burnt out, houses with boarded up windows. A section of waste ground that no one professed to own so was taken over by the wolves when it suited them. Tonight it was vacant.

After a few hours of what I thought was a pointless exercise, we were heading back to my house, our base, when something attracted Scratch's attention. Following Scratch we entered an underground garage under one of the two tower blocks on Shelbourne. The echoing chamber reverberated with our footfalls. There was no other sound and from the few remaining fluorescent lights that still clung to life we could see that it was deserted. The car park was for use by residents of the tower blocks that stood like giants over Shelbourne. At the outset it had seemed a great idea but no sensible person ventured there now and especially not at night. Locally the garage had the nickname 'The rape-room'. Men and woman had suffered, it was rumoured that thirty-three rapes had taken place. It only came to light after the first brave woman had found the courage to report her attack which then led to more women finding strength to do likewise, and finally, two men, one who later reportedly committed suicide.

Scratch led us to a dark corner where we skulked in the shadows.

"Why have we…?"

"Shush," was the reply from Scholar.

It soon became apparent as we heard tyres screeching on the concrete floor.

"But how did…?" I asked, and again I got shushed.

Headlights like search beams scanned the area but fortunately the dark corner where we stood was hidden from them. A car stopped, with engine still running. A few minutes passed before three people walked out from the shadows behind the car. Then two men, with guns clearly showing in their waistbands, got out of the black BMW and greeted the three men who were all dressed in dark clothes.

Scholar once again got out his notebook and started to mark the pages. I tried to look but it was too dark.

How did he know what he was doing?

We watched the proceedings for nearly thirty minutes, people came, discussions took place, before most people left. More car headlights broke the dark shadows from where the three men had come, more engines started and a number of cars rolled forward. A few parcels were passed from one vehicle to the BMW. After a parting gesture, the three men got into one of three cars, which had appeared from seemingly nowhere, and drove off, leaving the two men with guns standing at the boot of the BMW.

We slipped out unnoticed and headed back to my house.

"Your questions will be answered soon, now we sleep." Whispa gave me a knowing look as I turned the key in my front door.

Inside, obediently, I went back into my daughter's room again.

27

A restless night ensued with my family memories haunting me. Our first foreign family holiday, Joshua was six, Clare was three. We'd saved hard for this holiday, a reward for all the overtime I'd done. We flew to Faro Airport, Portugal, which was an hour and half's transfer time to the villa we'd hired for two weeks. It had its own private swimming pool and was only a couple of miles from the beach.

Perfect.

I made the mistake of letting it slip to Joshua and Clare as soon as we had booked it.

"Do you not like fish fingers anymore Clare?" Samantha asked.

"Josh said they were real fingers," Clare said, pushing them almost off of her plate, her frown showing her disgust.

"Joshua," I reprimanded.

"She wouldn't shut up about her Barbie Doll and she broke my Lego house."

"She didn't do it on purpose," Samantha replied.

"It's not fair, whenever she does anything wrong I always get the blame."

"JOSHUA!" I scolded. "You know that's not true. You should never tell lies." Joshua threw down his cutlery. "If you are going to behave like a spoilt child then you can go to your room. I won't have that sort behaviour at my table. And to think we were going to take you on holiday." The words were out before I could stop them. Samantha eye's went wide, scolding me. We had decided not to say anything knowing it would be difficult to control their excitement.

Clare stopped playing with her food and looked at Samantha. Joshua said excitedly. "Are we really going on holiday?"

I sighed heavily, trying to maintain parental control which floundered as I spoke. "Not if you carry on like that, we won't."

Joshua's face lit up. "Cool, a holiday. Where we going?"

"Portugal. Samantha added reluctantly, cutting up Clare's fish fingers in the vain hope of persuading her to eat them, which she refused to do.

They started preparing all the things they were going to take, almost immediately, even though they had three months.

Trying to get them to sleep at night became a nightmare, we used every trick we knew. Some nights I would take them for a ride in the car, Joshua would tell me all the things he was going to do, for the hundredth time. Eventually the gentle rolling of the car would rock them to sleep and I would have to carry them to their beds. The days couldn't pass quickly enough. It was a big adventure.

Two nights before we were due to fly out Joshua went very quiet. At first we couldn't understand why. He had been so excited. We pushed him for a reason but he remained silent, just shrugging his shoulders; after some encouragement and a bedtime story he finally opened up.

"Daddy, I'm scared," his small voice whispered.

"Why?"

"What if the plane falls?"

I tucked him up in bed and tried my best to explain the concept of planes and how they worked. Samantha and I had only ever been on one plane, before the kids were born, and I still marvelled at how such a big bulky thing could get off the ground. I was still apprehensive about flying but I couldn't let on. As much as he tried to understand and I tried to simplify it, Joshua couldn't quite grasp the principals of flying. In the end I decided we would go to the library and get some books on the subject. But even after studying the books he still needed a lot of reassuring that we would be alright. It was a good job Samantha had reams of patience with him.

On the day of the flight he clung to his mother's side until he got on the plane. Clare didn't seem to care, she had her favourite rabbit, Mincemeat, tied to her wrist and danced all the way along the moving walkways...

There was a gasp from a member of the press. "The what?" Peter made a mental note to talk the person afterwards, once he registered from whom it had come.

...to the departure gate. It was quite wearing for us, but you had to admire her enthusiasm.

Joshua insisted he wanted a window seat, although when he saw the wings stretching out as far as he could see, he changed seats to sit with Samantha, hugging her tightly. As the aircraft roared off down the runway he became excited at the full force of the initial thrust of the plane, which planted us firmly in our seats. His eyes became like saucers as the plane left the ground then instantly turned to terror. I tried to imagine what he must have been feeling, I held his hand tightly and he gripped it with more force than I thought possible.

Joshua was quiet all through the flight, despite Clare trying to annoy him, he didn't even eat. Once in Portugal, Joshua got back to his old chatty self talking ten to the dozen within minutes of getting off the plane. The villa was incredible with three enormous bedrooms, two bathrooms, dining room, lounge, and a veranda. The kids argued who was having which room until we designated rooms for them. They sulked for a bit but that was soon forgotten once they got into the pool in the bright sunshine. The cold water took them by surprise but as they splashed about the coldness became a forgotten memory. Samantha lay on her sun-bed, reading, whilst I tried to show my children how clever their father was by making the biggest splash, soaking Samantha in the process.

"Mark!" she scorned.

"Sorry?" I said whimsically, the children just laughed, Samantha softened and joined in. We laughed so much. That holiday made us who we were.

Samantha and I made love that night like we hadn't done in ages and afterwards sat out on the veranda wrapped in sheets, drinking wine and talking like lovers again. The children fell asleep quickly worn out by the day's excitement.

Our budget was tight but we wanted to make this the best holiday ever, so it was picnics on the beach and on the nearby hillsides; occasionally we'd stop in the small town nearby for our evening meal and if the children were good, we treated them to ice cream afterwards.

It was a million miles away from all our troubles back home. The estate had started to turn by then, the odd bit of vandalism had become more regular, car theft seemed to be rising and drunken behaviour was more commonplace, although we didn't realise what it would eventually become.

If we had, I think we would have left there and then, pulled the shutters down on it and got out before it was too late. But hindsight is *such a wonderful thing.*

Trying to pack on the last day of the holiday was gut-wrenching. The children didn't want to go home, there were tantrums and tears and much slamming of doors. They had made a few friends and vowed to keep in touch, but they never did. Driving home from the airport it all seemed a distant memory, another universe. We were all quiet. Joshua didn't worry about the flight home, just took it in his stride.

The estate appeared so grey and tainted to our sun dazzled eyes, an unwelcoming, unfriendly place. Only two weeks had passed, but a strange apprehension had descended. Now the lightly tanned bodies of our family, along with our memories, were all that was left of those two weeks.

Waking from this splendid dream, I fought to claw it back, to stay in that dream world with my family and that place. But it was gone and only harsh reality survived.

I went downstairs and watched from the lounge doorway as my three guests were engrossed in some form of meditation. Whispa's voice echoed in my head.

"Join us, we have work to do."

A palpable tension took hold of my body as the reality of the life I was stuck in hit me. I wanted to be with my family, I was sure they were in a better place. This was all too much. My cowardice kept me from making that final decision to join them, from making that most decisive of decisions. To end it all.

28

Tentatively, I sat down next to my Brethren. Without opening their eyes, Scratch and Scholar both reached across from their positions, each taking one of my hands. A static electrical force ran through me, making the hairs on my arm stand on end, then all too quickly, I found myself deeply immersed.

An oppressive atmosphere descended on the room, it hung like an intimidating gloom suffocating us, cloaking us in its morbid presence.

My breathing became slowed, rhythmic and hypnotic. An undercurrent of warmth exuded from my core. The deeper I succumbed, the more I felt in tune with my companions, my Brethren, our hearts beating as one, soothing and entrancing.

Scholar's voice broke into my subconscious. "The order of the Spirit of Four call upon Lucifer, the God of Darkness. Using the Key of Asdinoferal, we seek his presence, command his presence. We summon that he rides forth on the Path of Thenekium to our world. Sosotium herood de feroukium. Open the gate of Seriustifon." The last words rang out in a thunderous command.

Silence! Noise from the outside world evaporated.

Then nothing happened, I was surprised and felt a giggle start to rise inside me.

There was a tiny part of me that was not fully committed to this course of action and I was glad 'that nothing had happened'. That small part started to grow and shake me from the madness that I had invited in. Then an instant later a burning sensation eclipsed all those feelings, my heart thumped pounding its powerful beat, I wanted to grab my chest to soothe it but Scholar and Scratch held my hands tightly.

The immense pain was suffocating. Though I let out a scream, no sound was audible. Tears welled up in my eyes as the burning intensified, spreading to my lungs, then my kidneys, liver, finally my brain. Everywhere inside was raging with fire. I couldn't move. I couldn't shake it.

"Don't fight it. Let it consume you." Whispa was there again in my head. Something about his words eased the pain but as soon as his words were gone it intensified again. Excruciating agony enveloped every muscle, joint and fibre of my being. When I thought it could not get any worse, the pain engulfed my eyes. How could I still be awake and in so much pain? I hoped, wished for, death to take me.

"Welcome it. Don't fight it." Again the pain disappeared at Whispa's words, but as soon as his voice was gone from my head, the pain was back tenfold.

The smell of burning flesh entered my nasal passages, my burning eyes widened as I went to let out a scream that remained locked inside, deep inside. The putrid, acrid, stench made me want vomit. The tips of my fingers and toes felt like they were on fire. Paralysed with the pain, I tried to scream again, but still nothing came out.

As the intensity subsided I could hear chanting. "Sosotium herood de feroukium." Over and over again. Around me Scratch, Scholar, and Whispa were all deep in meditation. Their mouths were moving but the words seemed to be coming from elsewhere, another place, another time. Then, with great relief, the pain suddenly vanished. I sucked in a welcome breath of cool air, but before I could enjoy the relief of painlessness, it came back with a vengeance, excruciating, incomprehensible pain. Scratch and Scholar still held my hands so tight I couldn't move, despite the fact that I struggled to break free.

As quickly as it had come back, it was all over. Scholar and Scratch let go of my hands and I rolled backwards onto the floor gasping for air, the smell of burning flesh all around.

Staring at the ceiling, every part of my body refused to move, paralysed with fright.

My three guests were standing over me, looking on, satisfaction plastered across their faces. Hoisting me up, they effortlessly carried me from the room. There was very little I could do. I thought, I hoped, my time was finally over and that maybe, in an attempt to improve my situation, I had invited into my house my own executioners. My existence would now be erased from the book of life. A welcome relief that I had never been able to achieve by myself. Now, taken out of my hands.

I was laid out on the kitchen table like a man about to be prepped for an operation, my lifeless form unable to prevent anything, but my mind conscious of everything. In my peripheral vision I saw Whispa holding what looked like a curved dagger, a mini cutlass. My T-shirt was sliced open, exposing my bare chest. Scholar held a chalice above my face.

Inside, I resigned myself to the end, and a sense of calm washed over me. I just hoped it would be over quickly, without any more pain.

Scholar proceeded to mark out a figure or symbol on my torso with the thick liquid the chalice held. Whispa held his right hand above me and used the dagger to cut the palm of his hand with one swift, meticulous movement. Blood flowed freely down his forearm and, as the first drops landed on my stomach, they burned like acid making me flinch as life leapt back into my body. Every sinuous fibre alive with a raw energy, I wanted to get up, yet, when I tried I couldn't move. Scratch held his hand just in front of my face and, as if by magic, I relaxed, acquiescing to his silent command.

Scholar read a few words from the large tome he held in both hands. "Luto argotiyé. The Spirit protect. The Soul consume. The Earth release. Dark Lord rise up. Do not conceal your presence."

The oppressive atmosphere around me pulsed with fear and loathing.

"The Master is with us." Whispa spoke with subtle jubilation.

Scholar continued. "Then let him take half the soul we offer and possess the body and in return help us to be successful in our task." I wanted to bring the proceedings to a halt but was powerless, a living, breathing, dummy.

A low rumble emanated from the floor, the vibrations rattling through me, the ceiling light fitting swung and my head was bathed in a haze of blurry images, the room spinning.

Abruptly, everything went still, normal. Whispa and Scratch helped me off the table and onto to my feet, which didn't seem to belong to me, distant, almost surreal, as if viewing life through someone else's body. Disconnected.

I was helped to my daughter's room where I was laid on my makeshift bed.

"You will rest now." Whispa spoke, his voice softer, but still full of authority.

Sleep took me easily but it wasn't restful or disturbed, more a semi-conscious blur. An awakening of the mind, a growing sense of power and being.

***

The dawn light broke the darkness of the room and hurt my eyes. I tried

145

to stand up, but making simple movements was still difficult, my co-ordination gone. The muscles in my legs wouldn't work properly, three attempts to stand up left me reeling on the floor, confused. The noise I was making summoned my guests into the room.

"Aye, so y'awake then," Scratch drooled.

I merely peered quizzically at him, trying to focus and form words in my fuddled brain.

"It takes time to adjust to having only half a soul." Whispa's voice was cool.

"Haaaalth myyy soool buth." Each word I said was punctuated by the need to draw in breath.

"If you require the Master's help, then payment is needed and there is only one thing the Master wants, or needs," Scholar explained.

In my brain the answer swirled around like a tiny wisp of cloud, I tried to quantify what I was being told. What kind of nightmare had I let myself in for?

Whispa and Scratch helped me up, putting my arms around their shoulders for support. It was as though I had no will, a rag doll being carried around. As they took me downstairs, I found my limbs regained some of their lost strength and the more I moved the more invigorated I became, my three guests merely smiled their contentment.

I felt strangely powerful, even though I still pondered on what had happened. My fuzzy memory recalled the burning on my torso and upon looking down I saw my T-shirt in shreds. Strength was returning and I took my arm from around Scratch's neck to pull the T-shirt off my skin, revealing what was underneath. The movement was still disjointed but my legs could now support my weight. I ran my fingers over the texture of the marks on my skin then stumbled back upstairs to the bathroom to look in the broken mirror.

As my eyes focussed I saw an upside down triangle on my chest, the point of which was above my belly button, below this was a mark which I couldn't make out, no matter how long I stared at it. With my finger I stretched the skin, hoping it would become obvious, I traced it around with my index finger, again almost losing my balance.

Whispa spoke from the open doorway. "The mark of Dosca, the thirteenth key of Colboltius and the Gate of Acrodian." His voice soothed my silent questions.

"Our work can star' proper now," Scratch voiced excitedly, standing *behind Whispa.*

I was still dazed.

"Tonight, my friends, we start." Whispa's voice was clear in my head.

Beryl slumped exhausted to the floor as silence filled the hall. Cyril stopped writing and ran to her aid.

"Bravo, bloody marvellous," called an upstanding gentleman, producing a thunderously loud clap, despite wearing leather gloves. "Absolutely outstanding."

"Thank you, sir," Peter called, as Cyril glanced at both men, feeling nothing but contempt for them.

Unusually, the audience remained quiet, awestruck and the gentleman's claps became uneasy until someone else joined in. Peter felt embarrassed, wondering if something had changed the audiences opinion of Beryl, but, finally their reluctance to applaud disappeared and the hall resonated with jubilant cheers.

Cyril half carried Beryl to the dressing room, and after a drink, took her back to the B&B.

29

Garrett Hotel, Fulford

Cyril lay on the bed of yet another B&B room, staring into nothingness. After ringing Father James still no advice was forthcoming. The Bishop had advised the correct department and the case was being looked into according to procedures. Cyril was conscious that the events had been no different to the earlier ones, although Beryl was exhausted afterwards, Mark didn't appear to be causing her any actual harm. The audience loved the fact that Beryl acted it all out, but it hurt to see his aunt being used like a puppet. All attempts to trace any of the people mentioned by Mark were fruitless. But even knowing that didn't quell his fears. If only help or guidance from the church was forthcoming, it would ease his anxious mind. Finally Cyril fell into a fitful sleep.

Beryl lay awake, churning over thoughts in her head. Why was Mark so strong? What connected him to her? She wanted to know how she could prevent the spirit from taking her so completely. She had seen Cyril's concern and shared it, his eyes betrayed his thoughts every day.

Peter sat in the reception area and rang Edward to get an update on 'SHELBOURNE'.

"My cousin can not find mention of it anywhere as the name of an estate. There are records of buildings, houses, even streets, but no mention of an estate by that name."

"That's strange, surely it must be mentioned somewhere?"

"He's even checked back over a century and looked at colloquial names of places. Nothing. I am sorry Peter but you need to find out more from this spirit." He paused for a second. "Maybe Beryl can question the spirit."

"The spirit, Mark, seems to be the one in control."

"That's strange, the evenings weren't like that when I used to visit. She is alright?" Edward expressed his full concern and it wasn't lost on Peter.

"Of course."

"Peter, she is a friend and I would hate to see any harm come to her."

"I can assure you she is fine, a little tired that's all. I must admit there is definitely a different feel about these evenings, but I put that down to the fact that they are in halls. The audiences are loving it."

"I don't really care about the audiences. Take care of her, and yourself, of course." There was brief pause between the two friends. "If my cousin finds out anymore I will let you know."

"Thank you. Goodnight."

Peter was puzzled even more now. He wanted to know more about this place that Mark talked of. Another idea started to plant itself firmly in his mind, another way to make money from this tour. A follow up, a true account of 'Shelbourne'. He had a writer in his stable that was good at writing factual books...yes. 'Shelbourne – life in a living hell'. Perfect he thought. But he needed to know where it was located.

Thursday 26th October 1978
Community Centre, Redcar

The rest of the day was a blur. Detached, confused and looking for some kind of familiarity, I found myself once again in my safe haven, this time laying on the bare boards where my makeshift bed used to be. I closed my eyes in the hope that when I opened them I would find it had all been an illusion, my guests would be gone and my whole family would be around me.

When I did open my eyes, intermittently, I only saw the underside of the roof. Nothing had changed, no matter how hard I wished. Realising it was all real, I was gripped with a sense of foreboding; a feeling that was so strong the bile in my stomach started to rise and the loft began to spin. I sat up, narrowly missing a rafter. I wanted to hide, run to the darkest corner and disappear. Slowly the feeling passed and I lay back down.

Evening arrived, and I sat at the battered kitchen table with my

Brethren, I noticed they looked wired, their eyes shimmering in the dim light, pupils dilated, strange half smiles plastered across their faces. I had not witnessed anything like this before in the short time I had known them and it sat uncomfortably on my shoulders. Scratch had cooked a stew of some kind. I had no idea where the contents had come from. I certainly didn't have enough food for this feast, I was eating better than I had done since my family had gone and it tasted good. Fresh bread was a welcome joy as I broke off another piece from the loaf and dunked it in the hot warm liquid.

"Brethren, we are one. The power of four," Whispa announced abruptly, and then the room fell silent, with the exception of sipping the tasty stew.

Time in my safe haven had done nothing to quell my misgivings about what I had instigated. Deep down, I knew it was too late to stop it and somewhere inside a thought tugged at me that this was the right thing to do - for my family's sake. I had a score to settle and had to be content with that knowledge. The fight had to continue, regardless of the outcome. Reaching that conclusion only enhanced the feeling of raw power which had started to consume me, making me believe I was invincible, every fibre twitching with positivity.

"It is a good feeling?" Whispa broke my thoughts surprising me as he drained the last spoonful of his stew.

Feeling the strength, I answered. "Yes. I...I feel strong."

"Ain't noffing like it, believe me." Scratch nodded his head at me, waiting for my agreement. "The wolves won't know what has hit'em," He sniggered. "I think it's time to leave, don't you?" He looked in turn at each of us and pushed his bowl heartily to the centre of the table, his appetite sated.

"Hold, Scratch. Scholar is just getting ready."

"Whispa, why does he have to take so long. I can taste flesh." He licked the index finger on his left hand. The way he did it reminded me of when he had scratched the wolf's face. Again a wisp of steam rose up. "See, the flesh burns." He laughed menacingly, and I found myself enjoying it, caught up in the rapture. A wry smile slowly but surely spread across my face and I ate another mouthful of stew.

The aroma from the stew penetrated my nose, electrifying the senses, it smelt better than when I had first sat down. As I chewed the meat, strength grew inside me, thunder rising from the depths. It was good, *very good.*

Whispa and Scratch shared a glance which I caught out of the corner of my eye.

"You see, my friend." Whispa put his arm around my shoulder as I scooped up the last morsel of stew. "Our friend here has marked one of the said 'wolves'." He punctuated the air with two fingers from his right hand, "and now there is no getting away from us. That little wisp of steam is his flesh burning."

"If ya close enough ya can 'ear him howl with pain." I looked at Scratch, the menace in his eyes like a hungry beast. "So whaddya say we do lil' hunting t'night." The thirst in his voice dripped venom. "When Scholar can get his act t'gether that is." The pointed statement was full of frustration at having to wait.

30

"How did you all get together?" Their stares only managed to emphasize my own surprise at the question, I hadn't planned to say it.

"We'll save that question for another day." Whispa pondered my curiosity.

"Lets jus' say we were once men of the cloth." Scratch cleared the plates from the table, glancing sideways at Whispa.

Fifteen minutes later we left the house. This time I didn't feel uneasy, I was confident, my new found strength striking the right chord within me. Stopping occasionally, Scholar made some notes or sketched, I was curious as to what he was doing but somehow knew it was inappropriate to ask. I wondered what had been meant by 'Men of the cloth' – surely not the church?

"Your questions will all be answered." Whispa's voice was in my head again.

I relaxed and took in the cool night air without the usual apprehension, which had laid heavily upon me on previous excursions. My fear seemed a thing of the past 'just like the wolves were going to be' that thought punctuated my mind, filling me with mirth, Shelbourne was going to be taken back.

I looked at Whispa, studying him, trying to fathom who he was and why he was here.

"It is good, is it not?" Whispa spoke softly without turning to look at me. I tried to pretend not to be staring as he walked one step ahead of me. I nodded my agreement and, although he couldn't see me, he seemed to understand my silent reply. My three Brethren looked at each other in turn, they understood what I was experiencing.

I walked tall and felt strong. I was in control now. I could do anything.

Parts of Shelbourne…

Peter nudged Cyril indicating that he wanted a piece of paper and pencil and when handed them calmly wrote 'SHELBOURNE' in capital letters, underlining it three times as a statement, not to forget to mention to Beryl about what he had found out or rather not found out. Then he returned his attention to Beryl.

...had been abandoned by the normal folk, the good people of Shelbourne, fear keeping them away. Inside I knew tonight was the night that fear would be given its marching orders and the estate would start to be reclaimed.

The alley where I had almost lost my life loomed up, and I brushed off my usual intimidation and marched tall with my Brethren.

We were soon at the location of the hammer attack that I still felt responsible for. The pavement had been scrubbed, but even in the dim light of the quarter moon, dark bloodstains could still be seen on the ground. Tonight I could re-address some of that guilt, correct the wrongs of the wolves.

Whispa stood where the man had fallen. Closing his eyes he allowed himself to fall into a meditative state; I watched on bemused, turning to Scratch to ask 'What is happening?' but was met with the palm of his hand signifying for me to be quiet. Scholar made notes and I kept watch with Scratch. I was still curious about Whispa as his breathing became shallow. A thin mist appeared from nowhere, rising from the ground around his feet, rising up in columns to the tips of his long meaty fingers. I became aware of a noise made by Whispa, a slow intake of breath, lasting well over a minute.

Then, without a word, he came to, nodded to Scholar, turned and proceeded to walk on, with us all falling in line. I tried to sneak a look at what Scholar was writing but every time I came within viewing distance he would close the book, as if he knew, and I would feel ashamed for trying.

Eventually we came to five residential blocks, each containing thirty-two flats spread over three floors, each connected by pathways that ran from block to block on the second floor. Broken rotary washing lines littered flag-stoned areas at the base of each block, rusting away like ancient monuments of a better life. No one dared leave anything personal to dry outside, knowing that it would be stolen or ripped to shreds.

I had heard stories about these blocks, that the residents were the first to fall prey to the wolves. First the drugs took the sons and daughters, then the families would move out, transferred by the council, this was when they used to care. The flats would only be empty for a few hours before they were broken into by the pushers, dealers and prostitutes. News would spread like wildfire that another place was being vacated. When the families returned to gather their remaining possessions, they found it too late. In hindsight, they were the lucky ones, although they didn't think that at the time. After a while the council stopped transferring people and the residents were forced to live with the situation escalating around them.

Now people only came here to experience the darker, seedier side of life. I didn't know of anyone living here now who didn't belong to the wolves. Over time they could corrupt anyone, you could only fight for so long; in the end you learned to participate or die.

Staircases wound upwards inside brick columns that looked as though they had been stuck on the fronts of each block as an afterthought. The blocks formed a U-shape, someone's idea of community. On the ground floor of each block nearly all of the flats lay deserted, either boarded up with metal sheets or as burnt out shells. The residents of these flats had been the easiest targets for the wolves. I remember reading that one resident had been committed to a mental institution, driven mad by the incessant abuse, and the relentlessness the wolves showed in achieving their goals. At least he was out of it now.

Scratch's eyes scoured the buildings then raising the nail of his index finger to his nose picked up the scent of the scratched wolf. He resembled a maddened dog for an instant. The wolves remained elusive tonight as if they were in waiting, biding their time. I hoped recent events had made them think long and hard about their ways but probably they were just re-grouping.

The night air was broken by the sound of screeching tyres followed shortly by a radio belting out the beat of an unidentifiable tune, a siren to the wolves that their fix had arrived. Making our way towards the noise we saw a silver Mercedes parked at a nearby kerb. Already a crowd surrounded the vehicle, it was the equivalent of an ice cream van on a hot summer's day.

Two men dripping with gold stood point, handguns drawn at the ready. We hung back at one corner of the nearest block of flats, waiting, observing the blatancy of the brisk trade, knowing the police wouldn't or couldn't do anything to prevent it.

Footsteps echoed behind us and, as we turned, a group of three wolves, in their early twenties, approached menacingly. The one leading the pack had wild, spaced out eyes, his clothes were dirty and hung loosely on his emaciated frame. He was flanked by larger built wolves with shaven heads, their pot bellies hanging over the tops of their jeans, again their clothes were dirty. One had dark sunglasses on whilst the other had wristbands, which only managed to make his arms look more like meat cleavers. Rather than walk round, they stopped immediately in front of us. Standing our ground, we faced down the leader and his bodyguards. We were bigger and there were four of us but that didn't seem to make any difference, defiance was evident.

"Get out the fucking way, shit for brains, before I shuv a fucking knife in ya." Spaced-out sharply commanded, venom in his pubescent type voice, as he produced a seven inch hunting knife.

The audience audibly gasped, not expecting to hear that sort of language. Even Peter managed to look uneasy, his cheeks turning crimson as he too was surprised by the outburst, he had never even heard Beryl raise her voice. Peter observed the uncomfortable looks on some of the audience member's faces, but Beryl continued unabated and it was all forgotten again.

A few nights ago I would have been petrified. It took me a little by surprise to realise the inner strength I now possessed and the fact that I wasn't afraid anymore. I was not going to be beaten down by these animals.

Spaced-out didn't waste any time after getting no response and swung the knife at Scratch's throat. With lightning reflexes Scratch grabbed Spaced-out's wrist, blocking the swing, and with considerable speed and force twisted the arm sharply up behind his back, yanking it as high as it would go for good measure then forced him, face first, against a boarded up doorway, knocking the wind out of him. With his free hand he grabbed Spaced-out's throat and squeezed slowly. Spaced-out started to choke. The strains of him struggling to get his breath filled the air.

The flanking wolves, Sunglasses and Wristbands, made a move to help their leader. Whispa's fist flew at an incredible pace and hit Sunglasses square in the face pushing his nose upwards into his skull, causing it to explode, splattering blood over the ground. Going down like lead, he fell awkwardly, banging his head against the hard concrete where he remained still, blood oozing from his nose and a trickle appearing from the back of his head, at first I thought he was dead but I could see his chest gently rising and falling as if asleep. Wristbands launched himself towards me, I kicked with all my might, my foot finding its target, his crotch, surprised tears formed in his eyes as he fell to the ground holding himself and rolling around in agony, whimpering like a hurt dog.

Scholar was drawing in his book, leaving the fight to his comrades. Whispa stepped over to where Scratch was holding the leader.

"Turn him round Scratch, eh!" Scratch responded as asked.

The fight was still in Spaced-out's eyes but he was turning blue. Whispa put his face to Spaced-out's face. Spaced-out tried desperately to bite him, but Scratch just tightened his grip on the wolf's throat and he went limp as Whispa continued. The knife dropped to the floor with a clang, which attracted the attention of a pack walking away from the Mercedes, and they turned to see what was happening.

Spaced-out let out a long slow rasp as Whispa drew out his soul. Spaced-out's eyes became empty, all fight dissipated, a zombie for all intents and purposes. Scratch let go and he remained standing like a living breathing statue.

More imminent danger loomed as the pack from the car decided to investigate what was going on.

31

Scholar spoke out. "Frehidia cor heretita kimani." Repeating the words as Whispa, Scratch, and myself stood proud in front facing the pack of eleven wolves.

"What ya doing man?" The tallest one of them spoke his voice calm but brooking no nonsense, the others nodded in agreement, looking at the fallen ones behind us.

Wristbands had crawled around us to join the safety of the eleven strong pack.

Whispa spoke low and calmly. "Nothing that you need concern yourself with." There followed a few seconds of contemplation by the pack. Scholar was still repeating his incantation. "You may go now."

The lead wolf looked at him perplexed then slowly turned and walked away leading the pack with him, even the one holding his crotch was baffled, not comprehending why his crotch hurt so much.

"Just one more fing," Scratch added, walking over to the leader and shaking his hand, but keeping eye contact with him. The wolf's bemused expression gave way to a look of forgetfulness of what he was doing and he didn't notice the tiny scratch appear on the back of his right hand.

The pack dispersed lethargically, each going their separate ways, confused.

I had remained calm throughout, my heartbeat only rising slightly as the adrenalin had flowed in anticipation of a fight. I turned round to face Spaced-out and Sunglasses. Spaced-out's soulless form was lifeless suspended in a split second. Sunglasses tried to speak but could only cough up blood, I saw him try to move his right hand, although his eyes were blank, it moved two inches, then stopped, and I watched his life ebb away, a dark blood stain on the concrete would be all be that remained of him. Scholar pulled out a container from a pocket and collected some of the blood.

"What will happen to him?" I quizzed Whispa, pointing to Spaced-out.

"Whaddya care eh?" Scratch snarled.

"*Easy Scratch, our friend here is new to our ways.*" Scratch shook his head and kicked the lifeless form on the ground. "*One of two things, his body will either start to shut down because of withdrawal from the drugs and...other substances, eventually dying...or he will be locked up in some institution and put on a drip. Either way his life is over.*"

"*What did you do to him then?*"

"*Whispa took 'is soul. An' y' can't survive wiv out ya soul.*"

"*But you took my soul.*"

"*No.*" Came the stern reply, this time from Scholar. "*Half, as an offering.*"

Back in the dressing room Beryl sat trying to drink a cup of tea, her hand shaking uncontrollably. The door opened and in walked Peter with a ragged look on his face, making Beryl almost drop the cup.

"Can we keep the language clean Beryl? I have just had an ear bashing from Mr Collins, the caretaker, who was not impressed, I can tell you. I think I have managed to smooth things over though." Peter gave Beryl a stern look. She reciprocated with a look of consternation, then spoke calmly, placing the cup and saucer shakily on a nearby table.

"In this instance," she drew a breath, "I do not have the control as I would normally," she breathed deeply again. "I am sorry and I shall go and apologise." She moved as if to get up.

"No. No, it is done, I have already said we are sorry." Peter put his hand up to stop her.

Beryl frowned, she was starting to feel nothing but contempt for the man in front of her.

"As I have said before, this spirit, Mark, is stronger than I am used to and I must say I am finding it difficult to control him so I cannot edit what the spirit does or does not say, although I must..." She left the sentence unfinished, aware that Cyril had just entered. "I'll try my best Peter."

"Try your best at what Auntie?"

"Never mind, Cyril. Never mind." She drank some more tea.

"Thank you." Peter turned to walk out the door, but instead spun round holding the piece of paper he had scribbled on earlier.

"Beryl," Peter said inquisitively.

"Yes, Peter. What is it?"

Cyril interjected; "By the way I have nearly finished Samuel Preston. I think it will be ready by the time this tour ends." Cyril's excitement at the prospect of being an author in his own right was tainted as he saw the effect the tour was having on Beryl.

"Good, Excellent. Beryl?" he paused.

"Come on Peter you're not normally lost for words." Beryl was finding it hard to hide her distaste for the man.

Peter looked at Cyril. "Well, it's this Shelbourne. It doesn't seem to exist. I have had Edward's cousin checking for the last few days and he can't find hide nor hair of it."

"So?" Cyril questioned.

"So," Peter replied, "if this place exists, is there some way you can find out where it is, from the spirit?"

Cyril looked to Beryl for an answer.

"I am sorry Peter, I don't know." Beryl paused. "Mark seems to be hiding details. Spirits I have…been in contact with before tend to want to explain who they are and where they are, to help them pass over. I don't understand this one. And that is my honest answer." The room fell silent. "I'm sorry I can't be more helpful," Beryl finished.

"Yes, well…" Peter didn't know what else to add so left the room.

"Auntie, are you sure you want to continue with this?"

"Cyril, you've got a lot to learn about obligations. Besides, this will help with your book.Now let's hear no more about it and head back to the B&B."

32

Beryl and Cyril sat silently in the classroom being used as a dressing room with Cyril growing more and more anxious about his aunt. The audiences were oblivious to the nuances that gave Cyril indications that all was not well, a sense of foreboding growing as each evening progressed. It was like Mark waited for her, needed her. Was he losing his aunt?

"Do you fancy a short walk?" Cyril said, "We have got an hour to spare."

"I'm fine, you go." Beryl stared sullenly at the wall.

"Come on Auntie, it is nice out there and we haven't shared the fresh air for a while now."

"I'm okay Cyril. Why don't you ask Tracy?" Beryl's words lacked the normal sincerity and affection she had for Cyril.

"I'll buy you some fudge." Beryl loved fudge, it was her one weakness.

She smiled half-heartedly. "I appreciate the thought Cyril. You'll make someone a lovely husband one day. Go on, you go, and ask Tracy."

"He is close, isn't he?" Again Cyril ignored the comment about Tracy, she was very forward and although he fancied her, his experience with Valerie had given him the impression that all forward girls were rude and ungrateful.

Beryl looked into Cyril's eyes and he saw the strain there. "He is. I can feel him all around me. I don't understand the connection, I wish I did, it would make it so much easier. Look, go on, go for a walk, ask Tracy to join you, she likes you, don't let what happened with Valerie put you off."

Cyril could see he wasn't getting anywhere. "Maybe." He left the dressing room.

Strolling briskly across the hall he saw Tracy and Adele busy setting up the stall.

"Hi Cyril," Tracy said, lifting up another box of books. "Your aunt's books are certainly selling well."

"Hi." Cyril said. As much as he wanted to ask her to join him and felt the words rising in his throat, they just wouldn't come out. Tracy bent down to pick up another box of books and he couldn't help but look at her rear.

"Nice isn't it, Cyril?" Adele commented smiling.

"Erm." His cheeks flushed. "I'm just going out for a walk."

"You don't need to ask my permission, does he Trace?"

"No." She planted another box on the table. "One day he might ask me to go with him. I guess in the meantime I shall just have to keep waiting, won't I Ad?" Tracy added playfully, looking forlornly at Cyril.

Cyril stood nervously before his embarrassment got the better of him and he left.

"He will ask one day Ad."

"Yeah right, you might be claiming your pension by then."

***

Cyril walked along the road, gutted that he hadn't managed to ask Tracy, what was in effect such a simple question, and she said she wanted to. He cursed himself, and Valerie for shaking what little confidence he had. He smiled as the image off her backside flashed up in his mind. 'She was gorgeous' he thought, "I will ask her out, and soon," he uttered determined.

Finding a telephone box he rang Father James who answered on the third ring.

"Hello, it's Cyril Hewington, is Father James there?"

"This is he. Hello. I am guessing that the church hasn't been in contact yet, and that's why you're calling?"

Dejected he answered. "No, no they haven't. I am very concerned my aunt is not her usual self. I even tried to get her to come out for a walk but she said no, she never says no. She said she could feel the presence of Mark. I am worried."

"Mark?"

"That's the spirit's name."

"Oh. Have you been able to establish where he lived, as in county?"

"No, Mark is all we have. Oh, and his family, his has a wife, Samantha, and two kids, Joshua and Clare. But we still don't know where Shelbourne is, it doesn't seem to exist. Peter, Mr Phillips, has had someone in the government looking through records."

"That is most peculiar." Father James thought for a moment. "I'll tell you what, I'll ask someone I know in parish records, see if we can't dig up some information that might be able to help. You don't have the family's surname to go on?"

"No."

"Shame, we might have been able to go through death records, although that would be a long winded search if you don't know where Shelbourne is, or where he died." There was a pause. "I suppose we could try searching records using all four first names, yet without specifics it will make that task somewhat difficult to say the least, with so many possibilities and so many records. It certainly won't be easy. I will see what I can find out. I'm only sorry I can't be of more help."

"Thank you, anyway, and please see if you can hurry the church up, Father."

"You're welcome. I will see what I can do. In the meantime I will say another prayer for her."

"Thank you." Cyril replaced the receiver. Every which way he turned was drawing a blank.

***

Back at the hall Cyril watched the audience bustling round the bookstall like hungry birds, Beryl sat at a table to one side signing frantically, her eyes dull and lifeless. He noticed a vein in the side of her neck, throbbing like a worm under the skin, indicating that she was under stress. When she saw him she smiled weakly. Cyril joined her and added his own signature to some of the books. The frenzy continued for another twenty minutes before Cyril decided it was enough.

"Ladies and gentlemen, please excuse us, my aunt, Miss Wallace, really needs to prepare for this evening. So, if you don't mind." The noise of the barrage of people overwhelmed Cyril's quiet voice. Yet Beryl heard and her eyes thanked him. Cyril turned to Peter, who stood proudly surveying the throng of people, pleased with the success and dismayed that Cyril was trying to end it so soon. So what if the evening ran on later than intended as long as the people were happy. "Please, everyone can you give my aunt some room?" Again his words fell on deaf ears. With frustration and concern growing inside, Cyril stood up ignoring Peter's consternation and took the book which Beryl had just signed and overeagerly handed it back to a woman in a sheepskin coat. "I'm sorry but my aunt really needs to prepare herself." The words came out a little too forcefully and immediately he realised he had offended the gathered people, but his thoughts were for Beryl, who smiled her gratitude.

Before he could add anything else Peter butted in. "Ladies and gentlemen, I'm very sorry for my assistant's apparent rudeness," Peter shot a glance at Cyril, who became guilty at the rebuke. "But, unfortunately he is quite right time is running on and Miss Wallace does need to prepare herself with a little quiet time." Adding, just as the audience were about to verbalise their annoyance, "I'm sure Miss Wallace will be more than happy to continue after tonight's performance." That seemed to work as the men and women looked to her for her adherence. Beryl smiled reluctantly and nodded as Cyril helped her up and led her to the dressing room.

"Thank you," she offered, her energy already flagging.

The signing had lasted forty long minutes.

***

Back in the dressing room Beryl was searching her soul for the confidence to admit to Cyril that she was indeed afraid, but, as she opened her mouth to speak, Peter burst through the door.

"Are we ready then?" His words boomed into the dressing room.

Cyril looked at his watch, not believing that fifteen minutes had passed so quickly. Beryl acknowledged, her hollow eyes finding it hard to hide her true feelings. "Are you alright Auntie?" Cyril asked, the question lingering in the air.

"Of course we are." Beryl answered for the both of them ignoring Cyril's question, "we have a job to do." She sighed, resignation hanging on her weary shoulders. She was tired, so tired after the day they had had.

33

It had been a blur, Peter had arranged an interview with a local journalist, Matthew Gareths who was like an excited child, wanting Beryl to perform for him. Thankfully, Peter had intervened saying that Beryl needed to save herself for the night. Disappointed, Matthew had left an hour and a half later, very disappointed. Next a book signing had been organised at Aspinall Books, the largest bookstore in Gateshead. Three long hours in the afternoon, attracting queues of people, overwhelming both Beryl and Cyril, almost like the first time they had done a book signing at Grindley's books store, Leigh;

Saturday 9th October 1976

Local Author, Beryl Wallace, will be signing copies of her new novel 'Justice for John Johnson' at Grindley's in Leigh-On-Sea from 9am. Following the success of her first book 'Anne Farmer', Phillips Publishing and Literary Agency owner, Peter Phillips, said, 'It is an ideal opportunity for local people to meet a national phenomenon', adding, 'Miss Wallace has dedicated her life to serving local causes and it will be nice for people to meet the woman behind the name'.

Beryl caused quite a stir in the literary world, attaining the honour of "bestseller" for a first novel, an unusual event. 'Justice for John Johnson' is again a story of a spirit whose story has been told through Beryl. Beryl is quick to point out that her nephew, Cyril Hewington, who takes notes at the weekly meetings, has been the talent behind the team, even though his name does not appear on the front cover, credit remains with him.

Her weekly meetings have had to be temporarily curtailed due to their growing popularity, it seems the town wants to witness this ladies' 'gift', and her house is not big enough to accommodate everyone.

A third book is planned, but Mr Phillips is playing it close to his chest.

This reporter believes that a bright future lies ahead for Beryl Wallace.

Reporter: Jack Furrow

The crowd was bustling to get to the shop front. By eight o'clock the shop-owners were still not in sight and the police were struggling to organise the growing mass of people. Some had been queuing up since six o'clock. to get their hands on a signed copy of 'Justice for John Johnson'.

"What time's this author due here, Constable Stephens?"

"I don't know Sarge, about nine I think. I have never seen anything like it. Not here in Leigh. London maybe, and if it was the Rolling Stones, but an author."

"Times are changing Stephens. I wish they'd contacted us before, we could have cordoned off the street and diverted the traffic. Never mind, too late now."

"Excuse me, what's going on?"

"And can I ask who you are?" Sergeant Nichols enquired.

"I'm trying to get to Grindley's to open up, we have Miss Wallace arriving to do a book signing."

"This IS for Miss Wallace," sarcasm ringing loudly in Nichols' voice.

"Are you serious?"

"Yes miss, very serious. I hope you have enough books."

The woman looked worried. "Oh my word. We have only organised for two hundred copies to be here. I never expected this many people to turn up.

"Can I ask your name, miss?"

"Teresa. Teresa Marshall."

"Well, Miss Marshall, if you follow me I'll try and get you close to the door so you can open up. You might want to ring for some more help."

"Yes, yes, I will."

Sergeant Nichols started forcing his way through the massive crowd, which had grown in the last fifteen minutes, and was now extending toward Leigh Pet Centre a further 100 yards west along the road.

***

"Good morning, Beryl. How are you this morning?"

"Very well thank you Peter. Cyril is just finishing getting ready. Would you like a tea or coffee?" As Peter walked towards the kitchen at the back of the house Beryl closed the door and called up the stairs "Cyril. Peter's here."

"Be down in a few minutes." He replied.

Peter took, a seat noticing the article, written by Jack Furrow in the Southend Standard, was in a prominent position on the table. He also noticed how the house had not changed one bit since her foray as an author, despite the cheques Peter had given her for rather large sums of money. In a strange kind of way he admired that in her. She had done everything she said she would, given money to the church, set up a trust for runaway children as well as donate to other worthwhile local charities.

"It is a good article, Peter. Do you know I am actually starting to enjoy these little book signings." Peter's ears pricked up.

"I beg your pardon, Beryl Wallace," he said in astonishment.

"I said, I was starting to enjoy these book signings. I so hated them, when Anne's story was first published. I don't really know what I expected at the beginning but the people seem so nice and appreciative of Cyril's work. I think after all the initial interviews when I was just mocked, it sort of knocked me sideways. But with all the good work the money has enabled me to do it isn't so bad if you get into it. Here you go. Black, two sugars."

"Thank you. Glad to hear it Beryl. I really am. And you'll be glad to know today will only be a short one, a couple of hours at most. The orders for John's story have been steady and I'm quite sure sales will match those of Anne."

"Looks like I will have to search further afield for good causes then." Beryl poured herself another tea from the pot on the table and then heard Cyril's heavy footfalls on the stairs."

"I'm sure I can help you find them. In fact I'll get Valerie onto it first thing Monday morning."

"I think I will start my usual Wednesday evenings, again as I have certainly missed them. Demand was growing, that was why I stopped them, but I guess now the initial furore is dying down I can fit my regulars in again. I certainly don't want to push them aside."

"You should take over the church hall Beryl. Let everyone see you for what you are." The comment came out a little too jovial. "Sorry, that wasn't quite meant to come out like that."

"It's alright Peter, I think I know what you meant."

"Morning." Cyril chimed.

"Morning Cyril," Peter said, savouring his sweet coffee.

"By the way, I have been thinking about what you said about needing the next story." Cyril was really enjoying being a writer. He had certainly attracted attention from girls wherever he went. Although he hadn't been out on any more dates since Valerie, he still liked Tracy but was too scared to ask her out. Most that asked him out only seemed to want notoriety and they didn't seem interested in his personality or what he had to say, except Tracy, but the more they worked together the further away the question appeared to get. He couldn't stop thinking about her.

"I was searching through my notebooks trying to decide what you might think was a good story." Cyril poured himself a bowl of cornflakes.

"A-ha," Peter commented.

"And I think I have found another good one. Do you remember, about two years ago, that spirit that came to us?" The question was directed at Beryl.

"Which one, Cyril?" Beryl said, carrying her breakfast things to the sink.

"The 1920's mobster." Beryl stared at Cyril for a moment. "You know the one that had killed and tortured all those people before he fell victim to another crime family."

"Oh yes, I think I do. He didn't really stay around too long though as I remember."

"No, but I have been doing some research and, with what I have got from those evenings and my research, I think I could write a great book." Cyril was finding it difficult to hide his excitement. This was a chance to really test whether he had any talent or not. "What do you think, Peter?" Cyril shovelled a spoonful of cornflakes into his mouth.

Peter had another idea that was brewing, a twinkling of an

idea which had sprang to mind just a few moments before, something that seemed apt to cater for Beryl's Wednesday evenings and the demand from the public, but he needed to work out the details.

"Let me see what you have, but I'm not sure a mob story would go down very well with Beryl's readers. Anne and John's stories built empathy with the reader, I 'm not sure anyone would have compassion for a dead mobster."

"But how about if I change it slightly?"Cyril finished his last spoonful and slurped his tea noisily.

"Let me see what you have and we can discuss it." Peter spoke rather too coldly. "Right, are we ready then, don't want to keep your public waiting."

Cyril gulped at his tea. "Yep."

***

"Where is Harry?" Beryl asked Peter, after they had driven about a mile.

"His mother is ill and he needed to look after her so I thought I would oversee one of these book signings myself. It's been a long time since I came out of the office. Hope your hand is up to it."

"I'm sure it will be fine."

"Oh, I almost forgot." Peter pulled out an envelope from inside his jacket pocket and handed it to Beryl, who was sitting in the back of the car.

"What's this?"

"A cheque."

"But you only gave us one three weeks ago," Cyril interjected amazed.

"That's the way it works, you write the books, I sell them, we make money. But, if you don't want it? I will say this, you have been a godsend for my business. We had fallen on hard times recently. Edward can't believe how much work I am putting his way, he has had to run a second shift at his print shop just to keep up."

"I haven't seen him for weeks. How is he?" Beryl asked fondly.

"He is goo…my god what is going on?"

All three looked through the windscreen to see a mass of

people standing in the road with policemen trying to control the crowd. Peter drew his car to a halt and wound down his window to speak with the nearest officer.

"Excuse me. I am trying to get to Grindley's."

"You and every other person. Whoever that bloody writer is I hope she turns up soon otherwise we'll have all the shopkeepers moaning that no one can get to their businesses. You'll have to go back sir."

"You don't understand. This is…"

"I am sorry sir, you will have to turn round and come back later there's no way you'll get through the crowd," the officer said more forcefully.

"Officer this is…" Peter tried to state his case more firmly.

"Sir, please turn around…"

"This is the 'bloody' writer, officer," Peter stated in tones that rested just below a shout.

The officer looked into the car and turned bright red and, without saying anything more, he signalled to another officer, and they started to clear a path for the car, waving Peter through.

Beryl sat in the back, feeling intimidated by the large crowd. "This can't be for me, surely?"

"I think it is Auntie," Cyril stated, amazed.

"My, oh my."

There was a loud slap on the top of the car which shook all three. Then a head poked through the open window as Peter once again was forced to bring the car to a stop.

"This is as close as you'll get," said Stephens.

More officers appeared and they started to form a barrier so that Beryl, Cyril and Peter could make their way into Grindley's, which had two large half-bay windows either side of a glass-panelled door. Once inside the narrow, but deep, shop, Teresa greeted them.

"I'm sorry about this. I have never seen such a crowd. Would you like a tea or anything before we start, Mr Phillips?"

"Yes. Er! No, I'm fine thank you." Peter couldn't take his eyes of the front windows and the sea of faces staring in, all for Beryl.

Cyril and Beryl both shook their heads in disbelief.

"I've set you up over here," Teresa said pointing to a small table to the left of the shop, a little way along from the counter. "Your driver, Stan, delivered the books yesterday but I am not sure we will have enough. We only ordered two hundred."

"Have you got a phone I can borrow Miss..." Peter asked.

"Oh, Teresa Marshall."

"Teresa?"

"Yes, it is out the back. This way." She led Peter into a small office with a single desk and chair.

"I think it may be best to open the doors and start, don't you?"

"Yes, yes. Mark, Sue." Teresa called to two Saturday staff who were standing by the office door at the back of the shop. They sprung into action and, within minutes a steady stream of people were making their way to the table where Beryl and Cyril sat answering questions and signing books. The till rang out its gleeful tunes as money seemed to run like water from satisfied customers' hands as they held signed copies of 'Justice for John Johnson'.

Peter had organised another delivery, dragging Stan out of bed on a Saturday.

***

"I'm exhausted Auntie. I didn't realise signing books could be so tiring."

"Neither did I." Beryl added, opening and closing her hand to relieve the aching.

Peter sat at the back of the shop, aghast at the flow of people that had come in throughout the day. He looked at his watch which showed twenty-to-three.

"Unbelievable. Absolutely unbelievable. If I hadn't seen it with my own eyes." The door opened again and they all turned to looked at the customer who walked through. The lady did a double-take before hastily leaving again.

"Was it something we said?" Cyril invited.

"I think some lunch is in order," Peter finally said.

"More like afternoon tea, I'm famished," Cyril said, rubbing his stomach.

34

Beryl picked at her dinner, a fish and chip supper in newspaper, before arriving for the book-signing session at the hall. A crowd of people had already started to queue outside, making Beryl shudder at the pressure. From being bearable, this tour was starting to grate on Beryl, but she forced a smile for her fans and walked into the hall behind Peter.

"If you go to the dressing room, I'll make sure everything is ready," Peter said nonchalantly.

It was barely fifteen minutes later when Peter caught up with them both.

"Ten minutes, okay?" But it wasn't a question, more a statement of fact, which Cyril was about to respond to when Beryl tightened her grip on his arm and smiled gracefully at Peter.

Sitting in silence, they were both lost in their own thoughts, it was time and they proceeded into the hall for more book signing. A throng of people were standing holding copies of the first two books, eagerly awaiting Beryl's autograph, she faltered slightly.

"You okay?" Cyril enquired, taking her arm to steady her.

"Mmmm, just tired." Her weary words spoke volumes.

"Ladies and gentlemen, Miss Beryl Wallace," Peter exuded as they approached the table.

Time moved slowly as book after book was thrust in front of her, her hand still aching from the afternoon session, but finally it was time to prepare for the evening and, all too soon, Peter took to the stage, primed with the notes that Cyril had prepared for him. The threads of the story, the bare introductions to the characters. Cyril was clever with recaps, managing to avoid any outcry of the obvious questions, 'Where is this Shelbourne?' or 'When did this spirit die?', yet invoking a sense of intrigue, reinforcing his talent as a wordsmith. Peter had embraced his role as compére, jubilantly retelling the story so far and embellishing the words further, under Cyril's disapproving eye. In truth these evenings had surpassed even Peter's original plans, sales were going through the roof.

Beryl reluctantly and wearily took to the stage for this, the twelfth event, gone was the healthy looking woman. She looked drawn and pale, her eyes had a hollowness to them. The audience sat expectantly. How she hoped beyond hope that Mark would not find her, but he seemed to be drawn to her. Almost before she made it to centre stage Mark consumed her, he wanted to perform, he had an audience. She wanted answers but he was not willing to give them. Why did he torture her so?

It became apparent that Scratch seemed to be hunting someone or something, what, wasn't exactly clear. We were walking around the base of the third block of flats when Whispa halted in his tracks.

"Wait." He looked up at a window on the third floor where a light burned from within, casting a faint shadow over the ground below. "In there!"

Nothing more was said and, although I wanted to know to what or who he was referring, like a minion I followed, happy to be part of a larger force.

The concrete stairwells smelt of excrement and urine, the wafts filling our nostrils, emphasising the squalor that the wolves created. On the third floor we made our way along an open-sided landing with nothing but a metal railing preventing people from falling off. There had been accidents reported of people falling to their deaths, the circumstances suspicious, to say the least. The front doors to the flats had once been uniform in colour and materials, now they barely looked similar in any way, people used whatever they could, one was made from scaffold boards.

Outside number thirty-seven, we hesitated. The door had footprints on faded flaky red paint, showing it had been kicked in at some point. There was one Chubb and two Yale locks clearly visible. Someone had once tried valiantly to protect themselves and their property. All the windows next to the front doors on these landings had bars on them - this hadn't prevented the glass from being smashed, ply-board had been used to cover the damage.

Whispa placed his hands on the door. "She is gone! Scholar, do the honours."

Scholar replaced Whispa at the door and from one of the oversized pockets inside his jacket he pulled out a set of keys, about thirty in all.

"There ain't one lock Scholar can't open," Scratch explained.

"What about the book he keeps writing in?" The question slipped out, I fumbled to take it back, but it was too late.

Whispa came in close to me. "Grimoires are personal, it is not right to ask about someone's Grimoire without their permission." Scholar had ignored the question entirely

"I'm s…"

"Yes, I'm sure you are." Whispa let that hang in the air and his eyes pierced mine, as if he was searching for something. "But as you are now 'One of Four' we can let you into its secret; you see Scholar here is our Grimoire keeper."

"Well, I ain't learned to write," Scratch laughed.

"You need to keep a Grimoire, it orders events. Stops things becoming muddled in the mind. Also, it contains information about people; information that can be used at a later date. You may have noticed Scholar doing a lot of drawing. He draws faces and places that may be significant. Magick is powerful, and if you have the right tools, any information can be used to great effect, pictures or words."

"Door's open, Whispa," Scholar stated matter-of-factly.

He looked at me for a few more seconds then all three went inside, leaving me standing on the landing alone.

"Come," rang Whispa's voice, and I obeyed.

Inside, the putrid smell of rotting flesh hit my nose and I had to run to the front door again to take a breath of fresh air to avoid vomiting. Upon hearing voices further along the landing I quickly changed my mind, gulped in as much fresh air as possible, and braced myself to head back inside, shutting the door behind me, fighting the impulse to gag, as best I could.

The flat looked as though it hadn't been decorated for at least two decades. That shouldn't have surprised me as you needed money to decorate and, as the rot had set in, standards slipped, for most, if not all, the residents. They were scared of having anything nice, knowing it would attract unwanted attention. In the kitchen, which was the first room on my right, plates and cutlery lay on the draining board with a green fur coat of mould growing over them, a mouse perched up on its hind legs and looked at me before disappearing down the back of a worktop. Nothing had been moved for a long time. The plywood window made the place seem even more like a dingy prison cell. The first room on the left, after the bathroom, was the bedroom, the bed was neatly made ready for night to fall and its occupant to take up residence.

In the lounge I found my three friends standing over a body, sitting upright in a wing-backed chair, from the skirt I surmised it was a woman. She must have died some weeks before judging by the decay we witnessed. Another fact of the estate was that weeks could pass and no one would notice an elderly lady slip her earthly chains, no neighbours cared that they hadn't seen her - sad. The putrid smell emanated from this room and her decomposing remains. Suddenly, I noticed her eye moving but when I looked more closely a maggot fell out of the socket. I barely managed to hold in the remains of my stew. I turned to head out of the room, but my arm was grabbed by Scratch.

"Watch an' see justice bein' done." He grimaced.

Whispa stood behind the wing backed chair where the old lady had perished and rested his hands on the woman's rotting head. My stomach churned as the head rocked slightly to one side.

Scholar started to investigate the remainder of the premises.

"What are you doing?" I finally managed to say, holding back the strong urge to throw up.

Whispa didn't answer, lost in a trance-like state. I looked round the room, trying to fathom what sort of existence the woman had had, taking my thoughts off her rotting corpse. A wedding photo on the shelf showed a young couple getting married, the groom's brylcreamed hair reflected the bright sunshine of the day. The happiest day of her life, never a thought that she would end up a lonely, decaying corpse.

"It is done." Whispa spoke, removing his hands from her head.

"What have you done?" surprise filling my voice.

"I have transferred the soul of that wolf into the body of this woman," he stated

"Why?"

"You can only carry a live person's soul around for a limited amount of time before it will start to fight for possession of the carrier."

"But surely her soul is there? What will happen to her soul?"

Scholar chipped in. "Her soul departed upon her death, she is merely an empty vessel, no longer of any use. Her body can no longer hold her soul, there is nothing for it to cling to."

"If tha…"

Whispa's reticence to explain himself was starting to show. "My Brethren, the wolf's soul I have tied to this body. It is punishment. Wherever this body goes, the soul will go. It is a living hell."

"'magine an eterni'y of nuffingness, well that's what he got." Scratch came over to me. "'e can prob'ly see us now." He waved a hand at the corpse.

I shuddered at the power these people possessed. I was wary of it, however strong they made me believe I was, it faded in to insignificance against the Brethren. I didn't want to get on the wrong side of them, otherwise I might have an eternity in hell (if I didn't already have that lined up for me) or was I already in hell?

Leaving the flat, I announced the need to make a call from a phone box on the way home, to alert the authorities.

"As you wish," Whispa responded, his disapproving tones ringing through.

I knew the authorities wouldn't rush round but it was the least I could do under the circumstances, I was sad that she'd ended her days in that way.

As we left the flat I found myself, for the first time, leading my Brethren. I was uncomfortable at the front but they would not pass me. It seemed Scratch must have known about the elderly woman. How? Did he pick up on the knowledge of the wolves he scratched?

As I reached the stairwell and descended the stairs to the halfway concrete platform I realised I was on my own, my Brethren gone. Suddenly three heavy-set wolves descended from the landing above, they looked even more awesome from where I stood. Where were my Brethren?

"Trust," came the voice of Whispa in my head.

35

Starting to retreat, I looked into the eyes of the first wolf heading the group towards me. He was neatly dressed, Timberland boots, black Levi jeans and green bomber jacket over a crisp white T-shirt. I turned as if to run but was confronted by five more wolves making their way up the stairs from below. I backed myself against the wall as each pack came closer to me. I knew my fate was staring me right in the face, square on.

"Belief" There was Whispa's voice again in my head.

"Not so hard without your mates then." Terror must have been written over my face. "Not got much to say either, eh?" Up close, Bomber-jacket had a burn mark down one side of his face which ate into his hairline and made his ear appear deformed. All the wolves from both directions edged onto the landing, encircling me. The cold of the concrete wall penetrated my clothes as I edged as far back as I could. I saw my end getting closer. 'I'm sorry Samantha', I thought, 'I'll see you soon'.

The glint of metal broke my thoughts, even though I didn't catch the shape, I guessed it was a blade and was waiting for the heat of the first cut when, out of nowhere, a fist caught me unaware, sending mucus and spots of blood over Bomber-jacket. My head slammed sharply back against the solid brick. Bomber-jacket calmly wiped the blood away before hitting the offending wolf with a twelve inch baton stolen from the police. The wolf, who wore a thick gold chain around his neck and had deep-set eyes, went careering to the ground where he stayed, out of respect and the threat of another helping.

"I saw what you did to our friends earlier, an' I believe in an eye for eye." The words were spat out by Bomber-jacket.

There was a murmur of concensus among the group but none dared interrupt as Bomber-jacket grabbed my face, squeezing it tightly in his vice like grip, the power forcing me up on my toes and my head back against the wall. Gold-chain grabbed my ankles to prevent me from kicking out.

This was it, my time was coming.

Bomber-jacket passed the baton to a wolf with ginger crew-cut hair standing to his left and, with his free hand took a craft scalpel from another, the sheaf already off. The silver of the blade and handle reflected in the dim moonlight that just made it into this dark crevasse. As the scalpel drew closer to my eye, little droplets of salt water formed in the corner. I knew the pain would be intolerable. I wanted this to end. I struggled, wriggling as best I could, but two more wolves pinned me to the wall. Terror ran through me. I tried in vain to pull my head away from the blade but it was already tight against the wall and the grip on my face did not allow me to move sideways. My heart pumped the adrenalin that was building up around my body. I tried to scream for help but only a muffled muted sound came out.

"Time to suffer."

The point of the scalpel was barely millimetres from my right eye when a self-possessed resolve to fight, took over.

Noises from the landings, above and below, distracted the remaining wolves not involved with my torture. In my mind I could already feel the red hot pain as the scalpel pierced the lens of my eye. Without warning the scalpel started to glow red hot. Bomber-jacket's eyes widened as the pain trickled from his fingers into his brain, shock registering on his face. Shock changed to panic as he realised he couldn't let go, despite his best efforts to shake it from his grip, compelled to hold it as if it was a test of bravery. The other wolves watched on, bemused. Bomber-jacket danced backwards, relinquishing his hold on my face, his scream muted as he fought to conceal the pain. The three wolves holding me looked on, bewildered as their leader fell to his knees, trying to free the scalpel from the burning flesh, the acrid smell filling the stairwell. He held the wrist of his burning hand as tears started to stream down his face, followed by cries of pain, which could no longer be contained.

Beryl turned sharply on Peter and instantaneously he was playing the role of Bomber-jacket, emitting howls of pain which filled the hall, making the audience gasp in horror. Cyril stopped writing, unable to fathom this latest development. Beryl continued with her story and, as quickly as Peter had felt the pain in his hand, it was gone. He found himself kneeling on the floor, embarrassed and a little confused.

I watched on, still pinned to the wall. I felt a sudden pain as a blow to my head caught me off guard. The scalpel fell from Bomber-

jacket's hand, 'clinking' on the ground. Another fist flew at my face but this time I saw it. It stopped millimetres from my nose. The wolf, Lip-piercing, looked astonished as he tried to force his fist to make contact with my face. The other wolves looked on in amazement.

Lip-piercing's face contorted with surprise, but his eyes showed terror.

"Go on hit him," one called.

"I can't," Lip-piercing replied, mustering as much force as possible.

He screamed in agony as his forearm snapped in the middle. The sound echoing round the concrete walls, a shard of bone protruded through his shirt, blood exploded onto the floor. The scream from Lip-piercing only sounded for a few seconds, before he passed out on the floor.

Mesmerized, the wolves eyed their fallen comrades, unsure what to do. Bomber-jacket still held his badly burnt hand. When he realised everyone was watching him, he quickly regained some composure, stood-up and, brushing the wolves aside, moved his face to within inches of mine. I could see the bravado of the move, he was trying to maintain power over the others, yet I sensed terror in his soul. Living, breathing, terror, something that so many had faced under his rule, justice, that's what this was. I was sure the other wolves knew it too, but were probably too scared of the consequences if they acknowledged it.

"When you least expect it, we'll be waiting. For you, and your friends. Your days are numbered." The words were full of menace but the power behind them was gone.

Lip-piercing came round and, for a split second the pain was gone. When it came back, it came back ten fold, and he let everyone know it.

"Shut it!" Bomber-jacket stormed.

"But my arm!!" he cried.

"Shut it or you won't be worried about that arm anymore." His eyes never left mine, he was trying to work out what had just happened.

Slowly the wolves dispersed, unsure, quiet, taking their hurt comrades with them. As relief trickled through me, I heard the voice of Whispa in my head. "Well done my Brother you are now one of us. You are truly one of us."

I looked at Scholar, Whispa, and Scratch who were standing on the landing above me.

"Ain't it grand your first time, eh?" Scratch jollied.

"I don't…"

"You will, Sway. You will." Whispa laughed heartily. "Come, I think we are done for tonight, don't you?

The others nodded their agreement and followed Whispa down the stairwell, passing me on the landing, each placing a manly hand on my shoulder. I was officially in.

The applause leapt up, filling the hall, as Beryl landed heavily on the floor, some people even stood to show their admiration for tonight's performance. Cyril finished his note-taking, puzzled and frightened by Peter's sudden inclusion.

Peter hesitantly stepped forward to the front of the stage, unnerved by his participation. He kept his closing comments brief wanting to leave the stage. He had started to register some of the fright that Beryl and Cyril already felt. He thanked the audience before going to oversee the bookstall at the back of the hall. Standing behind it, he watched the money changing hands at a frenzied rate, but his glee had lost its shine.

36

Out of nowhere, a man made a beeline for him.

"Good show," the man called, but the sentiment was a little thin. Peter, a little abashed, couldn't decide how to reply so just smiled, dipping his head in acknowledgement.

"I couldn't believe how good she was. Never expected it, totally brilliant."

"Thank you," Peter replied uneasily. The man stood expectantly in front of Peter, making him uncomfortable. "Can I help you with anything else?" he finally said.

"No. Just in awe, absolutely brilliant."

"Oh. Well I'll pass on your comments, which I am sure Miss Wallace will appreciate.

"Excellent, thank you." Finally the man departed to Peter's relief, then he noted that he hadn't even bought a book. People were strange, he thought.

As the eagerness of people to part with their money continued unabated, Peter temporarily forgot that for an instant he had been caught up in the action on stage and, for that short time afterwards, he had been petrified. But, that was how he chose to deal with things.

Cyril's anxiety was high. "Do you mind if I leave you to go back with Peter?" he asked as they settled in the dressing room.

Beryl turned to him, her eyes still distant. "No, of course not."

There was no question of where he was going and that surprised him, but after a second or two contemplating he left anyway. He desperately wanted the church to intervene but they were taking their time responding, he would ring again now there was a new development - that of Peter being dragged under Mark's control.

Sleepers Guest House

Cyril was surprised to find Beryl still awake and sitting in the small lounge bar, a pot of tea on the table.

"What are you doing up? I thought you would have gone straight to bed. Where's Peter? He usually likes a nightcap."

"I think I'm old enough to stay up late, if I so wish. Peter went straight to bed, he didn't want to join me." Beryl replied, more cheerfully than he had expected.

"Oh. Sorry, I only meant..." He didn't finish the sentence but flumped down into a chair next to Beryl.

"I know what you meant. I wanted to make sure you were alright." She looked at him but he wouldn't make eye contact. "I know you are worried for me and I just want you to know I am okay. I know I have been quiet the last few days but I am puzzled by the connection Mark has with me."

Cyril stared at his aunt. "I've been thinking."

"Oh yes,"

"Maybe this book deal for me isn't right after all. I mean, I do enjoy it but this is not what we, I wanted. And I don't want you to continue just for my sake, I know you watch out for me, but it is not worth your health."

Beryl's haunted eyes sparkled briefly. "I am so lucky to have a nephew like you. Maybe we will talk with Peter in the morning, see if we can't come to some sort of arrangement." She felt Cyril's only chance to be an author in his own right slipping away, yet she was struggling and knew her health was going to fail to if she didn't stop soon.

***

Peter's brief possession by Mark replayed again and again in his frantic mind making up its own version of events, making his sleep fretful. He had no memory of the actual time that he had been taken and that scared him more than anything. Now he had an inkling of what Beryl was going through and he to wanted to be as far away as possible, but the old adage his father used to quote came hurtling back, 'business is business, personal considerations come later'.

Even when he thought he had put the memory at the back of his mind, it snagged his imagination, enveloping him like a cloak.

Peter rolled over again and banged his head on the bedside table before crashing to the floor. For a few minutes, in his confusion, he couldn't fathom whether he was awake or dreaming as his eyes stared into the blankness of the night, a child-like fear tearing at him. Suddenly, he was a boy of six years old, scared of the dark, pulling his knees tightly to his chest. His father would not tolerate nonsense about being scared of the dark, he had to be brave and face the fear. His father didn't like weak people. 'Son you have to be strong in business and in life', he would say. He had worked hard to start the Phillips Publishing and Literary Agency and Peter had to earn the company, prove he was worthy of taking the helm, which he had done, learnt to face his fears head on. But irrational fear still provoked the child in him, the side that was well hidden from public view.

Before retiring to bed he had made an anonymous phone call to a press office declaring that he had been an audience member the night before and at one point felt his life had been in danger – stating quite clearly that this woman needed to be stopped. Peter knew how to exploit the press to the best effect and to his own gain, they would jump on this story.

But in the loneliness of his bedroom with his bravado gone, he was petrified, and he had no one he could talk to about it. He closed his eyes tightly and prayed for morning to arrive.

***

By the time Peter was wiping the tiredness from his eyes, walking downstairs getting ready to face Beryl and Cyril at the breakfast table, four morning papers had run with a story about Beryl putting people lives in danger.

"Have you seen this?" Cyril stood up and thrust a paper at Peter as he arrived at the breakfast table, forcing him to take a step back. "It's outrageous. I think we should cancel tonight." Cyril sat down heavily, throwing his napkin onto his plate, anger suppressing his appetite.

"I can't believe it. No one was in danger. How on earth did the papers get hold of this?" Peter spoke incredulously, pleased with his display, forgetting his own fears.

"It doesn't matter, it can't go on. We won't go on." Cyril remembered his conversation with his aunt from the night before.

"It has to go on Cyril." Peter stepped forward, placing a hand on the back of Cyril's chair and leaning into him. "If we stop now then the papers have won." He straightened up. "Besides, I'm sure it was just a one-off." He gulped nervously as his mind raced to the thoughts of how he had felt in the dark, scared and alone. "I'm quite sure of it." Peter walked to the door of the breakfast room, hoping he had concealed his nervousness from Beryl and Cyril. "Mrs Bennings, can I have a pot of tea please?"

"Right you are," was the distant reply.

Cyril's temper was boiling under the surface, he had always been taught to respect his elders and people of authority. He caught Beryl's eye and in that moment knew that she didn't like the idea any more than him.

"No, I am going to put my foot down. We will not carry on."

Beryl watched as Peter grew angry. She could sense what he might say next so tried a different tack. "Peter, may we at least have a few days respite, I am exhausted and I think the time might well be spent recuperating at home."

"Beryl," Peter took his seat. "I understand, but the halls have been booked and, if they are like previous nights, then they will be packed and that is a lot of disappointed people." Peter applied the pressure. "There will be repercussions. And that costs money. Thank you, Mrs Bennings." Mrs Bennings placed a pot of tea in front of Peter.

"Would you like a full English, Mr Phillips?"

"Yes, please, but no bacon." Peter stirred the contents of the teapot. "Look, I will see what I can do about rescheduling a couple. I'll make no promises though."

"That's all I ask, Peter." Beryl acknowledged Cyril's exasperated look, her eyes placating him and telling him that no more was to be said. Cyril could only feel contempt for the man that sat beside him, a figure he had regarded as someone to look up to, that image was fading as the hard-nosed businessman took charge.

Back lane Community Hall, Long Marton

Peter took to the stage a little more hesitantly than usual. The events of the previous night still fresh in his mind. He had successfully re-arranged a couple of the later events, much to the appreciation of Beryl, but with all the publicity, most venues were keen to proceed, knowing the audiences would be drawn in by morbid curiosity, making a small fortune.

"Good evening, ladies and gentlemen." The general hubbub took a while to die down. The hall was overflowing with people, all seats taken and barely any standing room left. He cleared his throat again. "Good evening, ladies and gentlemen." Finally, the crowd quietened. "Thank you all for coming tonight. I know some have had a chance to meet Miss Beryl Wallace already and have had books signed by her, you can see for yourself that you are quite safe, despite the press coverage today." There was a muted snort from a few members of the gathered audience as Peter scanned the faces locking eyes with two members of the press that he recognised. They smiled cynically. "Spirits, whilst a little unpredictable, cannot harm us, we know that. They like to fool with us. Miss Wallace has had years of experience dealing with spirits and, indeed, hearing some of your questions to her earlier, I know this has been on your minds. But…you are still here."

The expectant audience sat patiently, waiting. Peter's own nerves started to take a hold as he considered seriously, whether he was really in danger. There was nothing he could do about it now, the path was set. Peter pulled Cyril's notes from his suit jacket pocket and proceeded to tell the story so far. When he finished, the audience gave a conservative applause.

Cyril eyed Peter with contempt, his exuberance with the notes was starting to grate and, along with everything else, only added to the low opinion that Cyril was garnering of him.

"…Miss Beryl Wallace."

Soft applause grew as Beryl took centre stage. A few moments passed as it died down and Beryl stood in silence, all eyes focussed upon her.

Nothing!

37

Peter turned to Cyril, who looked dumfounded, yet pleased. Had the spirit finally gone? Relief surged through his bones, his shoulders losing the slouch, even from behind, he could see his aunt's relief. But what now? The audience were gathered. One minute turned into two. The rustling of a sweet wrapper could be heard through the packed hall, and shuffling, as the standing crowd shifted their weight from one foot to another, waiting.

Inexplicable horror dawned on Peter as the silence ran into three minutes. Beryl started to fidget herself, her mind blank, thankful, yet curious. In the comfort of her own parlour this had never caused a problem, nothing was expected, but here, tonight, expectation emanated from the audience. Beryl could hear whispering as three minutes became four. She could feel Peter's eyes boring into her back.

Four minutes grew into five.

Peter decided enough was enough and stood up, the scraping of his chair giving a cue for other people to fidget.

"Ladies and gentlemen. It seems the spirits are not kind to us tonight…" Peter drew level with Beryl, who shot a hand onto his shoulder with such speed and ferocity that it made him stumble, the audience gasped.

"Ya did good Sway, ya did good." Scratch scowled into my eyes, seeing the inner strength, squeezing my shoulder tighter and tighter until finally he let go."

Peter fell to the floor holding his left shoulder, fear striking him.

The journey back to my house was uneventful, a strange reassuring strength resonated through me. I was at one with my Brethren, an equal for the first time. The red morning sky was a vivid glow above us. We saw the odd small pack of wolves but they were subdued after the night's activities and were returning home for a rest.

I started to wonder about my mysterious guests. Who were they? Where did they come from? I listened as they discussed the Grimoire openly for the first time since our meeting, It was as though I had passed the initiation.

"As usual, Scholar, you have done us proud." Whispa's words were that of a proud father as he took the book and placed it on the kitchen table. Turning the pages, I saw the pictures that Scholar had drawn, magnificent, detailed, pencil sketches picking up almost every ugly detail. Even the evil in the wolf's eyes was evident.

I was in awe "How did you…"

"Scholar's a master o' many things, ain't ya Scholar?" Scratch's voice resounded with joy at my amazement as he opened a bottle of beer and gulped the contents down in one go before grabbing another.

"It's a gift the dark one bestowed me with. I keep all the Grimoires of our…shall I say missions. You never quite know when the information or pictures will be of use."

"There's many a way for a comeuppance an' ya gotta be prepared. Ain't ya Scholar?" Scratch pulled out a chair, turning it in one swift motion before straddling it, placing his second bottle of beer on the table. Grabbing the Grimoire he spun it around so it was the right way up to him and then proceeded to run a finger nail down the face in the picture. Wisps of smoke rose from the paper and a mark appeared on the wolf's picture, Scholar's drawing.

I heard a scream, a faint scream as if it was miles away, and sat bolt upright listening, but it was gone. When I returned to focus on my Brethren they were looking at me.

"You understand now!" Almost blasé, Scholar spoke, his rounded tones always so placid, he spun the Grimoire back to him and studied the mark left by Scratch.

I was perplexed, and then Whispa spoke from the open back door where he had been viewing my garden. "My Brethren have experienced this before, but to clarify for the new amongst us." Whispa smiled at me. "You do not need to be present, you only need something of the wolves to satisfy the Magick. You know this, don't you?"

Like a trapped animal I thought as fast as I could, 'the shoe', 'the drawing'. Yes, I did know.

"You have tried, have you not?" Whispa walked towards me, his dark piercing eyes making me uncomfortable. Out of his pocket he pulled two newspaper articles relating to the incidents. My experiments with magick! How did he know?

A cold shiver ran through me, all eyes upon me. I went from feeling as one with my Brethren to suddenly being wary. Whispa looked into my eyes for a long time like a teacher trying to emphasize a point. Inside, I shrank and silence consumed the kitchen.

"We knew you were powerful." Whispa continued. "Not many have that power. But you had to show it, not only to us, but to yourself. And tonight you proved it."

"That was me?" I was astounded, although a part of me knew it at the time, now it was like another person had been there, not me at all.

"Did ya not feel it?" Scratch threw in.

"We knew when you contacted us that you were the fourth one. The one we were missing."

"What?" All three were standing now, towering above me, as I sat taking it all in.

"Do not be afraid." Whispa's hand landed on my shoulder, making me jump.

"We have been three for a long time. Searching. Waiting for the fourth to arrive and now you are here. We will continue our mission and then you will unite with us. Our Dark master has deemed it so." Scholar spoke with reverence.

"But all I want is to put things right. I want this place to be how it was once." Uncertainty was evident in my voice. My three Brethren looked at each other.

"You are the one. It is deemed. We have been set a test and we shall comply but then you shall join…"

"…us." Scratch added before Scholar could finish his sentence.

"But I…I just…"

Whispa changed tack and the atmosphere in the kitchen lightened. "Do not fear us, we are your Brethren, trust us, we work as one."

I smiled uneasily. The tension had at least been broken. A mixture of feelings coursed through me. What if the cure was worse than the disease?

"We must offer thanks to the Dark one." Scholar walked towards the lounge, swiftly followed by Scratch and Whispa. I hesitated before joining them, half sitting, half standing, but finally compelled to comply.

As I followed my Brethren into the lounge, I thought about the attempted ambush in the stair well, in particular Lip-piercing's arm and how it had broken. Did I really have something to do with that? I don't remember wishing any of it to happen. I thought that Whispa or Scratch had been responsible, protecting me from certain doom, but they hadn't intervened. They must have seen the trouble I was in. If they were right, and it was all me, then - was there a dark side to me that I was not aware of, that stepped in when trouble loomed. Was this real? I pinched my arm, the pain shot straight to my brain – I was awake!

All I had ever wanted was my wife and kids back. Them, here with me. Now it looked as though I wouldn't even keep my sanity.

I heard my new name, Sway, called and went to fulfil the Brethren's wishes, dutiful, yet sullenly.

Kneeling down at my chosen point on the star I closed my eyes, taking Whispa's hand in mine. Our thanks started in the form of a low sing song chant. .

"So dovovium vie carratagen dozzar," Repeated over and over. A dubious presence grew in the room. A dark force enveloped us with its macabre energy.

Doubt inexplicably took over.

Whispa's grip tightened, crushing my fingers. Nausea swept over me, my head swam with wild images. I was sure I heard Samantha calling me at one point. What was she saying? It was gone, and in that moment, I became released from the cloak that had shadowed my life for so long, enlightenment rang like a bell in the early morning silence. I was engulfed by a new faith. Guilt didn't rake me. An absolute strength from within gave me satisfaction. My mind was free, nothing could destroy me.

"We give our thanks Dark Lord that you allow us to serve you." Whispa's voice echoed through the room. Then, in unison again, we closed the ceremony.

"Wudlium kutania fu hizlazio."

Opening my eyes I saw the Brethren staring at me, they all looked pleased with themselves.

"It is time for rest," Whispa commanded - all obeyed.

Returning to my daughter's old room I sank down onto my so-called bed, daylight streamed through the windows but I couldn't keep my weary eyes open any longer and I let myself be taken by sleep. Contentment settled as my mind drifted back to the day when my whole life had been changed forever.

38

It was a rainy weekend in April. The kids were bored. They wanted to be out playing but Samantha wouldn't let them until the rain eased off. Finally at about two o'clock, I was able to take the kids to the park to play football. Clare wasn't very good but she loved to try. She loved the thrill of chasing the ball, sometimes though she would pick the ball up in her hands and carry it rather than kick it, which frustrated Joshua no end. He dreamt of being a professional footballer, he was very good; his schoolteachers had commented on the fact.

The grass was unsurprisingly wet and slippery, and when either of them or I slipped over, it brought on fits of laughter. Samantha, being practical, had told them to put old clothes on so that it didn't matter if they got dirty.

This was a time when the park was still an okay place to go to during the day. The wolves were present but not in a threatening way. Joshua was so happy to be running around outdoors, he hated being inside, unless it was to watch Liverpool play.

We'd been playing for about half an hour when we heard the roar of a motorbike revving up somewhere in the distance. The noise alone cast a dark shadow over us, we all knew what it meant, I tried my best to distract them and kicked the ball harder. Joshua ran as fast as his legs would carry him. Suddenly, he slipped and went crashing into a large puddle in the grass. I grabbed Clare and rushed over to him, we burst out laughing when we saw him spread-eagled in the water. It turned into a farce as he tried to get up and fell face down. He was completely drenched, I couldn't help myself as tears of joy started to roll down my cheeks. Joshua's face blushed red with his embarrassment and anger at our laughter. I went to help and then found myself slipping. I tried vainly to steady myself with my arms spinning round like a windmill but it didn't prevent me from crashing into the puddle too. Joshua's anger broke and he started to laugh.

We were both now soaked through and when we got up, I reluctantly suggested that we went home to change before we got cold.

I wished I could take back those times.

Joshua went to retrieve the ball as it had rolled out of sight, across a path and down a shallow bank on the other side.

A sudden loud cheer in the distance froze me to the core. I knew it was time to leave. The events after that were a blur. The loud revving of a bike. I held Clare's hand tightly in mine to protect her. Joshua was out of sight down the bank and my heart jumped. Then he re-appeared holding the ball, he waved, relief coursed through me.

"Come on, I shouted," not hiding the urgency in my voice. I had that fear a parent gets when they know something doesn't feel right. I wanted to leave the park. "Now!"

From out of nowhere the motorbike noise grew louder. Joshua started to run towards where Clare and I stood. The bike came into view behind Joshua. Instantly I saw what was going to happen. Any words of warning got stuck in my throat as I watched Joshua get run-over lengthways by the bike, knocking him to the ground, he took the full force of the weight of the machine. Panic swept over me as I screamed in horror but I too had to dodge the oncoming bike, pulling Clare tightly to me. We fell to the ground but were uninjured. Clare was frightened and in tears, I tried to calm her down but my concerns were for Joshua. We got up and watched as the bike and its rider roared off, back to the pack of wolves over on the far side of the park.

They were laughing.

I rushed to Joshua, he hadn't moved. A man and his dog were running towards him as well. My heart was in my mouth, I held Clare tightly in my arms, hugging her close to me. I skidded to a halt near to Joshua. Blood was running from his mouth and a tyre mark ran along his back, his favourite Liverpool top badly ripped exposing his pale muddied skin.

The man with the dog arrived.

"Is he alright?" the man asked, breathlessly. I put Clare down on the ground and shook my son gently, hoping for a reaction, hoping for him to turn round and say, 'Fooled you'. Nothing! I tried again. Nothing!"I'll get an ambulance," the man said, regaining some of his breath. I knew. I knew it was too late. He was gone.

I held my son's body tight, dragging Clare into the embrace. Tears streamed down my face. Clare put her arm around my neck but it barely registered as numbness took its hold.

"Why is Josh sleeping Daddy?" That was the last thing I heard until the sound of the sirens broke the hush of my broken world.

A hand landing on my shoulder made me turn sharply, the tears distorting my view. I only just missed thumping the police officer standing above me as I swung my arm round violently. Brushing my arm easily aside he slowly and patiently spoke to me, his words lost in a blur but his tone speaking clealy.Reluctantly I let go of Josh, eased back by the officer's gentle, but firm physicality. Holding Clare I became aware that she too was crying. Picking her up again I held her tightly. I felt worthless as I watched the array of bodies changing in front of me, different coloured uniforms, blue flashing lights in the background.

What could I do?

Nothing.

There was nothing I could do.

Time seemed to freeze. Josh's body was stretchered into a nearby ambulance. Clare and I were ushered to a police car; they must have asked me where I lived because they drove me home.

As soon as we pulled up Samantha was at the door.

"Stan told me. How is…"

She didn't finish her sentence. One look at me was enough to tell her everything she needed to know. She buckled at the knees overwhelmed with grief. I helped her up and we embraced each other with Clare caught in the middle, to her it was a big family hug like we had had many times, oblivious to the fact that she had just lost her older brother.

That was the day that changed our future, our lives would never be the same again. Making the funeral arrangements helped us to cope, there was so much to do. Joshua was popular at school and the tributes just kept pouring in.

The police came round to question me within a day or so, and that's when I knew things had changed between Samantha and me. We sat in the lounge holding each others hands for comfort, whilst another officer took Clare into the kitchen, the questions kept coming. Do I remember anything about the bike? Did I see a face? Would I recognise the kids again if I saw them?

I was empty, racked with guilt, I'd lost a son and couldn't recall a damn thing. Samantha let go of my hand, I turned to see the horror in her eyes, the dismay, the hatred building up.

"My son has just died and you don't know anything about what happened. Don't you care?" I sat gobsmacked as she threw my hand to one side. The WPC tried to ease the tension that was building, but

Samantha wouldn't let it go. She was right I had watched the event unfold and I hadn't prevented it. Then, came the accusations.

"You might as well have murdered him yourself, for all the good you are. How could you?" Tears were flooding down her red-flushed cheeks, the soreness of her eyes bright red, her hair limp and straggly instead of being the usual well kept bundle of softness, neatly tied back. Spittle came from her mouth as every word was spat at me.

There was nothing I could say to defend myself. The hatred in her eyes only emphasised her words. The WPC managed to manoeuvre Samantha out of the room before she could hit me. I stared into oblivion. Lost in a haze of disbelief.

"Grief can have that effect," was the sympathetic platitude from the WPC.

"But she's right! I murdered my son! I let it happen!" I believed it.

"Your wife will be okay. It's not your fault, unfortunately, at the moment, she just can't see that."

"But I did."

"No, you mustn't think like that. Unfortunately, I have witnessed it many times. You just need to let her get it out of her system." The words echoed around inside my head.

She never did get it out of her system. Life would not be the same again, I had let her down and she had lost a son. I lost my whole family.

Beryl was on the floor, tears streaming down her cheeks, wrapped in sadness. The audience sat in stunned silence, palpable sadness engulfing everyone.

One pair of gloved hands tentatively showed their appreciation, breaking the indefatigable sense of loss that hovered in the hall, Peter recognised the man from the previous night. A second passed before another pair of hands joined in. There was a sniff as a woman two rows back wiped her eye, then stood up and clapped. Soon she was joined by three more ladies, then a gentleman.

"Bravo, absolutely brilliant."

The small round of applause did nothing to soothe Beryl's own melancholy.

39

Commemorative Hall, Scroggs Lane, Helsington

Cyril left his aunt resting in the dressing room at the Commemorative Hall Helsington. He desperately needed Father James to urge the church to contact him soon as his despair was casting its shadow. He racked his brain for a way to end this whole thing but knew his aunt would have none of it. Even if he didn't turn up, Peter would only find someone else to make notes and he would lose his chance to publish under his own name. 'Damn!' he thought. 'Why do I want it so badly?' Everytime he thought he could happily walk away leaving that dream unfulfilled it snared him again.

Where was this Shelbourne? What of it? What was it that Peter had said, 'it doesn't appear to exist anywhere in the country'. So where was this Mark? Why was he so persistent, and so strong? Beryl had always managed to gain some sort of background from the spirits, however, this one was being particularly vague, detailing only the picture it wanted to paint – and nothing else. Why? What about the terms he uses laptop, surf the net – what on earth were they? If they were colloquialisms as Peter had tried to explain, then surely that would give a region, narrowing down his search. Was Shelbourne itself a nickname dreamt up by locals?

He needed to do more research on the matter.

Finding a phone box, he called Father James, but got no answer, he tried Father Andrew, but again got no answer.

Deflated, he glanced at his watch, and realised time had run away from him. Heading back to the hall he couldn't quite clear his mind of all the questions that buzzed around like frantic bees caught in a glass jar.

Arriving at the hall, he saw the queue of people stretching back from the door, scooting passed them he entered the hall.

Tracy and Adele were busy setting up the stall, piling it high with books from all the writers in Peter's stable. Tracy smiled at Cyril, the keenness in her eye immediately making his cheeks turn crimson.

Finding his voice, he asked. "Have you seen my aunt, Tracy?"

"She's out the back with Peter, he's got the proof for the cover of the new book, it looks really good. Martin from the art department mocked it up."

"Thanks," Cyril replied, distracted.

"When are you going to ask me out Cyril? You know I like you. You've known for nearly two years now." Tracy walked round the table to where Cyril was standing, making him feel even more uncomfortable.

Cyril stood nervously, not knowing what to say, he liked Tracy, sure enough, but after Valerie her frankness scared him. "I...I..."

"Am I not pretty enough? Is that it? You like Valerie's type?" Her playful sarcasm wasn't lost on him.

"No, no and no," Cyril stammered, feeling like a buffoon. "But I have to find my aunt."

"Fine," she said deflated, struck by her own persistence. As much as she had tried to forget about Cyril and date other men, whenever she was in his presence she felt complete, it was a most inexplicable feeling that she hated but loved at the same time. "I won't wait forever, you know." Tracy teased knowing full well that she probably would. He hesitated for a further second before scurrying to the backroom, a little hot under the collar. Tracy wolf whistled. Cyril turned, smiled awkwardly, and disappeared through a door at the side of the stage.

"Ah, Cyril, I was just showing your aunt the mock-up for the new book cover. What do you think?" He offered it to Cyril, who took a cursory glance.

"I need to speak to my aunt," and then added dismissively, "yes, it looks great."

"You could sound a little more convincing."

"I'm sorry. It's just that I would like to speak privately with my aunt before tonight," then added more firmly. "If I may? Please."

Peter rolled up the cover and slid it back into the cardboard tube it had arrived in. "Very well!" he said and left.

"What is it Cyril? Sit down." Beryl beckoned him into the chair opposite her.

"I don't like what these evenings are doing to you. I'm scared for you. We can't find hide nor hair of this Shelbourne, and what about the other things 'laptop' 'surf the net' if these were, are colloquialisms, surely we would know where to look. This whole thing doesn't feel right anymore."

"Cyril," she sighed wearily, her eyes looking tired, her face drawn and grey. "I have been trying to find those answers myself." She placed her hands on Cyril's. "I have my concerns as well, but I have agreed to do this, we have agreed to do this. I do concede that this Mark isn't like any other spirit that I have dealt with in all my time of doing readings and spirit writings.

The closest I can remember to feeling like this is...." her voiced trailed off before changing tack. "Do you remember the first time you came to my house, just after your mother died?"

Cyril's eyes still showed the bitterness of the loss even after fifteen years. "Murdered!"

"Yes..." Beryl lowered her head as her sister's death sprang back to her like an angry cat. "Remember how we tried to contact her, to find out who killed her, because the police were not having any luck."

"Yes."

"Do you recall how ominous the presence was in the room when we thought we had got through to her?"

"Yes." Cyril's answer was barely audible.

"This is like then, the same strange feeling, the same darkness. There is something not right. I do not have the power to control it. This Mark is as strong as that spirit was."

"So why go on? Let's go now, whilst we can," Cyril urged. "Why pursue this?"

"You don't remember, do you?"

Silence! Cyril's face contorted as the memories he tried to block out cascaded back into place.

"Once contact was made, that spirit, my so-called sister, wouldn't let go."

It wasn't his mother's spirit, it was the killer's. He had died within hours of murdering Cyril's mother, Brenda, run over by a drunk driver. Some might say poetic justice. The spirit was still persecuting Brenda's spirit and, by tuning in, Beryl became the next victim. The evening was still a vivid image in his mind;

***

"Auntie Beryl what are you doing?" Cyril screamed as panic swept through him.

"Auntie Beryl, Auntie Beryl." the spirit mocked.

"Please do something Maggie."

Beryl held a kitchen knife to her wrist.

"NO!" Cyril roared launching himself at her, grabbing her arm. The power the spirit instilled in Beryl made it difficult for Cyril to control her. "I can't hold her much longer, please do something Maggie."

Maggie splashed Beryl with Holy water, then grabbed two crystals from a velvet pouch she held. "Beryl if you can hear me, fight from within. You can do it."

Beryl turned to face Maggie shrugging off the young teenage, Cyril, as though he was nothing but an inconvenience. Maggie kicked Beryl's right hand breaking her grip on the knife sending it to the floor.

"Grab the knife Cyril, don't let her get hold of it." Cyril picked it up and retreated against a wall. Maggie ran forward and placed her hands in Beryl's, in her palms were two Merlinite crystals.

"Present and past let go. Break your earthly shackles. Shake free from your hold. I COMMAND THEE! ALLOW THIS EARTHLY VESSEL ITS FREEDOM." Maggie held on tight as the spirit fought to shake free, but finally he relinquished his hold and the room fell silent with Beryl falling into Maggie's embrace.

"Thank you," Beryl said.

"You're welcome. That was a close one. What happened?"

"We tried to contact my mother," Cyril said sheepishly.

Beryl slouched to the floor. "I wanted to find out who my sisters killer was, the police can't find anyone." Tears flowed from her eyes at the bitter memory.

"I'll guess we'll never know now." Cyril said deflated placing the knife on the side board.

"Actually," Beryl said, getting up, grabbing at a chair to help her. "I have got his name."

"What?" both Cyril and Maggie said in unison.

"In fact I have quite a bit of information about him, just from that temporary joining. We can help your mother, my sister, Cyril."

"I don't think you ought to try contacting her again," Maggie stated resolutely.

"Don't worry we won't."

"Then how about a cup of tea?" Maggie asked helping to straighten up the room.

"That would be lovely, thanks. I'll tidy the room."

"But my mother, what about her?"

"She will be fine Cyril. Once we tie up all the loose ends up in this mortal world, the spirit's will fall into line."

***

"The only difference this time is that the spirit doesn't seem to have a past that I can read. It's like he never existed before that first night. I don't understand. I have spoken to Maggie and she is baffled too. She has sent me this." Beryl pulled from around her neck a Rosary, except that this one had a locket attached. "Look." She opened it. The inside was full with herbs and spices to ward off evil spirits.

Cyril looked on solemnly, worried for his aunt. It had been a close call then. What did this situation have in store for them all?

The door burst open. "Are we ready then? Your fans are ready for autographs." Peter beamed, concealing the fear that he had managed to lock deep inside him, fear that, once again, he might be manipulated by the spirit.

Beryl looked at Cyril, who took a long deep breath, and reluctantly nodded his agreement.

"Excellent."

***

After the book-signing session the interval seemed shorter as she sat in the dressing room saying her prayers, clasping the rosary tight in her hand. She heard her introduction and her shoulders visibly sank as she left the dressing room.

In the sea of faces, which Beryl dared look at tonight, she recognised a few from previous nights, surprised to see them back, realising they must have travelled miles which only had the effect of adding pressure on Beryl's narrow shoulders. A part of her was pleased, but another part sickened by the morbid interest they portrayed. 'Maybe I'm just tired', she thought.

Quietly reciting the Lord's prayer to herself she took to the stage. Before she could finish, a darkness came over her and Mark was there…

40

Days went by. Samantha didn't say one word to me. I tried in vain to get an answer to even simple questions like 'Do you want a cup of tea?' 'How is Clare?' Silence was the response. The hatred was raw and evident in her eyes. I was only allowed into our bedroom to get clean clothes, forced to sleep on the sofa. I couldn't sleep in Joshua's room, it didn't feel right, the wound too fresh.

Occasionally I caught Samantha starting to break, her mouth would start to make the shape of a word, then, just in time she would catch herself. Notes became our only form of communication and, even then, they were brief and to the point, 'Tea oven', 'Out with Clare'. Eventually, even they stopped.

Clare was my only friend at home. Being only four she was aware that something wasn't right as she had not seen her brother and didn't understand, she would ask when he was coming home. We wouldn't hide the truth, but still she didn't seem to take it in, as if it was a game we were playing.

After two weeks of this frustrating performance, I resorted to trying to start arguments with Samantha just to get a reaction, anything. It was as if she switched off as soon as I opened my mouth.

My only way to deal with it was to work. More, and more overtime. Anything to keep me out of the house and, when I did return, I would only spend time with Clare and she would be in bed, so I'd sit by her bedside listening to her breathing and talking away in her dream world. I hoped her brother was with her. I didn't want her to forget Joshua.

The closest I came to having a conversation with Samantha was one Saturday when I said I was taking Clare out. Samantha launched into a tirade of anger.

"No you're bloody not," she bellowed. "I'm not letting you take my daughter out. I can't trust her life with you."

"She's my bloody daughter too."

"Not anymore, she's not."

Dismayed, I stood there like a lost child. Clare was upset, coat on and ready to go. I stared at Samantha for a few moments before she grabbed Clare from me, then took her own coat out of the cupboard, brushed me aside, and left.

I wanted to fight but not in front of Clare. Samantha's words had cut me down.

I had not even been allowed to help with any of the funeral arrangements for Joshua, becoming a mere bystander.

It was heart-warming to see so many people wanting to pay their respects and for a few hours Samantha had kept her counsel with me, albeit one word commands, but that would be the last time she ever spoke to me before she left.

***

The smell of fresh coffee woke me from my slumber, dragging myself up, for a moment I saw the room for what it once was; my daughter's room, awash with her toys and clothes.

Then, I saw Whispa standing there. He handed me a mug of steaming coffee. "Memories, eh!"

In a blink of an eye the previous night's events came flooding back. All that had happened. I dwelled on it for a moment, a little confused, before it was gone again. Then I felt the positive energy trickle back into me. Payback was finally going to be mine, revenge for tearing my life apart.

Whispa watched me for a moment, his eyes boring into me. "They keep us sane." and then, after a short pause, before he left the room, "sometimes they drive you mad if you let them."

More memories came flooding back, this time the court case - what a shambles that was.

***

The police caught the culprit, well at least the owner of the bike. He denied his involvement, saying that a friend must have borrowed his bike that day, he didn't know who, his friends often borrowed things without asking. He stood there in the dock, suited and booted, the epitome of respectability, running circles around the prosecution, it was all a game to him and he was winning. All the evidence was circumstantial, nothing definitive, nothing they could pin on him. During an interval outside in the waiting room I tried to comfort Samantha, but was met with a scolding glance that put me in my place.

The prosecution barrister kept me updated as best he could as I waited outside. When it was my time in the dock, my side of events sounded lame, even more so than I first thought, Samantha sat stone faced in the viewing gallery. A futile account is all I gave, everything still a blur, the defendant's lawyer ran circles around me, making me feel like the guilty one. 'I have lost a son', I shouted in desperation, but was told to keep to the point, I thought that was the point. I thought that was why we were in court.

I remember looking up at Samantha and, for the briefest millisecond, I caught her eye and saw the venom there. All was lost. I broke down and cried, helped from the dock by a court official. This boy would get off scot-free.

The trial went on for four days, and, in the end, after several people had stood witness to him being somewhere else at the time, the case was thrown out for lack of evidence. They couldn't even prosecute him for not having a licence because no one would stand against him and say that he had ridden the bike on anything other than private land. His parents stood there, clearly lying, painting a picture of pure innocence. What a joke! I was sickened to the pit of my stomach by the bravado he showed as he left the courtroom, a free person.

I, we, still had to live with this for the rest of our lives.

***

I choked on the coffee that Whispa had given me as the bile in my stomach started to rise, the sickness that I felt that day. Samantha walked out a broken woman.

In my mind, I had a clear picture of the boy's face and now I knew what I wanted, an eye for an eye. He would pay with his life.

Downstairs my three guests sat around the kitchen table. Since they had arrived, the house had taken on a new lease of life, it still looked trashed but it felt more alive, as if it was finally breathing again. Had a reason to be there.

"'Ow ya feeling then?" Scratch drank his coffee noisily as I entered the kitchen.

"Yeah. Good. I think."

"The first-timers can have strange reactions." Scholar spoke down to me. "I've seen them go running to the church to seek forgiveness. People ask for power and when they get it, they are suddenly scared of the consequences. Whispa can normally spot them a mile off, even before we meet them. You were different. We knew." I looked *inquisitively at him.*

The court case, fresh in my mind again. "Yeah, well, they deserve everything they get....we can dish out. It's about time this estate was returned to a state of normality and if this is the only way. Then so be it."

Whispa rose from his seat putting his arm around my shoulder and said, in a low drawl, "I hear what you say and I like it Sway, I like it. Don't we?" *They all looked at one another and smiled conspiratorially, Whispa easing me into his seat.* "Tonight though, I think we need to slip out the back way. The wolves know we are out for souls."

I looked at the clock, it was nearly three o'clock, I couldn't believe I'd slept for so long and how refreshed I was, despite my dream.

"Sway, I think you need to check on your neighbours." *Scholar spoke matter-of-factly.*

"My neighbours?"

Whispa leant in close "They're dead! You don't want them to remain like the old lady we found last night. Do you?"

I looked incredulously at Whispa, and then Scholar.

41

After ringing the police I waited for them to arrive whilst my guests made themselves scarce upstairs.

I was asked if they had any living relatives and it saddened me to think they didn't. The police broke down the front door after asking me a few searching questions as to why I was concerned. I explained that they were creatures of habit and the fact that the curtains were still drawn at four in the afternoon was a sign that there was something wrong, I emphasized that I had not heard any sound from them for two days.

As the door gave way, the cankerous smell of decaying flesh wafted out, free from its prison. The sudden urge to vomit hit me but I managed to hold in the contents of my stomach. The first police officer visibly baulked at the prospect of going in but knew it was his duty. Taking a deep breath, he rallied his composure, before entering with his hand over his mouth and nose.

Within a few seconds he was out again, confirming one body in the lounge. The officer looked dismayed when I re-iterated that there should be two people and he went back in to search the rest of the house, eventually confirming another two upstairs.

When I heard there were three bodies I was perplexed.

"But there should only be two, they didn't have any children."

"That may be so, sir, but there are definitely three bodies in all."

I tried to rush in but was stopped by the firm hand of the officer.

Forty-five minutes later the coroner and crime scene officers turned up to investigate. At this point I was asked to go in and officially identify the bodies of my neighbours, Jim & Eileen. Eileen was lying on the bed as if she had just gone to sleep in her clothes, placed in her hands was a note 'I love you with my heart so full. I will be with you shortly'

Sadness racked me, shivers shot down my spine, the power of the wolves. I almost broke down and cried, Jim and Eileen were always so peaceful and harmless, yet they had been driven to this. The officer then led me to the bathroom. They warned me that it was not a pretty sight, Jim was in the bath, his wrists littered with cuts, empty packets of Anadin and Paracetamol lay on the floor, discarded. I choked at the sight of my neighbour. It looked as though he had been in a fight.

They then led me downstairs to the lounge where a third body lay, this time a teenager.

"Do you know this person, sir?"

I stared at the body that lay sprawled across the coffee table, a kitchen knife stuck in his chest, a pool of blood, now black and congealed, covered the once immaculate carpet.

"The wolves." I let slip.

"Excuse me, sir."

"I mean, no, but he looks like one of the kids that ruin this estate." I felt the anger burst through. "Because none of you will do anything about it. We are left here to rot in hell whilst you are...." A hand on my shoulder turned me sharply, a WPC looked me straight in the eye and I let the tirade fall into silence, I was escorted from the house.

Outside, I overheard a conversation between another officer on his radio.

"...Probably deserved it anyway. The old man and woman are dead too. Not sure what the woman died of, the man was suicide. Looks like a struggle beforehand and a teenager was stabbed, looked like he took a while to d...."

I was suddenly aware that I was fronting up to the officer, despite the WPC trying to escort me away. So many conflicting thoughts cascaded through my mind, anger, frustration, rage, sadness, denial. I eyed the officer, he didn't say a word but looked concerned and, with a heavy heart, I let it go and walked back into my house.

I continued to watch the scene outside from the front bedroom window. It was early evening when the police finally left. The WPC had come round to check that I was alright and whether I wanted to talk to anyone, I plagued her with questions until she gave me what I wanted, which was that the wolf had got in somehow, there was a fight between Jim and the wolf and, in anger, Jim had grabbed at the nearest object. They were not sure whether Eileen had died before or after, but it looked like she had suffered a heart attack and Jim obviously couldn't take it anymore.

There were a group of wolves sitting and joking on the green opposite the house, scavengers, they would take the news back to the den. The house would then be targeted for material gain. I'd heard about it many times, usually within hours of the occupant leaving in the 'meat wagon', the wolves ransacked the house before family members even arrived to stake their claim. What they didn't take, they trashed, breaking many people's hearts, but they didn't care.

The police had arranged for the front door to be boarded up, where they had broken in but, within an hour, we heard a familiar noise of breaking glass and raised voices.

Scratch was watching from the kitchen window as a couple of them carried the TV out the back door towards the rear fence.

"Are we ready then, Brethren? Duties are a calling." Whispa spoke with glee.

We headed into the back garden, Scratch in front and me bringing up the rear. They never saw us as we scampered over the fence that separated the two gardens. Scratch whistled at them as if they were a pack of dogs. I felt dead inside, repulsed by what I had seen and the devastation caused, the wolves face from the courtroom was like a large laughing film poster in my mind and adrenalin started buzz through giving me a feeling of power - it was time again to exact some revenge.

42

The two wolves, one a tall wirey- framed wolf with a pale face, and a scar running down his right cheek, the other with wide saucer-like eyes, were carrying the TV set. They stopped in their tracks, calling to their mates inside. A wolf with a confident swagger and carrying a video recorder, marched out ready for a fight.

"Yeah, you wanna start somethin'?" Came the bold statement from Confident-swagger, who also had a crooked mouth and narrow shoulders. Dropping the video recorder, he strode towards Whispa.

Whispa said clearly and softly, "No, we want to finish something."

In that instant all ambient noise appeared to fade away, replaced by an eerie silence. For the minutest second something registered in the wolves' faces, an enlightenment that was too late to act upon.

Scratch stepped forward grabbing Confident-swagger by the throat with one powerful hand, squeezing tightly, before he could reach Whispa. Confident-swagger swung his arms wildly trying to break free from Scratch's grip but Scratch's hand only tightened further, causing him to gasp for air and quelling any strength that was there. Confident-swagger's fists never found their target as Scratch forced him back against the wall of the house, just as another wolf, with white hair, came out of the back door. Seeing us, White-hair dropped the bounty he was carrying, but too late to protect himself from Scratch clawing the side of his face with his free hand. White-hair's cheek burned as he fell to the ground in agony, holding his face.

Whispa was dealing with Wirey-framed, who had left Saucer-eyes to struggle down the garden carrying the heavy TV, until he had finally dropped it, screen first, onto the ground, shattering the thick glass and sending shards everywhere. Whispa's fists flew left and right, first knocking Wirey-framed's head one way and then the other, mucas and spots of blood splattered the ground. Wirey-framed didn't get the chance to defend himself as punches rained in quick succession.

Saucer-eyes's anger rose as he looked at the shattered TV set, then, turning towards Whispa, he stomped angrily towards him and I caught sight of the tattoos that littered his wrists, forearms, neck and ears. I called out to Whispa who turned sharply and landed a punch square on Saucer-eyes face, sending him reeling back down the garden crashing into the debris of the TV set.

A fourth wolf, wearing a red and white baseball cap, came running from the end of the garden towards me, and I stood ready to defend myself.

A sharp object caught me unaware on the shoulder and I stumbled to the ground. Baseball-cap kicked me as he ran past to help Confident-swagger, and I swung round to see my attacker, who wore a denim jacket covered in patches. I put my hands up to defend myself from a kick aimed at my face by Denim-jacket but Whispa intervened and in one swift movement had my attacker on the ground, his knees either side of Denim-jacket's chest locking his arms securely by the side of his body. Whispa placed his hands either side of Denim-jacket's head. The wolf struggled, but slowly the fight died away as Whispa bent down, putting his face to Denim-jacket's and extracting his soul.

When I looked at my shoulder, a broken piece of wood had been rammed into it and now protruded like a dagger.

Nausea overtook me as I tried to get up, but I persisted anyway, I wanted to help my Brethren. I reached for the piece of wood to pull it free but the world span around me. Half kneeling I looked around to see Denim-jacket lying motionless, just the gentle rise and fall of his chest signifying that he was still alive.

White-hair, in the meantime, had partly recovered from his burning cheek and had tried to attack Scratch, who easily pinned both, Confident-swagger and White-hair, to the wall like helpless bundles of rag. Although Scratch looked scrawny, I found it hard to believe the immense power he wielded so effortlessly. Baseball-cap had made his target and was on Scratch's back, trying to get him to release his grip on both wolves. Struggling up, I staggered forward, my shoulder registering its protest against movement, but I had to help my Brethren.

Shutting out the pain I grabbed Baseball-cap with my free arm…

Peter was drawn in to the action.

…he swung one arm violently round and caught the side of my head, making me more unsteady on my feet. Somehow I managed to

grab his wrist firmly.

Beryl grabbed Peter's wrist as he swung his arm at her. The audience drank in the scene played out so skilfully and accurately.

As I fought the burning pain of my shoulder I concentrated on crushing the bones in Baseball-caps hand. Baseball-cap slowly released his grip on Scratch's neck, sliding off of his back. I heard a bone snap like a twig, then another. Surprise registered on Baseball-cap's face before he issued a cry. I spun him round to face me, momentarily letting him go. Immediately he grabbed my hurt harm, I yelled at the pain.

Beryl's scream filled the hall surprising the captive audience, Cyril momentarily stopped writing, caught in indecision, fearing for his aunt and for Peter, who had somehow been dragged into it.

"Auntie? Peter?" But the words fell on deaf ears.

I stepped towards him and he backed into Scratch. I glared into Baseball-cap's eyes, channelling my aggression, forgetting my own injury and pain.

Peter stepped backwards as Beryl marched towards him.

His eyes became wide with terror, he knew the outcome was not going to be good. He was mine now, mine to control, a helpless puppet and I wanted to torment him. This was payback time. Why hadn't I done this earlier? Why use physical force when I had this power?

The pain from my shoulder was a distant memory, the focus was in front on me, my revenge, my plaything for everything that had happened to my family. I would show him how much I hated his kind.

Cyril rushed to his aunt, calling her, she was not there, neither was Peter, their minds taken by Mark.

I watched the reaction in Baseball-Cap's face as he guessed his fate was sealed. He attempted a half-hearted swing at me, which I stopped, inches before it landed, and I held it there, suspended in time.

Peter's swing caught Cyril on the cheek sending him reeling to the ground.

The wolf stood paralysed as I crushed his hand, using only the power of thought. Listening and feeling as every bone splintered, rendering his fist a mass of feeble flesh.

I blotted out what was going on elsewhere in the garden and relished the power I now had. His hollow screams echoed round the night sky.

His vocal chords were next on my list and I crushed them just like his hand. He gagged as his cries faded and his breathing became difficult. In his terror, he had wet himself but that was the least of his problems, each chord pinged like an overstretched rubber band. I smiled, I hadn't even laid a finger on him, just the pure strength of my mind. I didn't know I held so many dark thoughts or that I could commit such atrocities to another human being. But in those short seconds I could justify the actions, quantify the guilt, for the pain and suffering that so many of the residents had incurred. For what I had gone through, what I had suffered.

Using my mind, I threw him onto the ground, Baseball-cap's instant reaction was to break his fall instinctively putting out his crippled hand which buckled immediately under the weight. He hit the deck hard, crumbling under the pain, forcing him to land awkwardly on his other elbow. He tried to yell but only silence emanated from his lips. Struggling for breath, he tried to crawl away.

Peter crawled across the stage, watched by Cyril, who found himself helpless, whilst Beryl marched on, acting out everything as described, the audience watched in morbid fascination.

In my head I could hear the wolf's accelerated heartbeat thumping loud like a kick drum. The contorted face pleaded with me to stop, but nothing was going to stop me, I was in my element now I had found my freedom. I moved in closer, although I didn't need to, helplessly Baseball-cap edged back on the patio, every move another flinch of agony. I was feeding off his fear. I now knew what it was like to have what they had enjoyed for so long - Power.

Marching nearer to him I imagined his heart beating faster and faster, then faster still. His eyes glazed over before he twitched and slumped, helpless, on the ground.

Peter collapsed, still on the stage, the audience gasped in horror. Cyril got up and grabbed his aunt by the arms, shaking her, trying to shake the spirit loose from her. Her eyes were full of rage. Cyril could see she wasn't really behind them.

He was gone...

"Auntie Beryl, Stop. Stop!" Cyril cried, but it was no use.

...but I couldn't let go, in my mind I tore at his insides. I was lost, caught up in my anger, my rage, my revenge. I watched as the body moved and pulsated. Only the hand of Whispa on my shoulder

stopped me in my tracks.

"Leave him, he is done."

Beryl turned away from Cyril breaking his firm hold, all anger gone. Peter lay motionless on the stage.

I shivered as the rage dissipated at the touch of Whispa's hand, and I realised that I had crossed over into temporary insanity.

I looked at the wrecked form on the ground, the dull moonlight managed to make it look even more disfigured than it was. Inside I was calm.

I turned to look at Denim-jacket who was also motionless, where Whispa had left him on the ground. Scratch had allowed his two to get away, he saw my curious look.

"I got plans for those two. Don't you'se worries."

"What do we do now?" I asked pensively.

"We do nothing," Whispa stated matter-of-factly. "Look at that over there." He pointed to the end of the garden, I saw nothing, but then felt fire, as Whispa pulled the spike of wood from my shoulder. I cringed as I fought back the urge to cry out. The pain tearing at me. Holding my breath, I tried to get it under control. I placed my left hand on my injured right shoulder willing the pain to stop and was amazed as it slowly died down.

"Ain't the power grand Sway? Ain't it grand?" Scratch laughed. "Now we go."

43

I regained my composure. "We can't leave them here, it's a bit close to home, isn't it?"

Scratch put his hand on my other shoulder. "No one knows nuffin'." He squeezed my shoulder, smiling. Then one by one we headed through the back gate of Jim & Eileen's leaving the shattered wolves where they lay.

There were garages at the back of the gardens. Most were now merely ruins, burnt out shells filled with rubbish. An alley lay at one end, leading into a road beyond.

Rolling my shoulder, loosening it up, I was amazed how good it felt. The fierceness of my power was immense and made me wonder if I was becoming invincible. Walking proud I was not the man I had been, the frightened pawn that had kowtowed for so long.

Scratch was leading again. Thoughts of my own immortality put a spring in my step and a couple of times I found myself being held back from taking the lead.

"Easy Sway. This is Scratch's time." Whispa spoke.

Carrying on in silence, Scholar made notes in his Grimoire.

Stopping at a crossroads, Scratch appeared to be tuning himself into something or someone, hunting the scent, receiving his guidance. The estate had been swamped by an eerie quietness, an unfamiliar ambience as the streets lay deserted of wolves who had always been so prevalent. I wondered what the residents made of the mysterious events that had been taking place of late. Were they scared? Not sure if they were safe or indeed, next in line? Were they rejoicing that finally justice was being dealt? What would they think if they knew the truth? The secret. Would they bow down in appreciation or rise up and verbalise their disgust at the way in which peace would be granted to them? Would they be scared of the power a few people could exert? Scared that the cure could be worse than the disease, almost preferring to carry on living the nightmare the wolves had inflicted.

Scratch turned left and we followed the slow purposeful meander; destination unknown, yet we knew Scratch would find whatever it was he was hunting.

We entered a dark cul-de-sac where all the street lamps had been broken, half bricks littered the road. A burnt out car hid itself in the shadow of a tumble-down wall. The cul-de-sac was the back entrance to two rows of houses that lined it. A couple of back gates lay in tatters, where they no longer did their jobs, rotten and smashed. The houses beyond were caverns for the wolves. I knew of these houses, though I had never dared venture here before tonight. I had no reason to.

A cold shiver shot down my spine as I thought of how this cul-de-sac might once have been. House-owners washing their cars, kids kicking footballs, not a care in the world.

Scratch ventured into a house immediately to our right, trampling over the debris of the back gate. A missile came out of nowhere narrowly missing him. He walked purposely on, not acknowledging it. Out of the corner of my eye I caught the swift motion as Whispa also disappeared from view, entering a garden further down. He moved with stealth and cunning, a silent warrior.

Scholar watched Scratch's back and carried on drawing, instinctively, hardly glancing at the paper, the speed of which I had never witnessed. I stood as a sentry and observed as my Brethren knew their tasks without a word spoken between them.

I remembered how the estate used to be, it was so sad how it had deteriorated. The houses, when new, had radiated a warmth that brought a glow to the people who lived within. Pride.

There was a commotion going on inside the house that Scratch had entered. Scholar slammed the Grimoire shut and we followed the sounds. The stench hit our noses as soon as we moved over the threshold of the broken back door. The notes of filth, damp, urine and excrement, made for a foul concoction. The kitchen was just a shell, all the cupboards and work tops had been ripped out long ago, even the wall tiles had been taken, wallpaper torn down. A body lay on the floor and, in the dim light, barely moving. I guessed whoever it was, was stoned on something.

A noise from upstairs signified where we could find Scratch, and we followed the howls of pain.

Beryl flaked out on the stage, exhausted, tears in her eyes, eyes that pleaded for help.

Cyril stopped attending to Peter when Beryl finished talking letting a St. John's Ambulance medic see to him instead, he was disorientated but alright. The medic helped Peter to his chair, then poured him a glass of water from the jug on the table.

"What happened?" Peter gasped the strained words. Cyril heard and fought back the temptation to tell him what he really thought.

"A little participation, that's all." Satisfaction present in Cyril's delivery.

Peter gulped down the glass of water and quickly poured another. Cyril aided Beryl, who was struggling to stand up, before guiding her to the dressing room where she uttered words that sounded like heaven to Cyril. "I can't do this anymore." He sighed with relief. He didn't care about his own writing career now, things were getting out of hand.

The majority of the audience sat astonished and bewildered, not sure what to do next. Those that had been to previous evenings started to applaud.

"Good show," one called out.

A slow unsure applause then continued as the audience hesitantly dissipated. Peter, embarrassed and confused, sat momentarily trying to decide if he wanted to make any closing remark but then bolted from the stage, as the bile started to rise in his stomach, fear gripping him, his mind a fury of thoughts, trying to comprehend all that had happened.

A & J Arnold Guest House, Omskirk

"Peter, I couldn't give a damn about your business. My aunt's life is more important than any book sales. It was the second time that you have been a part of it, tonight. Don't you care?" The anger in Cyril's eyes was fused with hatred for the businessman who stood before him in the lounge of the guest house. Any ideas Cyril had about publishing 'Samuel Preston' were gone, he didn't think it was worth the risks anymore.

Peter tried to hide all signs of irritation; he had plied good money into this venture and a contract had been agreed. He was determined that it would be honoured, pushing his own involvement to the back of his mind. "Cyril, look, your aunt agreed to this, I have it in writing…"

Cyril raised his voice. "I don't care if she has it written in blood, she is not proceeding any further with this."

Mrs Arnold, the landlady, appeared at the lounge door, wrapped up in her pink dressing gown, Peter and Cyril turned immediately to face her, the agitation clearly showing on her face.

"Gentlemen, please, it's gone eleven. Guests have started to complain." The argument had started almost as soon as they had returned, some twenty minutes previously. "If you don't stop it, or at least start talking like civil people, I shall have to ask you both to leave and find somewhere else to sleep tonight." Her voice mimicked a schoolmistress.

Chastised, Cyril turned away and walked to the window, staring out into the blackness of the wet night, sighing heavily at his frustration that Peter didn't seem to care.

"I am very sorry, Mrs Arnold, of course." Peter was instantly a picture of respectability and as calm as a drifting iceberg.

"Cyril." The loving tone of a very tired Beryl broke in. She had hoped to avoid the confrontation that was seemingly inevitable. Cyril had her best interests at heart and she had let him make his point, however, the discussion had raged out of control and was going nowhere. "Leave it for tonight. Come on, let's go to bed, we can sort this out tomorrow." Then adding more pointedly, "can't we, Peter?"

Before Peter had a chance to reply Beryl's body contorted in pain. Cyril rushed to her side. "Quick, Mrs Arnold, some water."

Then, as quickly as it came, the pain subsided and Beryl's eyes became fiery, her stature grew. Gone was the tiredness. Cyril stepped back. Something wasn't right.

Beryl started to speak, both Peter and Cyril, recognised the voice, it was Mark again.

"No," Cyril exclaimed. "Auntie Beryl, please hear me. Can you hear me?" Cyril pleaded, but it was too late. "Please fight it. Please Auntie?"

Mrs Arnold jolted at the sight of Beryl's sudden transformation in demeanour and stature. "What on earth is going on?" When she didn't receive an answer, she added. "Right that's it. I have had enough. I want you all to pack your bags and go. Now!"

Peter stood flummoxed at the intrusion by Mark, and sank into a nearby chair, grabbing a handkerchief from his pocket to mop his fevered brow, fearful of what might follow, and ignoring Mrs Arnold. The earlier possession still fresh in his mind, the second he had experienced since this little tour had begun.

"Auntie, break the hold, you can do it." Cyril's pleas fell upon deaf ears.

Mrs Arnold pulled her dressing gown tighter, trying to emphasize her disgust at being ignored. "Did you...?

44

Upstairs, the putrid smell got worse, making me want to heave. Graffiti littered the walls and gave a good idea of the sort of person that inhabited this place from time to time, even if it was just to daub the walls with more luminescent artwork.

In the front main bedroom we found Scratch with Mack, the wolf we'd encountered the first night when my Brethren had joined my crusade. Scratch was teasing the mark on the side of his face, the mark that had appeared after scratching the picture Scholar had drawn of him. Small wisps of smoke rose as it burned. Mack howled as the pain tore through him, he looked smaller in stature than he had that first night. He scraped his face trying to ease the agony but only caused it to bleed. His girlfriend cowered in the corner, visibly shaking, silently pleading for Scratch to leave her alone. She didn't try to straighten her clothes to hide what they had been up to, her knickers still wrapped around one ankle, her top half way up her stomach exposing a pierced belly button. She tried to hide her make-up stained face behind her hands like a shield; if she couldn't see us then it wouldn't be real.

Scratch bellowed once more. "Who control' this 'state? I won't ask you again." His voice cut through the room like a knife. He licked his finger nail again and Mack cried in pain, more wisps of smoke billowed into the air.

"Excuse me," Whispa drawled, as he walked behind Scholar and me over to the girlfriend. Then, kneeling down in front of her. "Aren't you a pretty one?" He placed a finger under her chin, encouraging her to lift her head and not to be so frightened. For an instant she stopped muttering and faced Whispa. Her face brightened, eyes cautious, wondering whether she was going to get out alive.

"I didn't do nuffin', honest." She trembled, mustering as much confidence as she could to answer the rhetorical question Whispa had made.

Mrs Arnold skulked by the door as Peter moved towards her, acting out Whispa's part.

"I believe you my pretty one." Then he paused before speaking softly.

"So why do you lie to me?" Whispa now gripped her chin, supporting it between his right thumb and first finger, studying her. "It's no good, you can't hide the truth from me. I'm sure you have done plenty."

Peter held Mrs Arnold's chin and she took on the part of the girlfriend. Cyril stepped backwards into the room, terrified.

She started to cry, tears carrying her eye make-up down her cheeks. "I didn't. I didn't do nuffin' honest." Then she changed tack, a sudden realisation that her baby would be motherless if she didn't get out of here quick. "My baby, my little Kylie. I need to get back to her. I have to go." But Whispa held her chin tighter and the little swatch of courage vanished as quickly as it had come, she knew the end was near.

"Maybe I ought to do little Kylie a favour then?" He paused, looking into her eyes for a reason to save her.

"Please mister, please I'll do anyfing you want. I promise. Please." For an instant she flirted with Whispa, as if sexual favours would help her case.

Whispa pulled her face closer to his. "Yes, I'm sure you would." For a moment as his face drew closer to her, she thought she was safe, it was just going to be sex and then she could go, she hoped – she was used to men treating her like that. She closed her eyes, ready to receive his kiss. Her eyes widened in terror as Whispa drew out her soul. Then, within seconds she was just a vacant vessel, barely alive, leaving Kylie motherless. Whispa left her where she lay, eventually she would fade from this world through starvation.

Walking over to Mack, who was still being tormented by Scratch. "You look like you wanted to be close together."

Mrs Arnold stood vacant in the doorway. Peter walked over and clasped Cyril's head in his hands, Cyril fought as best he could but the grip was too strong.

"What! No! Wait!" Whispa took hold of Mack's head clamping both his meaty hands either side of his face. "Whatya doing?" Mack struggled, trying to twist his head away.

"Ain't love grand? Makes you wanna be t'gevver, don't it?"

Whispa transferred the girl's soul into Mack, who kicked as much as possible until Scratch held his legs firmly. When he had finished Whispa stood up. "Ah, isn't it nice to be close?" a beaming sarcastic smile on his face. "This can be so rewarding."

Mack's eyes danced before us, an inner battle raging. His face *twitched as the two souls started to fight with each other, the two lovers locked eternally together in one body. The torment turned his eyes bloodshot. Mack slapped himself hard, first with the left hand and then the right, the battle continued as we walked from the room, part of me found the scene amusing. They deserved it, they all deserved it. I wanted to watch the outcome of this battle, but my Brethren led me from the room.*

"It ain't right to see lovers fight, gotta respect their privacy. Ain't you Whispa?" Scratch imparted ruefully.

"That's right."

Mrs Arnold snapped back to life and looked at Cyril, confusion registering in her eyes. He could see her trying to fathom what had happened. Cyril watched on, disturbed, as Beryl continued.

As we walked down the stairs I thought I heard two voices arguing and wondered how long it would last.

"Normally drives them insane, one tries to kill the other," Whispa calmly answered. "Of course, that normally means the end for both."

I was the first one to speak after we left. "Where did you go to, Whispa, before you joined us? Did you find anything out?"

Whispa stopped and faced me. "Sway wants to know where I went." *I became very uncomfortable, then Whispa broke into a hearty laugh.* "I had to take a leak, is that alright?" *He slapped me firmly on my back.*

Scratch and Scholar laughed along with Whispa, and I nervously joined in, feeling foolish.

Two more guests in dressing gowns walked into the lounge, annoyed.

"Look, we are trying to sleep. Can you please keep…"

As they viewed the scene they recollected the news stories and watched in mild interest from behind Mrs Arnold.

We walked into the night and the heart of the estate, my brethren still looking for one definitive leader, although I knew that a few factions ran the estate, all had their own territory, occasional fights broke out when there was a battle for supremacy, but most lived harmoniously whilst the rest of the estate suffered their reign of terror. There was safety in knowing where to go and where not to go, although the boundaries were always changing. It needed to be halted.

We found ourselves back in the underground garage block, known as 'the rape room'.

"Why are we here? No one comes down here." I asked Whispa.

"Shush." Was his reply.

Scratch, who was leading us, stopped. We all followed suit. The echoes died away as the gloom filled with silence. Standing for a few minutes, I was about to ask something, when Whispa's voice broke into my thoughts. "Shush my friend. We have guests." I was still a little unnerved by Whispa's talent.

45

A squeal of tyres told us that we had company and a car's headlights swept through the darkness like search beams. We darted behind separate concrete pillars, listening, watching, waiting. The car pulled into a space by the metal lift doors. A continuous thump of music came from within as it idled, waiting, the engine humming. The headlights were left on like two eyes in the night shining in the opposite direction leaving us shrouded in darkness. Stealthily, we moved from our positions so we had a good view of the car and its occupants.

After a few minutes, three wolves got out, two flanking the third. A steady stream of wolves appeared from nowhere, and trade started. The two flanking wolves acted like bouncers, keeping a wary eye out for trouble. Business was brisk and orderly. The addicts got their fixes, some not wanting to wait, preferring to sit down near the concrete wall and take their potent death sentences. They acted like it was normal, lighters flickered under bent spoons until the contents were ready, then a hypodermic needle swallowed the contents, before being forced into a waiting vein.

As we watched, we caught the glint of a metal object from the waistband of one of the flanking wolves and, as one customer started to question the goods, the gun was swiftly pulled, subduing the complaint instantly.

Whispa's voice once again came into my head. "We work together on this, united power, Scratch, Scholar." They quickly nodded. "Sway?" I concurred. "You know what to do Scholar. Sway let us channel into your energy, it's the only way. 'Alacuskia matadia' will work."

"Wha…" I didn't get a chance to finish my question.

"It means the power of four," Whispa continued. "We all have certain power on a one-to-one basis. Two of them have guns and we are not immortal. If we focus our energies through one person it will temporarily unite our powers. That person will be you, Sway."

Before I could question it, Scholar picked up where Whispa had finished, this time whispering. "Everyone of us has a different power, yours is the most suited to this task. We need to form a diamond

220

configuration, you in front, then Scratch and Whispa, each with a hand on your respective shoulders, and I walk behind."

In the gloom of our hiding places, we had let ourselves relax in the safety of the shadows, Scholar's whisper had been picked up and, without warning, the first bullet narrowly missed us ricocheting off the wall behind.

"Who's there? Show yourself. That was just a warning." We remained silent.

Then I felt myself being pushed forward, thrust into the head of the diamond formation that my Brethren had talked about.

I wanted to protest, but it was a moot point now. I knew the power they possessed, although I still hadn't grasped the full extent of my own, and was not confident in what they were trying to prove here. "Trust us." Whispa's voice rang in my head.

Now our visitors were onto us, there was little choice left. I was shaking, knowing I wasn't immortal and knowing it could all end here, us four against guns, what power could we possess against guns?

The two guests at the door took the roles of the wolves with guns, whilst Cyril, Peter and Mrs Arnold looked on in horror.

I concentrated hard on letting them channel their energies and power into me, trying to let them guide me.

Second and third shots rang out their chorus.

"This is your last chance." The angry cry sang out.

Scholar started to speak, slowly and quietly, as we stood in the security of the blackness that enveloped us.

"Judacia Bruickna Deararay. Focus the force to one. Let the power ignite inside. Believe in us. Let us do your bidding. Dark Lord rise up. Let us show you our work. Dark Lord let us please you. Dark Lord let us not take your name in vain. Dark Lord....."

With Scholars words behind me and Whispa and Scratch to either side, we slowly marched forward from the darkness across the expanse of concrete. Confidence engulfed me and I knew what I needed to do. One of the wolves had got out a powerful hand held torch to scan the area, the bright bulb shone straight into my eyes, temporarily blinding me. Blinking I caught the movement of the gun from the second wolf. Another four shots were fired, their report reverberating around us. I wished the torch would get hit so we would stand a better chance.

"Focus Sway." Whispa's words inside my head, his hand gripping *my shoulder tighter. Suddenly a bullet hit the torch and the bulb exploded. The wolf holding it dropped it and the body of the torch shattered on the hard floor. We were about 150 feet away from them now and just at the border of darkness and light.*

The two bodyguards stood poised, guns at the ready, pointed directly at us.

The two guests stood with their arms outstretched, as if holding guns, pointing them at Cyril, Peter, Mrs Arnold and Beryl.

"You've had your warnings."

In my head I was instructing them not to fire. They remained stock still, guns pointing in our direction, but no triggers were pulled. As we got closer I saw them looking at each other, puzzled by their sudden inability to fire. The small group of customers at the back of the car dispersed, they didn't want to be involved.

The head wolf slammed the boot lid closed and shouted commands to his bodyguards to shoot us. "We can't." they both stammered, shocked.

The head wolf opened his long leather coat to reveal a machete holstered to his belt. We were now only thirty feet away.

"Do I have to do everything my bloody self? You two are fired." He took the machete from its holster and swung it with immense power as he reached the first of the two wolves, "I never did like you much anyways, Forrester." The machete sliced off the gun hand in one clean sweep.

Beryl swung her hand and caught one of the guest's wrists. The guest fell to the floor in a blood gurgling cry. Footsteps could be heard upstairs as more guests were disturbed.

Forrester's screams reverberated around the solid walls as he knelt on the ground, clutching his severed hand.

"As for you, Smithie, I'll deal with you later."

"But Grant, I can't fire. It's not my fault."

"Oh, fucking shut up! You make me sick. You're paid to do a job."
Grant swung his left fist at Smithie, catching him square on the jaw.

"It's not." Whispa spoke out loud.

"Who the fuck do you think you are? God or something?"

"We is the power. You ain't," Scratch spat out.

"What sort of bollocks is that?" Grant was getting closer to us and

within swinging distance of the machete, which hung menacingly at his side.

"Oh, it ain't," Scratch retorted.

A gun shot rang out. Forrester was snivelling on the ground, his whimpers getting weaker as blood oozed from his wrist. Smithie was surprised by the gunshot.

"What the hell are you doing? That nearly got me." Grant squealed, turning his back to us.

"It is not his doing." My voice sang out, but it wasn't me thinking the words.

"You are really starting to annoy me, now fuck off!"

"First, you tell us who's running this estate? And then we may consider it."

"I guess you boys aren't too bright are you. I said get the fuck out of here. NOW!" Grant raised the machete as if to charge.

"We're taking this estate back, so I suggest you get back in your car and get out of here before we do some damage to you." The confidence with which I spoke belied my true emotion.

Grant laughed loudly, filling this whole cavernous space. "Or, what you going to about it? BOYS!"

Two more shots rang out. Grant eyes widened upon realisation that he had been shot by Forrester.

Two more sets of car lights flooded the area, lighting us up like Blackpool illuminations. Suddenly I believed our mission was foolhardy, we were outnumbered. Where had the other cars come from?

Beryl, exhausted, fell to the floor, narrowly missing a chair. Cyril took a couple of seconds to realise that it was over.

46

"Auntie Beryl! Auntie Beryl!" Cyril called running to her. "Now you see PETER!" The words were full of venom. "This has to stop."

Peter found his normal calm exterior fading, he was trembling and couldn't find any words with which to answer Cyril.

Cyril helped Beryl up as she slowly came round. "What happened?"

"You're alright now, Auntie. You're alright."

The two guests aghast to find themselves involved in something so extraordinary, scurried out of the lounge and up to their rooms passing three other guests who had made their way downstairs. Mrs Arnold snivelled from her place on the floor, pulling a handkerchief from a pocket of her dressing gown. "Never, in all my days. Never." She got up and disappeared towards the kitchen.

"Come on Auntie I'm taking you up to your room. We'll go home in the morning. Goodnight, and goodbye Peter. I don't care about my book anymore."

Peter didn't reply.

***

Deciding it was best to be close to his aunt, Cyril spent an uncomfortable night in the armchair in her room. He knew he couldn't do anything if another possession took place but it gave him peace of mind to be near her. He still didn't understand how Mark could have such power over his aunt. Why was Mark so fixated with her? It was worse now and he was starting to intervene outside of organised events. The power Mark wielded was terrifying, especially as he could do it so readily using anyone in the vicinity, like a great puppeteer. There was no way his aunt could have foreseen this. He was relieved she had finally conceded to call an end to it.

Restlessly, Cyril tried to sleep, at one point moving onto the floor but to no avail. His aunt, however, slept peacefully, exhausted by Mark's activities; she had barely uttered a word after Cyril had helped her to her room.

In his room Peter was pacing, torn between business and the fact that this venture was turning sour, even he could see that. He thought back to his father's advice, which was usually a good source for him. 'Business first, always. It's always served me well and it will serve you well. Remember that'. He could even hear his father telling him, and for a moment he wondered whether Mark was nearby, playing games with him, toying with him. He shivered at the thought.

When he had suggested a book tour, nothing could have been simpler. With the first two books selling well and, with the increasing publicity 'Justice for John Johnson' had garnered, this third one would certainly capture the minds of the public, but now he was wondering if it would be for the right reasons. It was incredible how fast news was spreading of each event; and the so-called possessions. Even Peter, with his anonymous remarks telephoned into the newspapers, couldn't have predicted how it would all escalate. With the books selling rapidly at the back of the hall, Tracy and Adele were struggling to keep up, it was fast becoming the biggest news story of the year, referred to as a phenomenon. Spiritualists had been dragged out of the woodwork to cast their aspersions on what was happening, thinking it was 'hocus pocus' - merely a publicity stunt, but others believed. Peter felt the weight lift from his shoulders as these thoughts allayed the fears which had pre-occupied his mind so readily. Putting money before the lives of those around him seemed an easy task for him. It was probably that attitude that had kept him single all his life, the closest thing he had to family was a housekeeper. Money made it easier to deal with the loneliness.

His hand trembled as he tried to light another cigarette, his eighth since retiring to his room, he was still scared. He had never dealt with anything spiritual in his life, an atheist at heart, physical things were what he dealt in, and money was what he understood. He thought back to the first time on stage when he too had been taken, to act out a part. Shuddering, goose pimples rose on his skin like mole hills on the surface of a plush velvety lawn, he had no memory of those few minutes and that scared him more.

He lay down on his bed, stubbing out the remains of his cigarette, as a sickness in the pit of his stomach took hold. How could he go on? Then, taking out the last cigarette, he screwed up the packet and threw it across the room, wishing he had bought another earlier. His heart still pounded. He sat up, his hand still trembling, disbelieving how restless he was. Trying to forget about the bile rising inside him, he sucked in the smoke hoping it would calm him, but it did little to rescue his frantic mind. Stubbing out his last cigarette, he lay back down and turned the light off, then turned it back on almost immediately, as every little noise triggered his over-active imagination. Finally his eyelids closed, the bright 100 watt bulb doing little to keep him awake.

Wednesday 1st November 1978

"Morning Cyril," Beryl said as briskly as she could muster.

"Morning," Cyril replied stretching, trying to relief the ache in his back. "You okay?" he yawned amazed at how tired he still felt.

"Yes, I think I am. Thank you for watching over me." Beryl sounded the happiest she had been for a few days, which struck Cyril as odd knowing how frail and tired she had been but put it down to the fact that they were going home, it was over. "Look why don't you get washed up and I'll meet you for breakfast in about half an hour."

"Okay," Cyril yawned again getting up from the floor his back still stiff.

After Cyril had left, Beryl's decided to go outside for some fresh winter air before breakfast. As she reached the bottom of the stairs Mr Arnold called to her.

"Oh, Miss Wallace, a parcel arrived this morning for you."

"A parcel, Mr Arnold?"

"Yes, by 1st class." Mr Arnold handed the small package to Beryl, who took it cautiously, surprised to be receiving anything as she had not told anyone where she would be. Wandering into the small lounge, she sat down to open it. Inside were three silk wrapped crystals, with a note which read;

Beryl,
Please give me a call urgently when you receive this.
Hope you are okay.
Love Maggie.
xx

Beryl got up and rang Maggie from the telephone at reception. Mr Arnold started the timer as Maggie answered on the third ring.

"Hello Maggie, it's Beryl. It's not too early is it?" Her voice quiet as she still remained shaken by the previous night.

"No, no of course not, just glad my package got to you. I was concerned. My spirit guides advised me that you were in danger and I just needed to do something."

"Thank you." Beryl was so relieved to hear Maggie's voice that she almost broke down and cried.

"Are you alright Beryl? You sound upset."

"Oh Maggie, it is getting out of hand, I can't control the spirit, he has a will that is too strong, there is so much anger and love. I can still feel him now. Waiting for me."

"Then my guides were right. I'm sorry Beryl, I wouldn't normally interfere but when I read the stories in the papers, I had to, just had to."

"It's quite alright, I welcome your help. But how did you know where I would be?"

"I rang Phillips Publishing or whatever, anyway the secretary gave me details."

"Ah!"

"Now there are three crystals in my parcel. Merlinite, Rhyolite and Spinal. The Merlinite I have threaded on a leather lace, if you wear that round your neck it will help heal past-life and present-life, balancing the energies of both conscious and sub-conscious, healing any rift there might be. With the other two stones, just before you go on stage, meditate with one in the left hand and one in the right, doesn't matter which. The Rhyolite will help you to deal calmly with the spirit and the Brown Spinal will cleanse your aura and ground you. Using these together like this will help rejuvenate your energy, re-aligning your chakra. If you put the Merlinite on now you will start to feel its energy working with yours."

Beryl placed the phoned on the counter and did as instructed. A shiver ran through her spine and a sense of ease coursed through her, immediately relieving her aching mind.

"They are powerful."

"When you use them correctly they can be most effective and should certainly help you gain control. Just be careful though as there are no guarantees with anything."

"Thank you Maggie. I feel much better already. I feel that I have the strength that I need. Is that Sapphire I can hear purring? She is loud."

"Certainly is, she has just had her breakfast. How is Cyril? I do have to confess I did a little searching for him too and I think love is close by, but he does need to open is heart to it."

"He is fine. One couldn't ask for a better nephew. There is one girl he is keen on but I think, unfortunately, that date with Valerie knocked what little confidence he had and now he won't ask her out. Well, that's how I read it, he hasn't actually spoken to me about it. Young love eh?"

"Love will always find a way. Oh, there is one other thing."

"What's that?"

"This spirit, I remember when we last spoke you said he felt familiar to you. Well, my spirit guides can confirm this, especially Michael, he says that the bond is a maternal one."

"A maternal one?! I don't get it. That's impossible."

"I know, and you know my guides have never been wrong."

"Yes, yes, I know." Beryl was confused. "I don't suppose they know where Shelbourne is do they?"

"Unfortunately not. How many more days have you got left?"

"We are quitting today. Going home. I can't do this anymore. This Mark is too strong.

"But Beryl, he wont let you go. My guides say this is the only way." Beryl stood speechless, she had felt such relief that they were going, and now Maggie was saying she had to finish.

"Beryl, you still there?"

"Yes, yes." She said timidly.

"I'm sorry to be the bearer of bad news."

"It's alright. I understand." Beryls mind raced. She felt better, more at ease with Maggies gift but apprehension still rode her.

Anyway, it has been a great relief to talk to you, and thank you for your gift. You have certainly put my mind at rest. I feel a lot lighter already, ready to face the world at large again."

"You're welcome. Call me if you need to talk. Anytime."

"I will. Bye." Beryl replaced the receiver and studied her package, lifting each crystal up and feeling the energy course through her.

'A maternal bond' she thought!

47

"You alright Auntie?" Beryl hurriedly put the crystals back in the box and smiled at her nephew. "Yes. Yes I think I am. How do you feel after your hot bath?" she said brightly, her mind still uneasy at the thought of continuing.

"Better, still a bit stiff."

A sullen Peter appeared on the stairs.

"Morning," he grunted, his mind still racing from last night.

"Yes, it is." Was the stern reply from Cyril and the three walked to the breakfast room where Mr Arnold directed them to a table.

"Mr Arnold, can you charge that telephone call to my room please."

Peter looked haughtily at Beryl, who didn't elaborate. As the three sat down there was an awkward silence. They all noticed that Mrs Arnold was conspicuous by her absence. A strange, unsettled, quiet filled the room with the normal hubbub of conversation gone. The two other guests that had so inexplicably been drawn into the charade, sat at their separate tables, refusing to even glance in Beryl's direction. They ate at such a pace that one almost spilled his tea over his cereal. It was apparent no one wanted any contact, each overcome by a nervous energy.

Finally, the deadlock was broken.

"Peter," Beryl stated, with a new confidence. Peter looked on in anticipation, he had an idea what was coming. "I have decided to carry on with this tour." She glanced at Cyril as his face dropped in shock. It was not what he had expected. Beryl placed a reassuring hand on Cyril's, who was too dismayed to react. "It appears that this Mark has something to say and whatever we think, or do, he will not give up. He has chosen me. I don't know why, but it is so. Now there is only one way forward as I see it. To carry on."

Cyril withdrew his hand and threw his napkin down on

the table, stood up and left the breakfast room. Peter's looked surprised, his mouth half open.

Beryl continued, saddened by Cyril's exit. "I guess that is alright with you Peter?" she said to the man, who sat dumfounded. When he had woken he thought he would have to apply some pressure to get Beryl to continue, but here she was, agreeing so willingly. Jubilation sang its chorus to him, and he drank the remainder of his tea as if it was the best champagne, until his own concerns started to eat at him, making him wonder, 'maybe he wouldn't sit on the stage whilst Beryl performed, instead he'd take up a position at the back of the hall, where it might be safer, yes that would be best, distance'.

The Salvation Army Hall, Heswell

Cyril sat in the dressing room with his aunt, it was not very often that he sulked, refusing to speak, but he felt angry and betrayed. Her decision, her change of heart, hit him like a bullet. He had stormed out of the B&B and gone for a walk to calm down, but the further he walked the more wound up he became. Time had rolled on and he had almost made them late for the journey to the next venue. He had toyed with the idea of not showing up at all, but he just didn't have the strength to go through with it.

The journey had been a quiet one, all lost in their own thoughts. Checking into the B&B had been done with the minimal of conversation and now at the hall after a small tea, again, eaten in silence, they were ready for the evening.

Beryl had an air of confidence about her which Cyril couldn't help but silently note, she appeared brighter, more awake, more at ease. Guilt racked him, he should at least talk to her and, as he tumbled over the words in his head, the door sprang open.

"Ready?" Peter appeared less confident than previously. The book signing session had gone well but now the main event was here, a little trepidation crept into his bones.

"Yes, Peter we are ready. Aren't we Cyril?" Beryl replied, without the slightest hint of hatred or malice.

"Yes," Cyril uttered sullenly.

"Good," Peter said, and left.

"Don't fret Cyril, I think I know what I am doing. That was Maggie I spoke to earlier and she has helped me a great deal. Please don't be upset with me, I know what I said last night."

"But..." Cyril spoke hastily, but was interrupted by Beryl.

"I know, I know. And it must seem odd to you. There isn't anything that I can say that will explain my reasoning or what I feel. Mark is a part of me somehow. I know that makes no sense but I feel it deep inside." Cyril looked at his aunt, he had seen how withdrawn she had been, how exhausted and, after finally agreeing to put this behind her, she was facing it head on, against his better judgement and instincts. "Please trust me, Cyril. I need you with me. I need to know you support me."

"I." The words got lost, and he smiled reluctantly. "I'll go and get ready." He didn't understand, his own dreams of writing under his own name lacked the pull that they once had. He just wanted the quiet life again.

Peter's usual opening remarks were somewhat less enthusiastic compared to before and as Beryl eased onto the stage, he took his usual place forgetting to leave the stage as he had promised himself. Beryl started and dread filled him.

48

I gulped, as through the bright lights I saw another five wolves walking towards us. Where had they come from? As good as I was beginning to think we were, I didn't think we couldn't handle that many. The outlines of the wolves' shadows looked as though they were armed and ready for action.

Forrester was on the ground barely moving, the blood loss from his amputated hand making him weak. I could feel his life-force fading.

Smithie stood aimlessly, he had shot Grant. He had not been able to stop it, a hidden force making him do its bidding. He dropped the gun and it clattered on the ground.

"The harder they come, the harder they fall." Whispa's voice echoed inside my head again.

"We can do this, we are the power of four," Scratch added.

Concentrating hard on the guns that Smithie and Forrester no longer had, I became at one with them, almost hypnotised by them, sensing their being, feeling their cold metal and residual energy, the odour of smoky debris from the spent cartridges caught in my nose. Consuming the power my Brethren offered, I let their raw energy encompass me, taking me to a higher plane.

I breathed each gun, treated each like an extension to my own being. The guns started to move on the ground, rattling at first, the metal scraping on the hard concrete. The five wolves ignored the noise, focussed intently on us, swaggering confidently.

Smithie knew better and started to turn to run. "Don't do it. They're not right, they're not."

"Shut it," the lead wolf commanded, and then pulled a gun and shot Smithie, who for an instant, stood in disbelief as the shot shredded his insides. Then, as recognition registered, he coughed up blood and mucus then grabbed his stomach. Looking down at his hands, all human life evaporated, and he fell heavily onto his knees, before crashing face down on the ground. Dead!

I breathed the guns. I was the guns. I could feel their force.

Again the guns moved, this time the noise was more apparent and *two of the wolves looked around warily.*

"That's what waits for you lot," the shooter grunted.

"We are one, Sway." Whispa was there again in my head.

Mentally feeling the pressure of the triggers being depressed, I heard two shots ring out, followed by dull thuds and grunts as two more of the wolves fell down dead.

Now they were only three.

The lead wolf briefly turned to see his comrades fall.

"What the…" were the last words he spoke as the two guns draw level with his eyes, the hammers ready to fall and expel yet another bullet from each. The lead wolf didn't look so brave as the last of his pack bolted. How could they explain that they had seen two guns suspended in mid air, shooting their leader?

As they ran, two more explosions filled the car park. Before the wolves could get too far from us, I held them in their tracks, letting the guns fall to the ground their work done.

"Robbs, I'm stuck. I can't bloody move."

"Neivver me, Sparks."

"What's going on? Bloody hell. We gotta do something." Terror exploded in Robbs voice.

"No. Really?" Sarcasm hid the foreboding underneath.

We broke our diamond formation and approached the two wolves.

Robbs turned to face us. "Look. What do you want? If it's the goods they're there in the cars."

"We ain't come here for that," Scratch added incisively.

Whispa approached Sparks and took his chin in his right hand.

"What you gonna do?" Sparks asked in desperation.

"Never you mind." Whispa leaned in closer and withdrew Sparks' soul.

"What you done? What you bleeding done?" Scratch marked the face of Robbs, who grimaced, trying to conceal the pain, pretending to be brave.

"Payment for our Dark Lord," Scholar commented to me.

Scratch added. "Naw ya got two choices, right. Either tell us your associates and where we can find 'em, or…" Scratch laboured the point. "…or ya can be payment too. Choice is yours, 'don't care either way."

"I ain't telling you nothing. You just wait."

"Very well. Whispa?"

"Na, leave him Scratch."

"But Whisp... ah yes! Of course. Very well." Scratch marked Robbs once more, this time his skin burnt so hard he couldn't help but cry out in agony.

We left him, sobbing like a baby on the ground, surrounded by his fallen comrades.

I reflected on what we had achieved in just a few nights, the undoing of years of destruction. We were making this place safe and habitable again. We had the wolves on the run at last, our strength was their weakness. They were scared. At the grass roots we may have been just vigilantes, but the means justified the end and it felt good to be dealing it out for a change.

As we walked through the estate back to my house, now our base, and what I hoped would one day become my home again, I began to puzzle about my comrades and what had made them what they were. I sidled up to Whispa.

"Do you mind if I ask you something, Whispa?"

"You can ask anything you like. I might not ans...ah you want to know. Curiosity getting the better of you, eh? You know what curiosity did? Don't you?" Whispa looked at me with a half smile.

I didn't know how to take my Brethren, I was treated like one of them yet they knew more about me than I did about them and their beginnings. I didn't answer Whispa, preferring to let the matter rest, walking on in silence. The estate was quieter at night now. To some, the mysterious deaths and strange zombie-like wolves were a blessing that rested uneasily on their shoulders, caught between being pleased and wondering if they were the next to be struck down. So far though, they had only seen the wolves suffer.

Inside my house, at the altar they had made in my lounge, Whispa offered the fallen souls to our Dark Lord and we gave our thanks.

"Tomorrow we get a paper," Scholar stated matter-of-factly.

"Why just tomorrow? Why not previous days?" I asked.

"We need t'know what's been reported." Scratch spoke, before yawning. "Don't want to be being looked for, now does we?" Suddenly these guys were concerned about being found out. What twisted sense of morality was that? We were doing the police and the estate a favour, there was little evidence to link us to the actions and deaths. I began to think I had a twisted sense of right and wrong. Had I crossed the line?

Had I gone too far? Did I really believe this was right? Was I suffering some sort of mental breakdown?

"Dansabar Brethren 'take it easy' you are right." Whispa placed his hand on my shoulder, and I could still feel the raw energy trickling through me.

Scholar and Scratch went to their makeshift beds in the dining room. I was just about to go up when Whispa called to me.

"Sway. Come…drink with me." I stopped with one foot on the bottom tread of the stairs. Sitting at the kitchen table, Whispa opened a couple of bottles of beer using the edge of the table.

"Why do you want to know?"

The question vexed me until I remembered my own thoughts on the journey back. "Just interested, I guess. You all seem to work so well together I'm just interested, I s'ppose." I tried to cover up my nervousness.

Whispa took a swig of beer and started to talk slowly and thoughtfully. "A long time ago I had a normal life too, like you. I worked. I had a wife - she was pregnant with our first child. Nothing could be better, you know the sort of thing." He gave me a pointed look, seeing my family in my eyes. "Anyway, I worked for the council, a good job. Planning." The longing his eyes conveyed, the first real emotion he had expressed since being here.

"I didn't want much, I didn't need much, we were happy. We even went to church regularly. Then it happened, my…" He thought for a second and changed tack. "Your worst fears come true." He sat forward at the table, leaning into me. "Both things precious to you are taken away in one go." He sent a knowing look in to my eyes. "The baby came early. Then, what should have been the happiest day of my life, turned into the worst, the baby was born fine, however my wife died due to complications." Whispa gulped at his beer. "My child. My son survived for a whole week in intensive care, I even named him in the family tradition, taking our fathers' names and placing another in front. Matthew William Henry Ian Stephen Paul Austin. My father was Henry, my grandfather Ian. I always said I would abandon it when I had kids, otherwise the monogram would end up looking like an eye chart." Whispa sighed, and leaned back on his chair. "But, somehow, it seemed the right thing to do. I never held him whilst he was alive. He wasn't strong enough, and then his heart gave out."

Whispa's whole persona had changed, even his voice had softened, I let him continue.

"After that, life was a blur. I expect you know what that's like?" I drank my beer in silent contemplation. "Work gave me time to recuperate, but life didn't mean anything anymore. My home didn't seem like my home. So I went away, up North, Eardisely of all places. Just turned to a page in the map-book and drove."

Cyril couldn't believe his ears, finally a place name, and efficiently he made a separate note to follow it up later.

"I found a guest house when I got there, Punters', Hunters', something or other, I don't remember, it was a long time ago now." He snapped his fingers and smiled. "Happy Home Guest House." He paused, "I remember what happened next, quite clearly." Whispa stared at me intensely, before continuing.

49

"I'd been there for about five nights and was feeling, more at peace, shall we say; the landlady had made me really welcome and seemed to have an understanding about her. She let me talk about my wife, which helped me come to terms with my loss. Sometimes, with a stranger, it is easier to talk openly. They don't pre-judge you. Anyway, I was going to leave, and had just eaten breakfast when I saw the landlady." Whispa paused in thought. *"Elizabeth was her name. A lovely lady. Anyways this other woman, another guest, focussed her attention on me."* Whispa leaned in, pointing his beer at me *"Looked at me as though she knew me. I'd never seen her before in my life. She placed a firm, cold hand on my shoulder and then studied my face, like I was some sort of specimen. It was very strange.*

Up to this point I hadn't noticed a man lying on the floor, his shirt covered in blood. I remember feeling quite scared, I had just lost my wife and child and thought I was going to be joining them. Maybe that would have been best? When she finally spoke she called me by my names. All of them." Whispa paused, and gulped at his beer. *"William Henry Ian Stephen Paul Austin. That chilled me to the bone. Not many people would have a name like that. Would they?"*

"No s'ppose not but how did that lead you into...."

"She told me to join my wife and grabbed me by the throat. See." Whispa stopped and twisted his head slightly revealing tiny finger nail size scars on his neck, both sides. He then looked at me for the longest time, his dark eyes searching my soul, before abruptly changing tack. *"I think that's enough talk for one night."* Downed his beer and started to leave.

"But what happened? What about Scholar and Scratch?"

"Let's just say divine intervention eh? And their story is for them to tell."

Beryl remained standing as Mark left her, her strength obvious, no longer the puppet she had been. She turned to face Cyril, who took a couple of seconds to finish his notes. She smiled and he couldn't stay mad at her any longer, it was pleasing to see a glimpse of how things used to be.

Peter strolled confidently to the centre of the stage, relieved that no one had been drawn into the evening, especially himself, encouraging applause from the audience.

"Thank you, thank you. Ladies and gentlemen, there are books available at the back, we are also accepting pre-orders for this latest offering."

Cyril picked up his pad and pencils and walked off stage with Beryl, beaming at the transformation, back to her old self.

"We have a place name now Eardisely. It is so good that things are back to normal." Cyril was finding it hard to contain his happiness.

"They certainly are. Now come on let's go back to the B&B, I could murder a cup of tea."

Friday 3rd November 1978
The Village Hall, Wem

The hall was buzzing with energy, the scraping of chairs echoed around the stone walls. The bookstall was already doing a steady trade. Beryl was busy with autograph hunters, who eagerly queued to ask questions and get her signature emblazoned across the covers of her two books.

"Beryl Wallace, which is your favourite group, Thin Lizzy or Deep Purple?" A keen young man asked, thrusting a copy of Anne Farmer at her.

"I'm sorry, I don't know who you mean."

"What music do you listen to?" he asked.

"A little bit of classical, Beethoven or Mozart, sometimes Strauss…"

"How about Pomp and Circumstance?" another man interjected.

"How do you get your ideas for your books?" A woman spoke, trying to push her way through to get autographs on copies of 'Anne Farmer' and 'Justice for John Johnson'.

"They are not ideas, they are true stories." Beryl scrawled another signature across the cover as requested.

"What's the title of the next book? Another woman asked, passing her a copy of 'Anne Farmer'.

"Where do you go on holiday?" Came another question before she had time to answer the first.

"What car do you drive?" a tall, thin man asked.

The sea of faces grew thicker as questions were shot at her in quick succession, not giving her time to answer all of them.

"Please ladies and gentleman give my aunt a chance to answer." But Cyril's voice was lost in the chorus of questions.

Tracy was watching Cyril, who was standing behind his aunt, as best she could, as she and Adele busied themselves keeping stock replenished. When he noticed her glances, his cheeks turned crimson. Tracy still hoped he would ask her out, even though he seemed tied to Beryl's apron strings. She couldn't place what she fancied about him as he was far too much of a mummy's boy for her liking, but she couldn't fight the sometimes lustful feelings she had for him. She wondered if she would have to make the first move, although she couldn't be any more blunt, and she was sure he liked her.

Flushed with success, Peter surveyed the hall and, despite earlier occurrences which he had conveniently sent to the farthest reaches of his memory, was pleased with himself.

"How are things, Adele?"

"We are running low on 'Anne Farmer'. As for 'Justice for John Johnson', it's not doing as good but still selling well."

"Any pre-orders?"

Tracy butted in. "Had thirteen so far today which brings the total to…" She flicked through the order book "…279 so far."

"Not bad."

"Actually, Ad, 'John Johnson' is sold out. I got the last box out of the van earlier." Tracy informed Adele.

"No, there are two more boxes in the van. Aren't there?" Adele replied.

"No, we took those out the night before last."

"Sorry Peter, then we need those as well. As for Jack Friday – he is not doing so well, not really the crowd for spy thrillers. Gary Hatcher is going well, still got plenty here though. Oh and…" Adele scanned a pile of boxes stacked behind her. "…

Margaret Miller, we are almost out of hers. Can you think of any others Trace?"

"Peter Donald – 'Pictures of Avalon' we are okay, 'Hunting the Icon' we are low on, I think one more box." Tracy glanced around her. "One…mmm…yes, just one more box. As for Francis Ingle – 'A night by the Loch', 'Presence in the Scullery' and 'Mary Beth' all fine. Have you seen anymore of Harry Zenith, Ad?"

"No."

"We need some more of his books then, Peter."

"I'll get some more sent up for tomorrow." Peter turned to leave.

"Oh, Peter, Craig Phoenix, 'Ushered', is all gone, and 'Soulshadow', we've just got what's left on the table."

"Thanks girls. You're doing a tremendous job."

"Thanks." They spoke in unison, before returning their attention back to the waiting customers.

Peter walked behind the table, where Beryl was book-signing, smiling pleased with himself.

The papers had painted tall tales, they hadn't spoken favourably about Miss Wallace, except to say she could certainly create a story so cleverly woven that it grabbed you, and provided an entertaining evening, even if it wasn't true. They had done their own investigations about Shelbourne which had proved fruitless. However, it didn't seem to bother the audience.

At this rate, Peter knew the new book would become a best seller, very few had heard the whole story, the summaries Peter provided merely introduced the characters, whetting appetites. The possessions that had been witnessed had been interpreted as well-choreographed displays that only enhanced the evenings.

Tonight, Peter noticed familiar faces amongst the crowd, people drawn in and now following the tour to find out more. Two clergymen walked through the doors and caught his attention; he watched as they went to the stall, one picking up a copy of 'Soulshadow', whilst the other picked up 'Anne Farmer', scanning the preamble on the back, then flicking through the pages, before putting the books back and picking up others. They then watched the audience taking their places as they chose to stand to one side of the hall.

Peter checked his watch, it was time. He went over and reminded Cyril, who tapped Beryl's shoulder, before announcing to the crowd of autograph hunters that she needed to prepare. Beryl signed a few more copies before retiring to the dressing room to prepare.

As soon as Peter stepped on stage silence consumed the audience.

"Ladies and gentlemen, welcome to Wem Village Hall. Beryl Wallace will be joining us in a moment." A few of the new audience members looked on expectantly, not quite sure what to expect, some had contemplated the idea that she too was just a spirit that was visible to all. "But let me just provide you with an understanding of the story so far…" Peter's role had grown dramatically over the tour, as the story developed. His story-telling enthusiasm grew as the memory of his own involvement receded to the back of his mind.

Finally, he was ready to introduce Beryl. The audience applauded, some more vigorously than others, they were the ones who had attended previously. As Beryl walked on stage she could sense Mark nearby but after the last night was not concerned.

50

I'd seen a different side of Whispa but still he hadn't really answered the questions that were burgeoning me all the time. Who were my mysterious guests? What about their past? How did they meet?

I stood up and looked out of the kitchen window, the bodies of the wolves still lay on the ground next door, in Jim and Eileen's garden. For a nanosecond a hint of pity ran through me, even a bit of compassion that maybe they had just been unlucky throughout their lives. But it was just that, a brief hint. Like everyone, they had choices, they chose their path and knew the difference between right and wrong. They had to pay – it was the consequence of their decisions.

I turned and wandered through the house. At the dining room door, I paused and listened to rhythmic snoring. It seemed strange to me, that they shared a room, there was plenty of space in this house for a room each. In some ways I felt like an outsider, but in others, felt that I belonged.

As I made my way upstairs, I thought of all those times when I had been woken in the early hours of the morning to the sounds of the wolves destroying something, something of mine. It wasn't personal, they destroyed every possession that anyone owned, with no discrimination. That seemed to be in the past and I was pleased the tables were turning, too late for some though. If only the jobs would come back, then maybe things could be so much better.

In my daughter's room I lay down looking at the ceiling, feeling calm and relaxed, I was not tired and sleep would not come. My mind painted the plain surface with pictures of my family, such happy times, and I let them consume me for a few hours.

It was Clare's third Christmas (when she spent more time playing with the boxes than the actual gifts) and because the kids had got up so early, they were flagging by about seven, and Clare actually fell asleep in one of the boxes. I carried her upstairs, her warm body against mine, her head resting on my shoulder. She murmured with each movement but didn't wake up. I put her in her favourite pyjamas and gave her Mincemeat to cradle, then listened to her sleeping for what *like felt like hours.*

Samantha eventually came up carrying Joshua, who had fallen asleep on the settee, he was quite big and she struggled with him, but it was funny to see. After she had placed him in his bed she came into me.

"You can leave her you know, she'll be alright," she said softly, wrapping her arms around me, kissing the back of my neck. "You silly fool."

"I know. That's why you love me, though."

Samantha changed her tone. "I wouldn't go that far, I am just waiting for something better to come along."

"Oh, are you now?"

"Yes, someone extremely good looking, and incredibly good in bed." I turned to see her flirtatiously undo the top button on her dress.

"Not in front of the kids, they're innocent," I playfully replied

Samantha came in close and whispered in my ear. "It's alright she's asleep, and I might be if you don't come and join me next door. I thought we could do a little more practising." We stepped towards the bedroom door and I saw the silhouette of her breasts under her dress and felt myself getting aroused. "Unless you have something else to do? Which is fine. I'll please myself." She slipped her hand into her dress.

"Well, since you put it like that." I walked to the door and edged her out into the hall, closing the door to Clare's room. "I think the news is on about now."

"You want to watch the news?" Samantha's demeanour changed instantly.

"Well, there was an item about Scotland."

"About Scotland?" She stared into my eyes, she knew I was playing with her and changed tack again, taking my hand and placing it inside her dress. "So you don't want to have a little fun then?"

"Well I suppose I could be persuaded."

"Persuaded eh? And how would I go about that?" She eased in closer to me and kissed my neck. "Like this maybe, or..." She unbuckled my jeans, pulling the zip open, before rubbing me gently.

"Yes, that might work." I felt her lips tenderly touch mine, like a sweet intoxicating wine.

"Might it now? You sure?" She led me into our bedroom closing the door after first pushing me onto the bed. What a great way to end Christmas day.

***

Upon waking the next morning, I was surprised that the memory of that Christmas still lingered and as daylight filled the room, I decided I ought to decorate - a new start, a new life, a promise of something better.

Realisation took a hold of me and I knew that whatever I did would never bring them back.

A lonely tear rolled down my cheek. I had cried so much that there was very little left, so I just lay in my bed sorrowful and weary of the world I lived in, hoping for an end, waiting for daylight to break through the dirty windows.

Downstairs, an hour later, after I had managed to find some motivation, I found my guests sitting round the kitchen table with a pile of newspapers, all busy reading. Without a word I switched on the kettle and joined them.

The national newspapers hid the stories of Shelbourne amongst the various trivial matters. It was not big news for them, a local problem for local people. However, they had to take notice of the incidents of late which had been passed along the chain, gaining interest with every 'Chinese whisper'. The headlines couldn't be more vague - 'Gangland victim torn apart – girlfriend left too frightened to talk', to them it seemed gang warfare was at large on Shelbourne. Another paper reported, 'Mysterious infection leaves one person in a coma'. The sadistic side of me smiled, 'just desserts'. Local newspapers ran the stories on the front pages, they gave the victims names and families, made them into human beings, enraging me, How could they be sympathetic to the wolves? They were the lowest of the low. My blood boiled when I read the quotes from crying, loving parents saying 'how wonderful their son or daughter was'. A tainted picture, painted to mislead the rest of the world, only the dialogue indicating their lack of education.

Very few of the reports actually said the police were looking for anyone in connection with the crimes, there was a plea for witnesses, but that was it. Shelbourne was a place the rest of the world hoped would swallow itself up. Everyone would kill everyone else, innocent or guilty, it made no difference. The innocent casualties were just unfortunate weights on the scales of justice.

The police normally knew who the perpetrators were, knew who was involved, but also knew they couldn't do anything. It made me smile, knowing they wouldn't suspect me and my Brethren. It was highly unlikely the wolves would give any details anyway, they dealt their own justice and that was what had dragged this estate into this degradation in the first place, an eye for an eye, a tooth for a tooth. If I had any guilt in me, then I couldn't say. Were we just adding to the problem, just another faction to the cooking pot? But I saw us as the cure that would finally eradicate the poison.

Some things were lost forever, but hope wasn't. Hope was just hiding until it was safe to come out again. In my mind I had to believe that or else lose my sanity as well.

"You think in ideals." Whispa spoke in response to my thoughts, looking at me inquisitively, as if he was going to say more.

There was a knock at the front door which surprised me. We all glanced at each other.

Uneasily, I opened it, a man with a clipboard and a name badge David Tees – Sales Director for Lite Brite Windows, offered an introduction before I remembered I had arranged for a glazing company to come and quote for repairing my broken windows. I asked him to wait, whilst I warned the others and they took refuge in the lounge, closing the door.

I'd forgotten that in one of my positive moments, when things were on the up, I had thought about replacing the boards with glass hoping it would symbolise a new era for me. I knew it would take all the cash I could haul together but, at the time, it seemed like a good idea. I didn't feel like it today, but I led him round the house to all the rooms that needed doing. I could see his disgust at the place and, that opened my eyes to how bad the place had really become. The squalor that I lived in, how different this house, this home had looked once.

"You just bought this place then, obviously needs a lot of work, shame what squatters can do, should be nice when it's done. What's the area like? Can't say I know it very well, just moved here from London. Wanted to get away from the hustle and bustle. You know?" David tried to make polite conversation.

I smiled coldly. "You're not from around here are you?" He looked at me strangely with his deep set eyes, I realised then what he had been saying. "This is, and has been my home, for nearly ten years," His head dipped, showing me the thinning crown he was trying to cover up by combing the few remaining strands over it. He pretended to read information on his clipboard, trying to hold back anymore comments. He busied himself making the necessary measurements to expedite his visit and cover his obvious embarrassment. The enthusiasm on his face gone, he believed this was a lost call. At the door, I thanked him absentmindedly for his time and he left, saying he would put a quote in the post. I knew he would be as good as his word, even if it was just to show effort.

I stood on the doorstep watching David Tees get into his car, ignoring the wolves that had been eyeing it up. He had been lucky, a few more minutes and it probably would have been taken and eventually burnt.

I studied them a little longer from my half closed door. A strange uneasiness emanated from them, making them look lethargic and less troublesome. A removal van was parked outside a house three doors to my left, another resident moving out. I didn't know them, we had never spoken. I didn't even remember seeing them.

As I turned to go back inside I noticed the wolves had disappeared from the green. A strange atmosphere lingered in the air, maybe the estate was relishing in the news stories and the lack of wolf movement.

Were the wolves scared? Had we done enough to oust them, put them on the run? I noticed parents and children walking the streets, a slight spring in their step, enjoying the respite. Whether it was temporary or permanent, no one could tell.

Feeling confident, I did something very unusual, and opened the door again to step out on to the street. I actually dared leave the door open and walk more than a few feet away from it. A smile gradually spread across my face. It felt good. The sun was trying to break through the clouds, the birds were singing, the breeze rustling the leaves on the trees. Everything we were doing was right. We were winning.

The sound of police sirens broke my reverie, the people outside stiffened. I stumbled two steps backwards into my own front garden in time to see two police cars pull up outside. My heart lurched. They knew. How? But the officers ran past my front garden and into Jim and Eileen's. They didn't hesitate, bashing in the already damaged door. I stood quietly as I remembered the night before.

Running back into the house, slamming the door behind me, I went to the kitchen window to watch the police officers standing around looking at the bodies in Jim and Eileen's garden. I rushed upstairs to get a better look. An ambulance crew turned up minutes later to take away the wolf whose soul Whispa had extricated. To the ambulance men he would just appear in coma, vital signs faint. The dead ones were photographed and then taken away by the coroner.

I tried to conceal myself, but inadvertently made eye contact with an officer as he looked back at all the houses to see if anyone might have seen something. As he disappeared from view I knew what was next and, sure enough, there was a hammering at the door. I ran into the lounge where my guests were.

"I think you'd better answer the door." Whispa spoke before I could get a word out.

"Can't you do anything? Scholar?" I pleaded, I didn't want to answer questions as I was sure guilt would be written all over my face.

"Just answer the door, we'll stay in here," Whispa bid. I looked at my guests despondently then reluctantly went to the front door.

51

"Afternoon sir, may we have a word please?" It was a rhetorical question.

"Sure," I answered, my cheeks feeling flushed.

There was an awkward pause. "May we come in?" I looked at them, trying to decide what to answer.

"I'd rather not…"

They stepped forwards, forcing me backwards, until they were in. "We won't keep you long sir, we just want to ask you a few questions." Their faces registered their amazement at the state of my house, the threadbare, stained carpet that barely clung to the stairs, the wallpaper peeling, where there was some.

I walked the officers through to the kitchen, offering them a cup of tea - they refused, not surprisingly, when they saw the kitchen. They didn't even want to sit down.

"I'm PC Forster and this is PC Ghorelli. You live here alone?"

I thought and fumbled for my answer. "Yes," which just aroused their suspicion of me further.

"Do you know anything about the victims next door?" PC Ghorelli continued. "Did you see or hear anything?" They knew I knew, yet had not reported it, they probably wondered why.

"No," I answered again more assuredly this time.

"Were you in last night around midnight? That was what the coroner said wasn't it?" PC Forster threw in, with the second question directed at his partner, who nodded.

"Yes, I was probably asleep by then, I don't recall hearing anything out of the ordinary." I'd found my patter, although I could sense the nervousness in my voice. "You know what this estate is like? It's unusual if there aren't any untoward noises or anything."

"So you did hear something?" Ghorelli interjected quickly.

"No, nothing I was asl…"

"But you just said that it wasn't unusual if you didn't hear anything."

"Yes...but I was asleep." Mild panic swept through me, they were trying and succeeding in making me trip up. Resolutely, I added. *"It's amazing what you can sleep through after a while."*

"I'm sure it is." There was another awkward pause, and I saw PC Ghorrelli look past me to the lounge doorway and I was awaiting a question about my guests. *"So you can't tell us anything about..."*

"No," I butted in before he finished his statement come question.

"Well." He grimaced and glanced at his colleague. They knew I was keeping something from them. They couldn't prove anything and they certainly weren't that interested in ascertaining what had happened to the wolves. *"Thank you for your time...sir."* They hesitated by the lounge door, looking at my guests. *"Don't suppose you gentlemen saw or heard anything?"* PC Forster quizzed, knowing full well what the answer would be.

Scratch & Scholar shook their heads whilst Whispa stood up and looked the officer square in the eye, before answering the question with an almost menacing, *"No."*

That would be noted somewhere for future reference. I knew the officers would keep a close eye on us now, if they had nothing better to do.

Beryl stood proud, Marks power affecting her less as her strength appeared to be growing, she had taken control again, pleasing Cyril. The evening had passed uneventfully. Relief showed on Peters face too, as he took centre stage to address the audience.

"Ladies and gentlemen, please show your appreciation for Beryl Wallace." The applause was slow in coming, disappointment hung like a cloud.

"Well that was a disappointment Ida, papers says she acts it all out."

"Obviously we're not good enough, they're from the south."

"The great divide eh, Ide? Ere, what's the time?"

"'Bout nine-thirty, how about a quick drink?"

"You're on."

For Beryl and Cyril, this was what the evenings were actually about, the telling of a story and that was all.

Saturday 4th November 1978
St Jeremy's School Hall, Eardisely

Feeling more relaxed after the previous night's events, Cyril confidently walked onto the stage in readiness for Beryl's entrance. Emotionally lighter, confident that nothing untoward would happen, he had left Beryl preparing whilst he set up on stage. Staring to the back of the hall, as he waited, to where Tracy was busy with Adele restocking books, he imagined kissing her, feeling her body hugged close to his, suddenly she looked up and smiled at him, the pencil he had been playing with flicked out of his hands onto the floor in front of Peter, who was joining him on stage.

Peter picked it up and handed back to Cyril. "Yours?"

"Yes, thanks."

"I think we are about ready, don't you?" It was a rhetorical question and Cyril didn't answer just looked back to Tracy, wondering if she could read his thoughts. Shaking it from his mind he poured himself a glass of water, noticing that the same two clergymen that had attended the previous night were back. Father James had said someone would be sent, but when the event finished the previous night they had disappeared before he could approach them, making him think that they were not the ones. Perhaps, just a couple of curious clergymen making sure their congregation was not being corrupted.

Cyril left the stage using the four steps at the front and raising his hand to Peter, who was about to say something to him, implying he would only be a minute, leaving Peter standing resentful at the rudeness. The two priests watched as Cyril approached, the taller of the two held out his hand.

"Mr Hewington, I presume?" Cyril nodded. "I'm Father Frederick and this is Father David, who is observing. Father James told us your concerns." Father Frederick paused as a couple of members of the audience took an interest in the conversation, he made eye contact and smiled at them, they sharply turned away. "As I was saying, Father James told us your concerns and asked us to," he paused thoughtfully, "assist if we could."

"Thank you. But why didn't you introduce yourselves last night?" The question sounded more impatient than Cyril had intended.

"We needed to observe, Mr Hewington."

"Please call me Cyril."

"Cyril. It is foolish to act too quickly, irrationally, unless danger is imminent. And whilst there was definitely a presence here, I did not feel any unrest. I did not feel anyone was in any real danger. Your aunt?" Father Frederick dipped his head, raising his eyebrows questioningly, Cyril agreed. "Well, she seemed to be in control…"

"But the previous nights, it was different." The words rushed out, his pitch rising, enforcing his concern.

"Maybe so," Father Frederick offered. "But I can only act upon what I see and feel." Father David tapped Father Fredrick on the arm, gently indicating that Peter was about to start. "We will speak again later. I would like to meet your aunt, if I may?"

"Yes, yes, of course." Cyril walked back to the stage, a little flustered and disappointed by the priests. He didn't know what he had expected from the clergymen, but some sort of action, yet he knew that last two nights had been better, more like it should have been, even if it had disappointed the audience somewhat.

My house was now going to be under close scrutiny. With all the mysterious 'goings-on' on the estate, the police seemed to be taking a new and rather keen interest. Before, they just let things run. I was sure a few were on the take, how else could so many things go unresolved? Maybe that was how the estate worked, helping prevent ugly clashes between the wolves and the police. The police would do what they had to when someone had the guts to involve them, but they knew not push too far with the investigation as there were some powerful packs on the estate. Squealing to the police usually resulted in some swift retribution by the wolves.

Sometimes an officer would try to help beyond the bounds of his duty. Temporarily it made a difference, but generally proved detrimental in the end. One officer now lived life in a wheelchair, permanently brain damaged. *The only other officer to help was so badly beaten that it took three days for him to die.*

Ironically, now the tables were turning, the police seemed concerned for the wolves' safety even though the wolves had their own brand of justice. Hypocrisy! Look after the tormentors when they are being threatened. What a twisted reality I lived in. It sickened me to think that this was the way life had become, but pleased we were doing something about it.

After a few hours we were on the streets again, our mission well and truly underway. I didn't reflect on what the outcome for the estate could finally be, only what I wanted it to be. As if, by some magick, it would bring back my family and return us to the happy state we were in, so long ago. Disillusioned? - I certainly was, maybe even a little crazy, because no matter what I did, it would never change anything in the past, things would never be as they were.

Beryl stood on the stage and stared thoughtfully at the back of the hall as if remembering a poignant moment from long ago. A minute ticked slowly by, causing Peter to shift uneasily in his chair. Two more minutes went by and the audience could be heard whispering.

"Is that it?"

"I don't know, Mike."

Leaving via the back door we headed to the garage blocks at the end of my garden, alert and wary of watchers. As we walked the previous night's route we became aware of increased police presence on the estate. A two man, armed, foot patrol strolled across one of the greens. For the first time it seemed some good was being done around Shelbourne and the police were getting involved. Maybe they felt the unrest had finally come home to roost and were worried the fine line between order and chaos was going to be crossed. I wondered how many were on the payroll of the drug dealers? Maybe the Police Commissioner hated the Shelbourne name appearing in national newspapers, even in small articles, for whilst it remained hidden from the public, he could ignore it. Now it was gaining notoriety, something had to be seen to be done.

It never occurred to me that the four of us were quite a distinctive group, I almost considered us as being invisible. We walked with purpose and conviction, Scholar always at the back, continually making notes in his Grimoire; Scratch leading, he always knew where to go, Whispa and myself were the second row.

We went further afield tonight past where we had been last night, and into the outer reaches of the estate until we were standing outside 'The Brokers Arms', a pub with a reputation. I had blocked it out of my memory some years before, when it had started to turn bad and there had been rumours that the gangs used it to recruit people (although this was never confirmed). The rumours had ruined this once nice family-run pub which sat nestled in a piece of ground shaped like a bowl, the once well kept gardens and children's play area now looked nothing more than scraps of waste ground.

A black BMW screeched to a halt outside the pub and two large wolves got out, opened the boot, and to my astonishment, lifted out Robbs, the wolf we had let go the previous night. His battered bloodied body and torn clothes showed that he had been beaten to within an inch of his life. They placed him on the ground in the headlights of the car.

52

In the hall two male members of the front row stood up and assumed the roles of the two in the story and then, lifting a third member from her seat, dragged her to just in front of the apron of the stage.

Cyril heard the scraping of chairs and his heart sank, glancing first at Peter, who showed the first signs of terror, then to Father Frederick, who watched curiously not wanting to get involved, he silently pleaded with Father Frederick for help but to no avail.

A third wolf with cropped bleached hair, smartly dressed in a linen jacket, pressed trousers and shiny black brogues got out of the driver's side, Gold jewellery dazzled in the only streetlight that had survived vandalism. Bleached-hair walked into the pub after first checking the gun in the trouser waistband.

Another member of the audience, a woman, stood up and the rest of the audience began to smile, thinking how daft the people looked acting out the story. Yet pleased that this part of the show, that had been so talked about in the press, was back. Cyril nervously carried on writing, anxious to do something but not knowing what.

A few minutes later Bleached-hair walked out with two scrawny young wolves, who looked like identical twins, long dank hair hung down to below their shoulders, their bony features giving them a skeletal appearance as if fabric had been stretched across bone. Bleached-hair walked them over to Robbs who still lay on the ground. Something was said by Bleached-hair and the twins nodded vigorously then backed away.

Two more people stood up and joined the acting arena, replicating everything as it was being told. Father Frederick became wary as he sensed an ominous threat in the hall, never had he witnessed such a possession before. Was this a trick, a cleverly prepared farce by Peter? Nothing sinister had happened thus far, but with his foot he checked the black doctor's bag at his feet and turned to acknowledge Father David.

Bleached-hair ordered the two bodyguards to lift Robbs up so he was standing. Then raising the gun to Robbs' forehead and, without hesitation, Bleached-hair pulled the trigger, splattering bone and blood over the bodyguards. The shot rang out in the night sky like a shockwave.

The member of the audience who had assumed the role of Robbs collapsed on the floor. The audience craned their necks to see her lying on the floor, motionless.

The residents of the pub knew better than to come outside. The twins flinched as they heard the shot, like most, they probably talked big, acted big, yet when their lives were on the line they were as frightened as the next person.

Whatever we had started, it was being finished. There was only one solution in the wolves' world, death, or more precisely, execution. A show of strength always managed to make the errant ones toe-the-line.

The bodyguards handed the twins two milk bottles with rags dangling from them. It took a whole second for me to realise what was about to happen. The shooter then pointed the gun to the head of one of the twins. Kill or be killed appeared to be the choice that was being forced upon them. This was obviously what the police were afraid of, retaliation. Each twin was handed a cigarette lighter and reluctantly they lit the rags. Even at this distance I could sense their fear, fear for their own lives and the lives of their mates in the pub. The seconds seemed like hours as the flames surged up the rags, hesitantly the twins threw the bottles. One smashed on the front door of the pub, immediately smothering it in a shroud of flames, the second bottle crashed through a window and screams emanated from inside as the bottle broke, shooting liquid flames in all directions. Fear coursed through me for those inside. Did they really deserve this? Then I questioned myself; Hadn't I started this? Is this not what I wanted? The wolves tearing themselves apart, destroying each other until they were all gone.

We were the cure.

The flames engulfed the building rapidly as the alcohol inside caught light, sending out tentacles of fire, exploding the windows. Any second I expected to see people run out through the front doors. Then, as the first appeared, clothes alight, he was shot in the knee, causing him buckle and fall to the ground, screaming in agony. The wolves didn't put him out of his misery, only watched on mercilessly. The twins moved as if to aid the dying man but found guns directed at them and knew they had to watch, helplessly.

Another man started through the doors but quickly darted back inside as he heard a shot explode and narrowly miss him. Trapped. I wondered if there was a back door and, as if reading my mind, a wolf was sent round to the back of the pub.

The front doors wavered as the people trapped inside deliberated whether to make a break for it or die in the inferno. Finally, another braved the gauntlet. The end was inevitable. I caught myself reacting, as if to run and help them.

Scratch eyed me and I lowered my head in shame. I couldn't get the screams out of my head. Chairs broke the remaining windows letting plumes of black smoke waft into the night sky. Another wolf made a break for it through a smashed window but again was shot.

Sirens could finally be heard over the ferociousness of the flames and mini explosions, as bottles of spirits caught fire. When the sound of sirens reached the assassins' ears they coolly got into the car and drove off, leaving the twins standing, stricken at the devastation and deaths they had caused.

Abruptly, the car did a handbrake turn, stopped and the bodyguards got out and shot the twins before they realised what was happening. One of the bodyguards clocked us as he got back in the car, he barked a command and, at full acceleration, the car swung round, the headlights dazzling us. As it screeched to a halt in front of us we stood our ground, my heart pounding inside me. The two bodyguards got out and approached us menacingly. Both seemed taken aback that not one of us paid homage to their presence. The bodyguard on the left pulled the gun from his waist band and placed it to Scratch's forehead.

"You have two choices, you saw nothing. Or you die. The decision is yours." The three statements came slowly but beckoned only one answer.

Scratch said nothing, boldly holding his ground, looking deep into the bodyguard's eyes.

"Did you hear what I said? You deaf or something?"

Whispa stepped forward and brushed the gun to one side. "If you were going to shoot, you should have done it by now."

Immediately the bodyguard to the right drew his gun and pointed it at Whispa.

"You got balls mate. I'll give you that. But you die. Now!"

I stepped forward to take Whispa's place, grabbing the gun and pointing it straight at my own forehead, much to the astonishment of the bodyguard. Bleached-hair got out of the car.

"Just bloody shoot them will ya, we gotta get outta here." I realised then it was a woman as she screamed her command.

"I can't."

I concentrated hard on the bodyguard's eyes, penetrating his soul. I let my thoughts possess him. In one swift movement Scratch disarmed the bodyguard who had pointed the gun at him, surprising and subjugating him.

Focussing my energy on the bodyguard in front of me, I sensed his being, felt his life force, controlled his will. His eyes widened in terror as the gun slowly but surely turned on him. Inside, he fought it - I could see him fighting it, his arms shaking as the tendons stretched to their full extent then slowly pinged as he pulled the trigger twice in quick succession. The first bullet entered his right eye and the second grazed his forehead as he fell to the ground, dead.

"Do you really fink that's wise putting guns at people heads, eh?" Scratch spat out, venom in his voice, at the bodyguard he now held on the ground.

The woman, dismayed, fired off two shots at no one in particular then jumped back into the car and sped away.

I relaxed, laughing nervously, and watched as Scratch tormented the bodyguard. Little tiny scratches that burned like paper cuts, one neatly placed after the other, as the bodyguard howled in agony.

"It ain't nice is it?" Scratch added maliciously.

"What do you want?" the bodyguard spluttered out.

Scratch's voice suddenly changed. "Nothing from you, and, in one swift movement, snapped his neck.

The sirens were getting closer, but Whispa took a few seconds to take their souls, which hovered over their dead bodies, as if questioning the reality of death.

Two fire engines pulled into view, immediately followed by three police cars. We turned to walk away as a big explosion ripped the pub apart. The night sky was lit up and would be for hours to come.

A fourth police car stopped by us as we made our way back along the road, barely a hundred yards from the bodies on the ground. Out of it stepped two officers in stab vests with batons drawn.

"Up against the wall, all of you. Hands high." The command was barked and none of us proffered any resistance. They ran their hands up and down us checking for weapons, before turning us round one at a time.

"Where do you think you're going in such a hurry?" They said, believing they had caught the perpetrators.

Whispa spoke calmly. "We not going anywhere in a hurry, we just came to see what the commotion was about."

"Are you trying to joke with me?" The officer wanted to say more but there was four of us and only two of them. It was obvious the odds were against them regardless of training, and with the history of the estate and the memories of officers who had either perished or been severely handicapped for 'trying to help' they were less than confident.

"You asked a question and I answered it." The frustration showed on the officer's face, he didn't like this kind of cockiness, even if he was trying to tread carefully and not get on the wrong side of the wolves, who he supposed we were. 'We are the good guys.' I wanted to shout out but knew it was futile.

The frustration boiled over and the officer gave in. "Maybe we should take you in for questioning?" His voice was filled with subdued animosity.

"Maybe you should. What are you going to charge us with, though?" Scholar interjected calmly.

There was a mental stand-off as each sized the other up

I spoke up. "I saw a black BMW whizz off up the road but didn't get the number plate."

All focus turned to me and, in that instant, I wasn't sure if I had done the right thing. It seemed harmless and I thought would defuse the situation.

53

"A black BMW you say?" I nodded. *Both of the officers relaxed instantly and I could see that they knew who was to blame. They both sighed and walked away, but then the second officer turned back to face me again. "I know you, don't I?"*

"No," I replied sharply.

"Yeah, I do." He came in close to scrutinize my features. *"I'm sure I do. You look familiar. I'm sure it will come to me,"* and with that they quickly left. I looked round at the two dead wolves on the ground, staggered that the officers had not seen them.*

I wondered whether the police were in cahoots with the people who owned the Black BMW, or whether they just knew who she was and were not willing to push it further.

There was silence in the hall as the last note of the spirit echoed around the stone walls. The members of the public who had unwittingly got involved all looked confused. Then, an instant later all eyes fell to the woman who had played the part of Robbs, as she didn't get up. A minute went by and she still didn't move. One of the participators called out; "Is there a doctor in the house?"

Pandemonium instantly swept through the hall as people ran to the exits, not wanting to be part of it anymore.

Peter stood speechless on the stage, aghast at what he had witnessed. He hoped the lady was okay but, as a St John's Ambulance attendee saw to her, Peter could see the sadness on the attendee's face and knew that the woman that had played Robbs was dead. She looked too young to die from a heart attack.

In panic he jumped down from the stage and rolled the woman over, to the astonishment of those that had remained.

Clearly on the woman's forehead was a black mark, charred around the edges. After staring at it for a second or two he realised it was a hole, and his mind made the connection.

Stunned he commented. "A bullet hole?"

"What?" came the shocked reply from Father Frederick, who was now standing nearby.

The atmosphere chilled as a shocked silence descended on the hall. The mass exodus had caused the stall at the back to be knocked over, sending books, as well as Adele & Tracy, cascading to the floor. Recovering quickly they gathered themselves up and got busy packing the books neatly away in boxes, knowing they would not sell anymore tonight.

With the exception of the few that had witnessed the events and felt obliged to stay, and those whose curiosity had held them back, the hall was empty. The question of 'How could a woman be shot without a gun?' was on everyone's mind. Even the press representatives had left hastily, phoning the story in to their editors, this was going to be front page news, and could well be their make or break chance.

Everyone glanced at each other as they all felt the urge to know who had pulled the trigger, their minds were blank, they had no recollection of those few minutes. Father Frederick looked at the guilty party but decided that it would not be in the best interests to say anything at this time, he went to the body and said a prayer for the woman.

Beryl was comforted by Cyril and within a few minutes the emergency services had turned up. The ambulance crew only confirmed what everyone knew and stayed to help those involved suffering shock. As there had been no exit wound they were sure there was a bullet inside which would help capture the killer. All who had been unwittingly involved looked at each other questioningly, no one knowing who had done what to who, but silent accusations started to be made.

When the police arrived Peter made it his business to introduce himself,

"I'm Peter Phillips, if you have any questions then please do not hesi…"

"I'm PC Tritt and we won't," snapped the PC, who had read about these events and thought of them with contempt. "So can anyone tell me what happened? And, where's the caretaker?" The question was met with a wall of silence.

"Right, I see, like that is it."

"I'm the caretaker," said a sleepy looking man.

"Can you lock the hall please while we find out what happened."

"Are you going to be long? It's just that I have the local women's guild to set up for tomorrow."

"It will take as long as it takes," PC Tritt stated, annoyed. The caretaker walked away frustrated that it looked as though it was going to be a long night.

"Now. No one else has anything they want to say?" The other officer, PC Vickers, who had arrived with PC Tritt, let the question settle. "Looks like we are in for a long night, Terry."

"Yes. Okay, we'd better start taking statements before the DI arrives. He's gonna love this," PC Tritt concluded.

Both officers set up pairs of chairs at either side of the hall, instructing everyone else to keep quiet whilst they took statements. As they wrote down what they were told a bizarre picture started to unfold, only compounding PC Tritt's own personal views. He looked across at his colleague, who raised his eyebrows with bewilderment and shook his head to signify that he thought he was in the twilight zone.

Fifty minutes passed before the coroner turned up. In tow were DI Collins and DS Harris.

Mystified by the resumé they received from the two officers, both Harris and Collins went to look at the body, which had been covered with a couple of coats.

"It's a strange one," Harris commented.

"Definitely a bullet wound," Collins stated. "And no one heard anything or saw anything except the role playing.

"Bloody spiritual freaks," Harris muttered.

"Agree with you there," Collins said. "Right let's speak to the perpetrators. Where are they?"

"Over here." Harris guided Collins over to where Beryl, Cyril and Peter were sitting on the stage.

"So, what happened? Please tell me something different from what I've already been told," Collins said. Peter and Cyril looked at each other, whilst Beryl looked at the floor. "Nothing eh?"

"I'm sorry, it is as what has already been stated," Peter finally added.

"Great! Come on Harris see if the cloth have got anything sensible to add.

Father Frederick and Father David only confirmed the eye witness accounts.

"It's going to be a long night Harris."

A hammering at the door and a muffled shout caught everyone's attention, PC Vickers went to investigate.

"It's Simon Stiller from the Evening Standard, detective. Shall I let him in?" PC Vickers yelled.

"No," came the stern reply. "The press here already Tritt? They get worse, like scavengers, they could smell a flea on a dog's back from 200 yards." Collins remarked.

"I know. Do you want me to make a statement?" Harris asked knowing his superior would decline.

"No, let them rot outside for the moment."

"Excuse me."

"What is it? Peter isn't it?"

"Simon Stiller was here this evening, along with Gareth Johnson from the Mirror and Fred Davis from the Sun."

"Oh, great!" Collins face contorted into a grimace. "Harris, this is the lot that have been in the paper recently, some supernatural book writing hogwash or other."

"That's them," Harris curtly replied, amazed that it had taken Collins so long to realise.

"Great, that's just what we need. Let them in. And get statements." said Collins angrily.

54

Like a bunch of excited school girls the reporters rushed through the unlocked doors. Both officers rolled their eyes as the barrage of questions started almost immediately.

"SHUSH! Now I am going to say this once…" Collins raised his voice. "I said…" His voice boomed above the reporters questions. "Thank you. Now I understand you were all present when the 'unfortunate' incident happened." Simon Stiller was about to speak but was met with an intense glare. "And we will get to you shortly. However, I expect you will all say the same thing, so please be patient." He paused, knowing the next question was rhetorical, but he had to ask. "I am guessing from your absence when we arrived, you have all called this in?" The question was met with a wall of silence. "Great! The chief will love this one."

"Vickers." PC Vickers rushed over to Collins. "Take statements from this lot."

"Sir!"

Time dragged on as the formalities were taken care of. The caretaker grew impatient and paced near the door whilst Cyril started to think about how all this had begun and how he felt when Peter had shown them the finished product, 'Anne Farmer'.

***

"Well, Cyril what do you think? The final product. The culmination of your hard work."

"It's incredible." Cyril beamed, handling the book with pride, flicking the thin speckled tea-stained colour pages. He held it in his left hand and stroked the cover with his right, as if the colours needed soothing.

"Edward has done us all proud. Which is why he is very good at his work. Your thoughts, Beryl?"

Beryl sighed reservedly, then placed a hand on Cyril's back. "Well done I'm proud of you. I knew you could do it. Thank you Peter, I must say it is an impressive looking book, not a bit like I imagined." Beryl took the book from Cyril. "Anne Farmer," she whispered to herself. "I hope you like it. I hope we have served you well."

"I'm sure of it Auntie. I don't know, it just feels right, as if this is what she wanted. You always say that fate deals the hand that we have to follow. Well if Peter hadn't come in that night, last year, then we wouldn't be sitting here, would we?" Cyril hadn't realised how much this book mattered to him.

"No you're right. If only your parents could have been here to see you, they'd be as proud as me. Probably prouder."

"Cyril, why don't you go down to the warehouse, you can see the boxes of your books, I think you'll be amazed. I'm sure Tracy won't mind showing you. It's quite a sight to see for new authors."

"Do you mind?" Cyril directed at his aunt.

"Of course not." She couldn't help but feel his delight.

Cyril left the room almost at a run, the anticipation of seeing so many, of his, books in one place was nearly too much to bare.

"Peter?"

"Yes, Beryl." Peter slouched back into his chair.

"I thought I said I wanted Cyril's name on the front cover with mine, after all they are his words, not mine." Beryl's tone was cautious.

"Beryl, I had to look at this from a business perspective." He realised he was going to reap her wrath if he didn't tread carefully. "Our target audience will react better to a female name on the cover, especially as the title is female. It is something that has taken me years to learn. If Cyril's name were to appear it would create confusion."

"Peter, I have seen many collaborations on book covers and it has never confused me." Beryl's words were gentle with a tinge of forcefulness.

Peter got up and sat on the edge of his desk. "Beryl, I understand your reluctance on this point and I know we have talked about it a lot."

"Don't be condescending Peter." Suddenly Beryl had a mother's tone and it caught him off guard.

"Sorry, I wasn't trying to. I was merely trying to point out that I have a great deal of experience in these matters." Peter stood up as his voice rose. "Please, Beryl, trust me. I have insisted that Cyril gets full credit on the imprint page. Look."

"But it's on the inside. I want people to know how talented my nephew is. This is not for me." Beryl got up and walked to the window, which was in desperate need of a clean.

"They will, believe me they will, he will be with you at the book signings and you can tell everyone at the interviews."

"Book signings! Interviews! What book signings and interviews?"

"The ones I have planned to promote the book."

"I didn't agree to that."

Exasperated Peter sat down in his chair. "Beryl, in this business it is important to get out and meet your readers, it sells books. People will want to know who Beryl Wallace is. They will love the story. They will take you to their hearts. More so, when they see you. You're the face that they will trust, that can make them believe that everything in this book...," leaning forward Peter tapped the book that Beryl placed on the desk. "...is real. It was...it is going to sell this book and make the money that will enable you to help everyone you want to help."

Beryl looked sternly at Peter, or Mr Phillips as he was appearing to her now, just another businessman manipulating things, running roughshod over people's feelings. Over the last year he had managed to banish that image from her mind, but it was back like a ghost.

The door burst open and Cyril ran through.

"Auntie you have got to see this. It's amazing. I can't believe how many copies there are downstairs and they are all the same. It's incredible." Cyril picked up the copy from the desk "Can I keep this copy?" He studied the cover for the hundredth time; 'Anne Farmer' written in a garish green, the background in a blue hue, and Beryl Wallace in a plain font at the bottom. In between there was a haunting picture of a young girl.

"It's yours. Now why don't I arrange a taxi to take you home so you can celebrate?"

Silence filled the room as the atmosphere between Beryl and

Peter grew a shade darker.

"Thank you," Beryl said bitterly. Cyril, oblivious, almost danced out.

***

"How about fish and chips to celebrate Auntie?"

"It thrills me to see you so happy."

"Are you not pleased?" Cyril noticed his aunt looked down in the mouth. "You are happy about doing this aren't you?"

After a pause. "Yes." She thought about her answer a little longer. "It just seems in some way, less personal now. As if Anne would be upset having her dirty laundry shown for all to see."

"Maybe, but surely she would be happy with what we can do with the money her story makes, you know, helping more people like her. I mean that must be worth it surely."

Beryl cracked a smile. Cyril was right, it was what this project had been about, and Cyril looked truly alive for the first time since he had come to live with her. Although he had never been unhappy, but the jubilant air about him was like sunlight dancing on the early morning dew.

"Fish and chips it is. Would you mind just dropping us at the corner of Elderton Road please driver?"

"No problem," came the friendly retort.

"Let's enjoy it. It sounds as though we have a busy time ahead judging by what Peter said." Beryl looked forlornly out of the window. She hoped she was doing the right thing.

55

DI Collins was at a loss as to what he could do, no one was armed, no weapons were present, and statements had been taken. The man who had supposedly fired the invisible shot, when told, started to go into shock and the attending ambulance crew took him to hospital.

"What do you make of it Sir?" asked Harris.

"Weirdest case I have ever been to. Not much more we can do here now, so might as well let everyone go, as long as we have their details. Wait and see what the coroner says, but I think that will be pretty obvious judging by the wound."

Harris put two fingers in his mouth and whistled, quelling the hubbub that had filled the hall, all talk subsided and eyes stared at the detective.

"Right, I would like to thank everyone for their cooperation. We are going to let you all go." The caretaker sighed unexpectedly loudly. "Yes." Harris agreed. "We have your details if we need to ask you any more questions." PC's Vickers and Tritt nodded in agreement. "No point asking you lot 'not' to run with the story I s'ppose?" The question was directed at the reporters, and their lack of response confirmed what he knew.

"Oh, Miss Wallace," Collins called. "If you have any more of these events planned, may I suggest you cancel them before someone else gets hurt."

Peter answered for her. "She has, and I can assure you officer that we take every precaution possible. I'm sure there is a simple explanation for what happened tonight."

"It's Detective," came the annoyed response.

"Don't worry. I think this is the end of this PR exercise," Cyril added sardonically.

"Cyril, please."

"But Auntie."

"Cyril, leave it!" Beryl froze, all eyes upon at her, there was click from a camera as Simon Stiller took a picture, then Beryl continued talking, but it wasn't Beryl.

We walked on. I was subdued, thinking about my family and the day my wife died. The second officer had been at my house that day, he obviously had a good memory and that concerned me a little.

That was a six months after they had left me, a day I knew was going to be a bad before I even got up. I hadn't slept well. The settee's lumps and bumps were becoming uncomfortable. A month had passed since our son had been buried. Some nights, in the dark, I still cried myself to sleep. Samantha hadn't spoken to me in nearly all that time. My daughter was the only one that spoke to me and that was only if Samantha didn't grab her attention first.

That morning I left for work as normal, sad and lonely, I kissed Clare goodbye. She knew something wasn't right but she babbled on regardless, pretending, in her world, that everything was normal. I said goodbye to Samantha in the vain hope that it might break the stalemate but, as usual, I didn't get an answer.

I walked through the factory gate to the usual hustle and bustle of people talking about last night's TV and the football. Everything continued on around me, as it had done for years. I met up with Frank, a colleague, I always tried to put on a brave face but every day it was getting harder. I didn't want to let on what was really happening so I lied and made things up. People didn't really believe me. They probably didn't want to know the truth if they asked 'how are you?' so it was easier to lie and, I suppose, in some peculiar way, it made the days bearable. Whenever we were invited anywhere I made excuses as to why we couldn't go. They all knew about Joshua, sometimes I thought they were just being kind to me.

About ten o'clock an urgent meeting was called in the main canteen, 200 managers and supervisors crammed in to hear the announcement that would rock Shelbourne.

It was a bolt from the blue as we had been so busy. The factory was closing, but sales had been bad for a long time yet the inevitable had been delayed in the hope that times would change. Now the decision had been made, judgement day had arrived. 10,000 people out of work from the main source of employment for the area. It was effective immediately, and we were to relay the information to the workers on all three shift patterns. It wasn't even a case of being taken over or relocation or a few redundancies, it was just over.

The remainder of the day was like walking through treacle. People took the news so differently, some nodded acceptance, others got angry, sharing their anger with me. One threw the first thing to hand at a wall behind me, narrowly missing my head – it was a paperweight and it exploded as it hit the wall, I had almost wished that was me, others asked what were quite acceptable questions, What about my family? What about my house?

What about mine? I wanted to scream back, but no, I kept a calm demeanour throughout, almost detached.

I finally walked out of the factory gate for the last time at six o'clock in the evening, the end to a stressful, traumatic day.

I decided to drive a long route home, it was depressing at home anyway and now I had no reason to even leave in the mornings. Abruptly the whole area appeared to have accumulated a dark ominous cloud.

I remember pulling over in a lay-by and not knowing where I was, I couldn't remember the journey and I didn't care. Somehow I drove to the beach, and strolled along the promenade, the slight breeze helped to dissipate what was boiling up inside me. I sat on a bench and thought about food, but couldn't eat, hunger didn't seem to exist, I should have been ravenous having not eaten all day, but sheer despair kept it at bay. I needed divine intervention, a reason to carry on.

The thought of suicide seemed a good option, the best option for all.

Cyril looked at Peter, fear of what could befall his aunt at the mention of those words.

"Okay game's over," said Collins.

"This isn't a game," Cyril replied forcefully.

Collins grabbed Beryl's arm. "Right, if you don't stop right now you are coming down the station."

Beryl ignored the command.

"It's not her," Cyril pleaded, as Peter backed off, scared of the consequences.

I could walk into the sea and disappear for good, I knew I was thinking about it too long to go through with it. In my heart, I didn't have the strength, and thoughts of Clare and how she would feel losing her father after her brother, kept me safe. An hour passed as I watched the waves lap up onto the stony beach and then retreat, taking rafts of them with it. The time was approaching when I would have to return home and face reality, I couldn't put it off any longer.

Life seemed to be lurching horribly out of control and I needed to get it back on track. I resolved to talk to Samantha and force her to listen before we destroyed any hope of us being a family again. Our own upbringing had not been good, surely this should have made us pull together at times like these.

The only good thought I could conjure out of my redundancy was that I had been a manager and that would stand me in good stead for another job. First thing in the morning I would head to the job agency, maybe I could look at moving the family to a new town, start again with a better job, more prospects, new faces. Yes, that was it.

My heavy heart began to lighten and I was a little more jubilant by the time I headed home, charged with positive thoughts, dreams and aspirations of a better future, for us all. A new start.

56

It was nine-thirty that night when I pulled up outside our house. It looked deathly quiet. No lights, no flashing pictures from the TV. Apprehensively I put the key in the door and opened it - I was met with silence.

Frantically, I searched the house and garden. No sign of Clare or Samantha. I guessed she must have gone to a friend's house. Why should it surprise me that I didn't know? I didn't know what was going on anyway.

Hunger hit me and I searched the fridge for something to eat but instead found a beer. As I flumped onto the settee in front of the TV I toasted myself 'Cheers – isn't life just so bloody crap sometimes'. The '10 o'clock' news announced the job losses, talk about rubbing it in. I switched off the TV and listened to the silence, the emptiness, the house breathing, letting time wash over me.

I finished my beer and got another, then flicked the TV back on to break the silence, the repeated rubbish drifting mindlessly in front of me. A while later I wandered out to the kitchen again. Looking at my watch I noted it was nearly eleven-thirty and was puzzled by the fact that Samantha was still not home, although not totally surprised. The bleariness of the day's events and the beer, added to the fact that I had not eaten, left me in a stupor and devoid of clear thought.

Something under the kitchen table caught my eye. I banged my head and cursed as I attempted to pick it up. It was an envelope with something loose inside. I slumped down on the nearest chair with a sigh, placing my third beer on the table.

As I opened the letter two rings fell out, Samantha's diamond engagement ring and her gold wedding band. As I held them in the palm of my hand I sensed the first sting of tears. Utterly dismayed, my heart sank as I slipped them neatly onto the little finger of my right hand, almost choking as I took out the accompanying letter.

' Mark,
I can't go on like this. I don't want to blame you but I can't stop. I don't know how to cope anymore. I

can't speak to you because, in some ways, I hate you
for what happened. I know you could not have done
anything to prevent it, but in my head I still blame
you. My son is gone. Living this nightmare does not
change that. I can't stay.
Something inside me has changed, I feel isolated.
Seeing you only reminds me of the fact.
Please don't look for me, everything we had has gone.
As far as I can see there is nothing for us. Just get
on with your life.
I'm Sorry,

Samantha Roberts.

Clare

Clare had scrawled her name underneath as well.

Samantha had been crying when she wrote it, I saw the smudge of ink from the tears.

I looked at the rings disbelievingly. Somehow my brain couldn't comprehend what was written. I re-read it, again and again, everytime anger rising inside, burning me harder and harder.

"YOU'RE SORRY! What about me? WHAT ABOUT ME???" I shouted as loud as I could, swinging my arm out, clearing the kitchen table in one fell-swoop, my beer went careering to the floor. Standing up, I grabbed the chair by the edge of the seat and turned it upside down, then with as much force as I could muster I kicked it, breaking one of its legs clean off. I kicked at the other chairs one by one, they didn't smash so I kicked them harder, every ounce of emotion driving me on, fuelling the fire inside.

When they didn't break easily, I stamped on them till they were in pieces. Tears streamed down my face, the letter a crumpled mess in my hands.

I marched to the kitchen door and grabbed awkwardly at the handle, missing it. In my frustration I punched it so hard that one of the panels gave way. I was oblivious to the blood on my knuckles until I was halfway up the stairs. Checking both my room and Clare's, as if it would make a difference, then I went to Joshua's. I'd missed the signs when I first came home. Clothes, a few toys, Samantha's perfumes, all *gone. She'd even taken the duvet, leaving me just a couple of blankets.*

I slammed the door of Clare's room so hard the walls vibrated. 'BITCH!!' I bellowed. 'How could you?'

In Joshua's room all his baby photos had gone, as well as his favourite teddy bear. I kicked the bed, I kicked the door, I kicked his wardrobe, which collapsed. The anger inside hurt so much that I couldn't release it, no matter what I punched, hit or kicked, it was like an elastic ball, the harder you hurled it against the floor the more it bounced with charged- up energy. Tears blurred my vision, sweat from my efforts, mixed with the salty tears, stinging my eyes. I marched through the house again and again, searching and finding nothing until I finally collapsed in a heap in the hallway downstairs. The exertions of my anger, the final acceptance that Samantha and Clare were gone, and the lack of food taking their toll.

Tears and snot amalgamated, streaming down my crumpled face as I finally admitted defeat. I was crushed.

I still had the two rings on my little finger. I pulled them off and studied them, before throwing them in the direction of the kitchen, they sounded like pins dropping onto the stone floor as they came to rest. I sobbed relentlessly until I fell asleep where I was.

The next day and the day after, were a blur of images, anger, denial, shock, confusion, even sympathy raked through me at some point. I barely ate and didn't wash, that I do remember, and the slightest provocation from any inanimate object would provoke my anger, I'd punch it, or kick it, or hurl it across the room.

It was days before I came to my senses and knew I had to do something or I would destroy myself. I found the screwed up bit of paper that was the letter and re-read it, it dawned on me that Samantha had actually signed her maiden name. It really was the end.

I sat on the bottom step of the stairs, all shades of anger gone, just defeat staring down at me. The startling realisation was that I had to let her go. If I chased her now she would run forever. If I gave her space, maybe, just maybe, there could be hope, at least to see my daughter again. I desperately missed them both.

I needed to do something about where we lived. I couldn't possibly hope to get her back whilst this was still meant to be our home. I would sell the house for whatever I could get. I couldn't lose any more than I already had. I wouldn't be any worse off. So I'd owe the bank some money, but at least I'd be free of Shelbourne. I would find another job somewhere then maybe things would change! I had to live with that, otherwise all would be lost, and if I didn't have hope then my life was over.

Beryl collapsed onto the floor. It took her a few seconds of recovery before she took in the scene in front of her. DI Collins was being helped up by his colleague from the pile of chairs that he now lay in the middle of. Father David was clutching his left eye, an angry cut below it was bleeding profusely. Father Fredrick, pale and fraught, was being helped up by Cyril. Peter was sitting down in his chair, dazed and confused. Things no longer looked rosy. The caretaker was nowhere to be seen, he had split the moment things had taken a dramatic turn. The press had snapped as many photos as possible before being ushered out of the hall by PC Tritt, but they had the violent rage on film, black and white photos showing the true nature of these events.

Beryl looked into the pairs of eyes that now looked back at her. She saw fear, hatred, and anger and, in Cyril's, pleading, as he held his right arm.

57

"Miss Wallace, you're under arrest for striking an officer," Harris announced, producing a pair of handcuffs and spinning her swiftly round in one smooth movement.

"But it wasn't her fault, it's not her…" Cyril tried to defend his aunt, but the police officers were still sceptical about what they had witnessed. Cyril unthinkingly grabbed Harris's arm to gain his full attention, and was immediately slammed into an arm-lock and forced up against a nearby wall.

"Do you want to be arrested too?" It was more a statement than question. "You've been warned," he grunted.

Harris released him and Cyril rubbed his arm, fearful for his aunt. She looked forlornly at him. "It's okay Cyril."

"But Auntie," said Cyril, sounding like a tempestuous child.

A scream of pain caught everyone's attention. The gash on Father David's cheek started to burn. Steam rose in wisps, before dissipating. Tears ran down his cheeks. Father Frederick calmly went to attend to his colleague.

Father David looked frantic clawing at his burning cheek, a mad frenzied look appeared in his eyes as a dark force started to unlock itself. Father Frederick gulped, he had seen this type of thing before, a soul slowly being taken, possessed by something from outside this realm. Instinctively, he reached into his doctor's bag and pulled out a small vial of Holy Water, uncorked it and sprinkled the contents freely over Father David.

"I command the unclean Spirit, leave this vessel." Father David howled in pain as the water burnt his skin like acid, filling the hall with an acrid stench. "Rejoin your world, you are not welcome here. Your time has passed. Leave, unclean Spirit your mortal bonds are broken." Father David put his hands to his face as Father Frederick repeated the procedure, the Holy Water burning. Suddenly Father David's scrawny frame grew as he fought back the pain, marching on Father Frederick, forcing him further and further back until he was against the wall on the far side of the hall.

"Did I do this Cyril?" Beryl spoke with remorse.

"No, of course you didn't," Cyril snapped, trying to reassure her but his words just sounded angry. "I'm sorry."

Father David struck out, catching Father Frederick firmly on the side of the head. Father Frederick staggered sideways, disorientated, the world spinning in front of him. Father David spoke, but the voice that came forth was not Father David's, and Father Frederick's eyes widened in terror.

"Ain't it grand." Father David looked at his right hand, studying it like a scientist, before licking his index finger. Father Frederick stood up again, but his legs were like jelly, his strength failing him. He tried to say something. His lips moved, but no sound came out. Then he stumbled, as if drunk, crashing to his knees, his eyes like gyroscopes, as steam rose from a cut on the side of his head. He looked at Collins and Harris, then back to Father David, who merely stared on, smiling.

"See ya in hell."

Tritt and Vickers ran to hold Father David but he shook them off with ease, his sudden strength overwhelming them. Father David ran to the door and no one else tried to stop him, too shocked at what they had seen.

Beryl was still being held by Harris when she started to speak again, and the atmosphere grew ominous around her, a foreboding that grew as a wild shadow. Beryl's voice grew darker and more determined. Harris instinctively let go, fearing for his own life

The redundancy money came through quickly although it was still scary finding myself with no job, no wife, no son and no daughter. For the first time I realised how insular we had been. I couldn't think of one person I could talk to. I had been given a reasonable settlement for the eight years of dedicated service and immediately set about sorting myself out, putting my life back in order. I redecorated the house and sent off my CV for potential new jobs, fresh with hope of a rosy future and a new place to start again - to try and win my family back. I shut the estate from my mind. There was light at the end of the tunnel and I didn't want my energies distracted from my goal, my chance to get back everything I had worked so hard for. I contacted an estate agent and they valued the house, it looked as though I would loose a few thousand pounds but that was of no consequence compared to what I would gain.

Quite a few people had the same thought so there was a glut of properties on the market. I had to make an effort, make it so shiny and bright that anyone would instantly want to buy it. I continued redecorating in earnest after signing up with various job agencies, especially the national ones. I told them I wanted to make a new start and didn't mind where it was. This made them smile, they said it would be easy to place me with my experience and 'on the job' training. All seemed hopeful.

For all my efforts at decorating the estate agent gave good feedback, said it would be no problem to sell, at the right price, which was a little less than he had originally suggested a few weeks before. A relatively small penalty to pay to get my family back. I put the house on the market.

I spent the next few weeks oblivious to what was really going on around the estate and the effect 10,000 job losses was having on the area (over a third lived on Shelbourne). I had interviews lined up, some as far as 150 miles away, a new start looked possible. I kept myself busy, I couldn't let this positive feeling slide away from me.

I had a couple of viewings, and one offer, well below the asking price, which I turned down, hoping it was the right thing to do. I had a couple of interviews but nothing solid came from them. I scoured the area for a part time job, anything to keep me busy, but with hundreds of people doing the same, it looked hopeless.

Some of the employers said I was over qualified, I countered saying 'does it matter? Use me for other things, please'. It didn't make any difference. I bolstered my hopes every day, telling myself 'it will get better, it must get better'. The house and gardens were pristine, in fact, so well maintained, that there was nothing to do.

Two months drew to a close. No other offers on the house were forthcoming and no offers of a job – the rejection letters were racking up. Jim & Eileen were great, they had made a point of popping round to make sure I was alright and inviting me in for coffee. The support they gave helped me enormously. They even suggested I rang the estate agent and ask if that original offer was still on the table. I thought about if for a while and then decided maybe it would be worth a try. I rang up but the couple in the end had decided against the area.

Slowly, my resolve was ebbing away. I started to watch more TV, leave the garden for a day or two so there was more to do, two days became three, three turned to four, and so on. I stopped looking every day for jobs, resorted to once or twice a week. As time went by a melancholy engulfed me, wrapped me up in its warmth.

I had no family, having been given away at birth. If I knew my parents I would love to hate them for it. I had various foster parents but could never settle. I was always my own worst enemy, always fighting for attention and most just got tired of me and returned me back to the children's home. I became a hard person to place for adoption and the older I got, the worse it became.

I didn't make many friends, I kept my own company and used threats to obtain help from weaker spirits. That was until I met Samantha.

We hated each other at first, doing anything to wind each other up, between us we caused the carers no end of hassle. One day they finally threatened to call the police, we ignored them, baiting them even more. They did. The police came and unceremoniously slapped us both in handcuffs. We were only thirteen at the time and it scared the shit out of us. It was our wake up call, the wake up call we needed, to stop us tossing our lives down the sewer.

In the back of the police car I started to cry, my whole facade broken down, the bravado gone. I expected Samantha to take the piss out of me. She surprised me by unexpectedly saying, 'Sorry!'

Something so simple, changed everything. We were bundled out of the police car and thrown into the cells for a few hours to think about our behaviour. It was the loneliest time I can remember. The cold, white-washed walls, the toilet in the corner which stank of disinfectant, the thin mattress on a solid base. In that cell the only comfort I had was that one word from Samantha, 'Sorry', whilst in there it came to mean so much.

Samantha and I were dropped off back at the home in time for a late supper, not that we deserved it. Joe, our carer, sat us both down in the dining room, dishing up our re-heated tea, telling us that it had all been a set up, a last ditch attempt by them to break the strangle hold we had over the home, and the nightmare we were causing everyone else. It was also a reflection of what could happen should we continue *on the path we had chosen. It had the desired effect. The police officers were friends of Joe's, and it had been his idea, that's how he told it on our wedding day.*

We grew closer and closer over the next three years, until we left the home, using each other for support, as we tried to change our ways. Together our lives were improving and together we got through everything. We were each other's saving grace and all we needed and trusted. We didn't become lovers until one night not long after Samantha's fifteenth birthday when one thing led to another, a sort of 'have you had sex yet?' It was hardly a steamy night of passion, more the fumblings of two people who didn't really know what they were doing, with a 'Oh my god is that it!' at the end. We were each other's first. It was another seven months before we tried again and then it was quite a different story. It sealed our fate.

With Joe's help we found jobs and he arranged for us to go into separate half way houses as they wouldn't let us stay together. We saw each other every night, discussed work, our life ahead. We didn't socialize with work colleagues, content with it just being the two of us.

Samantha had been put up for adoption when she was only one year old which led to her learning not to get attached to anyone as she was disowned when she was two. The friends we did have, were people that would only drag us down, thinking it was a joke that we wanted to improve our lives, better ourselves. They thought life was shit and they took what they could. If we had never met each other, we probably would have ended up just like them.

One night we saw some of these 'so-called' friends driving around in a Ford Escort. They stopped and asked if we wanted to come out with them, they were going cruising, the car certainly looked flash enough. Bobo kept goading us, just to shut him up I was tempted, but Samantha wanted us to go for a quiet drink somewhere, she was always the strong one.

"Come on," I said. "It could be fun."

"You go if you want," she told me.

"Woah, we not good enough for ya now." Trish shouted from the backseat. Samantha turned and walked away and, for a moment, I nearly didn't go with her.

"Sorry guys," I finally decided.

The car tyres squealed as they pulled away giving various finger salutes.

"Fuck off and die losers."

"Mark," Samantha said afterwards, "if we are going to change our lives then we need to leave them behind us. They don't care about us or who they take with them." I had to concede she had a point.

Some kids from the home had started drinking at twelve, others getting into drugs by fourteen, stealing to feed the habit. I thought Bobo, Trish and Fin were okay though, but Samantha meant more to me.

We became quite insular, Joe was the only person we regarded as a 'real' friend, he had our best interests at heart.

Two days later we found out that Bobo had been arrested for car theft, it was his fourth time, and would be his second stretch inside. This time he was going to a 'man's' prison. I saw him briefly before he went down. He was all bravado, saying it was going to be the easiest time ever.

He hung himself after only three weeks inside.

It shook me. He had always been so strong. It gave me the push to really make a difference, to move away from the area completely, a long, long way, even if it did take a year to get enough money to rent a small bed-sit and find a job. A new start for two less than fortunate young adults who wanted to change their destiny. Joe helped as much as he could, speaking to people he knew. He liked to see kids make a success out of the hardest starts.

We were married at a registry office. Joe was the there. He had arranged the witnesses for us, friends of his.

Life was so good. We worked hard for two years, living in that first bedsit, scrimping and saving. I read books, anything to better myself. Then I had an offer of a job with a new factory that was opening up, 10,000 jobs being created. I was selected for a fast track management programme which paid enough for us to finally buy our first house.

Samantha gushed with pride when I told her and we celebrated. Fourteen months later we had our new home and Joshua, and felt like royalty. We aimed to give him everything we'd never had, love, family, a proper home, the ideal. It was so good.

In the weeks since Samantha had left, the few phone calls I had received from parents of the kids that knew Joshua, helped keep Samantha's essence strong inside me. I made excuses at first, telling them that she wasn't there, until I finally ran out of excuses and the truth came out. At first I took their sympathy, they were kind, but they didn't really know what to say to me. They hardly knew me. They knew Samantha. I started to push people away, it was easier than trying to hold, often awkward, conversations with someone who I believed only rang out of sympathy. Time dragged on. There were no buyers for the house, the low employment opportunities in the area were putting people off and sending shockwaves to the house values. I saw our house fall £20,000 over two months. I reduced the price just to sell it and get out, but it didn't help.

My redundancy was paying the bills but that was running out fast, reluctantly, I attached the 'for sale' notice to my car. It was heartbreaking, it was freedom from this place. But you couldn't eat a car.

In the night that followed, I was awoken by a loud noise. It took me a while to fathom where I was and if I was really awake. I looked out of the bedroom window and saw my car on fire. My heart sank. 'No', I cried at the bedroom window, but it was too late. I saw wolves in the distance, laughing and shouting.

58

The police were 'kind' enough to tell me that this was the first car fire they had attended on Shelbourne. It didn't make me feel proud, only help draw in the depression that was already nibbling at me.

I consoled myself with the fact that maybe they had done me a favour and I could claim on the insurance, the car had been in a bad way anyway. However, I was not prepared for the fact that the insurance had expired two weeks previously. I couldn't believe I had missed the renewal notice, it only added insult to injury. I was gutted.

Depression was setting in fast. After I stopped crying at my bad fortune, I looked out at the estate from my open front door, for hours at a time, some days. Homes had already started to look jaded. The loss off the main employer was starting to hit everyone hard, redundancy monies were running out, causing futile disputes. The arguments grew and started to involve members of every family, soon they spilled out onto the streets.

Those that had found work were resented by friends they'd known for years. The whole system was breaking down in front of me.

The wolves fed off it, they picked up the vibes, picked up new recruits who had nothing better to do with their time and could be easily led. Before this the wolves had only caused minor irritations in the area, now they were on a feeding frenzy. My car being burnt was the metaphorical last straw that broke my back.

I saw Jim & Eileen as I stared at the street from outside my front door, they saw the defeat in my eyes as I stood like a condemned man.

Jim guided the bewildered and broken man that I had become into his house. Numbly, I sat there drinking tea while they spoke to me like the caring people they were. I didn't answer, just sat in silent contemplation, staring into oblivion, not listening.

In the following weeks I only got dressed to go out for food, I didn't shave, didn't care whether I washed or not, sometimes I had to force myself to go shopping. A part of me wanted to sit down and never move again, just wait for starvation and death to take me from this world. Opening the mail became a waste of time, the red bills piled up on the doormat. I just pushed them to one side if I wanted to go out. Any callers I ignored, in the hope they would just go away.

My neat and tidy gardens faded into an overgrown jungle. The house took on a jaded, desolate look that matched my mood. Each day I battled with my lack of motivation. Any hope I had of getting off the estate was fading.

In my mind I could still hear the children playing in the house and Samantha's voice laughing with them, occasionally I caught myself talking to them out loud, re-enacting times gone by.

I had ignored my bills for so long that one day the bailiffs came round, banging on the door. At first I pretended I wasn't in, in fact, I don't think I actually heard it for a while. When they stopped banging, I went to the window upstairs, the most energy I had expounded in quite some time and I watched them drive away. I recognised the van, I had seen it on the estate over the past few months. I knew they'd be back and for the first time adrenalin coursed through me. I was still alive. Still alive inside this shell. I took my most valuable items up into the loft. I didn't know how thorough the Bailiffs were going to be and there were a few treasured possessions I needed to save, even though Samantha had taken most, just a handful of reminders of the children left.

The Bailiffs returned four days later with a police escort and I opened the door reluctantly. I knew what was coming, they presented me unceremoniously with the court order and set about the task, the police observing. By the time they were gone every room was bare, they even took a couple of broken bits of furniture I had carefully arranged in case of potential viewings. In two hours, my children's rooms were stripped except Joshua's broken bed and wardrobe which had no value. Anything that belonged to family had been fair game. It was like they were being erased, piece by piece. The police officers stood and watched. They had the grace to look ashamed and uneasy, but they were just doing their job, and I knew they would forget about it after their shift finished.

The council had pleaded with the local courts not to take people's homes from their owners because of the exceptional circumstance that surrounded Shelbourne. In hindsight, it might have done me a favour if they had; they could have re-housed me somewhere new. The handouts I got went mostly to the mortgage company.

The house felt cold, detached and soulless. Lampshades had been taken, leaving naked bulbs. I was surprised they didn't take those. The police didn't allow them to take saucepans or the kettle, although they had to fight for that, such was the determination of the bailiffs to treat me as if I was the scum of the earth.

They didn't search the loft, my stash was safe.

As Beryl finished, everyone in the hall showed the same signs of letharg. Peter sat long-faced feeling the desolation of a lost cause. Cyril hugged his aunt. The police officers didn't seem to care whether they took Beryl in or not.

No one took much notice of Father Frederick lying on the floor.

59

By ten in the morning Cyril, Beryl, and Peter had been allowed to return to Happy Home guest house. Nobody had spoken during the taxi ride back, all had too many thoughts rattling around their heads, and tiredness added to their already subdued mood. DI Collins had decided to let Beryl off with a caution, noting the exceptional circumstances that had caused the fracas in the first place, together with some unexplained happenings. Once the coroner had examined the bodies, he might want to ask more questions, but for the time being he had finished. Besides, he was having a problem trying to understand what had happened and, hating to be mocked, he would rather turn a blind eye.

Back at the guest house, each collected their room keys and retired without a word. Peter was very aware of Cyril's growing animosity towards him, Beryl just appeared shocked. Cyril was in turmoil over his aunt's safety and his own career.

Struggling to sleep Cyril only managed a few fitful hours, as he replayed the images of the woman being shot and how it had appeared harmless enough. No noise, no explanation as to how she could have possibly been shot, and Father Frederick lying dead from a supposed heart attack. It had all been too much. Cyril longed for the time before this when it all seemed like a happy whirlwind. Pacing the room he could feel the pangs of hunger, he could still remember the taste of the dinner when the idea of a holiday had been mentioned after the success of 'Anne Farmer'.

***

"Are you alright Auntie? You seem very quiet."

"I'm fine, Cyril. Do want some more peas?"

"No, thank you."

Cyril finished setting the table whilst Beryl dished up dinner. Cyril poured the tea into Beryl's favourite china cups. She sat down with a heavy heart, weary from the past few days, Peter's idea of a holiday still circulating around her mind. She had not had a holiday for many years, there had never seemed the need.

"It's so nice to have a civilised meal. It seems like this circus has gone on for months."

"Auntie?" Cyril said, chewing a mouthful of food. "Are you happy about how it is all going? It's just that you don't seem to be enjoying it."

"You know me, Cyril, I like, liked my quiet life. I miss the quiet evenings we shared with a few guests. Peter says that maybe we should take a short holiday after the next round of book signings. What do you think?"

"Where to? Do you mean abroad?" Cyril almost couldn't believe it, the possibility of going on holiday out of the country.

"Well we can certainly afford it now, that's for sure." In just a few short months the public had lapped up the books like hot cakes. She was pleased that Anne's story had been taken to the hearts of so many.

"What did Father Andrew say when you gave him the cheque for the church roof?"

"Let's just say that for once he was lost for words. In fact I am sure I saw him turn rather pale at the shock. But he was pleased. He has put me in contact with a shelter for runaway young girls as well." She ate another mouthful of steak and kidney pie, enjoying it fully. "Peter has given me the name of someone who can help us set up a trust, then we can sign the royalties from book sales over to them and hopefully it will be self perpetuating."

"That's good. But you still don't seem over-pleased at the prospect," Cyril said, chasing peas round his plate."

"Cyril." Beryl placed her knife and fork on either side of the plate and took a sip of tea. "It's been like a whirlwind and I can't believe that Peter wants to get John's story out so soon after Anne's." Beryl started to slice another piece of pie.

"I must admit I was a little surprised, but I suppose we had all the notes already and, as you have said to me before, strike while the iron's hot."

"I see, hit with my own advice."

"Sorry, I didn't mean it like that."

"No, I know. And I see what you mean, and it will help with the Trust. In fact, at this rate, we will be able to set up more than one. But I do hate the way the newspapers and radio turn it into some sort of joke."

***

"And that was 'Ballroom Blitz' by The Sweet and after 'Lost in France' by Bonnie Tyler we will be talking with the new writing sensation, Beryl Wallace, who says her books are stories from spirits beyond the grave. Spooky. Whooo, Scary stuff, listeners. Anyway, let's get on with the music."

Beryl's face dropped, this was the ninth interview she had done and all interviewers took to mocking her. Cyril had enjoyed all the attention as he had been on the periphery of it. The focus remained on Beryl, leaving him to enjoy the benefits, after all, it was not him they wanted to talk to, but Beryl insisted that he be with her. She would put his name into the mix hoping that people would talk to him. He had been eyeing all the expensive equipment the studio contained, he thought his Bush clock radio was high-tech, it was a far away world from the one he lived in. Beryl had looked after him and, in her own way, protected him from the world outside. He had enjoyed it, but now the world seemed to be opening up around him.

The first few chords of 'Lost in France' reverberated around the studio.

"Hi Beryl and…"

"Cyril," Cyril added.

"Of course, yes. I'm Paul O. Thank you for coming in today. Can we just get a sound check? If you wouldn't mind speaking into the microphone."

Reluctantly Beryl smiled and spoke. "Hello."

"A little bit louder please."

"Hello," she repeated, feeling her annoyance of interviews growing.

"That's better. And now you Cyril."

"Hi."

"A little bit more than that."

"Sorry. Hello my name is…"

"Excellent. So this is your first book, Beryl, and it's about Anne Farmer?"

"Yes, that's quite right, She lived…"

"Whoa steady, we'll talk more on the air, I just want to get a few facts straight first," Paul O interrupted.

"Have you always lived in Southend?"

"Yes."

Paul O sat expecting more elaboration. "Okay. How did Phillips Publishing and Literary Agency discover you?"

Beryl sat quietly for a moment, she had answered the same questions again and again in other interviews, and hated repeating herself. Cyril saw Beryl's discomfort and interjected.

"It was more a case of Mr Phillips came to see my aunt one night when she, I mean we, ran our spiritual guidance nights."

"I see, so you are mediums?"

"No, well not me, but my aunt is."

Beryl took over. "I talk with spirits that are all around us, here and now, they are everywhere. Most people are not tuned into them, but they are there for those that want to listen."

Paul O's expression turned to one of 'right of course they are'. "Anyway, I'll ask you a few questions when we go live in about forty seconds, try and keep the answers short and sweet as we don't have much time. Our listeners enjoy their music." Paul O replaced his headphones over his ears and looked across to his technical team through the large glass pane that separated them.

Beryl and Cyril watched as the seconds were counted down on the hands on one of the technicians, who wore the loudest shirt Cyril had ever seen.

"Three…two…one."

"And we are back. Thanks Bonnie Tyler. What a great voice that woman has. Now, here in the studio with me today we have medium turned author, Beryl Wallace. Say hello Beryl."

"Hello," she said flatly.

"She is with us today to talk about her new book 'Anne Farmer' which is taking the literary world by storm. Quickly, can you tell us what the story is about?"

As the routine started again she had to remind herself why she was doing this, the good causes, the church.

"The story is one of a young girl who died about nine years ago in 1967."

"And let me get this right, you didn't research this girl, this is the story that was told to you by a ghost."

"No, not a ghost." Beryl was trying not to sound annoyed. "A spirit. I'm a medium and I talk, or rather they communicate with me. My nephew is the one who is responsible for…"

"It is certainly a compelling story and it is based here in Southend-on-Sea, was that intentional?"

Beryl looked at Paul O incredulously. "I cannot control where the spirits come from. Only those that want to talk actually do. Their world is not a physical one like ours, and that is a concept that needs to be understood. If you would imagine one huge room and the world sits inside that. The spirits that roam this world are, therefore, in theory, all in one place."

"Right," Paul O said vaguely. "Earlier you said you had lived in Southend-on-Sea all your life. Were your parents mediums?"

"Yes, I have lived here all my life and no they weren't."

"So how did you discover the skill?"

"As children we are open to all manner of things that as adults we choose to discredit. Some of us choose to keep believing."

"Thank you. Now for some music before we get back to Beryl and her books. And, yes, I did say books.But first, for your ears we have 'Lola' by The Kinks." Paul O pushed a button and the music cut in.

"Excellent, you're doing brilliantly. So what's your nephew's role in all this?"

"He takes minutes of the spiritual evenings and adapts his notes into the books." Beryl picked up the copy of 'Anne Farmer' they had brought with them and opened it to the imprint page. "See."

"So who is the talent behind Beryl Wallace, the author?"

Cyril butted in before his aunt could answer. "It is not a competition, we work as a team, my aunt has the gift but I like to work with words. I love the way you can create images using words and not pictures. They are stronger images when you can fire someone's imagination." Beryl beamed her appreciation of Cyril's explanation.

"Eloquently put Cyril." Cyril blushed.

"Right," Paul O added, not sure what to make of the two people that sat in front of him. He was starting to think they were a couple of eggs short of a dozen. "We'll be back on air in a minute." The studio fell silent except for the crackle of the needle on vinyl. Again the countdown came from the technicians.

"Three...two...one."

"And that was The Kinks and 'Lola'. Now back to my guests, Beryl Wallace and Cyril..." Paul O realised he didn't know his surname. Cyril went to add it but was cut short by Paul O. "... who writes the stories. So one could say he is the brains behind Beryl Wallace. So, are you married Cyril?"

The question was so off the field that Cyril grimaced, only just making an audible sound. "No."

"So you live alone."

"I live with my aunt. What has this got to do with the book?"

"My listeners like to get to know my guests. What do you think of your aunt's gift?" Paul O slyly looked at Beryl, who didn't look amused.

"She has a very special gift and a lot of people think so." Cyril sounded defensive.

"Are there anymore books in the pipeline, or is this a one-off?"

"Actually there is. It is called 'Justice for John Johnson' and it will be out in time for Christmas."

"And what is this book about?"

"A man wrongly accused of a crime and punished by the local community, and how he seeks justice after his death." Paul O looked at Cyril disbelievingly.

"Sounds a bit James Herbert."

"Who?" Cyril added.

Paul O had had enough. "Well thank you for coming in and good luck with the books. We look forward to hearing more from you in the future. And now back to the music and Mott the Hoople and 'All the Young Dudes'." The record started.

"Thank you for coming in," Paul O said, sorting records.

A technician came in and led Beryl and Cyril unceremoniously from the studio.

***

"Yes, that Paul O was so obnoxious." Cyril said.

"Yes, he was."

"And as you say…" Beryl looked at Cyril, light-heartedly displaying displeasure at having her words used against her for a second time. "It's only because they don't understand. As you say, people are wary of what they don't know."

"You are going to have to stop listening to me. You're remembering too much and using it against me,"

"Sorry,"

"Don't be," Beryl placed a hand on Cyril's. "I like the fact that you listen to me. You're a good lad. Lad! I mean young man now. I am surprised a girl hasn't snapped you up yet. You've got such lovely eyes,"

Cyril wondered if his aunt knew he fancied Tracy. Everytime she was near he couldn't take his eyes off her. For a month after the date with Valerie she wouldn't talk to him, making him dread going into Peter's office, so he was reluctant to ask Tracy out, in case it went the same way.

"One day," he smiled, thinking of Tracy.

"What shall we do tonight after dinner? As we have a night to ourselves," Beryl inquired.

"It's the Generation Game, that's normally funny to watch. I love the way Bruce talks to the guests,"

"Why don't you see some of your friends? You haven't seen any of them for ages."

"They all have girlfriends and last time we went out I ended up playing gooseberry. Besides it will be nice to spend an evening in. As you said…"

"There you go again, hitting me with my own words."

"…only that it has been madness the last few weeks." He laughed.

"I'll tell you what. I have a bottle of Blue Nun in the cupboard. I'll put it in the fridge and we can have a quiet celebration. None of those fancy restaurants Peter seems to love,"

"That sounds nice. This pie is really nice,"

"It is one of Fred's handmade ones. He certainly has a craft. There's more in the kitchen if you would like it?"

"Yes please. If only he could move on eh?" Cyril said getting up. "It's alright I'll get it.

"Yes, such a waste. He would make a lovely husband, if he would give someone else the chance,"

"I suppose it just takes time."

"Let's hope he doesn't leave it too long," Beryl called out to the kitchen where Cyril was cutting another large slice of pie.

"Yes."

"Where's the wine? I'll put it in the fridge."

"It's in the larder on the second shelf."

60

Cyril's thoughts ran to his aunt and whether he ought to check on her to make sure she was alright.

Beryl sat at the end of her bed thinking long and hard about the two deaths, distraught that she was in some way responsible. She hadn't had any sleep, despite laying down wishing it would consume her.

"Mark, oh Mark what is it that you want from me?" she asked out loud. She gasped as she felt a presence all around her, this time it was darker and more oppressive.

"Mark, please go away. Please Lord God protect me from evil spirits…"

I was broken from my melancholy by Whispa.

"Looks like it's started."

I shook my head to throw off the shadows in my mind, but they were too strong. Whispa was right, the burning of the pub had ignited the tension that had been like touch-paper running through the estate. People came running out of their houses to view the thirty foot high flames and hear the explosions as the fire took its hold. It was the sign the wolves were waiting for. A night of complete anarchy, could, at last, be the final nail in the coffin of Shelbourne.

If people had avoided taking sides before, it was no longer an option. As we walked past families huddled together I could feel the despair and condemnation for everything this estate had descended into. Once, it was meant to be the definition of 'community' living. Their sorrow was mine. I felt their dismay. Would they have anything left after tonight? Would they even still be alive? Had I really started this? Had I been the one to push this? After wallowing in my own self pity for so long, had I wanted to bring everything down to my level?

*"Easy Brethren, fate is what we make. Don't be hard on yourself. They made their choices a long time ago, now justice has been dealt."
Whispa's voice was consoling and, at the same time, distant from me. I knew what he meant, but I'd created this.*

Scholar looked as if he was about to add something, then decided not to. Scratch spoke instead. "Outta the ashes a new way will rise, the strong survive. The weak, some find strenf, others, well, there always has to be casual'ies." He half smiled, as if that would justify what we had started.

Right now I missed my family more than ever as the distance grew between their memories and me.

The night was awash with sirens and blue lights flashing against the night sky. Soon the emergency services would be here en masse. I wondered what would happen to them, they were just trying to do their duty, serve and protect the innocent. I knew the wolves would descend on them to work out their anger and frustration, and have what they called 'fun'.

This would get the attention of the world. Some wolves needed actions like ours to act as their cue, a reason for persecution on a larger scale. Others jumped on regardless, no cause, no justification, anything to sap the marrow out of life and make existence as unpleasant as it can be, and they succeeded. The fire would bring out the local press, and the onslaught to follow would bring out everyone else.

Outside Beryl's room Cyril was surprised to find the landlady, Elizabeth Harker, a tall elegant looking woman, along with a cleaning lady, equally as tall but gaunt in the face, listening at the door.

"What the hell…" Cyril began to demand, but was interrupted by Elizabeth.

"I'm very sorry, sir, but there's a man voice inside and I know for a fact that no one has entered the room since Miss Wallace went in. He sounded threatening so Lucy, our cleaning lady, came and got me. I tried knocking on the door but Miss Wallace does not answer. I was about to get you, Mr Hewington."

"Do you have a master key?" Cyril rattled off impatiently.

"Yes, Mr Hewington, but there is a key already in the lock."

Cyril impatiently banged on the solid oak door with both fists, calling out his aunt's name, but only managed to attract the attention of other guests, who came to investigate, Peter amongst them. Cyril tried ramming the door with his shoulder, much to the disgust of Elizabeth, but the door was too solid.

"Auntie? Auntie Beryl? If you can hear me, open the door, please," he shouted.

There was no reply. He hoped she was alright. Cyril knew that, up to now, the spirit had not harmed her, although it appeared dangerous to people around her, causing him great concern. Would he be better off staying outside until the spirit had finished? No, he had to get in and make sure she was okay.

Cyril started to think logically. "Mrs Harris, do you have a ladder?"

"Harker," Elizabeth replied, correcting Cyril.

"What?" Cyril questioned sharply.

"Mrs Harker, not Harris."

Cyril tried to remain calm, but his concern for his aunt was making him jittery.

"Please, Mrs Harker, do you have a ladder?" Peter interrupted, seeing that Mrs Harker's name was the least of Cyril's worries.

"Oh, I don't know, I guess my husband must have one in the shed."

"Can you check please, I might need to climb in through the window. I take it, it will reach?" Cyril glared up at Peter.

"I really couldn't say."

"Well, can you find out…please." Cyril's words were full of anxiety and sounded a little bitter to Elizabeth, who extended her neck haughtily, before asking Lucy to find Alfred, her husband, and get a ladder up to the window. When she didn't react immediately, Elizabeth said more firmly, "Now! Mrs Carr."

Cyril knelt by the door. "Auntie, we are going to get a ladder. Can you hear me?"

"What's going on Cyril?" Peter leaned over the banisters of the stairs above. Cyril ignored him.

"Miss Wallace has a man in there and…"

"Shush!" Cyril commanded.

"Now don't talk to me like that young man or I'll…"

"Will you please be quiet, Mrs Harker, I'm trying to see if my aunt is alright."

"Well, I never in all my…"

"Mrs Harker," Cyril said in a controlled bellow.

Elizabeth folded her arms across her chest and then, exasperated, walked away, talking to herself.

Peter joined Cyril at the door, much to Cyril's annoyance,

and both listened to the voice inside.

Uneasily, I followed my Brethren back the way we had come.

"I fink our work t'night here is done. Don't you?" Scratch said satisfactorily. "Won't b' long before they destroy themselves."

I turned to face him, confusion in my mind, this is what I had wanted, but now I wasn't so sure, too many innocents could get caught up in it. In truth, I was starting to despise my Brethren, my invited friends. It was fine whilst we were ridding the estate of wolves, but now innocent people were going to get caught up, baited, and possibly killed, it didn't sit comfortably on my shoulders. We had released the beast from its cage to do justice, we were no better than the wolves.

Whispa tried to calm the tension in me. "There is always cost. It has to be expected. It is the end result that you must focus your mind on. They will destroy themselves. Other costs are acceptable."

How had I let this happen? I was so ravaged by thoughts of revenge, so focussed on the wolves that I had not looked at the bigger picture.

I flinched as a nearby window was smashed by a missile, thrown on this night that would change the estate forever.

"It is set. Best we get out of here," Whispa urged. "We can do no more tonight."

"Where do you propose we go? Nowhere is going to be safe now, look what you've started?" *The words were out before I thought them through. Scholar took a step towards me and I flinched.*

"We did not start anything, as I recall, you were the one who wanted our help."

I felt the power of Whispa, Scratch and Scholar tighten around me and I conceded the point. I knew then I had betrayed them.

"Good, let's get under cover," Scholar hastened. *I had never witnessed Scholar as an aggressive person but I could see the fire in his eyes and, I wondered, 'Who was really the leader of this small group?'*

Making our way back to my house (to enter via the back door) we passed groups of wolves on their way to prepare for the full release of their anarchy. They didn't have a mission as such, just wanted to be part of the destruction. This night was going to turn into a free-for-all. A riot.

A car sped past, nearly catching my arm, the tyres squealed as it barely slowed to take a corner, one of the many drug dealers, making a hasty exit, they knew it would not be safe here tonight. The fight didn't interest them, they merely provided the method to help screw up the system, twist people's minds and lower their expectations of life. Money was their only incentive and they wanted no part of this mindless violence, they only did what was necessary to keep control of their own domain.

A pack of wolves were blocking our entrance to the alley that led to the garages at the end of my garden. They were armed with bats that had nails half bashed in, pieces of scrap wood, one had a pair of nanchukas, although he didn't look as if he knew what to do with them as they sat clumsily in his hands. They marched towards us without fear and with conviction that they were going to win any confrontation. It was the night of the wolves as far as they were concerned.

61

Standing our ground, Whispa and Scratch pushed me to the front, forming the diamond shape as before, laying their hands on my shoulders so they could focus their strength through me. The wolves marched on, excited at the prospect of a fight, boisterously taunting us. I was tempted to let them do their worst, I'd started this and now I was feeling guilty about it. I had lost everything in this world that I cared about. But something inside still egged me on, kept me going, moving along in this pointless life.

The wolves started to charge, the ferocity and anger in their eyes shone like beacons. Self preservation kicked in and I concentrated my mind, utilising the power of all four of us. My mind was jumbled in its thoughts, I just needed to teach them a lesson. Random ideas of attack. I heard a snap, followed quickly by another and I saw the lead wolf's knees buckle underneath him and he fell crashing to the ground, a look of astonishment on his face, a second before the pain kicked in. The rest of the pack still advanced, leaving their fallen comrade. A brick flew at us from the back of the group, I was too late to do anything about it and it caught me square on the shoulder, breaking our formation.

Behind, Scholar was chanting. As the wolves reached Scratch, he struck out at one of them with blinding speed, catching him in the throat and ripping it out with such ferocity that blood and matter splattered over me. I convulsed as I saw the dark crimson liquid flow freely over the tangle of torn veins. Momentarily dazed, the wolf stumbled to his knees gasping for breath, holding his throat with both hands, with utter disbelief in his eyes, gradually he fell vacant, his body slumping to the ground.

Bent over and holding my shoulder, I was struck again between the shoulder blades, leaving me a crumpled heap on the ground. As I looked up I saw a second strike coming at me. Focussing my dazed mind, I managed to eliminate the pain. The baseball bat stopped inches from my face, the killer blow, the nails like spikes ready to mash my features to a pulp. I breathed in its force, its energy, its presence. The wolf who wielded it was short and stocky, and startled that the bat had stopped so abruptly after he had mustered all his power into the blow. Now he stood shaking, trembling from sheer exertion, trying to make the bat continue with its course, time had seemingly stopped, he was unable to let go of the bat, and unable to carry on. The trembling grew steadily more exaggerated as if the bat had a life of its own now. Confusion showed in his eyes.

In my own mind I tightened his grip on the bat, making his eyes widen like saucers. If he wanted to use the bat as a weapon then it would become part of him. Blood was starting to seep from his hands, from round his fingernails. The more focussed I became, the tighter his grip, he screamed loudly. I blotted out everything around me. Tighter and tighter. Suddenly, I couldn't think clearly and the bat dropped from Stocky's hands, the handle was stained red. I saw Stocky drop to the ground, unable to support his own weight, tears in his eyes. I became nauseous and dizzy, everything blurred as I fell to the ground, but pain instantly registered in my shoulders and everything went black.

***

When I came to, I was inside, my daughter's bedroom. Every time I moved my head throbbed, so I remained still and let the darkness comfort me. I couldn't hear much going on outside, in fact the whole house was eerily silent.

I hoped I had been dreaming.

There was a loud pounding on the front door that wouldn't stop.

I struggled unsteadily to my feet, my legs weary. Stumbling down the stairs, my throat was dry, the world spinning. Something was different about the house, yet my addled brain couldn't identify what. I opened the front door just as the pounding stopped. The bright sunlight blinded me briefly, until I shielded my eyes with my hands. Two figures in black and white stood before me. I blinked to make sure. My balance went and I started to teeter to one side. A hand shot out to help me.

I said something, but the words were like a stranger's. I was guided to the kitchen and placed on a seat at the table. One of the figures busied themselves, putting the kettle on, the other figure sat opposite me. I saw the mouth moving, but it was just a weary muffled sound, white noise. One word entered my world, 'wife'. Almost, in an instant, I snapped awake.

"What?"

"Your wife was pronounced dead at the scene. Your daughter is in intensive care, in a coma."

"How? What? What happened?" I spoke, every sound and syllable crystal clear, although I had a sense of distance from the scene.

"Your wife was walking near the park...."

"Near the park, but she left me. What day is it? She left me. Went. Never coming back." I stood up, my heart hammering in my chest, I rocked on my feet as the world started to spin again.

"Here, drink this, it will help." The second figure handed me a mug of coffee but, as I went to take it, it slipped from my fingers and crashed to the floor. I sat down, again as nausea swept over me.

"I don't understand. Where am I?"

"Sir?"

"Where am I? What's going on?"I shouted.

The first figure continued, " Sir?... it's Tuesday. You are in your house.Unfortunately, your wife is dead. I'm sorry to say a stolen car mounted the pavement and crashed into a wall which then toppled onto your wife." He paused. "She died instantly. Your daughter was crushed but survived, she is in a critical condition."

A sudden realisation struck me and I said out loud, "Daughter? Wife?" I knew where I was, everything was crystal clear in my head. "She was coming back. After all this time, she was coming back to..." Tears of joy sprang from my eyes and started to fall 'she was coming back'. I was halfway through smiling when I remembered what I had just been told. "Nooooooo." My voice started to break and I sank further into the chair, sobbing.

"My daughter. I've got to see my daughter." I was awake again.

"Certainly, we can take you."

I rushed to get dressed, thoughts cascading over and over in my mind, apologies, messages of love, all the things I wanted to say. I was driven to the hospital in a daze, all recent events erased from my memory, just one focal point. My daughter, Clare. My precious Clare. The journey seemed to take forever.

I watched her, saw the wires coming out of her and held her hand tightly, pleading for her to wake up. 'Daddy's here'. She looked so much like her mother.

The police needed me to officially identify Samantha. Her body was laid out on a table, covered by a sheet. I fought with tears, all my love for her like a ball inside ready to explode. She looked jaded but peaceful. I went to touch her but stopped, withdrew my hand, and put it in my pocket.

"Samantha, I love you so much." My fingers found two rings in the pocket of my jeans. Pulling them out, I stared at them, before placing them in their rightful place. I whispered, 'I love you', then held her cold hand for a long moment.

As I was escorted from the morgue and the rings were returned to me

"I'm sorry these can't stay on her just now. But if you wish to return them to her later, you may." The officer's voice was compassionate and caring.

I went and sat with my daughter, afraid to leave her side.

Beryl fell silent and started sobbing softly her tears full of anguish.

Cyril rapped gently on the door. "Auntie Beryl! Auntie Beryl! Are you okay in there?" Beryl could be heard blowing her nose and sniffing. The key turned in the lock and Beryl's tear-stained face appeared, Cyril took her in his arms and walked her back into the room, shutting out prying eyes. On the landing, everyone stared at each other in astonished silence before gradually dispersing, embarrassed. Peter knew, for once, it was best to leave things alone.

62

The Sleeper's Rest House in Stroud was the next proposed stop. Peter, Beryl and Cyril were due there by the afternoon, to prepare for the event at the Memorial Hall nearby. Peter conceded that this was not going to happen after the unexpected late night at the police station and Beryl, who was struggling with the spirit for the second time outside one of the planned events. This whole tour had seemed such a good idea to Peter, but he could not have foreseen what would happen and how it would all unravel.

Tentatively, Peter plodded down to reception, wary that the landlady was not happy with his little party.

"Mrs Harker, can we retain our rooms for a further night please." He tried hard to hide his abject disappointment with the way things were disintegrating.

"I'm not sure, Mr Phillips," was the off-hand reply. "Normally, I would be happy to accommodate my guests, but I do not expect to be spoken to as I was, in my own guest house."

The front door opened, and in walked Mr Harker carrying a bucket of water and a leather. "Lucy said you wanted me, Liz."

"Never mind, Alfred, the problem has been resolved."

"Oh." Alfred's shoulders dropped as he sighed. "Very well. I'll be tending to the veg' then." With that he turned and left.

"Look, Mrs Harker, I can assure you, Cyril, Mr Hewington, is not normally like that." Peter smiled, keeping his growing dislike of Cyril hidden. "He is a very polite young man who cares about his aunt very much, and these have been trying times. That's all. I'm sure when he sees that his aunt is well, he will apologise to you. In fact, I'll make sure of it."

Elizabeth continued to flick through the register. "Well, as long as he does," she replied curtly. "As it happens, I can let you have those rooms for another night." Her begrudging words had a hollow ring to them.

"Thank you, Mrs Harker. Have you got a payphone I can use?"

"Just over there." She pointed to a booth to the left of the front door.

Peter rang Adele and Tracy who were staying at 'The Knight's Rest' in Stroud ready for the next event.

The phone rang twice, before being picked up by a chirpy sounding woman. Peter pushed two coins into the slot as the pips sounded.

"Good morning, Knight's Rest, how can I help you?"

"Good morning, it's Mr Phillips of Phillips Publishing here." Peter's business voice made him sound like royalty. "Is Adele Larchwood there?"

"Hold on, let me just check." Peter could hear the rustling of pages being turned. "Yes, her and Tracy Goodman. Would you like to speak with them? I believe they are still here."

"Yes, if you would be so kind. Either will do."

"Hold on." Peter heard the receiver being put down on a hard surface and then voices in the background, suddenly the pips started to sound again.

"Oh bother." He searched through his pockets and found some more coins, which he quickly pushed into the slot. It was about two minutes before Tracy came to the phone.

"Hello," Tracy said cautiously, "Mr Phillips?"

"Adele."

"Tracy."

"Well, Tracy then. Things are not going as planned, I'm going to have to cancel tonight at the Memorial Hall, can you please contact Robert…Robert," Peter flicked through an address book he had pulled out of his inside jacket pocket, "Robert Davies, and let him know. The deposit has been paid. Send him my apologies. Then carry on as planned for tomorrow."

"What do you want us to do for the rest of today?" Hope rang in Tracy's voice.

"Well, there's not much to be done, is there?" Peter sounded as if he was talking to a child. "Stan should be delivering those books to you, so once you have got them loaded into the van then, I suppose, the day is yours."

"Very well, Mr Phillips. Good…" Peter had already replaced the receiver.

"Yes!" Tracy quipped, punching the air with delight. "We've

got a day off as Stan's already been."

Adele looked on incredulously, her face questioning what had happened.

"Don't ask me." Tracy smiled. "Oh well, let's enjoy ourselves then. Shame Cyril's not here, I'm sure I could have found something to occupy my time."

"In your dreams, honey, in your dreams." Adele smiled.

"He's interested. He just doesn't know it yet, but I'll bring it out of him."

Like giggling schoolgirls they ran up to their rooms to get ready to go out.

***

Cyril spent the afternoon in his aunt's room, wary of the spirit's return but reluctant to leave her alone. He had apologised to Mrs Harker who had arranged for some sandwiches to be brought to the room. Peter had tried twice to talk with Beryl and Cyril but had been politely but firmly turned away. Peter had spent a considerable time on the phone to his office, who had been hounded by the press since the news had broken about the deaths. Luckily, they did not have the location of the guest house, although he thought it wouldn't be long before someone let that out.

What had started out as a highly intriguing business proposition, had turned sour, but Peter knew that any publicity was good for business, and this would only heighten interest in the book, especially if he embellished it a little, and his devious mind started to work out ways to do just that. If he could get Beryl to continue with the tour then all would be perfect. Memories of his own participation vanished from his mind as pound signs flashed like crazy neon. He could force the contractual agreement but felt Cyril and Beryl would not care about the penalties, and he guessed that Cyril's overriding concern for his aunt would render any pressure being applied to his own writing career as null and void. He knew he needed another means of persuasion, but what? He sat down in the lounge to ponder this, ordering a coffee.

Beryl was suffering from melancholy with which the spirit had enveloped her. With a heart heavy, she found it difficult to comprehend that two people had died as a result of her actions.

Never had such a thing happened in all her time of spiritual writing, it scared her almost to death.

"Cyril, I need to go home, I need to see Maggie. Can you arrange it?" Her voice was quiet yet firm and broke the silence that had rested between them for an hour.

"Of course. What do you want me to tell Peter?"

"Whatever you like, I don't care anymore. I never meant anyone to get hurt, let alone killed." Her eyes were red and sore.

"I know, I know." Cyril was relieved, although bitterness at losing his own possible writing career still registered.

"Cyril?" Beryl's voice brightened.

"Yes?"

"I think Tracy is a nice girl, she'd be good for you." Cyril blushed. The statement caught him off-guard, and, for a second or two, he didn't answer.

"But she is so forward sometimes. Valerie was like that."

"Don't let Valerie tarnish your confidence. Not all girls are like that. It'd be nice to see you with someone. You deserve someone special in your life. She may be as forward as Valerie but that doesn't mean she isn't shy and using it as a defence."

Cyril half-smiled, his thoughts and concerns were of the spirit, and the effect he was having on their lives, and not about his love-life. It surprised him that his aunt was thinking about that.

"I'll go and ring Maggie, and the train station, to see what time the trains are."

"Thank you, Cyril."

"You're welcome."

"And, I'm sorry."

"What for?"

"When we leave I'm sure Peter won't take you on as a writer. I know that is what you wanted, and I would have loved to see your name on the cover."

Cyril knelt down in front of his aunt, who was sitting on the bed.

"I don't care...okay, I do care, but you are more important to me now. You are my family and I need to know that you are safe. You always said to me 'what will be, will be'."

"Even at times like these you use my own words against me."

Beryl smiled, and rubbed Cyril's head playfully.

***

Peter was still in the small lounge area when Cyril walked in. Peter dipped his head in acknowledgement, but didn't say anything, leaving the first words to be said by Cyril.

"Peter!" Cyril stood his distance and took a deep breath. "My aunt and I have discussed the situation very carefully and…"

"Cyril before you finish that sentence," Peter stood up sharply, his temper rising, he had expected this, "let me just warn you that both yourself and Miss Wallace signed a contract to finish this book promotion and I can hold you to it." Peter's annoyance didn't quite have the force that he intended, in truth, for the last ten minutes he had been worrying about his participations, even though he didn't know what actually happened, he did fear for his life. He had also been contemplating contacting the police and finding out about Father Frederick's untimely demise, as well as looking for another way to persuade Beryl and Cyril to continue, but when Cyril had walked in, his contempt for the young man had come to the fore."I realise that your aunt may have…" he paused, searching for the correct word. "…misgivings, shall we say, but the fact remains, a contract was signed and agreed."

Cyril was dismayed that the man before him showed no signs of compassion.

"You are absolutely unreal. Two people have died and all you care about is the blasted book." Cyril knew he was wasting his breath, but he couldn't stop himself. "Two lives extinguished for the sake of a few words for entertainment purposes, and all so you can make a few pounds. Have you no heart? Do you not feel anything?" Cyril's voice rose then there was a moment's silence. "Well, we're going home. Do what you have to do."

Peter took in Cyril's words, then appeared to discount them, his voice taking on a condescending tone. "My dear boy, there a few things that you need to learn about the real world and one of those is that you have to use every situation to its best advantage." The remorse Peter had been on the verge of faded. Cyril went to respond, but Peter quickly continued, "and… whilst I agree with you that the current circumstances are not 'ideal', shall we say? They have happened, and I do feel for the families of the people that have died." He sat down again, feeling superior once more. "But what's happened has happened and we can't change that. Life moves on. Now I have cancelled the next event, as a sign of respect, but we will carry on as usual in two days time." He flicked through his pocket diary. "No, three days actually. That will be Wednesday, 8th November."

Cyril stood dumfounded at the complacency with which Peter took everything.

"We are heading home tonight." Cyril turned and walked out of the little lounge, almost crashing into Mrs Harker.

"Fine, but if that's what you wish, just make sure you are at…" Peter grabbed a piece of paper out of his pocket. "…the Ely Guest House, Peasedown St John, near Bath for Wednesday, 8th November."

"Please, Peter, can you keep your voice down? This is a guest house not an office."

"Apologies, Mrs Harker, but some people can be so exasperating."

Cyril stomped up to his aunt's room, slamming the door behind him.

"I cannot believe that man. The arrogant bas…" He caught himself before he finished, knowing his aunt hated bad language. He stormed over to the small bay window that looked out over the well maintained side gardens.

"I take it Peter…"

"No, he didn't," Cyril snapped. "Sorry." He sighed heavily, expelling some of his anger.

"What exactly did he…" Beryl was again lost to the spirit.

"Auntie, Auntie Beryl." But the voice that came back was not hers and all Cyril could do was listen.

63

Clare was in a coma for three days and I hardly left her bedside, watching as the doctors and nurses fussed over her, tending to her, doing their best to help her. I kept talking to her, telling her stories, hoping and praying that she would wake up and we could go home. But no matter what they did, it made no difference and, finally, she passed away without ever regaining consciousness. I didn't know if she knew how much I had loved her and her mother.

I couldn't cry as I sat numb from the heartache, watching her still body, expecting to see her open her eyes and cry, 'Daddy'. I was led from her room by a nurse. I felt like a zombie. I had forms to fill in but don't remember what they were. I was handed the clothes and possessions that she had had with her at the time of the accident, her murder; amongst them was Mincemeat. I held onto it so tightly, letting big retching sobs tumble out of me, as I sat in the corridor, not knowing what to do next.

I was lost and alone in a world that didn't seem to care about me. Just a forgotten one. All my family gone, forever. I wanted to join them.

I couldn't believe my family had been so close to coming home when they were taken away so cruelly, snatched from me at the last minute. Never even getting to say goodbye or tell them how much I loved them. What would have been our first words when Samantha had arrived home? What would have been my reaction?

Lost, I walked out of the hospital carrying Mincemeat. I walked the streets. Walked and walked. I didn't know where I was going. I didn't care anymore, I just wanted to get away, as far away as possible. I don't remember where I went. I don't remember eating, just walking as the day faded into night and back into day, I must have rested at some point, but was oblivious as to where and when.

I remember a bridge. I remember standing there contemplating ending it all. I stood there for a long time in a trance-like state, then climbing over the hand rail and standing at the brink of no return. My hands anchored me securely, Mincemeat still clutched by his left ear. I couldn't let go, some hidden power made me hold on, making me go on *fighting for life. But why? Life seemed to hate me so much.*

Go on for what?

A gust of wind blew through my hair and I registered the cold bite it had, my right foot slipped and I twisted to hold on, desperate to continue living.

In my panic, Mincemeat slipped from my clutches, bouncing on the ground, then toppling through the railings.

"Noooo," I screamed as I made a grab for him, but he was out of my reach and I watched, as it in slow motion he fell forty feet into the stream below, I tried desperately to secure my own grip on the bridge. Mincemeat landed on his back, his happy, smiling face teasing me as he rolled over along the rapidly flowing stream, lost forever.

Voices. I heard voices. Then felt a hand on my wrist, followed by another, two men were wrestling me back to safety. I looked at them, desolation in my eyes. Their words mingled with the wind, I wanted to go with Mincemeat. I sighed and looked down at the stream, the waters sounding their welcoming call. I released my grip but did not fall.

"Please let me go," I pleaded so calmly that the two men almost stopped what they were doing. I wanted to go, I wanted to follow Mincemeat.

"Please let me go, there's nothing here for me now."

Another pair of hands grabbed at my clothes and I found myself being hauled back over the railings like a sack of grain and plonked unceremoniously on the ground.

I lay there and, in the distance, I could see Mincemeat, gleefully riding out his journey. My last connection gone.

I found myself back at the hospital from where I had started. From there, I was referred to a care facility, to be observed. They all knew my story. They talked to me as if everything was going to be alright, tried to convince me there was hope. But I had been through so much, I couldn't face anymore.

The State arranged for the cremation of Samantha and Clare's bodies long before I left the care facility, just another missed opportunity for me. They didn't realise where I was, a trail lost in paper and bureaucracy.

I was psychologically evaluated and found to be of sound mind, enough to be allowed home, or rather back to my house, where I *sank deeper into misery. I was meant to keep appointments with a psychiatrist, but I just let them slip by, what could they tell me? How could they help me? I spent hours staring at the walls of the house. I didn't remember eating, but I must have done, somehow I kept going.*

One day a brick came through the lounge window, landing barely a foot away, it was only then that I realised that I was sitting in my own excrement. I looked around, disillusioned and ashamed that I had let life take this path. The brick was my wake up call. I had lost everything, but I was still alive, still breathing. No miracle had taken the last breath from my body, so I had to change it, or end it.

Maybe Samantha was watching over me, and I thought how ashamed she would be to see me like this. I started to put my affairs in order. The mortgage had been covered by the insurance, now my wife had gone it was all mine. Little comfort. I had back payments of bills to sort out, unemployment to claim. I didn't know what the future held. Loneliness seemed the obvious scenario, but I had to push that from my mind, I had to make the best of the situation.

I replaced some of my furniture with the small payments that the social gave me. Food was basic, I didn't like drink so that was an easy abstention. The scariest moment came when I started to look for a job, it seemed the world had moved on so quickly and left me behind. I knew it would be easy to let things defeat me. I decided to treat myself if I achieved just one small goal a week, applying for a job deserved one, so with the little money I had, I bought a small tin of paint, to cover the grubby wallpaper. The house was looking habitable again, basic, but habitable.

I was sleeping on the floor upstairs, half awake, listening to the wolves decimate the estate, little by little, night by night. The howls of high octane fun penetrated my empty room, destroying any chance of joining the realms of a complete sleep. As an escape, I filled my dreams with Samantha, Clare, and Joshua. The nights belonged to the wolves and, gradually, over time, they became braver and braver, as less people stood in their way.

My life was in some semblance of order now, and as long as they left me alone, maybe I could get along. That wish was too much. As much as I tried to keep myself to myself, the wolves inevitably got round to focussing their attentions on me. One night, whilst I sat in Joshua's bedroom, a missile broke the window, the missile caught my shoulder, tore my shirt and stained it with blood. I went to the window and looked down at them, they laughed, baying at me like demented idiots. How could they hold so much power over so many? This was to be the first of many attacks on my house over the coming weeks they would destroy everything that I was trying to rectify and send me to my safe haven up in the loft.

"Sway, you alright?" Scholars voice broke into my thoughts, and clumsily I tried to work out what was going on. As the fog cleared, I realised I was still outside, by the alley that led to the garages.

64

I looked up into the face of Scholar, who had a trail of blood running down his cheek from a wound to his head, hidden by his hair. Fallen wolves littered the ground; Whispa had stolen their souls for presentation to our Dark Lord and now, soulless, they lay quite still, eyes blankly staring into nothingness.

Scratch and Scholar helped me to my feet and then into the house. I was weak, my neck and back hurt from the blows I'd received. All around, the noise and general hubbub was increasing, as the estate descended into anarchy, the wolves relentless in their endeavours. Flames lit the night sky with an orange glow. The ranting war cries heralded the end of civilised life for tonight. The screeching of tyres signalled that someone else had lost yet another possession.

As I was seated on a chair in the kitchen I questioned who it was the wolves thought they were fighting and what they were fighting for. Mindless acts against innocents.

"We've got to do something. We can't let this go on, people will die."

"This is cleansing, a few innocent victims is par for the course," Scholar voiced carelessly.

"Cleansing!" I felt my blood boil. "They'll murder anyone who gets in their way."

Whispa walked over to where I was sitting. "That is not our problem."

"Plus they'll kill each uvver as well," Scratch added.

"You're all bloody mad, you are." I started my tirade aimed at my Brethren. "This is our problem!" But standing up I became woozy and had to sit down again.

"We need to sit tight now and prepare." Scholar looked pointedly at me. "Come on, let's thank our Master." They all started to leave the kitchen. "That goes for you too, Sway."

"My names Mark, not Sway, and no, I don't."

Scratch was on me like lightning, his hand round my throat. The chair rocked back with the force of my bodyweight then teetered off *balance and sent us crashing to the floor - Scratch still didn't let go, "I see, now we done your bidding, you don't wanna know. Is that it, eh?"*

Scratch's grip was tight and I could barely get the words out. "My bidding? I didn't ask for this," I spluttered.

Scratch stood up and hauled me to a standing position on tiptoes. Whispa came and stood in front of me. "Oh, but you did." His voice was menacing, and a warning. Should I heed it?

I wanted to reply, but Scratch's grip prevented me, and I was frogmarched into the lounge, Scratch's hand still firmly holding my neck, the door was slammed behind me. I was forced to my knees at my given position on the star. As Scratch's grip was released I caught a couple of gasps of air and twisted my head from side to side, rubbing my neck. Up to now I hadn't experienced the physical strength that he possessed. I was frightened and angry. It had all seemed so mundane, and I had even enjoyed the feeling of power, the dignity that it gave me. However, it seemed I couldn't have it without repercussions.

As the others knelt down, I looked back at the door, sizing up my options. Whispa's voice cut in to my thoughts. "Don't even think about it. The deal is done. We are one."

I was trapped. I had gone from one type of prison to another, and escalated the whole situation. I heard the others start the ritual with the opening words, praying to the Gods of the North, South, East and West, invoking their power, each taking their turn, until it came to my turn. There was a deafening silence and all eyes fell upon me. If I were to speak again, would I be able to rid myself of these people? Was I caught up in something too deep to get out of?

"Sway!" commanded Scholar. "The Dark Lord awaits."

I gulped. Slowly, I started to get up, stumbling backwards. Whispa's hand grabbed my shoulder, it felt like someone had placed a concrete block there. "You anger the Dark Lord. Do not." The warning was stark and glaringly obvious.

As I knelt back down, Whispa's grip loosened. The three Brethren all looked at each other.

Scratch drew a knife from behind his back, a seven inch glistening silver blade.

"What's it to be, eh?" Was the ominous question.

"I...I..." Fear stopped me answering. I had been fooled when these three strangers had arrived, regarded them as my saviours, this estate's

saviours. Had I really been all that different to the wolves?

"Auntie Beryl, no. Please, no." Cyril screamed as the seven inch knife Beryl had pulled, came close, resting on Cyril's throat.

Suddenly Beryl's eyes were hers again and she looked down at the knife she was holding. Shock registered.

"I'm sorry, I'm so sorry." Dropping the knife, Beryl scampered backward on her knees. Tears welled up in her eyes, remorse dancing behind them. "I'm sorry, Cyril, so sorry," she pleaded.

Cyril hugged her close to him. "It's alright Auntie, it's alright." He felt the racking sobs as she let out her emotions.

Beryl clung to her nephew with all her might. Her physical and mental strength fading. Cyril knew he was losing her to the spirit. The clergy, who had turned up to help, had been ill-prepared for the task and, in the end, it had cost one his life.

"Cyril help me, please help, I can't go on like this. He's too strong."

"But I don't know what to do." Cyril could see her exhaustion. Why had they agreed to such a thing? Peter had a persuasive manner and they had been taken in by the prospect of helping others. Cyril cared about the good they were doing with the money but his Aunt was his number one priority. The first port of call was a church, where he thought they might be able to gain some respite from the spirit, that was fast becoming a tormentor.

"Come on, let's go. I'm taking you somewhere safe." Cyril lifted her easily off the floor, her small frame offering little resistance.

"I'm sorry, Cyril…"

"It's alright." Beryl's face showed her confusion, the anguish she felt.

Beryl clung tighter to Cyril and he knew time was of the essence, dread was filling every part of his being. He headed for the door, struggling to get a hold of the handle. Suddenly there was a knock.

"Open it, please, whoever it is," Cyril shouted. "It's alright, Auntie." He could feel a presence, and knew the spirit was close by.

Peter stepped purposefully into the room, followed by

another man dressed like Father Frederick and Father David, forcing Cyril backwards.

"This is Father Gareth." He had broad shoulders and neatly trimmed, slicked back hair, wearing tiny, round glasses, and could only have been about thirty. The moment Peter spoke the atmosphere became oppressed, and a putrid smell of burning flesh wafted around the room. The door slammed shut.

"Is Beryl alright?" Peter's false concern didn't fool Cyril.

"Stuff your pseudo concern, Peter." The venom was lost on Peter. "Now, open the door!"

Peter grabbed the handle and tried to turn it, but it wouldn't budge.

65

Beryl started to fidget and Cyril found it hard to hold her as a disturbing energy consumed her. She pushed herself from Cyril and half fell and half jumped to the floor.

Father Gareth moved in front of Peter to watch Beryl, who now knelt on the floor, her voice growing thicker and darker.

I thought about the power I had exerted on the wolves and focussed it onto Scratch, who seemed to be the most lethal. His eyes widened, but not in terror, more in humour, as if I was toying with him. I was trying to restrict his vocal chords, trying to attack by stealth, which Whispa sensed.

"That's not very nice, Sway!"

Scholar picked up his Grimoire, opened it to the back page, and started to read.

"Sayswaforacium guthara."

Within seconds a burning sensation flowed through me.

Beryl held her chest, her face grimacing in pain.

I tried to fight him with the power of my thoughts, but it had no effect, Scratch had recovered and was angrier than ever, a sly, mean look on his face. I keeled over backwards onto the floor, tearing open my T-shirt to try and relieve some of the pain, the intensity of heat made me feel like my skin was on fire.

Beryl ripped open her cardigan to the astonishment of Peter who looked on, frightened and bewildered. Filled with dread he scrabbled with the door handle to try and force the door open, a loose feeling filling his bowels, as panic swept through him.

"Open, damn you! Open!" he said, through gritted teeth, pearls of perspiration forming on his brow.

My heart pumped madly and I could feel the pounding in my chest. Scratch, Whispa and Scholar started chanting.

"Sayswaforacium guthara."

Months ago I would have invited death, now I didn't want it. I shouted out. "Please, Dark Lord, I repent. I beg forgiveness, let me do your bidding." My three Brethren were still chanting, but the burning subsided immediately.

"The master is pleased," expressed Whispa.

I lay there, trying to grasp the full consequences of my actions. The sweat from my brow trickled down the sides of my face, my every nerve was alive and tingling with electricity.

The Brethren returned almost immediately to their worship. I rubbed my chest and felt the sign inscribed on it from when they first came into my life. I was a marked man. My fingers followed the edges of the hard raised scars. I'd invited in the devil, gained the powers I needed, and now was to pay the cost. Life would never be the same again.

I returned to my position on the star, reluctantly, obediently. Whispa disposed of the souls he'd collected and, as he did so, faint screams filled the room before slowly fading. I drank from the proffered chalice, produced by Scholar. In my mind, I questioned what the red liquid was, my hesitance only drew unnerving glances from the others. It seemed I had no real power without them. Together we completed the picture. 'We are one', that was what he, Whispa, had said, he had waited for me to complete them, 'The power of four'. Maybe their power lay in the fact that they - we - worked as a team? Maybe a lot of my strength came from uniting with them, making me believe that I was strong?

What about the early experiments? They had been successful. What about my parentage? Was there darkness in there? In life, I guess I would never know.

I had tried once to find out about my parents, who they were? Why had they left me? Every channel I pursued led to a dead end, it was as if my life had just been invented. I had a certificate but no names were mentioned on it, no father, no mother, no birthplace except a hospital where, I guessed, I had been left. How? Why?"

Father Gareth started to sprinkle holy water over Beryl, but it had no effect. He uttered the Lord's prayer.

"Our father, which art in heaven. Hallowed be thy name. Thy kingdom come. Thy will be done, on earth as it is heaven..."

This was not what Cyril had expected when he had spoken with Father James and he wondered now whether the church had taken him seriously enough.

"What good is the Lord's prayer? Can't you do anything else, this is killing my aunt." Cyril sounded more controlled than he actually was.

"I'm doing the best I can." The words had a ring of innocence about them that shook Cyril to the core.

"Auntie if you can hear me, fight it please. Please fight it, Auntie?" Cyril knelt beside her, placed his hands on her upper arms. With the force of a cannon he was thrown back straight into Peter, knocking the wind out of him and pinning him to the door. Cyril slumped to the floor, unhurt, but baffled.

My thoughts rambled on as my three Brethren continued in worship.

I had gone from one prison to another. Any hope of breaking free vanished the moment I let these people into my life. What had I done? If only I could turn back the clock.

"I'm so sorry, Samantha," I said to myself.

Whispa's eyes glared at me. I focussed on the ceremony which I was now compelled to join in, before closing down the portal in the usual way.

Scholar pulled out a small pocket book from inside his jacket, it was barely notebook size and had a torn red cover. He then proceeded to instruct us all in a new ceremony - which made me very uneasy, but I knew better than to argue.

Scholar read the opening words aloud as the atmosphere oozed like cement. My unrest was magnified as the others spoke at the requisite time.

"Solcoldia madafarasia Lucifer." Scholar spoke loudly and clearly.

Peter found himself saying the words in unison with Beryl. Father Gareth stood dismayed and lost.

"Oh Lord give me strength," Father Gareth said, wishing that Father Frederick was there to guide him, but he was dead, apparently from a heart attack. Father Gareth had been sent to offer prayer for Beryl.But prayer was something he knew was inadequate.

"Hataria cogracia Lucifer," Scratch continued.

Now Father Gareth found himself part of the proceedings.

"Hibothium jurifia de hagerarian Lucifer," Whispa finished.

Finally, Cyril, who had barely recovered from being thrown across the room, also found himself involved.

Whispa, Scratch and Scholar all held hands and I was urged to do the same; both myself and Scholar placed our free hands on the altar. They then repeated what they had just said. I was not to join in, and this filled me with trepidation.

Peter took Father Gareth's right hand in his left, Cyril then took his left and they sat in a half circle around Beryl, as if praying to a god. Cyril and Peter placed their free hands on a nearby chair.

I was compelled to continue what I had started.

A pulse surged through me, making every hair on my body stand to attention. It didn't feel ominous, but filled me with a strange euphoria. A faint aroma of burning sugar and cinnamon filled my nostrils.

I was filled with doubt. Had I got them all wrong?

I was alive, like never before. My fingers prickled with tiny electric shocks that tickled, rather than hurt. In my mind I was at one with everything and everyone in the room, a slow dawning, as if I had attained a higher order in life, an understanding of the energy that existed in any object, in any person.

Had I passed the initiation? Was this my reward? It was hard to resist, all painful memories erased, all anger and love the same.

The atmosphere in the room swarmed with a vaporous presence which rapidly grew heavier, seemingly consuming all of us. The candles glowing an effervescent purple which turned to a deep red. I glanced at the others, their eyes were closed in deep meditation.

Suddenly cramp spasmed in my calf muscle. Automatically I let go of Whispa's hand, to ease it. Inexplicably, I was hurled to the wall behind, knocking the breath out of me. Instead of falling to the floor, I remained half way up the wall, with my feet dangling about a foot from the carpet, suspended like a picture.

Beryl's body launched itself at the wall behind her, temporarily making her lose the power of speech.

Fear took a stranglehold and the treacle-like atmosphere choked me, giving me a sense of being examined. A foul stench of burning flesh surrounded me. The cramp in my leg still registered in my brain, yet I was unable to move. The cramp expanded, incorporating my thigh, then my other leg. All hope of eliciting a cry of pain abandoned as I found myself under someone else's power.

I fought with every bit of strength to break free, but I was locked in place, held captive by an invisible force. Whispa's voice broke into my thoughts.

"Don't fight it, my friend. Welcome it. It will be so much easier."

Summoning every bit of inner strength, I could, I found my voice. "I'm....not...your...friend." I had to fight to get the words out, as I stifled the pain from the cramp, which continued to grow at an unbearable rate.

"It makes no odds, soon our Master will be here."

"Roadia vorgaia," Whispa, Scholar and Scratch chanted together, "take our offering, so you may once more walk the Earth."

A knock at the door remained unanswered as all in the room were forced to play out their parts. Mrs Harker raised her voice.

"Miss Wallace, I insist you open this door this instant otherwise I am calling the police." Her words sounded hollow. "Miss Wallace, do you hear what I am saying?" She waited for a reply but the scene continued unabated. "Lucy, go find Alfred." Lucy turned to go. "Oh, and Lucy, go and get Peter, he is in the lounge. Tell him I want him here immediately."

"Yes," Lucy replied.

With horror, I now had a grasp on what my purpose in all of this was. I could feel the beast all around me, sniffing me, trying me out, the acrid stench repulsive, the air oppressive. Each gulp I took into my lungs only succeeded in intensifying the feeling of strangulation. Inside I was fighting for my life, the life that I had wished away, ebbing away with every second. All my internal organs were crying out, threatening my brain with shutdown.

Agony roared as the cramp became a distant thought, as my muscles burned from the struggle, every fibre alive, yet dying at the same time.

Scratch, Whispa, and Scholar remained in silent contemplation.

My body lurched like a rag doll from the wall to the centre of the star mapped out on the floor, and the pain intensified. I was still alive but burning inside, my blood like boiling acid in my veins.

Beryl lurched from the wall and came to rest in front of Cyril, Peter and Father Gareth.

I fought, but to no avail. I willed myself to stop breathing but nothing would end the ordeal. I convulsed as if I was going to retch, nothing came out, except a long awaited, ear splitting scream.

Mrs Harker took her ear from the door as Beryl's scream swept through the guest house, alerting all the remaining guests that something was not right.

I sucked air into my lungs, it cooled my raw throat, making me cough and splutter. Despite my enormous efforts to breathe in large amounts of air, it was never enough to fill my lungs. My heart throbbed inside my chest, whilst all my other organs started to work again I experienced more discomfort as things started to return to normal.

The room fell eerily quiet.

Scholar, Scratch, and Whispa stared on in admiration.

66

I sat up and looked at all three. I'd allowed myself to be betrayed. Or had I betrayed myself?

For the first time I took in the sounds of the outside world. Shelbourne. I heard everything as if my ears were radars, every voice, every scream, every frightened soul.

All hell had been let loose tonight.

I stood up and walked over to Whispa, placing my hand on his head. It surprised me

"Thank you, Dark Lord. I am here to do your bidding," Whispa announced.

It was only then that I realised I wasn't in control anymore, I was at the mercy of the Master. The one we had prayed to. Lucifer himself.

What astounded me was that I still had my own thoughts, but didn't have control. I turned and looked at Scholar and Scratch.

"We go," I said. "There are many souls to take tonight and my time is short." I strolled purposefully out of the lounge and into the street. My three Brethren followed. I walked across the green to where a pack of wolves were throwing half bricks at a house. Within ten feet of them, their attention turned to me. I was unfazed.

"What do you want assface?" a wolf, who had short cropped hair with long side burns and a turned up, broken nose, shouted in distaste, followed by laughter from the rest of the pack.

"Your souls," I returned, straight faced.

The laughter died away as they fronted up to me, Cropped-hair pulled a flick knife from his back pocket. "Don't fink he's all there, do you boys?" He swung the knife in a wide arc, fast and furious. I turned like lightning, grabbing his fist, the next second he was a lifeless form, standing as a statue for all to see. The jeers quickly died away as the rest of the pack became aware of their fallen comrade.

Cyril, Peter and Father Gareth stood up and mimed throwing bricks, the mirror on the dressing table smashed as an imaginary brick landed. Then a window shattered, as another imaginary brick went through it.

Mrs Harker stood open mouthed in the hall, as the room reverberated with the sound of crashing glass.

"My beautiful guest house."

Peter swung his arm at Beryl, who grabbed it, twisting it sharply up behind his back, snapping the elbow. Peter started to yell but fell silent as his soul was taken by the mysterious spirit. He tumbled to the floor, hitting the corner of the bed on his way down, cracking his ribs and tearing his suit jacket.

Father Gareth found himself free from control and, after a second spent recollecting where he was, pulled a silver cross from his trouser pocket.

"Spirit, I beseech you to leave this place." His thrust the silver cross at Beryl, who recoiled.

Whispa, Scratch and Scholar had moved surreptitiously around the pack, blocking off any escape. Glances shot from one to the other as the realisation came too late. The six remaining wolves were left as soulless entities, living statues, as we walked away.

Because of the pandemonium on the estate no one noticed us, no one cared about us. The innocent ones knew they were in for a rough night, and some remained inside, barricaded in where possible, praying for it to end. Others had taken their most prized possessions and left, not knowing if they would still have a home to return to, if they could return.

We marched on, a band of warriors under the moonlit sky. We walked along the alley we had taken on the first night and out to the roads beyond. The violence was escalating rapidly, growing wilder and wilder. I could hear windows being smashed and commands being shouted out. Police sirens rang out in the distance.

I turned left, walked up to a house and kicked at the front door. Effortlessly it swung open, wood splintering. There was a great commotion from the lounge as people bustled out into the hallway. I placed a hand on the first to appear and, within a second, they fell to the ground, soulless. The others that followed quickly succumbed. I knew there was a person missing. I marched upstairs and found the one I was looking for, naked, in bed with another wolf. I touched the naked girl and took her soul, she fell silent immediately. I faced the wolf. He went to run, then saw my friends in the doorway, and stayed where he was. I stared into his eyes and touched the mark on his face that Scratch had placed there.

I was awash with the knowledge of different hideouts and dwellings, faces, names. I took away my hand, to the relief of the wolf, he tried to say something, but I took his soul before he uttered a word.

"...command thee spirit leave this earthly body." Father Gareth was reading from a small pocket book of Father Fredrick's like an informed scholar. He hoped he was doing it right, it certainly felt right.

The atmosphere in the room lightened and only the voice of Father Gareth could be heard. Beryl collapsed in a heap on the floor. Cyril stood vacant and lifeless, only the rising and falling of his chest showing him to be alive.

Peter rolled over in agony as he came round, but as soon as he started to move he passed out again from the pain of his shattered elbow.

Mrs Harker was still pushing at the door when it sprang open unexpectedly, sending her flailing into the room. She gasped at the sight of the debris.

"My beautiful mirror. What have you done?"

Beryl wearily looked up at Mrs Harker.

"Someone is going to pay for this," Mrs Harker steamed.

Beryl stared at Mrs Harker like a snarling beast, sending Mrs Harker stumbling backwards out of the room, filled with dread.

From the half-landing, on the first set of stairs, a guest, a tall broad man, with well groomed, rough features, called out, "There you go, Mrs Harker! I just wanted to thank you for a lovely stay, it was just what I needed. You and your husband have made me feel so welcome, I almost feel complete again. Well, at least, at peace again."

Mrs Harker turned sharply towards the man, her voice teetering on the brink of uncertainty. "Thank you Mr Austen, and how are you today?" She tried to maintain her professional front.

"Very well. Ready to face the real world again."

"You're most welcome..."

Beryl followed Mrs Harker from the room, upon hearing the man's voice, a voice she recognised and, cocking her head to one side, took in Mr Austen. Trembling she stepped towards him. Mr Austen looked on dismayed.

"Please, Miss Wallace, you're disturbing my guests." Mrs Harker pulled a small lace handkerchief from her sleeve and blew her nose delicately. "Now pack your bags. I want you to leave. I'm sorry but I can't have someone so flagrantly destructive in my establishment." The emotional turmoil showed on her face.

"I know you," Beryl said, after a lengthy gaze into Mr Austen eyes, "yes, I do," she finished, scowling.

67

Cyril staggered to the door in time to see his aunt take the first few steps towards Mr Austen, her hands held high, clawing at the air, as if ready to strike him. Mr Austen edged back, almost toppling down the stairs and just managing to maintain his balance by grabbing the handrail.

"I think you are quite mistaken, Mrs...?" he let the question hang briefly whilst he composed himself. Beryl didn't answer, but took another step closer, placing a hand on his shoulder. Mr Austen shuddered as the hand moved to his neck. He gulped down a mouthful air and gripped the banister rail behind him tightly- stiff with fright.

"Auntie?" Cyril gasped unsteadily, struggling to get his breath back, his body weary and fatigued.

Beryl turned to look at him, craning her neck, recognition registering, but the spirit's hold was too strong.

"Auntie, it's me, your nephew, Cyril!" He reached for her, but she batted his hand away.

The door behind Cyril banged against the wall as Peter tripped through the doorway holding his left arm, perspiration dripping down his pale face, his eyes bloodshot and glazed. He looked as though he would fall down any second, and used the doorway to steady himself.

"Can...someone...please get me an amb..." He slid down the frame of the door, clutching his arm. His shirt had a growing dark crimson stain on it. Loosening his tie he gulped down more air, finding the nausea that was building in the pit of his stomach difficult to fight.

Instinct gripped Mrs Harker as she switched into first aid mode, diverting her attention from Beryl to Peter.

"Mr Phillips? Listen to me, you need to stay awake." She lifted his suit jacket to investigate the bleeding. "Can someone call an ambulance from recept..." she glanced into the room behind Peter and saw the body of Father Gareth lying outstretched on the floor motionless. Her composure started to crack. "What the hell have you done?" She wasn't frightened anymore. Full of anger at the ruination of her nice family-run business, no one would want to stay here after this.

Beryl turned back to Mr Austen, who just stared on at the mad woman in front of him.

"Look, I don't know who you are, but I suggest you do as Mrs Harker says, otherwise, I will call the police." Finding an inner strength, he said, "I'll go...and...call them, Mrs Harker."

"Thank you. Ambulance and Police. We need them here urgently. Mr Phillips looks as though he has lost a lot of blood. Mr Phillips, stay with me." She unbuttoned his shirt to see the extent of the wound. She saw the crimson liquid seeping from a triangular flap of skin measuring about three inches along each diagonal side and, putting a handkerchief to her mouth, she fought the urge to vomit. Never had she seen such a wound.

Mr Austen turned to go down the stairs, breaking the grip that Beryl had on him, but she spun him round like lightning, placing both her hands on his shoulders, forcing him tight against the banister rail until it dug into his back. An ice cold chill spiralled down his spine, sending shivers through his body.

"You! You must die," she said with venom.

Mr Austen looked on, shocked and incredulous. He didn't know this woman.

"I'm sorry, I ..."

"William Henry Ian Stephen Paul Austen. I want you to join your wife and child." Beryl's voice was filled with malice.

"This isn't funny, whoever you are." William pushed Beryl back, his mind frantic as the loss of his wife and child came to the fore. "My wife is dead. You malicious woman." William's mouth contorted as he fought to control the rage building inside.

"I know. So why don't you join them?" Beryl launched herself at William, who lost his footing on the stairs, and went crashing towards the ground floor lobby. Beryl stumbled down the stairs with him. As they came to rest she grasped his throat like a demented madman, trying to choke him.

"You must die!"

Cyril tried to make it down the stairs to pull Beryl off William, but his body still did not feel like his own, his limbs moved only with extreme effort, his brain lethargic.

William's eyes were bulging and his face started to turn blue, he could not believe a woman could overpower him so easily. He grabbed at her wrists and kicked with his feet as panic swept through him.

Cyril finally reached his aunt and, placing his hands on her shoulders, attempted to pull her off.

"Oh, my god, you're alive! Thank God," Mrs Harker stuttered as she became aware of a figure walking from Beryl's room. It was Father Gareth, dishevelled, but otherwise seemingly, unharmed. He had grown in stature, his eyes full of control, looking like a man who had been released from a character he had been playing at, a hidden, untapped knowledge, flowing from within.

Speaking with passion and commitment he said, "by the power invested in me by the Lord Almighty above I command thee to leave this earthly body. You are banished to your domain." Father Gareth stepped over Peter and Mrs Harker, moving in closer to Beryl, throwing a few drops of Holy Water on her, as he recited an exorcism ritual.

William was fading, his eyes showed his life force was ebbing away, his legs stopped thrashing about and his grip loosened on Beryl's wrist.Father Gareth continued, bravely, his voice feeling the power within the words, "I command thee to leave this earthly body. You will obey the words of the righteous one. Be gone, banished from this world, unto your own."

Beryl released her grip on William and started up the stairs, focussing on Father Gareth on the landing above.

"You! I know you too. Scholar." Beryl stated.

"I do not know you. Now leave, you are not welcome here. Cease. Lord above guide this spirit from the taken one, banish it from this realm…"

William inhaled loudly, as if he was a balloon inflating, then coughed and spluttered, as the air tickled his throat and his lungs burned from the exertion. Rubbing his throat he tried to sit up, still coughing. His body was sluggish. Attempting to speak, only a rasp came out, making him cough even more. The colour filtered back into his cheeks.

"Leave now, I command thee," Father Gareth spoke with authority.

Cyril looked on, alarmed, his eyes pleading for Beryl to be returned to him. She was lost to the spirit. The spirit, which had once appeared harmless, was now in complete control. Father Gareth held out the silver cross with his right hand.

"Unclean spirit go. I command thee, leave this earthly body." Father Gareth's voice grew louder and he sprinkled a few more drops of Holy Water on Beryl, this time they started to scald her. Her face contorted with anger, the veins in her neck raised, taut as if ready to explode.

"Go now, I command thee."

Father Gareth started to back away, fearful as Beryl took more steps towards him, the strength behind his words diminishing.

Alfred appeared on the stairs below.

"Elizabeth, what's going on?" he questioned curiously.

"Call an ambulance, now," she shouted, "and the police."

"But Liz."

"Just do it, Alfred!" He turned to leave, yet curiosity made him look back.

Beryl struck out at Father Gareth, who stepped back out of reach, only to trip over Mrs Harker. They both went crashing into a nearby table, knocking over the vase of flowers that had been so well presented, water cascaded onto the carpet.

"Damn it," exclaimed Mrs Harker.

"Argh!" Father Gareth held the back of his head and cried out at the pain. As the initial stab of pain subsided, he removed his hand and looked at the blood on it.

Beryl bore down on Father Gareth, who looked up in astonishment.

"I'm sorry, Auntie, I'm so sorry." Tearfully Cyril raised the vase and reluctantly hit her on the back of the head. He couldn't let the spirit continue this massacre.

It took a second or two for the blow to register, but when it did, she turned and looked at him. The eyes this time were Beryl's, racking Cyril with guilt. He went to hold her, still wary of the spirit.

"Thank you," she said, and fell heavily towards the floor, with Cyril struggling to catch her before she hit it.

68

Everyone looked at each other as, finally, silence descended on the hallway. Was it over? What had happened? Peter coughed, attracting everyone's gaze. A bubble of blood appeared at the corner of his mouth as he gasped his last breath, before slipping away unceremoniously.

Mrs Harker couldn't hold back the flow of emotions as she surveyed the carnage of her once beautiful guest house. She stood bolt upright and very stoutly announced, "excuse me." Her handkerchief firmly held in front her mouth, she walked up the second set of stairs to the next landing and her private bedroom. Then, closing the door quietly behind her, she broke into sobs.

Cyril slumped to the floor with his aunt's lifeless form cradled in his arms, his tears falling into her hair. William managed to get to his feet just as Alfred reappeared.

"Ambulance is on its way, Liz. Police too." Alfred took the stairs two at a time up to the first half landing, where William was groggily trying to establish what had happened. When Alfred couldn't see his wife he stopped and glared at Cyril and Beryl.

"She went upstairs, Mr...," Cyril whimpered.

Alfred launched himself past everyone, hardly avoiding stepping on Peter's body. He caught a glimpse of Beryl's room and saw the debris. "What the hell happened? I knew you lot were trouble" The comment was not aimed at anyone in particular, and he continued up the stairs.

"Liz, Liz, you alright love?" He lightly tapped on the door before entering. "Come here." The door closed and Mrs Harker's muffled sobs could be heard.

Dazed, William helped Father Gareth to his feet, leading him downstairs to the lounge, away from the carnage.

***

Beryl came round on a stretcher that was being carried

downstairs to the waiting ambulance. A second ambulance crew had been called to deal with the other injured parties. Beryl's sorrowful, hollow, eyes looked through Cyril, who refused to leave her side, as guilt festered within him.

"I'm sorry." He gripped her hand tightly, trying to avoid her gaze.

She smiled meekly, exhausted. "It's okay Cy…"

Her hand tightened around Cyril's, crushing his fingers. "Ow," he pleaded, before he heard the voice that was now so familiar to him, driving a stake of fear through him. The attending ambulance crew stared on in bewilderment.

Leading us out of the house, I had routes and people firmly etched in my mind, where the wolves' hideouts were and who I was looking for. In the distance what had started out as a fire and confrontation between two individuals, was now escalating into a riot. The sound of breaking glass, interspersed with explosions, was getting louder and closer every minute. More lives would be lost tonight.

The first hideout was a burnt-out garage. Abandoned. I guessed the inhabitants were participating in the riot, helping to stir up events and perpetuate the violence. The wolves were good at that. The second hideout, a two bed-roomed flat in a converted house, was pretty much the same except for a stoned druggie in one corner. I took his soul and left him there to slowly die of withdrawal.

Whispa, Scholar, and Scratch marched on behind me, allowing me to do my work. Where necessary, and without instruction from me, they did help gather the wolves, allowing me to consume their souls.

We entered Shelbourne Heights and, breaking through a door at the top of a stairwell, gained access to the roof. The roof was an excellent vantage point to watch the destruction expanding from the pub, like ever increasing circles. Flames were lighting the night sky.

We saw police with riot shields trying to quell the crowds, but the missiles were too numerous and, as soon as one piece of debris was battered away, another would find its target.

Death floated over Shelbourne this night and I savoured its sweet aroma, welcoming it. We heard war cries as the wolves were buoyed with foolish confidence. For a few minutes I became immersed in the atmosphere.

"Come, we have souls to take," I commanded my followers, and

they were followers now, not my Brethren. The dynamic had changed, I was 'the one'.

As we made our way down the stairwell we came face to face with two wolves who were not even teenagers. They ran at us, armed with batons of wood, pierced with nails. One was wearing army surplus gear, the other had his hair tied back in a ponytail. Army-surplus swung his weapon in a magnificent arc and I put up my hand to prevent it hitting my head. Two nails pierced my hand. Army-surplus, taken by surprise, looked at his mate for back-up. I merely withdrew my hand, feeling the nails slowly retract from the holes they had made. I squeezed my fist closed and let the blood ooze out. I licked it like an ice cream.

Beryl tried to lick her hand but the straps across the stretcher held her firmly. The crew lifted her into the ambulance. Cyril was fraught, afraid that any moment he or the crew would be taken under Mark's control.

Ponytail was being held by Scratch, screaming to be let free.

"You are mine," I stated matter-of-factly to Army-surplus, and took his soul. Ponytail fell silent, no longer struggling, abject fear evident on his baby face. A dark patch appeared on Ponytail's legs, he turned, trying to break Scratch's hold, but I grabbed his Ponytail and yanked it with such incredible force that a wad of hair was torn from his head. Ponytail's screams reverberated around the hollow stairwell as I watched him sink to the floor, filled with a hot, stinging, burning pain. I enjoyed it, relished every second of his discomfort.

Stepping past Army-surplus, who stood motionless, I bent down to Ponytail, placed a finger under his chin, and lifted his screwed-up face to mine.

"Don't worry, pain is merely a stepping stone." Astonished, he glared at me, almost ignoring the pain he was suffering. "Have some more." I took his right arm, which was doing its best to cover the wound, and wrenched it so hard the snap cracked through the stairwell. Ponytail's eyes shone like beacons then faded as he passed out.

"You're no fun anymore. But I'll leave you 'til later. Scratch." I indicated for Scratch to mark him, he duly did so, and I took in the smell of burning flesh. "Onwards! We have souls to collect! We'll come back for this one later. I like to feel him suffer."

Out of the double doors at the bottom of the stairwell we followed the sounds of violence. A policeman was stumbling towards us, blood pouring from a head wound, disorientated, he pleaded for help.

"Of course." I grinned. I took his head and with both my hands twisted it sharply, the snap sounded like a twig breaking. I shot out a hand just above his head and grabbed his soul as it tried to ascend the white stairway to heaven "Not tonight. You are mine tonight."

Ambulance crews tried to get to the fallen, but the violence was immense and, some of them too, fell victim to the wolves.

Two or three houses were now on fire but the fire crews could do nothing, as they were blocked from getting there. Screams penetrated the night and could be heard over the general commotion.

My attention was caught by a wolf wearing thick gold chains around his neck, standing behind the front line. He was about to throw a petrol bomb, but as he threw it, he slipped on a piece of debris and fell backwards. He let go of the bottle and watched in horror as it smashed on the ground next to him, splashing its contents over his arm igniting it like touch paper. 'Whoosh', the flames engulfed the rest of his body. He rolled around on the ground, trying to smother the flames, all the time howling in pain. The more he rolled the more the fire engulfed him. A tall scrawny wolf nearby danced around Gold-chains, laughing and attracting the attention of more of his conspirators.

"Never like ya much anyhows," the scrawny one shouted, trying to kick Gold-chains' head like a football, the final insult.

Finally Gold-chains lost his battle and became a burning mannequin. As his soul rose, I opened my arms and beckoned it in with a smile.

For the next couple of hours we watched and waited as the wolves and police fell. The violence eventually seemed to focus on a few streets. We watched as more wolves began to join in.

There had been a plan after all, the police were being drawn forward under the assumption that the wolves were retreating. As I watched from the bedroom window of a house where I had stolen a few more souls, I saw the police lulled into a false sense of security, before the signal that would end the police fight, a single shot, which momentarily halted the commotion, but sent a police officer falling backwards off his horse. I welcomed his soul.

The wolves charged relentlessly from all directions, surrounding the police. The police didn't stand a chance without sufficient back-up. I picked up another thirty-three souls as the brutal killings and merciless beatings went on. Even when they were dead, the beatings continued.

Cyril urged the ambulance crew to get Beryl to the hospital, fearful for the crew's safety.

"Can't you knock her out, please, before it's too late?"

"I'm sorry, not until I have established what's wrong."

"But she not safe, you're not safe. Don't you see?"

"Please be quiet or you can get out." The command beckoned no reply.

Mark continued to tell his story.

As the last one went down, a cheer went up. The pack thought they had proved something and marched through nearby streets, chanting and throwing bricks and missiles at houses, just for the sake of it.

"It is time." I said.

We left our vantage point and walked down to the street, following the route the pack had taken. We were in diamond formation as Scholar started reading from his Grimoire. The immediate area around us went quite still.

The back of the pack were ahead of us, jubilantly celebrating their hollow victory.

"Come here, my pretty ones," I said, as we came within reach of the pack. A wolf turned, ready to shout, but I touched his forehead and he fell silently to the ground, where he remained motionless. A fellow wolf caught the movement out of the corner of his eye, but was not quick enough to react, he too went down. Scholar was keeping us under some sort of cloak, invisible to our victims until we were just a few feet away from each of the wolves, and by the time they realised what was happening, they too were gone.

The chanting grew quieter, and the lead wolves started to take note, as the volume died away. We quickly moved into the shadows as the wolves looked behind and saw their fallen comrades. A deathly silence descended. Puzzled expressions appeared on their faces.

I was playing with them, tormenting them. The more souls I took, the greater the euphoria I felt, this was good.

"Master, you have only one hour left," Scholar stated.

I gave Scholar a look of disgust, but he held my gaze. I did not take it any further.

I whistled loudly, attracting the attention of a few of the wolves, who stepped towards us, like the mindless animals that they were. I took their souls in seconds, giving them no time to react. There were only six wolves left now and they no longer jubilantly celebrated, they looked confused and scared. They saw their comrades littering the streets, mere empty carcasses, living, breathing art, who would gradually fade away until they died.

The six wolves spotted us in the shadows and beckoned for us to leave the safety of the seclusion and join them. They would not come to us. We obliged. Soon they too were gone.

The noise of the estate was now just a murmur, in stark comparison to a few hours ago. Fires still blazed uncontrolled. Horses frantically charged about trying to escape the burning obstacles.

Two more wolves came from nowhere, after finding the courage to rush us. They paid with their souls.

"It is time now, Scholar," I commanded.

69

We walked back to the house. I'd collected 343 souls, innocent and guilty, I didn't care, I felt their anger and rage, which enriched me and made me stronger. They would spend an eternity in hell, with me. I laughed, and it reverberated around the dead streets.

Back at the house, we sat in our positions in front of the altar. Opening the gate, I let the souls I'd collected pass through. The euphoria was gone. I was struggling to breathe.

"Master, it is time." Whispa spoke. I merely looked at him.

"You have served me well, Whispa, Scholar, Scratch."

"We are here to do your bidding, Master," Scholar replied dutifully.

"Yes," I retorted somewhat tiredly.

"And now, to rid myself of this physical being." With a wrench I felt my body become weak, every organ burned and screamed at me. I flopped to the floor to see the shadow of Lucifer dance around the room, like a free animal, my three Brethrens' faces filled with merriment.

I lay quite motionless, exhausted and paralyzed. Then Lucifer, the beast, looked me right in the eyes and waited for my imminent death with a smile on his ugly face.

"We are done here now, Scholar, Scratch, gather our things we leave tonight." Whispa commanded.

"Aye, Whispa."

As Lucifer faded from sight, Whispa's face drew close to mine.

"Thank you for your hospitality, Mark Smith. Remember, you will fade gradually. Enjoy." Mirth wrapped itself across his face, and then he laughed, before leaving the lounge to help the rest of the Brethren collect their belongings.

The front door slammed shut as the three Brethren left. Now I was an empty vessel waiting for my body to fade. I would now suffer the fate that I had help mete out. I felt nothing, no pain, no life, it was like being in suspended animation.

I could hear the estate outside becoming peaceful. A muddle of people trying to sort out their lives.

The illusion was shattered by smashing glass, followed by the

*whooshing of liquid fire engulfing the room. I could see the flames start
to lick at my body but felt nothing except my own damnation. All I
could do was watch as the fire engulfed me.*

*I welcomed death. It was what I deserved. My life was ending.
Lucifer had won.*

*In those last few seconds I heard the laughing howls of two wolves
who had followed us back to seek revenge.*

What had I achieved? What had I achieved?

Beryl released her grip on the ambulance man and relaxed
into the stretcher, breathing out a long breath and closing her
eyes. He retreated sharply to the other side of the vehicle,
rubbing his arm to get the blood flowing again, looking at Cyril,
astounded and frightened.

"What's going on? What just happened?"

"You alright Bill?" the driver shouted.

"Don't know mate. Not sure."

The ambulance lurched to a halt and Beryl was stretchered
into A&E, with Cyril following wearily behind.

"Mark, Mark, don't leave me," Beryl mumbled her eyes still
shut tight.

"What Auntie?"

"Clare's rabbit, I can see her rabbit, Mincemeat, it's coming
back to me."

"Auntie what are you saying?" Cyril knew he was losing her.

"Don't go, Mark, I'm your mother? I can help you. Please
stay."

"Auntie, what are you on about?"

Beryl was wheeled into a cubicle and the curtain pulled
around. A nurse tried to drag Cyril away but he refused to go –
he wanted to stay close to his aunt.

"You found me. Mark. I didn't know."

"Sir, please would you come with me, we have some forms
that need filling in." Cyril ignored the nurse's request. "Sir?
Please."

"No," Cyril shouted. "I need to stay with her."

"But, sir." Cyril shook the nurse's hand from his arm.

"Please, don't go Mark. Let me be your mother. I want to see
my grandchildren. My beautiful grandchildren."

"Auntie Beryl, please look at me."

To Cyril's surprise, Beryl's eyes opened.

"He is my son, Cyril. I can see it now. He is my son, my only son. And I let him down."

"But you don't have any children Auntie."

The nurse left the cubicle.

"I do, Cyril, he is so beautiful, only in death can all connections be made, disguises broken down. He is mine."

Dismayed, Cyril stood looking at his aunt, sorrow filling his heart. She had broken.

"Excuse me sir, I'm Dr Joyston. I understand this is your aunt?" The doctor had a pleasant face, with a ruddy complexion.

Tentatively, Cyril answered, "Yes, yes, she is, Beryl Wallace."

"Very well, we'd like to examine her now. If you wouldn't mind stepping outside with Nurse Simmonds, she'll look after you."

"But, my aunt."

"It's alright, we'll look after her, but please let Nurse Simmonds look after you whilst we check her out, and then you can come back in. Okay?"

Reluctantly, Cyril was led out of the cubicle to another vacant one, where he too was checked over.

Ten minutes later the general hubbub was disturbed by Beryl screaming.

"Don't take my Mark away. He is mine. Give him back to me."

Cyril pushed Nurse Simmonds out of the way and rushed to where Beryl was. Another nurse was trying hold Beryl down whilst the doctor administered an injection.

"No, no, you can't take him, he's mine. Mark. Mark…" Her fighting subsided as the drug started to take effect.

"Mr Wallace?" the doctor asked, after straightening his clothes. Cyril stared blankly at him.

"Mr Wallace."

"Yes. No, it's Hewington."

"Oh. Where is your aunt's son?"

"She doesn't have one. She's never had any children."

"Well, she seems to think she does. Did he die during

childbirth?"

"No, no, she has never had any children. I've known her all my life."

"So who was she talking about, because unless we get this 'Mark'," he raised two fingers of each hand and mocked speech marks in the air, "we will have to keep her sedated."

"Honestly, she has never had any children. Is she going to be alright?"

The doctor looked at Cyril, and then the nurse, before answering.

"Physically, yes, but..." the sentiment hung in the air. "... other than that I don't know. Whoever this Mark is, he has had quite an effect on her. We'll put her on a ward and keep her in for observation."

Cyril walked round the bed to hold his aunt's hand, gently brushing the hair from her grey face. She looked so peaceful.

"I'm sorry aunt, I should have done something."

70

"Mr Hewington, your aunt is in good hands." Dr Richards was tiring of Cyril's persistence. "We are doing everything we can for her. She is in the best possible place."

Cyril stared appealingly at Dr Richards, who shuffled papers around his desk.

"But she has been here nearly three weeks and you won't let me see her. Why?" Cyril hated the situation, but seemed unable make any headway.

"Time, Mr Hewington. Your aunt has suffered very severe trauma. Her mind is in a delicate balance. She has to want to return to us. Seeing you will only set that recovery back, and you wouldn't want to do that, would you?"

Cyril sighed heavily. Beryl had been transferred to the clinic a week after being admitted to hospital. No one had managed to get a coherent conversation out of her at the hospital, and she had attacked two nurses, accusing them of taking her baby, Mark, away from her. Cyril had visited her every day in the hospital and sat with her, although she was always so distant. He blamed the drugs that they had used to sedate her. Her eyes were tormented and lost as if she was in a place she didn't want to be. Cyril pleaded with her to recover, but it was all in vain.

She had been so persistent and convincing that the nurses had checked, double-checked and even treble-checked her records, almost certain there must have been an omission somewhere down the line, but they could find no errors or omissions. The doctors had even done a physical examination and found no signs of pregnancy.

Cyril was their last hope, until she struck out at him. It took three nurses to restrain her. It had left him shaken, but not as disturbed as when the attending doctor recommended she be moved to a clinic, Jacobs Hall in Shoeburyness, Essex, near her home, in the hope that she would make a full recovery.

Cyril fought the decision, but it was out of his hands. With the news story hot in the press, with the headline of, 'Author kills 1 and injures 4 in rampage', it was deemed the right thing to do, a secure mental hospital.

Once there, Cyril had not been allowed to see her. He never got close. Every day he had turned up, and waited hours to see someone, but they had just kept him hanging around in limbo. He hated the clinic, the cold sterile conditions, the screaming and shouting from patients, which sent shudders down his spine. It was a cold, heartless, soulless place and he knew she would never recover whilst there. She needed her family around her, him.

Dr Richards stopped shuffling papers and looked at Cyril. "Mr Hewington, I understand your concerns, but what she needs right now is what we are doing. Now please, we will contact you when she is ready for visitors, but just let her get on with recovering."

"But, I..." Cyril felt his world crumbling around him. Tracy placed her left hand reassuringly on his right. He didn't react, just sat there. The thought of returning to the house where they had lived, once so content, racked him. It was tainted, and he rattled around it like a lost soul. Tracy had done her best to be a friend to him after the tour collapsed, and he'd welcomed her warmth as a consolation for his aunt's absence. But still, little had its appeal without Beryl there. He stood up, and Dr Richards offered his hand, but Cyril stared blankly at the carpet, turned, and left solemnly, Tracy trailing behind.

Outside, Cyril stood looking at the formidable grey building.

"I will get you out Auntie, I will," he said, making a promise to himself.

Tracy rubbed Cyril's arm compassionately. "Maybe we could try the courts, I'm sure they will be able to help, at least get you visiting rights."

Cyril turned to Tracy. "Thank you for being here," he said, holding her tightly. "I'll see Fred Robertson in the morning, he has been our solicitor for years."

"Come on, let's take you home," Tracy said, pulling back from Cyril's hold, but he was reluctant to leave, even though it would do no good to stay, the courts were his only possibility.

***

Beryl Wallace sat in a chair in the cold undecorated room, her fingers toying with the edge of the green gown she wore, dark roots gave her lank, once vibrant bleached hair, a two tone look. Her pale complexion gave her the appearance of a ghost, her eyes vacant, lost in their own world, devoid of emotion.

Everything about the room contradicted all that Jacobs Hall openly stated they were trying to achieve.

Very few people had ever been known to leave the place. Thankfully, Cyril knew little of its reputation, and he was still full of hope.

The turning of the lock in the heavy wooden door broke the silence. Beryl didn't react, her feet swung beneath the chair, her bare toes brushing the hard concrete floor.

Dr Richards strode purposefully into the room, letting the door slam shut behind him, the noise loud in the sparsely furnished room.

"Afternoon, Beryl. How are you today?" Silence was the reply as Dr Richards took a seat opposite her. She didn't look up. "I had a visit today from your son..." Beryl brightened.

"Mark, my Mark," her eyes filled with life, and a contorted smile coursed across her face. She leaned into Dr Richards.

"...sorry, nephew, Cyril." Dr Richards read from the notes in the file he carried.

Beryl's smile faded. "Where's Mark? I want to see Mark. You took him away from me. You all took him away from me," her demeanour turning instantly to rage.

"Beryl you don't have a..."

"You liar. You all lie. You've taken him," Beryl screamed, as she stood up. "Where have you taken him?" Her voice became a high pitched shrill.

Dr Richards shrank backwards, trying to remain confident and calm, but her voice rattled his nerves. "Beryl sit down... please." He stared at the figure in front of him as she tried to fathom where she was, as if, in her rage, she had forgotten all that had happened. "Beryl, it is important that you sit down and remain calm."

"Mark. Where is Mark?" Her voice was calm as she sat back, folding one leg under her on the seat. "I want to give him this for Clare, it's her favourite rabbit, Mincemeat."

Dr Richards stared incredulously at the furry white rabbit Beryl was holding. It was dripping wet, and formed a puddle on the floor.

"Beryl, where did you get that?" Dr Richards said sharply.

"It's Clare's, Mark gave it to me. Where is Mark?"

Dr Richards stood up, nervously scouting the room whilst moving urgently to the door; he rapped on it. The heavy bolt slid back, the door opened and a male nurse appeared.

"Take her back to her room." Dr Richards' voice was full of urgency, and angrily he added, "I want to know where she got that rabbit from."

"Rabbit, what rabbit?" the male nurse asked, perplexed, glancing briefly into the room.

"The one in her hand dammit. Look!" Dr Richards grabbed the nurse by his arms and shoved him into the interview room, "see?"

Beryl turned. "Where is Mark? Have you seen Mark?"

Dr Richards stared on, amazed, the puddle and rabbit were gone.

"Get her back to her room. NOW!" Dr Richards stormed off.

The nurse raised his eyebrows, smiling to himself. He didn't like Dr Richards much and was pleased to see a patient get the better of him.

"Come on Beryl. You've been a naughty girl," the nurse said playfully.

He marched her back to her room, where she was locked up again. The room was basic with a bed, a chair and a bedside table, all bolted to the floor. There were bars on the windows, which prevented her even getting close to the glass beyond. Very little daylight penetrated the room.

She sat on her bed, quietly muttering to herself, lost in her world again, creating a life with Mark, Samantha, Joshua and Clare. Slowly the day faded into night, and she was given her tea, then put to bed.

***

"Martin, how are you? Wife okay now?"

"Yeah, not so bad. Doctors have given her the all-clear. Just needs to take it a little easier. I told her not to start decorating the nursery, said I'd do it when I'm off, but will she listen. Will she heck as like. She's so bloody impatient. Told her she's gotta watch her blood pressure, but, 'no' she says."

Michael's eyes started to wander around the office, wishing he'd never asked, Martin did like to ramble on. "I know what you mean. Look, I'm going to do the rounds, we've got a new one since you've been off."

"Who's that then?" Martin enquired.

"Room 31. A Beryl Wallace. A psychic who went cuckoo and killed a few people, apparently."

"What that woman who was in the paper?"

Michael looked at the clipboard, which was hung on a hook on the wall. "That's the one."

"She looked quite tasty though, I'll have to check her out."

"You're sick, Martin." Michael grimaced.

"What? No harm in looking." Martin licked his lips, his mind already thinking of Beryl and the picture of her that had appeared in the paper. How sallow she looked, how frail and beaten. How, from that picture, he had felt an urge thread through him like poison. The first stirrings rang like a bell on a crisp morning. He knew he couldn't stop it until the urge was fed.

"You alright, Martin?" Michael pulled the clipboard from the hook and flicked through the leaves of paper. "Looks like we need to keep an eye on 113 and 17, they've been playing up a little lately. Michael grabbed a set of keys from another hook. "I'll check the cupboard to make sure the day crew have actually left the right drugs out this time. Martin! Hello!"

"Sorry, I was just thinking."

"Thinking what?"

"Oh, nothing. Look, I'll do the rounds. When are you on til?" Martin found it hard to conceal his delight at the temptation that presented itself.

"Right through to eight in the morning. Cards later?"

"Yeah. How much do you owe me now?"

"I am just lulling you into a false sense of security."

"Dream on, dream on." Martin walked from the office his mind racing. Thoughts of Beryl Wallace pulsed through him, every fibre alive with anticipation. He knew he would be taking a risk, but hadn't he done it before? Many times before, and got away with it. No one cared anyway, not that he'd be caught. Michael normally spent an hour checking the less secure floors. Martin didn't need an hour. He repeatedly threw the keys up in the air and caught them. He could smell her.

***

Beryl slept peacefully, the voices in her head gone. She didn't even wake when the lock of the door turned.

Martin pushed the heavy door open, the well oiled hinges silent. Locking it behind him he stood looking at Beryl, asleep, her breathing a murmur. Martin started to salivate as the urge started to grow inside him. He could feel it beckoning him like a familiar friend, a compulsion he knew was wrong, but it was too strong to fight. What would his wife think if she knew? She didn't care now anyway, she had what she wanted, another mouth to feed, he thought to himself.

He knelt down beside Beryl's bed and gently, affectionately, moved her hair away from her face, biting his bottom lip, as it tingled. Still she didn't stir. Martin's hand skimmed down Beryl's rounded shoulder until it cupped one of her small breasts, he squeezed gently, feeling the urge grow inside him.

"Yes, you're nice. Cute. Don't worry, I won't hurt you," Martin stroked her cheek.

"Mark, Mark is that you?" Beryl opened her eyes. "Away! Away!" Beryl shouted.

Martin withdrew his hand and eyed her erect nipple, pressing tightly against the fabric of the gown, as she twisted, trying to get further away from him, bringing her knees up to her chest to protect herself. Martin reached for her ankles to pull her closer to him and Beryl pushed his hands away.

"Feisty. I like a little fight. But I don't want you to get too feisty now, do I?" Martin wrestled her away from the wall, and after a struggle, was sitting on her. The more she fought the more excited he felt.

Terror grew in Beryl's eyes as she fought to get free, but finally Martin managed to use his tremendous strength against her, pinning her contorted and struggling body to the bed.

With one hand he awkwardly pulled out a syringe from his pocket, removing the protective sheaf. Martin forced the needle into her arm. "Now, night, night." he beamed.

Beryl tried to fight him but the sedative kicked in and she just stared blankly up at Martin who laid her out like a corpse. Running his hand under her gown, he felt her soft delicate skin. He felt himself getting aroused. Her thigh was smooth and silky to touch.

"Oh yes. You feel nice."

He unzipped his trousers.

***

Fifteen minutes later Martin walked from Beryl's room, satisfaction glued across his face, whistling as he walked back to the office.

"You ready to lose now, Michael?"

"You look pleased with yourself."

"No, just feeling good, that's all. Five card stud alright?"

"Yeah, okay."

71

The planning meeting was rambling on over a small extension to The Gables, a Victorian manor house, built in the 1800's.

"Gentlemen! Gentlemen! Please! This is getting us nowhere. QUIET! I realise there are a lot a points raised by this planning application and..." A grumble from one of the members of the committee drew the attention of all eyes "...and there is need for more discussion, but let us take a vote on it. Okay? Geoff?" Hands were raised and duly counted. "Right, that's a no then."

Frederick wrote 'rejected' in big red letters next to the point on his agenda, before continuing. "This brings us to point 3.8, the planning application submitted by Gripley's, in conjunction with MetaHouse Construction. The application proposes to build 8,000 new homes and a car plant on the 150 acre site that was, until recently, Autumn Acre Farm. We have all seen the application and its proposal, and we have here representatives of both companies, who wish to address the meeting. Discussion will take place after they have spoken, when any questions will be answered." Frederick looked at a stout, well dressed, gentleman sitting just a few feet away, in a section of seating set aside for speakers. "The floor is yours, Mr Simpson."

"Thank You." Mr Simpson stood up, his brown pin-striped suit shimmered under the fluorescent lighting. Stroking his thinning hair, he took up position behind a lectern, in front of the committee, which sat at two oblong wooden tables. He purposefully withdrew a few prompt cards from inside his jacket pocket and cleared his throat.

"As you are aware, the Steel and Coal industries are some of the largest industries this country has, and the future is bright. I could quote you figures until I am blue in the face, about the hundreds of thousands of tons of coal drawn up from the ground, and the miles and miles of steel manufactured in the factories. These figures look set only to increase in the future, to cope with our ever-growing population. I don't think anyone can dispute those opinions, so I won't bore you with countless figures." Mr Simpson eyed his captive audience; they were listening intently.

"The majority of these businesses are up North, creating great opportunities for employment. However, it leaves a dearth of opportunities here in the South.

Yes, we have London, not thirty miles away, but that is for the intellectual business side of things. My client represents a car manufacturer who wants to invest heavily in this country. He feels we can offer the right calibre of people.

He also feels that Southend is the best location for his business as it lies within close proximity to Tilbury which, with the help of his business, looks set to grow exponentially over the next few years, creating a pool of jobs...and lucrative employment opportunities for thousands.

However, my client wishes to establish more than just a factory, he wants to establish a sense of community, he believes that the strength of a factory lies in the sense of community spirit that surrounds it. After all, has this not already been proved when Cadbury set up his factory, building homes and schools, and catering for a whole manner of other community needs, doctors and dentists. I could go on." He let the gathered party absorb his passion.

"But, and this is a big but, if we don't build the proposed homes, then my client feels he will be forced to move elsewhere. Forced to move to where the human resources can be found, rather than pay the high cost of transporting people, resources and materials on a daily basis..."

A sudden knock on the door caught everyone's attention. A tall blonde woman entered and walked over to the table, handing Frederick a message. He dipped his head apologetically to Mr Simpson and quickly scanned the note.

"Thank you, Miss Bridge. I'm very sorry to interrupt your speech Mr Simpson but I have a very important message for Mr Hartridge." Frederick turned to face his colleague. "Well, John, it looks like you're the proud father of a baby girl called Shelley Louise."

The committee erupted into cheers of congratulations, making Mr Simpson feel awkward, his train of thought temporarily broken, his winning patter interrupted. John blushed and, for a moment was too stunned for words, the baby wasn't due for another week. Frederick reached across the table to shake his hand and, at the same time, pat his back like a proud father.

"Well done, John."

"Thank you," was the rather shocked reply.

"First one, John?" asked Roy.

"Yeah," John replied, almost overwhelmed with emotion.

As the congratulations continued, John saw the look on William's face, where deep sadness was obvious.

"I'm sorry, I realise it must be har…"

"No. Look it's fine. I'm happy for you." The awkward moment caused a little embarrassment until William stood up and shook John's hand with feeling. "Just love and cherish every moment with them. You never know what is around the corner." The general murmur died down as William fought back the tears of his own sadness. All eyes were on William and John, who stood at two ends of the spectrum of life, John enjoying the first delights of a new life, and William still mourning the loss of his family. John felt guilty, yet totally overwhelmed at being a father.

"You haven't got any family-naming traditions, have you?" William said dryly.

"Sorry?" John replied, caught out by William's strange question.

"My monogram. It looks like an eye chart."

"What?" John looked curiously at William, who had a distant look in his eye.

"William Henry Ian Stephen Paul Austen. Each generation adding another name to the beginning. My son almost beca…" William stopped mid flow, the memories still too painful.

"Oh, I see," John replied. "No we haven't."

"Nice name, Shelley. Poetic." William sat down.

John felt for William, but his own jubilation soon

overwhelmed him, making him forget William's loss.

"Maybe you'd like to continue, Mr Simpson?" Frederick said, remembering that they were actually meant to be listening to arguments for and against the proposed project.

"Thank you. Where was I?" he fumbled with his notes. "Oh, yes. Congratulations by the way." John nodded. "My clients' think this town is the most suitable" He cleared his throat finding it hard to regain his patter then, pausing, composed himself again. "You have the countryside, you have seaside, both within easy reach. Good road and rail links. They feel the benefits to be gained from such a venture far outweigh any detrimental arguments. We can build on these foundations. Build a bigger, better, community where business takes care of the community.

Community is foremost in my clients' minds. They see this as a positive step, important for the local area in providing all the amenities that they could ever need, to make this a place where people want to live long and prosperous lives," he let the comment linger.

"Thank you for your time, gentlemen." Mr Simpson took his seat, disappointed that he had been interrupted, but pleased with how it had gone.

"Thank you, Mr Simpson, a very heartfelt speech that I'm sure we will all bear in mind. Now the proposal is for 8,000 new homes, incorporating small rise blocks of flats with connecting walk ways and community garden areas, surrounded by a few terraced streets with private gardens and greens at the centres. A parade of shops, a park, and a school.

Does anyone wish to make any comment?"

Julian spoke up, "and what about our green belt land?" There was a moan from the committee. "We are continually seeing our countryside disappear. If we let this continue, where will it end? I say we should put a stop to…"

"You are always going on about our countryside, yes, it's nice, but without jobs all we'll have is countryside and plenty of time to enjoy it."

Murmurs of, "hear, hear," came from other members around the table.

Frederick stood. "I think this is the way forward. Look at

our history. Villages were built around farms, around orchards, around churches. We need to sustain this town and provide for the future. Towns are becoming diverse. Our sense of community is being lost. Here is our chance to greet a company that wishes to promote those family values."

John added, "I've got a new child, what kind of future can I offer her if we don't allow this to proceed. I want to see her be part of a community, something to be proud of."

"What about the countryside, you lose that then you have nothing. Nature is beautiful. I'm not saying don't do some building, but think of other options rather than stampeding this through," Julian continued.

Harry, who had sat quietly contemplating all the arguments, stood up. "I have to agree with Julian, we have to be careful. Look at the rate at which land is being taken up by industry, motorways, roads, and factories. How long can we sustain it? We have limited resources."

William sat silently, suddenly reminded, so innocently of his own deceased family, letting the arguments rage on around him before Frederick finally called the meeting to order.

"I think a vote is in order. All those 'for' raise your hand." Four out of the seven seated at the table, raised their hands. "All those against." Two hands were raised. "William, are you abstaining?"

William didn't hear Frederick as he flicked through, in his mind, the memories of how his life had been, how raw the 'cut' still was.

"William. Are you abstaining?" Frederick repeated.

William looked all around the room. His heart wasn't in this anymore. He looked at Mr Simpson and the two owners of the company that sat behind him, awaiting the fate of their proposal. William sighed, "For."

"Then it is passed in principle. Now it just needs to go out for public consultation." Frederick declared.

"What is this estate to be called?" William asked lamely, surprising himself.

Puzzled expressions and glances shot from one to another.

One of the company's owners stood up, "Trafalgar Estate."

"I think you should name it after John's good news tonight," Harry interjected, with a hint of humour.

"I think the name of the estate should be as per my clients' wishes and should not be for the planning committee to decide," Mr Simpson added sternly.

A hand was placed on his shoulder and a company owner stood up. "I am Stephen Forster, owner of MetaHouse construction. What do you propose the name should be? I feel it should be something that encapsulates what we want to create."

"Well, John's daughter is called Shelley, she was born tonight. Your plan in principle has been agreed tonight. How about Shelbourne. It's quirky but..." Harry didn't get a chance to finish. Stephen Forster looked at his partner and they both smiled, rolling the proposed name around in their minds, it was catchy.

"We agree. A new birth. New life to this town. A sense of prosperity for all."

A round of applause went up and John stood up, "Thank you," he said, fumbling for words, "I don't know what to say except, thank you."

"I think that concludes our meeting, unless there is any other business?" Frederick paused, waiting for any last remarks. "Well, I draw to a close our meeting of Friday, 16th February 1979. Thank you, gentlemen. Time to adjourn to the pub to celebrate John's new arrival, I think."

"Here! Here!" came the responses.

William stayed sitting, forlorn, he didn't feel like celebrating, and hoped the others wouldn't notice if he just stayed back a little while.

72

The door to the office crashed open and Sandra rushed through, gasping for air.

"Room 121 has just gone into labour. You'd better call an ambulance."

Dr Roberts and Francis stopped talking.

"WHAT?" exploded Dr Roberts. "How the hell did that happen?"

"Look, I don't know. I mean I knew she was putting on weight, but she hardly shows." Sandra was anxious for answers, and knew there would be a full investigation. Beryl had been in Jacobs Hall barely ten months. "Sharon's down there now looking after her."

Francis dialled the emergency services. "Ambulance please, Jacobs Hall, Shoeburyness. We have a patient in labour," she explained calmly.

Dr Roberts rushed with Sandra to Beryl's room, where her screams were starting to stir the other patients on the floor.

"Francis has called an ambulance, I'm sure it won't be long," Sandra said.

"I don't think its going to wait, we need water and towels," Sharon replied, mopping Beryl's brow.

Beryl screamed harder as she pushed, she could feel the baby wanting to come out. Tears streamed from her eyes. "Mark," she cried, her voice reaching fever pitch. "Mark, my son, Mark."

Sharon looked at Sandra, then at Dr Roberts.

"It's coming," Sharon said.

"Tell her to stop pushing," Dr Roberts commanded.

"It's a bit late for that Tony," Sandra added sarcastically

Beryl let out an almighty cry as she pushed as hard she

could. A baby's head appeared, followed by its body, and then its cry was heard. "Mark...Mark," Beryl sobbed, delighted with her little bundle.

Sharon cut the cord, all her years of midwifery training coming to the fore. She wrapped Mark in a towel, before cradling him in her arms.

"It's definitely a boy. I don't know how she knew," Sandra smiled at the baby.

"Get it out of here," Dr Roberts shouted.

"Mark, Mark," Beryl stretched out her hands to hold the bundle.

"I don't think it's a good idea now. You know you can't keep him," Sandra said.

"Mark. My baby."

"No, Beryl. How the hell did this happen? She wasn't pregnant when she came in." Francis joined them, and now all four members of staff looked at each other quizzically. "Now get it out of here, and sedate her," commanded Dr Roberts.

"Come on, Doctor, surely a few minutes..."

"No, Sandra, we need to get it out of here, now." Dr Roberts left the room, muttering to himself.

"Mark. Give me Mark," Beryl was getting agitated.

"You'd better sedate her now." Sharon passed the baby to Sandra, before applying a wet flannel to Beryl's head.

Beryl got more agitated as she saw Mark being taken from her. "Mark, Mark," she screamed, her voice rasping. A phial of liquid was emptied into Beryl's arm and her eyelids became heavy, as her struggling subsided.

"Ma..."

"There's going to be trouble over this one," Sandra reproached.

"Tell me about it. But who? She hasn't had any visitors and only sees Dr Richards." Sharon stopped, "No!" she exclaimed.

"Surely not him," Sandra replied.

"You two have no proof of that and I doubt he would anyway. Those sort of rumours could cost him his job." Francis tried to squash the rumour before it started, even though doubt inexplicably found its way into her thoughts.

"Well who else then?"

"I don't know. But it's the child I feel sorry for. Look at him." Sharon and Francis looked at the baby cradled in Sandra's arms. "So innocent."

"Looks like it will be adoption for you little one," Sharon added playfully, enjoying the feeling of holding a new baby in her arms, it had been so long since her family had left home.

"What an awful start for him." Francis looked gooey-eyed.

"Well, he'll never know his origins, that's for sure."

"What do you mean?" Sharon asked.

"Well we can hardly tell them where this baby came from, it will kick up all sorts of fuss, and Dr Roberts won't allow that, not here."

"How about naming him?" Sharon asked.

"We'll let social worry about that," Sandra stated. "

Francis and Sharon nodded their agreement, before Sharon added.

"Surely we can at least give him a name?"

"Mark, is his name. I don't see a problem with leaving it at that."

"Mark Wallace," Francis said out loud.

"No!" Sandra commanded, I don't want him to ever be able to trace his origins back to this place. The investigation is going to be bad enough without him ever finding out the truth."

Sullenly all three agreed.

***

Dr Roberts sat in his office after his difficult conversation with Sandra about what to do, considering the big favour he had to ask of the registrar, wondering how much whisky it was going to cost him. Having friends in the right places was handy, but expensive.

Finally, he picked up the phone and dialled the number he knew by heart, it was answered on the third ring.

"Yep," was the annoyed and abrupt response.

"Clive, it's me, Harry,"

"Harry old mate, long time, long time. How are things cookin'?"

"Not good. Look I'll get straight to the point, I've got something that needs burying, that requires a small favour." Harry let the words settle.

"I'm listening."

"No, I think this needs to be done in person."

"I see." Suddenly Clive sounded more interested.

"Usual place, about eight?"

"Okay, I'll see you there. And don't forget..."

"I know, I know. Eight!" Harry replaced the receiver. This was a risky business that could cost him his job, but, then again, so could the truth.

***

'The big brekkie' was a transport café that opened late into the night to serve all the lorry drivers with their king-size breakfasts. Clive, a large rotund person, was already waiting with his plate piled high when Harry showed up.

"See you started without me."

"You're late," Clive said, spooning a massive forkful of food into his enormous mouth.

"Cut the crap, you just wanted a second breakfast didn't you?" Harry hated watching Clive eat, it was disgusting, but a necessary evil. "Tea please love," Harry called to the tall slim woman behind the counter.

"Shall we?" Clive stated, washing down his food with a mouthfull of tea.

"We have had a bit of an incident that I need to make disappear. I need a birth certificate with no mention of the mother's name on it."

"How about the father's?"

"I want no other names to show on it, I also need the date adjusted slightly,"

"I see," Clive smiled, as he drew his own conclusions. "Anything is possible, I'll have to go around the usual channels, but it can be done."

"Good. The name's Mark Smith."

"How very original."

"It will do, anyway you'll get your usual delivery, twelve bottles of Glenfiddich."

"I think twenty-four this time," Clive said, wondering if he was pushing his luck.

"Whatever, just make it so."

"I'll get you the certificate tomorrow."

"Excellent."